THE 5TH WAVE

THE 5TH WAVE

RICK YANCEY

G. P. PUTNAM'S SONS
AN IMPRINT OF PENGUIN GROUP (USA) INC.

G. P. PUTNAM'S SONS
an imprint of Penguin Random House LLC
375 Hudson Street, New York, NY 10014

Library of Congress Cataloging-in-Publication Data
Yancey, Richard.   The 5th Wave / Rick Yancey.   pages   cm   Summary: "Cassie Sullivan, the
survivor of an alien invasion, must rescue her young brother from the enemy with help from a boy
who may be one of them"—Provided by publisher. [1. Extraterrestrial beings—Fiction.
2. Survival—Fiction. 3. War—Fiction. 4. Science fiction.] I. Title. II. Title: Fifth Wave.
PZ7.Y19197Aah 2013   [Fic]—dc23   2012047622

Printed in the United States of America.
ISBN 978-1-101-99651-5
1 3 5 7 9 10 8 6 4 2

Design by Ryan Thomann. Text set in Sabon.

For Sandy,
whose dreams inspire
and whose love endures

IF ALIENS EVER VISIT US, I think the outcome would be much as when Christopher Columbus first landed in America, which didn't turn out very well for the Native Americans.

—*Stephen Hawking*

THE 1ST WAVE: *Lights Out*

THE 2ND WAVE: *Surf's Up*

THE 3RD WAVE: *Pestilence*

THE 4TH WAVE: *Silencer*

THE 5TH WAVE

INTRUSION: 1995

THERE WILL BE NO AWAKENING.

The sleeping woman will feel nothing the next morning, only a vague sense of unease and the unshakable feeling that someone is watching her. Her anxiety will fade in less than a day and will soon be forgotten.

The memory of the dream will linger a little longer.

In her dream, a large owl perches outside the window, staring at her through the glass with huge, white-rimmed eyes.

She will not awaken. Neither will her husband beside her. The shadow falling over them will not disturb their sleep. And what the shadow has come for—the baby within the sleeping woman—will feel nothing. The intrusion breaks no skin, violates not a single cell of her or the baby's body.

It is over in less than a minute. The shadow withdraws.

Now it is only the man, the woman, the baby inside her, and the intruder inside the baby, sleeping.

The woman and man will awaken in the morning, the baby a few months later when he is born.

The intruder inside him will sleep on and not wake for several years, when the unease of the child's mother and the memory of that dream have long since faded.

Five years later, at a visit to the zoo with her child, the woman will see an owl identical to the one in the dream. Seeing the owl is unsettling for reasons she cannot understand.

She is not the first to dream of owls in the dark.

She will not be the last.

I

THE LAST HISTORIAN

1

ALIENS ARE STUPID.

I'm not talking about real aliens. The Others aren't stupid. The Others are so far ahead of us, it's like comparing the dumbest human to the smartest dog. No contest.

No, I'm talking about the aliens inside our own heads.

The ones we made up, the ones we've been making up since we realized those glittering lights in the sky were suns like ours and probably had planets like ours spinning around them. You know, the aliens we imagine, the kind of aliens we'd *like* to attack us, human aliens. You've seen them a million times. They swoop down from the sky in their flying saucers to level New York and Tokyo and London, or they march across the countryside in huge machines that look like mechanical spiders, ray guns blasting away, and always, always, humanity sets aside its differences and bands together to defeat the alien horde. David slays Goliath, and everybody (except Goliath) goes home happy.

What crap.

It's like a cockroach working up a plan to defeat the shoe on its way down to crush it.

There's no way to know for sure, but I bet the Others knew about the human aliens we'd imagined. And I bet they thought it was funny as hell. They must have laughed their asses off. If they have a sense of humor . . . or asses. They must have laughed the way we laugh when a dog does something totally cute and dorky.

Oh, those cute, dorky humans! They think we think like they do! Isn't that adorable?

Forget about flying saucers and little green men and giant mechanical spiders spitting out death rays. Forget about epic battles with tanks and fighter jets and the final victory of us scrappy, unbroken, intrepid humans over the bug-eyed swarm. That's about as far from the truth as their dying planet was from our living one.

The truth is, once they found us, we were toast.

2

SOMETIMES I THINK I might be the last human on Earth.

Which means I'm the last human in the universe.

I know that's dumb. They can't have killed everyone . . . yet. I see how it could happen, though, eventually. And then I think that's exactly what the Others want me to see.

Remember the dinosaurs? Well.

So I'm probably not the last human on Earth, but I'm one of the last. Totally alone—and likely to stay that way—until the 4th Wave rolls over me and carries me down.

That's one of my night thoughts. You know, the three-in-the-morning, oh-my-God-I'm-screwed thoughts. When I curl into a little ball, so scared I can't close my eyes, drowning in fear so intense I have to remind myself to breathe, will my heart to keep beating. When my brain checks out and begins to skip like a scratched CD. *Alone, alone, alone, Cassie, you're alone.*

That's my name. Cassie.

Not Cassie for Cassandra. Or Cassie for Cassidy. Cassie for Cassiopeia, the constellation, the queen tied to her chair in the northern sky, who was beautiful but vain, placed in the heavens by the sea god Poseidon as a punishment for her boasting. In Greek, her name means "she whose words excel."

My parents didn't know the first thing about that myth. They just thought the name was pretty.

Even when there were people around to call me anything, no one ever called me Cassiopeia. Just my father, and only when he was teasing me, and always in a very bad Italian accent: *Cass-ee-oh-PEE-a.* It drove me crazy. I didn't think he was funny or cute, and it made me hate my own name. "I'm Cassie!" I'd holler at him. "Just Cassie!" Now I'd give anything to hear him say it just one more time.

When I was turning twelve—four years before the Arrival—my father gave me a telescope for my birthday. On a crisp, clear fall evening, he set it up in the backyard and showed me the constellation.

"See how it looks like a W?" he asked.

"Why did they name it Cassiopeia if it's shaped like a W?" I replied. "W for what?"

"Well . . . I don't know that it's for anything," he answered with a smile. Mom always told him it was his best feature, so he trotted it out a lot, especially after he started going bald. You know, to drag the other person's eyes downward. "So, it's for anything you like! How about *wonderful*? Or *winsome*? Or *wise*?" He dropped his hand on my shoulder as I squinted through the lens at the five stars burning over fifty light-years from the spot on which we stood. I could feel my father's breath against my cheek, warm and moist in the cool, dry autumn air. His breath so close, the stars of Cassiopeia so very far away.

The stars seem a lot closer now. Closer than the three hundred trillion miles that separate us. Close enough to touch, for me to touch them, for them to touch me. They're as close to me as his breath had been.

That sounds crazy. Am I crazy? Have I lost my mind? You can only call someone crazy if there's someone else who's normal. Like good and evil. If everything was good, then nothing would be good.

Whoa. That sounds, well . . . crazy.

Crazy: the new normal.

I guess I could call myself crazy, since there is one other person I can compare myself to: me. Not the me I am now, shivering in a tent deep in the woods, too afraid to even poke her head from the sleeping bag. Not this Cassie. No, I'm talking about the Cassie I was before the Arrival, before the Others parked their alien butts in high orbit. The twelve-year-old me, whose biggest problems were the spray of tiny freckles on her nose and the curly hair she couldn't do anything with and the cute boy who saw her every day and had no clue she existed. The Cassie who was coming to terms with the painful fact that she was just okay. Okay in looks. Okay in school. Okay at sports like karate and soccer. Basically the only unique things about her were the weird name—Cassie for Cassiopeia, which nobody knew about, anyway—and her ability to touch her nose with the tip of her tongue, a skill that quickly lost its impressiveness by the time she hit middle school.

I'm probably crazy by that Cassie's standards.

And she sure is crazy by mine. I scream at her sometimes, that twelve-year-old Cassie, moping over her hair or her weird name or at being just okay. "What are you doing?" I yell. "Don't you know what's coming?"

But that isn't fair. The fact is she didn't know, had no way of knowing, and that was her blessing and why I miss her so much, more than anyone, if I'm being honest. When I cry—when I let myself cry—that's who I cry for. I don't cry for myself. I cry for the Cassie that's gone.

And I wonder what that Cassie would think of me.

The Cassie who kills.

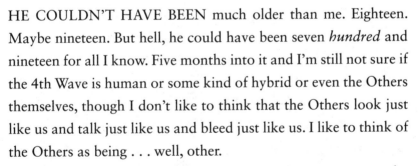

HE COULDN'T HAVE BEEN much older than me. Eighteen. Maybe nineteen. But hell, he could have been seven *hundred* and nineteen for all I know. Five months into it and I'm still not sure if the 4th Wave is human or some kind of hybrid or even the Others themselves, though I don't like to think that the Others look just like us and talk just like us and bleed just like us. I like to think of the Others as being . . . well, other.

I was on my weekly foray for water. There's a stream not far from my campsite, but I'm worried it might be contaminated, either from chemicals or sewage or maybe a body or two upstream. Or poisoned. Depriving us of clean water would be an excellent way to wipe us out quickly.

So once a week I shoulder my trusty M16 and hike out of

the forest to the interstate. Two miles south, just off Exit 175, there're a couple of gas stations with convenience stores attached. I load up as much bottled water as I can carry, which isn't a lot because water is heavy, and get back to the highway and the relative safety of the trees as quickly as I can, before night falls completely. Dusk is the best time to travel. I've never seen a drone at dusk. Three or four during the day and a lot more at night, but never at dusk.

From the moment I slipped through the gas station's shattered front door, I knew something was different. I didn't *see* anything different—the store looked exactly like it had a week earlier, the same graffiti-scrawled walls, overturned shelves, floor strewn with empty boxes and caked-in rat feces, the busted-open cash registers and looted beer coolers. It was the same disgusting, stinking mess I'd waded through every week for the past month to get to the storage area behind the refrigerated display cases. Why people grabbed the beer and soda, the cash from the registers and safe, the rolls of lottery tickets, but left the two pallets of drinking water was beyond me. What were they thinking? *It's an alien apocalypse! Quick, grab the beer!*

The same disaster of spoilage, the same stench of rats and rotted food, the same fitful swirl of dust in the murky light pushing through the smudged windows, every out-of-place thing in its place, undisturbed.

Still.

Something was different.

I was standing in the little pool of broken glass just inside the doorway. I didn't see it. I didn't hear it. I didn't smell or feel it. But I knew it.

Something was different.

It's been a long time since humans were prey animals. A hundred thousand years or so. But buried deep in our genes the memory remains: the awareness of the gazelle, the instinct of the antelope. The wind whispers through the grass. A shadow flits between the trees. And up speaks the little voice that goes, *Shhhh, it's close now. Close.*

I don't remember swinging the M16 from my shoulder. One minute it was hanging behind my back, the next it was in my hands, muzzle down, safety off.

Close.

I'd never fired it at anything bigger than a rabbit, and that was a kind of experiment, to see if I could actually use the thing without blowing off one of my own body parts. Once I shot over the heads of a pack of feral dogs that had gotten a little too interested in my campsite. Another time nearly straight up, sighting the tiny, glowering speck of greenish light that was their mothership sliding silently across the backdrop of the Milky Way. Okay, I admit that was stupid. I might as well have erected a billboard with a big arrow pointing at my head and the words YOO-HOO, HERE I AM!

After the rabbit experiment—it blew that poor damn bunny apart, turning Peter into this unrecognizable mass of shredded guts and bone—I gave up the idea of using the rifle to hunt. I didn't even do target practice. In the silence that had slammed down after the 4th Wave struck, the report of the rounds sounded louder than an atomic blast.

Still, I considered the M16 my bestest of besties. Always by my side, even at night, burrowed into my sleeping bag with me, faithful and true. In the 4th Wave, you can't trust that people are still people. But you can trust that your gun is still your gun.

Shhh, Cassie. It's close.

Close.

I should have bailed. That little voice had my back. That little voice is older than I am. It's older than the oldest person who ever lived.

I should have listened to that voice.

Instead, I listened to the silence of the abandoned store, listened hard. Something was close. I took a tiny step away from the door, and the broken glass crunched ever so softly under my foot.

And then the Something made a noise, somewhere between a cough and a moan. It came from the back room, behind the coolers, where my water was.

That's the moment when I didn't need a little old voice to tell me what to do. It was obvious, a no-brainer. Run.

But I didn't run.

The first rule of surviving the 4th Wave is don't trust anyone. It doesn't matter what they look like. The Others are very smart about that—okay, they're smart about everything. It doesn't matter if they look the right way and say the right things and act exactly like you expect them to act. Didn't my father's death prove that? Even if the stranger is a little old lady sweeter than your great-aunt Tilly, hugging a helpless kitten, you can't know for certain—you can never know—that she isn't one of them, and that there isn't a loaded .45 behind that kitten.

It isn't unthinkable. And the more you think about it, the more thinkable it becomes. Little old lady has to go.

That's the hard part, the part that, if I thought about it too much, would make me crawl into my sleeping bag, zip myself up, and die of slow starvation. If you can't trust anyone, then you can trust no one. Better to take the chance that Aunty Tilly is one of them than play the odds that you've stumbled across a fellow survivor.

That's friggin' diabolical.

It tears us apart. It makes us that much easier to hunt down and eradicate. The 4th Wave forces us into solitude, where there's no strength in numbers, where we slowly go crazy from the isolation and fear and terrible anticipation of the inevitable.

So I didn't run. I couldn't. Whether it was one of them or an Aunt Tilly, I had to defend my turf. The only way to stay alive is to stay alone. That's rule number two.

I followed the sobbing coughs or coughing sobs or whatever you want to call them till I reached the door that opened to the back room. Hardly breathing, on the balls of my feet.

The door was ajar, the space just wide enough for me to slip through sideways. A metal rack on the wall directly in front of me and, to the right, the long narrow hallway that ran the length of the coolers. There were no windows back here. The only light was the sickly orange of the dying day behind me, still bright enough to hurl my shadow onto the sticky floor. I crouched down; my shadow crouched with me.

I couldn't see around the edge of the cooler into the hall. But I could hear whoever—or whatever—it was at the far end, coughing, moaning, and that gurgling sob.

Either hurt badly or acting hurt badly, I thought. *Either needs help or it's a trap.*

This is what life on Earth has become since the Arrival. It's an either/or world.

Either it's one of them and it knows you're here or it's not one of them and he needs your help.

Either way, I had to get up and turn that corner.

So I got up.

And I turned the corner.

4

HE LAY SPRAWLED against the back wall twenty feet away, long legs spread out in front of him, clutching his stomach with one hand. He was wearing fatigues and black boots and he was covered in grime and shimmering with blood. There was blood everywhere. On the wall behind him. Pooling on the cold concrete beneath him. Coating his uniform. Matted in his hair. The blood glittered darkly, black as tar in the semidarkness.

In his other hand was a gun, and that gun was pointed at my head.

I mirrored him. His handgun to my rifle. Fingers flexing on the triggers: his, mine.

It didn't prove anything, his pointing a gun at me. Maybe he really was a wounded soldier and thought I was one of them.

Or maybe not.

"Drop your weapon," he sputtered at me.

Like hell.

"Drop your weapon!" he shouted, or tried to shout. The words came out all cracked and crumbly, beaten up by the blood rising from his gut. Blood dribbled over his bottom lip and hung quivering from his stubbly chin. His teeth shone with blood.

I shook my head. My back was to the light, and I prayed he couldn't see how badly I was shaking or the fear in my eyes. This wasn't some damn rabbit that was stupid enough to hop into my camp one sunny morning. This was a person. Or, if it wasn't, it looked just like one.

The thing about killing is you don't know if you can actually do it until you actually do it.

He said it a third time, not as loud as the second. It came out like a plea.

"Drop your weapon."

The hand holding his gun twitched. The muzzle dipped toward the floor. Not much, but my eyes had adjusted to the light by this point, and I saw a speck of blood run down the barrel.

And then he dropped the gun.

It fell between his legs with a sharp *cling*. He brought up his empty hand and held it, palm outward, over his shoulder.

"Okay," he said with a bloody half smile. "Your turn."

I shook my head. "Other hand," I said. I hoped my voice sounded stronger than I felt. My knees had begun to shake and my arms ached and my head was spinning. I was also fighting the urge to hurl. You don't know if you can do it until you do it.

"I can't," he said.

"Other hand."

"If I move this hand, I'm afraid my stomach will fall out."

I adjusted the butt of the rifle against my shoulder. I was sweating, shaking, trying to think. *Either/or, Cassie. What are you going to do, either/or?*

11

"I'm dying," he said matter-of-factly. From this distance, his eyes were just pinpricks of reflected light. "So you can either finish me off or help me. I know you're human—"

"How do you know?" I asked quickly, before he could die on me. If he was a real soldier, he might know how to tell the difference. It would be an extremely useful bit of information.

"Because if you weren't, you would have shot me already." He smiled again, his cheeks dimpled, and that's when it hit me how young he was. Only a couple years older than me.

"See?" he said softly. "That's how you know, too."

"How I know what?" My eyes were tearing up. His crumpled-up body wiggled in my vision like an image in a fun-house mirror. But I didn't dare release my grip on the rifle to rub my eyes.

"That I'm human. If I wasn't, I would have shot you."

That made sense. Or did it make sense because I wanted it to make sense? Maybe he dropped the gun to get me to drop mine, and once I did, the second gun he was hiding under his fatigues would come out and the bullet would say hello to my brain.

This is what the Others have done to us. You can't band together to fight without trust. And without trust, there was no hope.

How do you rid the Earth of humans? Rid the humans of their humanity.

"I have to see your other hand," I said.

"I told you—"

"I have to see your other hand!" My voice cracked then. Couldn't help it.

He lost it. "Then you're just going to have to shoot me, bitch! Just shoot me and get it over with!"

His head fell back against the wall, his mouth came open, and a terrible howl of anguish tumbled out and bounced from wall to wall and floor to ceiling and pounded against my ears. I didn't know if he was screaming from the pain or the realization that I wasn't going to save him. He had given in to hope, and that will kill you. It kills you before you die. Long before you die.

"If I show you," he gasped, rocking back and forth against the bloody concrete, "if I show you, will you help me?"

I didn't answer. I didn't answer because I didn't have an answer. I was playing this one nanosecond at a time.

So he decided for me. He wasn't going to let them win, that's what I think now. He wasn't going to stop hoping. If it killed him, at least he would die with a sliver of his humanity intact.

Grimacing, he slowly pulled out his left hand. Not much day left now, hardly any light at all, and what light there was seemed to be flowing away from its source, from him, past me and out the half-open door.

His hand was caked in half-dried blood. It looked like he was wearing a crimson glove.

The stunted light kissed his bloody hand and flicked along the length of something long and thin and metallic, and my finger yanked back on the trigger, and the rifle kicked against my shoulder hard, and the barrel bucked in my hand as I emptied the clip, and from a great distance I heard someone screaming, but it wasn't him screaming, it was me screaming, me and everybody else who was left, if there was anybody left, all of us helpless, hopeless, stupid humans screaming, because we got it wrong, we got it all wrong, there was no alien swarm descending from the sky in their flying saucers or big metal walkers like something out of *Star Wars* or cute little wrinkly E.T.s who just wanted to pluck a couple of leaves, eat some Reese's Pieces, and go home. That's not how it ends.

That's not how it ends at all.

It ends with us killing each other behind rows of empty beer coolers in the dying light of a late-summer day.

I went up to him before the last of the light was gone. Not to see if he was dead. I knew he was dead. I wanted to see what he was still holding in his bloody hand.

It was a crucifix.

5

THAT WAS THE LAST PERSON I've seen.

The leaves are falling heavy now, and the nights have turned cold. I can't stay in these woods. No leaves for cover from the drones, can't risk a campfire—I gotta get out of here.

I know where I have to go. I've known for a long time. I made a promise. The kind of promise you don't break because, if you break it, you've broken part of yourself, maybe the most important part.

But you tell yourself things. Things like, *I need to come up with something first. I can't just walk into the lion's den without a plan.* Or, *It's hopeless, there's no point anymore. You've waited too long.*

Whatever the reason I didn't leave before, I should have left the night I killed him. I don't know how he was wounded; I didn't examine his body or anything, and I should have, no matter how freaked out I was. I guess he could have gotten hurt in an accident, but the odds were better that someone—or something—had shot him. And if someone or something had shot him, that someone or something was still out there . . . unless the Crucifix Soldier had offed her/him/them/it. Or he was one of them and the crucifix was a trick . . .

Another way the Others mess with your head: the uncertain circumstances of your certain destruction. Maybe that will be the 5th Wave, attacking us from the inside, turning our own minds into weapons.

Maybe the last human being on Earth won't die of starvation or exposure or as a meal for wild animals.

Maybe the last one to die will be killed by the last one alive.

Okay, that's not someplace you want to go, Cassie.

Honestly, even though it's suicide to stay here and I have a promise to keep, I don't want to leave. These woods have been home for a long time. I know every path, every tree, every vine and bush. I lived in the same house for sixteen years and I can't tell you exactly what my backyard looked like, but I can describe in detail every leaf and twig in this stretch of forest. I have no clue what's out there beyond these woods and the two-mile stretch of interstate I hike every week to forage for supplies. I'm guessing a lot more of the same: abandoned towns reeking of sewage and rotting corpses, burned-out shells of houses, feral dogs and cats, pileups that stretch for miles on the highway. And bodies. Lots and lots of bodies.

I pack up. This tent has been my home for a long time, but it's too bulky and I need to travel light. Just the essentials, with the Luger, the M16, the ammo, and my trusty bowie knife topping the list. Sleeping bag, first aid kit, five bottles of water, three boxes of Slim Jims, and some tins of sardines. I hated sardines before the Arrival. Now I've developed a real taste for them. First thing I look for when I hit a grocery store? Sardines.

Books? They're heavy and take up room in my already bulging backpack. But I have a thing about books. So did my father. Our house was stacked floor to ceiling with every book he could find after the 3rd Wave took out more than 3.5 billion people. While the rest of us scrounged for potable water and food and stocked up on the weaponry for the last stand we were sure was coming, Daddy was out with my little brother's Radio Flyer carting home the books.

The mind-blowing numbers didn't faze him. The fact that we'd gone from seven billion strong to a couple hundred thousand in four months didn't shake his confidence that our race would survive.

"We have to think about the future," he insisted. "When this is over, we'll have to rebuild nearly every aspect of civilization."

Solar flashlight.

Toothbrush and paste. I'm determined, when the time comes, to at least go out with clean teeth.

Gloves. Two pairs of socks, underwear, travel-size box of Tide, deodorant, and shampoo. (Gonna go out clean. See above.)

Tampons. I'm constantly worrying about my stash and if I'll be able to find more.

My plastic baggie stuffed with pictures. Dad. Mom. My little brother, Sammy. My grandparents. Lizbeth, my best friend. One of Ben You-Were-Some-Kind-of-Serious-Gorgeous Parish, clipped from my yearbook, because Ben was my future boyfriend and/or/ maybe future husband—not that he knew it. He barely knew I existed. I knew some of the same people he knew, but I was a girl in the background, several degrees of separation removed. The only thing wrong with Ben was his height: He was six inches taller than me. Well, make that two things now: his height and the fact that he's dead.

My cell phone. It was fried in the 1st Wave, and there's no way to charge it. Cell towers don't work, and there's no one to call if they did. But, you know, it's my cell phone.

Nail clippers.

Matches. I don't light fires, but at some point I may need to burn something or blow it up.

Two spiral-bound notebooks, college ruled, one with a purple cover, the other red. My favorite colors, plus they're my journals. It's part of the hope thing. But if I am the last and there's no one left to read them, maybe an alien will and they'll know exactly what I think of them. In case you're an alien and you're reading this:

BITE ME.

My Starburst, already culled of the orange. Three packs of Wrigley's Spearmint. My last two Tootsie Pops.

Mom's wedding ring.

Sammy's ratty old teddy bear. Not that it's mine now. Not that I ever cuddle with it or anything.

That's everything I can stuff into the backpack. Weird. Seems like too much and not enough.

Still room for a couple of paperbacks, barely. *Huckleberry Finn* or *The Grapes of Wrath*? The poems of Sylvia Plath or Sammy's Shel Silverstein? Probably not a good idea to take the Plath. Depressing. Silverstein is for kids, but it still makes me smile. I decide to take *Huckleberry* (seems appropriate) and *Where the Sidewalk Ends*. See you there soon, Shel. Climb aboard, Jim.

I heave the backpack over one shoulder, sling the rifle over the other, and head down the trail toward the highway. I don't look back.

I pause inside the last line of trees. A twenty-foot embankment runs down to the southbound lanes, littered with disabled cars, piles of clothing, shredded plastic garbage bags, the burned-out hulks of tractor trailers carrying everything from gasoline to milk. There are wrecks everywhere, some no worse than fender benders, some pileups that snake along the interstate for miles, and the morning sunlight sparkles on all the broken glass.

There are no bodies. These cars have been here since the 1st Wave, long abandoned by their owners.

Not many people died in the 1st Wave, the massive electromagnetic pulse that ripped through the atmosphere at precisely eleven A.M. on the tenth day. Only around half a million, Dad guessed. Okay, half a million sounds like a lot of people, but really it's just a drop in the population bucket. World War II killed over a hundred times that number.

And we did have some time to prepare for it, though we weren't exactly sure what we were preparing for. Ten days from the first satellite pictures of the mothership passing Mars to the launch of the 1st Wave. Ten days of mayhem. Martial law, sit-ins at the UN, parades, rooftop parties, endless Internet chatter, and 24/7 coverage of the Arrival over every medium. The president addressed the nation—and then disappeared into his bunker. The Security Council went into a locked-down, closed-to-the-press emergency session.

A lot of people just split, like our neighbors, the Majewskis. Packed up their camper on the afternoon of the sixth day with everything they could fit and hit the road, joining a mass exodus to somewhere else, because anywhere else seemed safer for some reason. Thousands of people took off for the mountains . . . or the desert . . . or the swamps. You know, somewhere else.

The Majewskis' somewhere else was Disney World. They weren't the only ones. Disney set attendance records during those ten days before the EMP strike.

Daddy asked Mr. Majewski, "So why Disney World?"

And Mr. Majewski said, "Well, the kids have never been."

His kids were both in college.

Catherine, who had come home from her freshman year at Baylor the day before, asked, "Where are you guys going?"

"Nowhere," I said. And I didn't want to go anywhere. I was still living in denial, pretending all this crazy alien stuff would work out, I didn't know how, maybe with the signing of some intergalactic peace treaty. Or maybe they'd dropped by to take a couple of soil samples and go home. Or maybe they were here on vacation, like the Majewskis going to Disney World.

"You need to get out," she said. "They'll hit the cities first."

"You're probably right," I said. "They'd never dream of taking out the Magic Kingdom."

"How would you rather die?" she snapped. "Hiding under your bed or riding Thunder Mountain?"

Good question.

Daddy said the world was dividing into two camps: runners and nesters. Runners headed for the hills—or Thunder Mountain. Nesters boarded up the windows, stocked up on the canned goods and ammunition, and kept the TV tuned to CNN 24/7.

There were no messages from our galactic party crashers during those first ten days. No light shows. No landing on the South Lawn or bug-eyed, butt-headed dudes in silver jumpsuits demanding to be taken to our leader. No bright, spinning tops blaring the universal language of music. And no answer when we sent our message. Something like, "Hello, welcome to Earth. Hope you enjoy your stay. Please don't kill us."

Nobody knew what to do. We figured the government sort of did. The government had a plan for everything, so we assumed they had a plan for E.T. showing up uninvited and unannounced, like the weird cousin nobody in the family likes to talk about.

Some people nested. Some people ran. Some got married. Some got divorced. Some made babies. Some killed themselves. We walked around like zombies, blank-faced and robotic, unable to absorb the magnitude of what was happening.

It's hard to believe now, but my family, like the vast majority of people, went about our daily lives as if the most monumentally mind-blowing thing in human history wasn't happening right over our heads. Mom and Dad went to work, Sammy went to day care, and I went to school and soccer practice. It was so normal, it was damn weird. By the end of Day One, everybody over the age of two had seen the mothership up close a thousand times, this big grayish-green glowing hulk about the size of Manhattan circling 250 miles above the Earth. NASA announced its plan to pull a space shuttle out of mothballs to attempt contact.

Well, that's good, we thought. *This silence is deafening. Why did they come billions of miles just to stare at us? It's rude.*

On Day Three, I went out with a guy named Mitchell Phelps. Well, technically we went out*side*. The date was in my backyard because of the curfew. He hit the drive-through at Starbucks on his way over, and we sat on the back patio sipping our drinks and pretending we didn't see Dad's shadow passing back and forth as he paced the living room. Mitchell had moved into town a few days before the Arrival. He sat behind me in World Lit, and I made the mistake of loaning him my highlighter. So the next thing I know he's asking me out, because if a girl loans you a highlighter she must think you're hot. I don't know why I went out with him. He wasn't that cute and he wasn't that interesting beyond the whole New Kid aura, and he definitely wasn't Ben Parish. Nobody was—except Ben Parish—and that was the whole problem.

By the third day, you either talked about the Others all the time or you tried not to talk about them at all. I fell into the second category.

Mitchell was in the first.

"What if they're us?" he asked.

It didn't take long after the Arrival for all the conspiracy nuts to start buzzing about classified government projects or the secret plan to manufacture an alien crisis in order to take away our liberties. I thought that's where he was going and groaned.

"What?" he said. "I don't mean *us* us. I mean, what if they're us from the future?"

"And it's like *The Terminator*, right?" I said, rolling my eyes. "They've come to stop the uprising of the machines. Or maybe they *are* the machines. Maybe it's Skynet."

"I don't think so," he said, acting like I was serious. "It's the grandfather paradox."

"What is? And what the hell is the grandfather paradox?" He said it like he assumed I knew what the grandfather paradox was, because, if I didn't know, then I was a moron. I hate when people do that.

"They—I mean we—can't go back in time and change anything. If you went back in time and killed your grandfather before you were born, then you wouldn't be able to go back in time to kill your grandfather."

"Why would you want to kill your grandfather?" I twisted the straw in my strawberry Frappuccino to produce that unique straw-in-a-lid squeak.

"The point is that just showing up changes history," he said. Like I was the one who brought up time travel.

"Do we have to talk about this?"

"What else is there to talk about?" His eyebrows climbed toward his hairline. Mitchell had very bushy eyebrows. It was one of the first things I noticed about him. He also chewed his fingernails. That was the second thing I noticed. Cuticle care can tell you a lot about a person.

I pulled out my phone and texted Lizbeth:

help me

"Are you scared?" he asked. Trying to get my attention. Or for some reassurance. He was looking at me very intently.

I shook my head. "Just bored." A lie. Of course I was scared. I knew I was being mean, but I couldn't help it. For some reason I can't explain, I was mad at him. Maybe I was really mad at myself for saying yes to a date with a guy I wasn't actually interested in. Or maybe I was mad at him for not being Ben Parish, which wasn't his fault. But still.

help u do wat?

"I don't care what we talk about," he said. He was looking toward the rose bed, swirling the dregs of his coffee, his knee popping up and down so violently under the table that my cup jiggled.

mitchell. I didn't think I needed to say any more.

"Who are you texting?"

told u not to go out w him

"Nobody you know," I said. **dont know why i did**

"We can go somewhere else," he said. "You want to go to a movie?"

"There's a curfew," I reminded him. No one was allowed on the streets after nine except military and emergency vehicles.

lol to make ben jealous

"Are you pissed or something?"

"No," I said. "I told you what I was."

He pursed his lips in frustration. He didn't know what to say.

"I was just trying to figure out who they might be," he said.

"You and everybody else on the planet," I said. "Nobody actually knows, and they won't tell us, so everybody sits around guessing and theorizing, and it's all kind of pointless. Maybe they're spacefaring micemen from Planet Cheese and they've come for our provolone."

bp doesnt know i exist

"You know," he said, "it's kind of rude, texting while I'm trying to have a conversation with you."

He was right. I slipped the phone into my pocket. *What's happening to me?* I wondered. The old Cassie never would have done that. Already the Others were changing me into someone different, but I wanted to pretend nothing had changed, especially me.

"Did you hear?" he asked, going right back to the topic that I said bored me. "They're building a landing site."

I had heard. In Death Valley. That's right: Death Valley.

"Personally, I don't think it's a very smart idea," he said. "Rolling out the welcome mat."

"Why not?"

"It's been three days. Three days and they've refused all contact. If they're friendly, why wouldn't they say hello already?"

"Maybe they're just shy." Twisting my hair around my finger, tugging on it gently to produce that semipleasant pain.

"Like being the new kid," he said, the new kid.

That can't be easy, being the new kid. I felt like I should apologize for being rude. "I was kind of mean before," I admitted. "I'm sorry."

He gave me a confused look. He was talking about the aliens,

23

not himself, and then I said something about me, which was about neither.

"It's okay," he said. "I heard you don't date much."

Ouch.

"What else did you hear?" One of those questions you don't want to know the answer to, but still have to ask.

He sipped his latte through the little hole in the plastic lid.

"Not much. It's not like I asked around."

"You asked somebody and they told you I didn't date much."

"I just said I was thinking about asking you out and they go, Cassie's pretty cool. And I said, what's she like? And they said you were nice but don't get my hopes up because you had this thing for Ben Parish—"

"They told you that? Who told you that?"

He shrugged. "I don't remember her name."

"Was it Lizbeth Morgan?" *I'll kill her.*

"I don't know her name," he said.

"What did she look like?"

"Long brown hair. Glasses. I think her name is Carly or something."

"I don't know any . . ."

Oh God. Some Carly person I don't even know knows about me and Ben Parish—or the lack of any me and Ben Parish. And if Carly-or-something knew about it, then everybody knew about it.

"Well, they're wrong," I sputtered. "I don't have a thing for Ben Parish."

"It doesn't matter to me."

"It matters to me."

"Maybe this isn't working out," he said. "Everything I say, you either get bored or mad."

24

"I'm not mad," I said angrily.

"Okay, I'm wrong."

No, he was right. And I was wrong for not telling him the Cassie he knew wasn't the Cassie I used to be, the pre-Arrival Cassie who wouldn't have been mean to a mosquito. I wasn't ready to admit the truth: It wasn't just the world that had changed with the coming of the Others. We changed. I changed. The moment the mothership appeared, I started down a path that would end in the back of a convenience store behind some empty beer coolers. That night with Mitchell was only the beginning of my evolution.

Mitchell was right about the Others not stopping by just to say howdy. On the eve of the 1st Wave, the world's leading theoretical physicist, one of the smartest guys in the world (that's what popped up on the screen under his talking head: ONE OF THE SMARTEST GUYS IN THE WORLD), appeared on CNN and said, "I'm not encouraged by the silence. I can think of no benign reason for it. I'm afraid we may expect something closer to Christopher Columbus's arrival in the Americas than a scene from *Close Encounters*, and we all know how that turned out for the Native Americans."

I turned to my father and said, "We should nuke 'em." I had to raise my voice to be heard over the TV—Dad always jacked up the volume during the news so he could hear it over Mom's TV in the kitchen. She liked to watch TLC while she cooked. I called it the War of the Remotes.

"Cassie!" He was so shocked, his toes began to curl inside his white athletic socks. He grew up on *Close Encounters* and *E.T.* and *Star Trek* and totally bought into the idea that the Others had come to liberate us from ourselves. No more hunger. No more wars. The eradication of disease. The secrets of the cosmos unveiled. "Don't you understand this could be the next step in our evolution? A huge leap forward. Huge." He gave me a consoling hug. "We're all very fortunate to be here to see it."

Then he added casually, like he was talking about how to fix a toaster, "Besides, a nuclear device can't do much damage in the vacuum of space. There's nothing to carry the shock wave."

"So this brainiac on TV is just full of shit?"

"Don't use that language, Cassie," he chided me. "He's entitled to his opinion, but that's all it is. An opinion."

"But what if he's right? What if that thing up there is their version of a Death Star?"

"Travel halfway across the universe just to blow us up?" He patted my leg and smiled. Mom turned up the kitchen TV. He pushed the volume in the family room to twenty-seven.

"Okay, but what about an intergalactic Mongol horde, like he was talking about?" I demanded. "Maybe they've come to conquer us, shove us into reservations, enslave us . . ."

"Cassie," he said. "Simply because something *could* happen doesn't mean it *will* happen. Anyway, it's all just speculation. This guy's. Mine. Nobody knows why they're here. Isn't it just as likely they've come all this way to save us?"

Four months after saying those words, my father was dead.

He was wrong about the Others. And I was wrong. And One of the Smartest Guys in the World was wrong.

It wasn't about saving us. And it wasn't about enslaving us or herding us into reservations.

It was about killing us.

All of us.

6

I DEBATED WHETHER to travel by day or night for a long time. Darkness is best if you're worried about them. But daylight is preferable if you want to spot a drone before it spots you.

The drones showed up at the tag end of the 3rd Wave. Cigar-shaped, dull gray in color, gliding swiftly and silently thousands of feet up. Sometimes they streak across the sky without stopping. Sometimes they circle overhead like buzzards. They can turn on a dime and come to a sudden stop, from Mach 2 to zero in less than a second. That's how we knew the drones weren't ours.

We knew they were unmanned (or un-Othered) because one of them crashed a couple miles from our refugee camp. A *thu-whump!* when it broke the sound barrier, an ear-piercing shriek as it rocketed to earth, the ground shuddering under our feet when it plowed into a fallow cornfield. A recon team hiked to the crash site to check it out. Okay, it wasn't really a team, just Dad and Hutchfield, the guy in charge of the camp. They came back to report the thing was empty. Were they sure? Maybe the pilot bailed before impact. Dad said it was packed with instruments; there wasn't any room for a pilot. "Unless they're two inches tall." That got a big laugh. Somehow it made the horror less horrible, thinking of the Others as being two-inch Borrower types.

I opted to travel by day. I could keep one eye on the sky and another on the ground. What I ended up doing is rocking my head up and down, up and down, side to side, then up again, like some groupie at a rock concert, until I was dizzy and a little sick to my stomach.

Plus there are other things at night to worry about besides drones. Wild dogs, coyotes, bears, and wolves coming down from Canada, maybe even an escaped lion or tiger from a zoo. I know, I know, there's a *Wizard of Oz* joke buried in there. Shoot me.

And though it wouldn't be *much* better, I do think I'd have a better chance against one of them in the daylight. Or even against one of my own, if I'm not the last one. What if I stumble onto another survivor who decides the best course of action is to go all Crucifix Soldier on anyone they come across?

That brings up the problem of my best course of action. Do I shoot on sight? Do I wait for them to make the first move and risk it being a deadly one? I wonder, not for the first time, why the hell we didn't come up with some kind of code or secret handshake or something before they showed up—something that would identify us as the good guys. We had no way of knowing they would show up, but we were pretty sure something would sooner or later.

It's hard to plan for what comes next when what comes next is not something you planned for.

Try to spot them first, I decided. Take cover. No showdowns. No more Crucifix Soldiers!

The day is bright and windless but cold. The sky cloudless. Walking along, bobbing my head up and down, swinging it from side to side, backpack popping against one shoulder blade, the rifle against the other, walking on the outside edge of the median that separates the southbound from the northbound lanes, stopping every few strides to whip around and scan the terrain behind me. An hour. Two. And I've traveled no more than a mile.

The creepiest thing, creepier than the abandoned cars and the snarl of crumpled metal and the broken glass sparkling in the

October sunlight, creepier than all the trash and discarded crap littering the median, most of it hidden by the knee-high grass so the strip of land looks lumpy, covered in boils, the creepiest thing is the silence.

The Hum is gone.

You remember the Hum.

Unless you grew up on top of a mountain or lived in a cave your whole life, the Hum was always around you. That's what life was. It was the sea we swam in. The constant sound of all the things we built to make life easy and a little less boring. The mechanical song. The electronic symphony. The Hum of all our things and all of us. Gone.

This is the sound of the Earth before we conquered it.

Sometimes in my tent, late at night, I think I can hear the stars scraping against the sky. That's how quiet it is. After a while it's almost more than I can stand. I want to scream at the top of my lungs. I want to sing, shout, stamp my feet, clap my hands, anything to declare my presence. My conversation with the soldier had been the first words I'd said aloud in weeks.

The Hum died on the tenth day after the Arrival. I was sitting in third period texting Lizbeth the last text I will ever send. I don't remember exactly what it said.

Eleven A.M. A warm, sunny day in early spring. A day for doodling and dreaming and wishing you were anywhere but Ms. Paulson's calculus class.

The 1st Wave rolled in without much fanfare. It wasn't dramatic. There was no shock and awe.

The lights just winked out.

Ms. Paulson's overhead died.

The screen on my phone went black.

Somebody in the back of the room squealed. Classic. It doesn't matter what time of day it happens—the power goes out, and somebody yelps like the building's collapsing.

Ms. Paulson told us to stay in our seats. That's the other thing people do when the power goes out. They jump up to . . . To what? It's weird. We're so used to electricity, when it's gone, we don't know what to do. So we jump up or squeal or start jabbering like idiots. We panic. It's like someone cut off our oxygen. The Arrival had made it worse, though. Ten days on pins and needles waiting for something to happen while nothing is happening makes you jumpy.

So when they pulled the plug on us, we freaked a little more than normal.

Everybody started talking at once. When I announced that my phone had died, out came everyone's dead phone. Neal Croskey, who was sitting in the back of the room listening to his iPod while Ms. Paulson lectured, pulled the buds from his ears and wondered aloud why the music had died.

The next thing you do when the plug's pulled, after panicking, is run to the nearest window. You don't know why exactly. It's that better-see-what's-going-on feeling. The world works from the outside in. So if the lights go off, you look outside.

And Ms. Paulson, randomly moving around the mob milling in front of the windows: "Quiet! Back to your seats. I'm sure there'll be an announcement . . ."

There was one, about a minute later. Not over the intercom, though, and not from Mr. Faulks, the vice principal. It came from the sky, from them. In the form of a 727 tumbling end over end to the Earth from ten thousand feet until it disappeared behind a line of trees and exploded, sending up a fireball that reminded me of the mushroom cloud of an atomic blast.

Hey, Earthlings! Let's get this party started!

You'd think seeing something like that would send us diving under our desks. It didn't. We crowded against the window and scanned the cloudless sky for the flying saucer that must have taken the plane down. It had to be a flying saucer, right? We knew how a top-notch alien invasion was run. Flying saucers zipping through the atmosphere, squadrons of F-16s hot on their heels, surface-to-air missiles and tracers screaming from the bunkers. In an unreal and admittedly sick way, we wanted to see something like that. It would make this a perfectly normal alien invasion.

For a half hour we waited by the windows. Nobody said much. Ms. Paulson told us to go back to our seats. We ignored her. Thirty minutes into the 1st Wave and already social order was breaking down. People kept checking their phones. We couldn't connect it: the plane crashing, the lights going out, our phones dying, the clock on the wall with the big hand frozen on the twelve, little hand on the eleven.

Then the door flew open and Mr. Faulks told us to head over to the gym. I thought that was really smart. Get all of us in one place so the aliens didn't have to waste a lot of ammunition.

So we trooped over to the gym and sat in the bleachers in near total darkness while the principal paced back and forth, stopping every now and then to yell at us to be quiet and wait for our parents to get there.

What about the students whose cars were at school? Couldn't they leave?

"Your cars won't work."

WTF? What does he mean, our cars won't work?

An hour passed. Then two. I sat next to Lizbeth. We didn't talk much, and when we did, we whispered. We weren't afraid of the principal; we were listening. I'm not sure what we were listening for, but it was like that quiet before the clouds open up and the thunder smashes down.

"This could be it," Lizbeth whispered. She rubbed her nose nervously. Dug her lacquered nails into her dyed blond hair. Tapped her foot. Rolled the pad of her finger over her eyelid: She had just started wearing contacts and they bugged her constantly.

"It's definitely something," I whispered back.

"I mean, this could be *it*. Like *it* it. The end."

She kept slipping the battery out of her phone and putting it back in. It was better than doing nothing, I guess.

She started to cry. I took her phone away and held her hand. Looked around. She wasn't the only one crying. Other kids were praying. And others were doing both, crying and praying. The teachers were huddled up by the gym doors, forming a human shield in case the creatures from outer space decided to storm the floor.

"There's so much I wanted to do," Lizbeth said. "I've never even . . ." She choked back a sob. "You know."

"I've got a feeling a lot of 'you know' is going on right now," I said. "Probably right underneath these bleachers."

"You think?" She wiped her cheeks with the palm of her hand. "What about you?"

"About 'you know'?" I had no problem with talking about sex. My problem was talking about sex as it related to me.

"Oh, I know you haven't 'you know.' God! I'm not talking about that."

"I thought we were."

"I'm talking about our lives, Cassie! Jesus, this could be the end of the freakin' world, and all you want to do is talk about sex!"

32

She pulled her phone out of my hand and fumbled with the battery cover.

"Which is why you should just tell him," she said, fiddling with the drawstrings of her hoodie.

"Tell who what?" I knew exactly what she meant; I was just buying time.

"Ben! You should tell him how you feel. How you've felt since the third grade."

"This is a joke, right?" I felt my face getting hot.

"And then you should have sex with him."

"Lizbeth, shut up."

"It's the truth."

"I haven't wanted to have sex with Ben Parish since the third grade," I whispered. The third grade? I glanced over at her to see if she was really listening. Apparently, she wasn't.

"If I were you, I'd go right up to him and say, 'I think this is it. This is it, and I'll be damned if I'm going to die in this school gymnasium without ever having sex with you.' And then you know what I'd do?"

"What?" I was fighting back a laugh, picturing the look on his face.

"I'd take him outside to the flower garden and have sex with him."

"In the flower garden?"

"Or the locker room." She waved her hand around frantically to include the entire school—or maybe the whole world. "It doesn't matter where."

"The locker room smells." I looked two rows down at the outline of Ben Parish's gorgeous head. "That kind of thing only happens in the movies," I said.

"Yeah, totally unrealistic, not like what's happening right now."

She was right. It was totally unrealistic. Both scenarios, an alien invasion of the Earth and a Ben Parish invasion of me.

"At least you could tell him how you feel," she said, reading my mind.

Could, yes. Ever would, well . . .

And I never did. That was the last time I saw Ben Parish, sitting in that dark, stuffy gymnasium (Home of the Hawks!) two rows down from me, and only the back part of him. He probably died in the 3rd Wave like almost everybody else, and I never told him how I felt. I could have. He knew who I was; he sat behind me in a couple of classes.

He probably doesn't remember, but in middle school we rode the same bus, and there was an afternoon when I overheard him talking about his little sister being born the day before and I turned around and said, "My brother was born last week!" And he said, "Really?" Not sarcastic, but like he thought it was a cool coincidence, and for about a month I went around thinking we had this special connection based on babies. Then we were in high school and he became the star wide receiver for the team and I became just another girl watching him score from the stands. I would see him in class or in the hallway, and sometimes I had to fight the urge to run up to him and say, "Hi, I'm Cassie, the girl from the bus. Do you remember the babies?"

The funny thing is, he probably would have. Ben Parish couldn't be satisfied with being the most gorgeous guy in school. Just to torment me with his perfection, he also insisted on being one of the smartest. And have I mentioned he was kind to small animals and children? His little sister was on the sidelines at every game, and when we took the district title, Ben ran straight to

34

the sidelines, hoisted her onto his shoulders, and led the parade around the track with her waving to the crowd like a homecoming queen.

Oh, and one more thing: his killer smile. Don't get me started.

After another hour in the dark and stuffy gym, I saw my dad appear in the doorway. He gave a little wave, like he showed up at my school every day to take me home after alien attacks. I hugged Lizbeth and told her I'd call as soon as the phones started working again. I was still practicing pre-invasion thinking. You know, the power goes out, but it always comes back on. So I just gave her a hug and I don't remember telling her that I loved her.

We went outside and I said, "Where's the car?"

And Dad said the car wasn't working. No cars were working. The streets were littered with stalled-out cars and buses and motorcycles and trucks, smashups and clusters of wrecks on every block, cars folded around light poles and sticking out of buildings. A lot of people were trapped when the EMP hit; the automatic locks on the doors didn't work, and they had to break out of their own cars or sit there and wait for someone to rescue them. The injured people who could still move crawled onto the roadside and sidewalks to wait for the paramedics, but no paramedics came because the ambulances and the fire trucks and the cop cars didn't work, either. Everything that ran on batteries or electricity or had an engine died at eleven A.M.

Dad walked as he talked, keeping a tight grip on my wrist, like he was afraid something might swoop down out of the sky and snatch me away.

"Nothing's working. No electricity, no phones, no plumbing..."

"We saw a plane crash."

He nodded. "I'm sure they all did. Anything and everything in the sky when it hit. Fighter jets, helicopters, troop transports . . ."

"When what hit?"

"EMP," he said. "Electromagnetic pulse. Generate one large enough and you knock out the entire grid. Power. Communications. Transportation. Anything that flies or drives is zapped out."

It was a mile and a half from my school to our house. The longest mile and a half I've ever walked. It felt as if a curtain had fallen over everything, a curtain painted to look exactly like what it was hiding. There were glimpses, though, little peeks behind the curtain that told you something had gone very wrong. Like all the people standing on their front porches holding their dead phones, looking up at the sky, or bending over the open hoods of their cars, fiddling with wires, because that's what you do when your car dies—you fiddle with wires.

"But it's okay," he said, squeezing my wrist. "It's okay. There's a good chance our backup systems weren't crippled, and I'm sure the government has a contingency plan, protected bases, that sort of thing."

"And how does pulling our plug fit into their plan to help us along in the next stage of our evolution, Dad?"

I regretted the words the instant I said them. But I was freaking out. He didn't take it the wrong way. He looked at me and smiled reassuringly and said, "Everything's going to be okay," because that's what I wanted him to say and it's what he wanted to say and that's what you do when the curtain is falling—you give the line that the audience wants to hear.

7

AROUND NOON on my mission to keep my promise, I stop for a water break and a Slim Jim. Every time I eat a Slim Jim or a can of sardines or anything prepackaged, I think, *Well, there's one less of that in the world.* Whittling away the evidence of our having been here one bite at a time.

One of these days, I've decided, I'm going to work up the nerve to catch a chicken and wring its delicious neck. I would kill for a cheeseburger. Honestly. If I stumbled across someone eating a cheeseburger, I would kill them for it.

There are plenty of cows around. I could shoot one and carve it up with my bowie knife. I'm pretty sure I'd have no problem slaughtering a cow. The hard part would be cooking it. Having a fire, even in daylight, was the surest way to invite them to the cookout.

A shadow shoots across the grass a dozen yards in front of me. I jerk my head back, knocking it hard against the side of a Honda Civic I was leaning against while I enjoyed my snack. It wasn't a drone. It was a bird, a seagull of all things, skimming along with barely a flick of its outstretched wings. A shiver of revulsion goes down my spine. I hate birds. I didn't before the Arrival. I didn't after the 1st Wave. I didn't after the 2nd Wave, which really didn't affect me that much.

But after the 3rd Wave, I hated them. It wasn't their fault, I knew that. It was like a man in front of a firing squad hating the bullets, but I couldn't help it.

Birds suck.

8

AFTER THREE DAYS on the road, I've determined that cars are pack animals.

They prowl in groups. They die in clumps. Clumps of smash-ups. Clumps of stalls. They glimmer in the distance like jewels. And suddenly the clumps stop. The road is empty for miles. There's just me and the asphalt river cutting through a defile of half-naked trees, their leaves crinkled and clinging desperately to their dark branches. There's the road and the naked sky and the tall, brown grass and me.

These empty stretches are the worst. Cars provide cover. And shelter. I sleep in the undamaged ones (I haven't found a locked one yet). If you can call it sleep. Stale, stuffy air; you can't crack the windows, and leaving the door open is out of the question. The gnaw of hunger. And the night thoughts. *Alone, alone, alone.*

And the baddest of the bad night thoughts:

I'm no alien drone designer, but if I were going to make one, I'd make sure that its detection device was sensitive enough to pick up a body's heat signature through a car roof. It never failed: The moment I started to drift off, I imagined all four doors flying open and dozens of hands reaching for me, hands attached to arms attached to whatever they are. And then I'm up, fumbling with my M16, peeking over the backseat, then do-ing a 360, feeling trapped and more than a little blind behind the fogged-up windows.

Dawn comes. I wait for the morning fog to burn off, then sip some water, brush my teeth, double-check my weapons, inventory

38

my supplies, and hit the road again. Look up, look down, look all around. Don't pause at the exits. Water's fine for now. No way am I going anywhere near a town unless I have to.

For a lot of reasons.

You know how you can tell when you're getting close to one? The smell. You can smell a town from miles away.

It smells like smoke. And raw sewage. And death.

In the city it's hard to take two steps without stumbling over a corpse. Funny thing: People die in clumps, too.

I begin to smell Cincinnati about a mile before spotting the exit sign. A thick column of smoke rises lazily toward the cloudless sky.

Cincinnati is burning.

I'm not surprised. After the 3rd Wave, the second most common thing you found in cities, after the bodies, were fires. A single lightning strike could take out ten city blocks. There was no one left to put the fires out.

My eyes start to water. The stench of Cincinnati makes me gag. I stop long enough to tie a rag around my mouth and nose and then quicken my pace. I pull the rifle off my shoulder and cradle it as I quickstep. I have a bad feeling about Cincinnati. The old voice inside my head is awake.

Hurry, Cassie. Hurry.

And then, somewhere between Exits 17 and 18, I find the bodies.

9

THERE ARE THREE OF THEM, not in a clump like city folk, but spaced out in the median strip. The first one is an older guy, around my dad's age, I guess. Wearing blue jeans and a Bengals warm-up. Facedown, arms outstretched. He was shot in the back of the head.

The second, about a dozen feet away, is a young woman, a little older than I am and dressed in a pair of men's pajama pants and Victoria's Secret tee. A streak of purple in her short-cropped hair. A skull ring on her left index finger. Black nail polish, badly chipped. And a bullet hole in the back of her head.

Another few feet and there's the third. A kid around eleven or twelve. Brand-new white basketball high-tops. Black sweatshirt. Hard to tell what his face used to look like.

I leave the kid and go back to the woman. Kneel in the tall brown grass beside her. Touch her pale neck. Still warm.

Oh no. No, no, no.

I trot back to the first guy. Kneel. Touch the palm of his outstretched hand. Look over at the bloody hole between his ears. Shiny. Still wet.

I freeze. Behind me, the road. In front of me, more road. To my right, trees. To my left, more trees. Clumps of cars on the southbound lane, the nearest grouping about a hundred feet away. Something tells me to look up. Straight up.

A fleck of dull gray against the backdrop of dazzling autumnal blue.

Motionless.

Hello, Cassie. My name is Mr. Drone. Nice to meet you!

I stand up, and when I stand up—the moment I stand up; if I had stayed frozen there a millisecond longer, Mr. Bengals and I would be sporting matching holes—something slams into my leg, a hot punch just above my knee that knocks me off balance, sending me sprawling backward onto my butt.

I didn't hear the shot. There was the cool wind in the grass and my own hot breath under the rag and the blood rushing in my ears—that's all there was before the bullet struck.

Silencer.

That makes sense. Of course they'd use silencers. And now I have the perfect name for them: Silencers. A name that fits the job description.

Something takes over when you're facing death. The front part of your brain lets go, gives up control to the oldest part of you, the part that takes care of your heartbeat and breathing and the blinking of your eyes. The part nature built first to keep your ass alive. The part that stretches time like a gigantic piece of toffee, making a second seem like an hour and a minute longer than a summer afternoon.

I lunge forward for my rifle—I had dropped the M16 when the round punched home—and the ground in front of me explodes, showering me with shredded grass and hunks of dirt and gravel.

Okay, forget the M16.

I yank the Luger from my waistband and do a sort of running hop—or a hopping run—toward the closest car. There isn't much pain—although my guess is that we're going to get very intimate later—but I can feel the blood soaking into my jeans by the time I reach the car, an older model Buick sedan.

The rear windshield shatters as I dive down. I scoot on my back till I'm all the way under the car. I'm not a big girl by any stretch, but it's a tight fit, no room to roll over, no way to turn if he shows up on the left side.

Cornered.

Smart, Cassie, real smart. Straight As last semester? Honor roll? Riiiiiight.

You should have stayed in your little stretch of woods in your little tent with your little books and your cute little mementos. At least when they came for you, there'd be room to run.

The minutes spin out. I lie on my back and bleed onto the cold concrete. Rolling my head to the right, to the left, raising it a half inch to look past my feet toward the back of the car. Where the hell is he? What's taking so long? Then it hits me:

He's using a high-powered sniper rifle. Has to be. Which means he could have been over a half mile away when he shot me.

Which also means I have more time than I first thought. Time to come up with something besides a blubbery, desperate, disjointed prayer.

Make him go away. Make him be quick. Let me live. Let him end it . . .

Shaking uncontrollably. I'm sweating; I'm freezing cold.

You're going into shock. Think, Cassie.

Think.

It's what we're made for. It's what got us here. It's the reason I have this car to hide under. We are human.

And humans think. They plan. They dream, and then they make the dream real.

Make it real, Cassie.

Unless he drops down, he won't be able to get to me. And when he drops down . . . when he dips his head to look at me . . . when he reaches in to grab my ankle and drag me out . . .

No. He's too smart for that. He's going to assume I'm armed. He wouldn't risk it. Not that Silencers care whether they live or die . . . or *do* they care? Do Silencers know fear? They don't love life—I've seen enough to prove that. But do they love their own lives more than they love taking someone else's?

Time stretches out. A minute's longer than a season. What's taking him so damn long?

It's an either/or world now. Either he's coming to finish it or he isn't. But he has to finish it, doesn't he? Isn't that the reason he's here? Isn't that the whole friggin' point?

Either/or: Either I run—or hop or crawl or roll—or I stay under this car and bleed to death. If I risk escape, it's a turkey shoot. I won't make it two feet. If I stay, same result, only more painful, more fearful, and much, much slower.

Black stars blossom and dance in front of my eyes. I can't get enough air into my lungs.

I reach up with my left hand and yank the cloth from my face. The cloth.

Cassie, you're an idiot.

I set the gun down beside me. That's the hardest part—making myself let go of the gun.

I lift my leg, slide the rag beneath it. I can't lift my head to see what I'm doing. I stare past the black, blossoming stars at the grimy guts of the Buick as I pull the two ends together, cinch them tight, as tight as I can, and fumble with the knot. I reach down and explore the wound with my fingertips. It's still bleeding, but a trickle compared to the bubbling gusher I had before tying off the tourniquet.

I pick up the gun. Better. My eyesight clears a little, and I don't feel quite so cold. I shift a couple of inches to the left; I don't like lying in my own blood.

Where is he? He's had plenty of time to finish this . . .

Unless he is finished.

That brings me up short. For a few seconds, I totally forget to breathe.

He's not coming. He's not coming because he doesn't need to come. He knows you won't dare come out, and if you don't come out and run, you won't make it. He knows you'll starve or bleed to death or die of dehydration.

He knows what you know: Run = die. Stay = die.

Time for him to move on to the next one.

If there is a next one.

If I'm not the last one.

Come on, Cassie! From seven billion to just one in five months? You're not the last, and even if you are the last human being on Earth—especially if you are—you can't let it end this way. Trapped under a goddamned Buick, bleeding until all the blood is gone—is this how humanity waves good-bye?

Hell no.

10

THE 1ST WAVE took out half a million people.

The 2nd Wave put that number to shame.

In case you don't know, we live on a restless planet. The continents sit on slabs of rock, called tectonic plates, and those plates float on a sea of molten lava. They're constantly scraping and rubbing and pushing against one another, creating enormous pressure.

Over time the pressure builds and builds, until the plates slip, releasing huge amounts of energy in the form of earthquakes. If one of those quakes happens along one of the fault lines that ring every continent, the shock wave produces a superwave called a tsunami.

Over 40 percent of the world's population lives within sixty miles of a coastline. That's three billion people.

All the Others had to do was make it rain.

Take a metal rod twice as tall as the Empire State Building and three times as heavy. Position it over one of these fault lines. Drop it from the upper atmosphere. You don't need any propulsion or guidance system; just let it fall. Thanks to gravity, by the time it reaches the surface, it's traveling twelve miles per second, twenty times faster than a speeding bullet.

It hits the surface with a force one billion times greater than the bomb dropped on Hiroshima.

Bye-bye, New York. Bye, Sydney. Good-bye, California, Washington, Oregon, Alaska, British Columbia. So long, Eastern Seaboard.

Japan, Hong Kong, London, Rome, Rio.

Nice to know you. Hope you enjoyed your stay!

The 1st Wave was over in seconds.

The 2nd Wave lasted a little longer. About a day.

The 3rd Wave? That took a little longer—twelve weeks. Twelve weeks to kill . . . well, Dad figured 97 percent of those of us unlucky enough to have survived the first two waves.

Ninety-seven percent of four billion? You do the math.

That's when the Alien Empire descended in their flying saucers and started blasting away, right? When the peoples of the Earth united under one banner to play David versus Goliath. Our tanks against your ray guns. Bring it on!

We weren't that lucky.

And they weren't that stupid.

How do you waste nearly four billion people in three months? Birds.

How many birds are there in the world? Wanna guess? A million? A billion? How about over three hundred billion? That's about seventy-five birds for each man, woman, and child still alive after the first two waves.

There are thousands of species of bird on every continent. And birds don't recognize borders. They also crap a lot. They crap five or six times a day. That's over a trillion little missiles raining down each day, every day.

You couldn't invent a more efficient delivery system for a virus that has a 97 percent kill rate.

My father thought they must have taken something like Ebola Zaire and genetically altered it. Ebola can't spread through the air. But change a single protein and you can make it airborne, like the flu. The virus takes up residence in your lungs. You get a bad cough. Fever. Your head starts to hurt. Hurt bad. You start spitting up little drops of virus-laden blood. The bug moves into your liver, your kidneys, your brain. You're packing a billion of them now. You've become a viral bomb. And when you explode, you blast everyone around you with the virus. They call it bleeding out. Like rats fleeing a sinking ship, the virus erupts out of every opening. Your mouth, your nose, your ears, your ass, even your eyes. You literally cry tears of blood.

We had different names for it. The Red Death or the Blood Plague. The Pestilence. The Red Tsunami. The Fourth Horseman. Whatever you wanted to call it, after three months, ninety-seven out of every hundred people were dead.

That's a lot of bloody tears.

Time was flowing in reverse. The 1st Wave knocked us back to the eighteenth century. The next two slammed us into the Neolithic.

We were hunter-gatherers again. Nomads. Bottom of the pyramid.

But we weren't ready to give up hope. Not yet.

There were still enough of us left to fight back.

We couldn't take them head-on, but we could fight a guerilla war. We could go all asymmetrical on their alien asses. We had enough guns and ammo and even some transport that survived the 1st Wave. Our militaries had been decimated, but there were still functional units on every continent. There were bunkers and caves and underground bases where we could hide for years. *You be America, alien invaders, and we'll be Vietnam.*

And the Others go, *Yeah, okay, right.*

We thought they had thrown everything at us—or at least the worst, because it was hard to imagine anything worse than the Red Death. Those of us who survived the 3rd Wave—the ones with a natural immunity to the disease—hunkered down and stocked up and waited for the People in Charge to tell us what to do. We knew somebody had to be in charge, because occasionally a fighter jet would scream across the sky and we heard what sounded like gun battles in the distance and the rumble of troop carriers just over the horizon.

I guess my family was luckier than most. The Fourth Horseman rode off with my mom, but Dad, Sammy, and I survived. Dad boasted about our superior genes. Not something you'd normally do, brag on top of an Everest of nearly seven billion dead people. Dad was just being Dad, trying to put the best spin he could on the eve of human extinction.

Most cities and towns were abandoned in the wake of the Red

Tsunami. There was no electricity, no plumbing, the shops and stores had long since been looted of anything valuable. Raw sewage was an inch deep on some streets. Fires from summer lightning storms were common.

Then there was the problem of the bodies.

As in, they were everywhere. Houses, shelters, hospitals, apartments, office buildings, schools, churches and synagogues, and warehouses.

There's a tipping point when the sheer volume of death overwhelms you. You can't bury or burn the bodies fast enough. That summer of the Pestilence was brutally hot, and the stench of rotting flesh hung in the air like an invisible, noxious fog. We soaked strips of cloth in perfume and tied them over our mouths and noses, and by the end of the day the reek had soaked into the material and all you could do was sit there and gag.

Until—funny thing—you got used to it.

We waited out the 3rd Wave barricaded inside our house. Partly because there was a quarantine. Partly because some pretty whacked-out people roamed the streets, breaking into houses and setting fires, the whole murder, rape, and pillaging thing. Partly because we were scared out of our minds waiting for what might come next.

But mostly because Dad didn't want to leave Mom. She was too sick to travel, and he couldn't bring himself to abandon her.

She told him to go. Leave her behind. She was going to die anyway. It wasn't about her anymore. It was about me and Sammy. About keeping us safe. About the future and hanging on to the hope that tomorrow would be better than today.

Dad didn't argue. But he didn't leave her, either. He waited for the inevitable, keeping her as comfortable as possible, and looked at maps and made lists and gathered supplies. This was around the time the whole book-hoarding, we-have-to-rebuild-civilization kick started. On nights when the sky wasn't totally blanketed in smoke, we went into the backyard and took turns with my old telescope, watching the mothership sail majestically across the backdrop of the Milky Way. The stars were brighter now, brilliantly bright, without our man-made lights to dim them.

"What are they waiting for?" I would ask him. I was still expecting—like everybody else—the saucers and the mechanical walkers and the laser cannons. "Why don't they just get it over with?"

And Daddy would shake his head. "I don't know, pumpkin," he would say. "Maybe it is over. Maybe the goal isn't to kill all of us, just wean us down to a manageable number."

"And then what? What do they want?"

"I think the better question is what they need," he said gently, as if he were breaking some really bad news. "They're being very careful, you know."

"Careful?"

"To not damage it more than absolutely necessary. It's the reason they're here, Cassie. They need the Earth."

"But not us," I whispered. I was about to lose it—again. For about the trillionth time.

He put his hand on my shoulder—for about the trillionth time—and said, "Well, we had our shot. And we weren't handling our inheritance very well. I bet if we could somehow go back and interview the dinosaurs before the asteroid struck . . ."

That's when I punched him as hard as I could. Ran inside.

I don't know which is worse, inside or outside. Outside you feel totally exposed, constantly watched, naked beneath the naked sky. But inside it's perpetual twilight. Boarded-up windows that block out the sun during the day. Candles at night, but we're running low on candles, can't spare more than one per room, and deep shadows lurk in once-familiar corners.

"What is it, Cassie?" Sammy. Five. Adorable. Big brown teddy-bear eyes, clutching the other member of the family with big brown eyes, the stuffed one I now have stowed in the bottom of my backpack.

"Why are you crying?"

Seeing my tears got his started.

I brushed past him, headed for the room of the sixteen-year-old human dinosaur, *Cassiopeia Sullivanus extinctus*. Then I went back to him. I couldn't leave him crying like that. We'd gotten pretty tight since Mom got sick. Nearly every night bad dreams chased him into my room, and he'd crawl in bed with me and press his face against my chest, and sometimes he forgot and called me Mommy.

"Did you see them, Cassie? Are they coming?"

"No, kiddo," I said, wiping away his tears. "No one's coming."

Not yet.

———— **11** ————

MOM DIED ON A TUESDAY.

Dad buried her in the backyard, in the rose bed. She had asked for that before she died. At the height of the Pestilence, when hundreds were dying every day, most of the bodies were hauled to the outskirts and burned. Dying towns were ringed by the constantly smoldering bonfires of the dead.

He told me to stay with Sammy. Sammy, who'd gone zombie-like on us, shuffling around, mouth hanging open or sucking his thumb like he was two again, with this blankness in his teddy-bear eyes. Just a few months ago, Mom was pushing him on a swing, taking him to karate classes, washing his hair, dancing with him to his favorite song. Now she was wrapped in a white sheet and riding on his daddy's shoulder into the backyard.

I saw Dad through the kitchen window kneeling by the shallow grave. His head was down. Shoulders jerking. I'd never seen him lose it, not once, since the Arrival. Things kept getting worse, and just when you thought they couldn't get any worse, they got even worse, but Dad never freaked. Even when Mom started showing the first signs of infection, he stayed calm, especially in front of her. He didn't talk about what was happening outside the barricaded doors and windows. He laid wet cloths over her forehead. He bathed her, changed her, fed her. Not once did I see him cry in front of her. While some people were shooting themselves and hanging themselves and swallowing handfuls of pills and jumping from high places, Dad pushed back against the darkness.

He sang to her and repeated stupid jokes she'd heard a thousand times, and he lied. He lied the way a parent lies to you, the good lie that helps you go to sleep.

"Heard another plane today. Sounded like a fighter. Means some of our stuff must have made it through."

"Your fever's down a bit, and your eyes look clearer today. Maybe this isn't it. Might just be your garden-variety flu."

In the final hours, wiping away her bloody tears.

Holding her while she barfed up the black, viral stew her stomach had become.

Bringing me and Sammy into the room to say good-bye.

"It's all right," she told Sammy. "Everything is going to be all right."

To me she said, "He needs you now, Cassie. Take care of him. Take care of your father."

I told her she was going to get better. Some people did. They got sick, and then suddenly the virus let go. Nobody understood why. Maybe it decided it didn't like the way you tasted. And I didn't say she was going to get better to ease her fear. I really believed it. I had to believe it.

"You're all they have," Mom said. Her last words to me.

The mind was the last thing to go, washed away in the red waters of the Tsunami. The virus took total control. Some people went into a frenzy as it boiled their brains. They punched, clawed, kicked, bit. Like the virus that needed us also hated us and couldn't wait to get rid of us.

My mother looked at my dad and didn't know him. Didn't know where she was. Who she was. What was happening to her. There was this, like, permanent, creepy smile, cracked lips pulled back from bleeding gums, her teeth stained with blood. Sounds came out of her mouth, but they weren't words. The place in her brain that made words was packed with virus, and the virus didn't know language—it knew only how to make more of itself.

And then my mother died in a fury of jerks and gargled screams, her uninvited guests rocketing out of every orifice, because she was done, they'd used her up, time to turn off the lights and find a new home.

Dad bathed her one last time. Combed her hair. Scrubbed the dried blood from her teeth. When he came to tell me she was gone, he was calm. He didn't lose it. He held me while I lost it.

Now I was watching him through the kitchen window. Kneeling

beside her in the rose bed, thinking no one could see him, my father let go of the rope he'd been clinging to, loosened the line that had kept him steady all that time while everyone around him went into free fall.

I made sure Sammy was okay and went outside. I sat next to him. Put my hand on his shoulder. The last time I'd touched my father, it was a lot harder and with my fist. I didn't say anything, and he didn't, either, not for a long time.

He slipped something into my hand. Mom's wedding ring. He said she'd want me to have it.

"We're leaving, Cassie. Tomorrow morning."

I nodded. I knew she was the only reason we hadn't left yet. The delicate stems on the roses bobbed and swayed, as if echoing my nod. "Where are we going?"

"Away." He looked around, and his eyes were wide and frightened. "It isn't safe anymore."

Duh, I thought. *When was it ever?*

"Wright-Patterson Air Force Base is just over a hundred miles from here. If we push and the weather stays good, we can be there in five or six days."

"And then what?" The Others had conditioned us to think this way: *Okay, this, and then what?* I looked to my father to tell me. He was the smartest man I knew. If he didn't have an answer, there was no one who did. I sure didn't. And I sure wanted him to. I needed him to.

He shook his head like he didn't understand the question.

"What's at Wright-Patterson?" I asked.

"I don't know that anything's there." He tried out a smile and grimaced, like smiling hurt.

"Then why are we going?"

53

"Because we can't stay here," he said through gritted teeth. "And if we can't stay here, we have to go somewhere. If there's anything like a government left at all . . ."

He shook his head. He hadn't come outside for this. He had come outside to bury his wife.

"Go inside, Cassie."

"I'll help you."

"I don't need your help."

"She's my mother. I loved her, too. Please let me help." I was crying again. He didn't see. He wasn't looking at me, and he wasn't looking at Mom. He wasn't looking at anything, really. There was, like, this black hole where the world used to be, and we were both falling toward it. What could we hold on to? I pulled his hand off Mom's body and pressed it against my cheek and told him I loved him and that Mom loved him and that everything would be okay, and the black hole lost a little of its strength.

"Go inside, Cassie," he said gently. "Sammy needs you more than she does."

I went inside. Sammy was sitting on the floor in his room, playing with his X-wing starfighter, destroying the Death Star. "Shroooooom, shroooooom. I'm going in, Red One!"

And outside, my father knelt in the freshly turned earth. Brown dirt, red rose, gray sky, white sheet.

12

I GUESS I have to talk about Sammy now.

I don't know how else to get there.

There being that first inch in the open, where the sunlight kissed my scraped-up cheek when I slid out from under the Buick. That first inch was the hardest. The longest inch in the universe. The inch that stretched a thousand miles.

There being that place on the highway where I turned to face the enemy I couldn't see.

There being the one thing that's kept me from going completely crazy, the thing the Others haven't been able to take from me after taking everything from me.

Sammy is the reason I didn't give up. Why I didn't stay beneath that car and wait for the end.

The last time I saw him was through the back window of a school bus. His forehead pressing against the glass. Waving at me. And smiling. Like he was going on a field trip: excited, nervous, not scared at all. Being with all those other kids helped. And the school bus, which was so normal. What's more everyday than a big, yellow school bus? So ordinary, in fact, that the sight of them pulling into the refugee camp after the last four months of horror was shocking. It was like seeing a McDonald's on the moon. Totally weird and crazy and something that just shouldn't *be*.

We'd been in the camp only a couple of weeks. Of the fifty or so people there, ours was the only family. Everybody else was a widow, a widower, an orphan. The last ones standing in their family, strangers before coming to the camp. The oldest was probably in his sixties. Sammy was the youngest, but there were seven other kids, none except me older than fourteen.

The camp lay twenty miles east of where we lived, hacked out of the woods during the 3rd Wave to build a field hospital after the ones in town had reached full capacity. The buildings were slapped together, made out of hand-sawed lumber and salvaged tin, one main ward for the infected and a smaller shack for the two doctors who tended the dying before they, too, were sucked down by the Red Tsunami. There was a summer garden and a system that captured rainwater for washing and bathing and drinking.

We ate and slept in the big building. Between five and six hundred people had bled out in there, but the floor and walls had been bleached and the cots they died on had been burned. It still smelled faintly of the Pestilence (a little like soured milk), and the bleach hadn't removed all the bloodstains. There were patterns of tiny spots covering the walls and long, sickle-shaped stains on the floor. It was like living in a 3-D abstract painting.

The shack was a combination storehouse and weapons cache. Canned vegetables, packaged meats, dry goods, and staples, like salt. Shotguns, pistols, semiautomatics, even a couple of flare guns. Every man walked around armed to the teeth; it was the Wild West all over again.

A shallow pit had been dug a few hundred yards into the woods behind the compound. The pit was for burning bodies. We weren't allowed to go back there, so of course me and some of the older kids did. There was this one creep they called Crisco, I guess because of his long, greased-back hair. Crisco was thirteen and a trophy hunter. He'd actually wade into the ashes to scavenge for jewelry and coins and anything else he might find valuable or "interesting." He swore he didn't do it because he was a sicko.

"This is the difference now," he would say, chortling, sorting through his latest haul with crud-encrusted fingernails, his hands gloved in the gray dust of human remains.

The difference between what?

"Between being the Man or not. The barter system is back, baby!" Holding up a diamond necklace. "And when it's all over except for the shouting, the people with the good stuff are going to call the shots."

The idea that they wanted to kill *all* of us still wasn't something that had occurred to anyone, even the adults. Crisco saw himself as one of the Native Americans who sold Manhattan for a handful of beads, not as a dodo bird, which was a lot closer to the truth.

Dad had heard about the camp a few weeks back, when Mom started showing early symptoms of the Pestilence. He tried to get Mom to go, but she knew there was nothing anyone could do. If she was going to die, she wanted to do it in her own home, not in some bogus hospice in the middle of the woods. Then later, as she was entering the final hours, the rumor came around that the hospital had been turned into a rendezvous point, a kind of survivor safe house, far enough from town to be reasonably safe in the next wave, whatever that was going to be (though the smart money was on some kind of aerial bombardment), but close enough for the People in Charge to find when they came to rescue us—if there were People in Charge and if they came.

The unofficial boss of the camp was a retired marine named Hutchfield. He was a human LEGO person: square hands, square head, square jaw. Wore the same muscle tee every day, stained with something that might have been blood, though his black boots always sported a mirror finish. He shaved his head (though not his chest or back, which he really should have considered). He was covered in tattoos. And he liked guns. Two on his hip, one tucked behind his back, another slung over his shoulder. No one carried more guns than Hutchfield. Maybe that had something to do with his being the unofficial boss.

Sentries had spotted us coming, and when we reached the dirt road that led into the woods to the camp, Hutchfield was there with another guy named Brogden. I'm pretty sure we were supposed to notice the firepower draped all over their bodies. Hutchfield ordered us to split up. He was going to talk to Dad; Brogden got me and Sams. I told Hutchfield what I thought about that idea. You know, like where exactly on his tattooed behind he could stick it.

I'd just lost one parent. I wasn't too keen on the idea of losing another.

"It's all right, Cassie," my father said.

"We don't know these guys," I argued with him. "They could be just another bunch of Twigs, Dad." *Twigs* was street for "thugs with guns," the murderers, rapists, black marketers, kidnappers, and just your general punks who showed up midway through the 3rd Wave, the reason people barricaded their houses and stockpiled food and weapons. It wasn't the aliens that first made us gear up for war; it was our fellow humans.

"They're just being careful," Dad argued back. "I'd do the same thing in their position." He patted me. I was like, *Damn it, old man, if you give me that g.d. condescending little pat one more time . . .* "It'll be fine, Cassie."

He went off with Hutchfield, out of earshot but still in sight.

That made me feel a little better. I hauled Sammy onto my hip and did my best to answer Brogden's questions without popping him with my free hand.

What were our names?

Where were we from?

Was anyone in our party infected?

Was there anything we could tell him about what was going on?

What had we seen?

What had we heard?

Why were we here?

"You mean here at this camp, or are you being existential?" I asked.

His eyebrows drew together into a single harsh line, and he said, "Huh?"

"If you'd asked me that before all this shit happened, I'd have said something like, 'We're here to serve our fellow man or contribute to society.' If I wanted to be a smartass, I'd say, 'Because if we weren't here, we'd be somewhere else.' But since all this shit has happened, I'm going to say it's because we're just dumb lucky."

He squinted at me for a second before saying snarkily, "You are a smartass."

I don't know how Dad answered that question, but apparently it passed inspection, because we were allowed into camp with full privileges, which meant Dad (not me, though) was allowed to have his pick of weapons from the cache. Dad had a thing about guns. Never liked them. Said guns might not kill people, but they sure made it easier. Now he didn't think they were dangerous so much as he thought they were ridiculously lame.

"How effective do you think our guns are going to be against a technology thousands, if not millions, of years ahead of ours?" he asked Hutchfield. "It's like using a club and stones against a tactical missile."

The argument was lost on Hutchfield. He was a marine, for God's sake. His rifle was his best friend, his most trusted companion, the answer to every possible question.

I didn't get that back then. I get it now.

13

IN GOOD WEATHER, everyone stayed outside until it was time to go to bed. That ramshackle building had a bad vibe. Because of why it was built. Why it existed. What had brought it—and us—into these woods. Some nights the mood was light, almost like a summer camp where by some miracle everybody liked one another. Someone would say they heard the sound of a helicopter that afternoon, which would set off a round of hopeful speculation that the People in Charge were getting their acts together and preparing for the counterpunch.

Other times the mood was darker and angst was heavy in the twilight air. We were the lucky ones. We'd survived the EMP attack, the obliteration of the coasts, the plague that wasted everyone we knew and loved. We'd beaten the odds. We'd stared into the face of Death, and Death blinked first. You'd think that would make us feel brave and invincible. It didn't.

We were like the Japanese who survived the initial blast of the

Hiroshima bomb. We didn't understand why we were still here, and we weren't completely sure we wanted to be.

We told the stories of our lives before the Arrival. We cried openly over the ones we lost. We wept secretly for our smartphones, our cars, our microwave ovens, and the Internet.

We watched the night sky. The mothership would stare down at us, a pale green, malevolent eye.

There were debates about where we should go. It was pretty much understood we couldn't squat in these woods indefinitely. Even if the Others weren't coming anytime soon, winter was. We had to find better shelter. We had several months' worth of supplies—or less, depending upon how many more refugees wandered into camp. Did we wait for rescue or hit the road to find it? Dad was all for the latter. He still wanted to check out Wright-Patterson. If there were People in Charge, the odds were a lot better we'd find them there.

I got sick of it after a while. Talking about the problem had replaced actually doing something about it. I was ready to tell Dad we should tell these douchebags to stuff it, take off for Wright-Patterson with whoever wanted to go with us and screw the rest.

Sometimes, I thought, strength in numbers was a highly overrated concept.

I brought Sammy inside and put him to bed. Said his prayer with him. "'Now I lay me down to sleep . . .'" To me, just random noise. Gibberish. I wasn't sure exactly what it was, but I felt that, when it came to God, there was a broken promise in there somewhere.

It was a clear night. The moon was full. I felt comfortable enough to take a walk in the woods.

Somebody in camp had picked up a guitar. The melody skipped along the trail, following me into the woods. It was the first music I'd heard since the 1st Wave.

"And, in the end, we lie awake

And we dream of making our escape."

Suddenly I just wanted to curl into a little ball and cry. I wanted to take off through those woods and keep running until my legs fell off. I wanted to puke. I wanted to scream until my throat bled. I wanted to see my mother again, and Lizbeth and all my friends, even the friends I didn't like, and Ben Parish, just to tell him I loved him and wanted to have his baby more than I wanted to live.

The song faded, was drowned out by the definitely less melodic song of the crickets.

A twig snapped.

And a voice came out of the woods behind me.

"Cassie! Wait up!"

I kept walking. I recognized that voice. Maybe I'd jinxed myself, thinking about Ben. Like when you're craving chocolate and the only thing in your backpack is a half-crushed bag of Skittles.

"Cassie!"

Now he was running. I didn't feel like running, so I let him catch up to me.

That was one thing that hadn't changed: The one sure way of not being alone was wanting to be alone.

"Whatcha doing?" Crisco asked. He was pulling hard for air. Bright red cheeks. Shiny temples, maybe from all the hair grease.

"Isn't it obvious?" I shot back. "I'm building a nuclear device to take out the mothership."

"Nukes won't do it," he said, squaring his shoulders. "We should build Fermi's steam cannon."

"Fermi?"

"The guy who invented the bomb."

"I thought that was Oppenheimer."

He seemed impressed I knew something about history.

"Well, maybe he didn't invent it, but he was the godfather."

"Crisco, you're a freak," I said. That sounded harsh, so I added, "But I didn't know you before the invasion."

"You dig this big hole. Put a warhead at the bottom. Fill the hole with water and cap it off with a few hundred tons of steel. The explosion turns the water instantly into steam, which shoots the steel into space at six times the speed of sound."

"Yeah," I said. "Somebody should definitely do that. Is that why you're stalking me? You want me to help you build a nuclear steam cannon?"

"Can I ask you something?"

"No."

"I'm serious."

"So am I."

"If you had twenty minutes to live, what would you do?"

"I don't know," I answered. "But it wouldn't have anything to do with you."

"How come?" He didn't wait for an answer. He probably figured it wasn't something he wanted to hear. "What if I was the last person on Earth?"

"If you were the last person on Earth, I wouldn't be here to do anything with you."

"Okay. What if we were the last *two* people on Earth?"

"Then you'd still end up being the last, because I'd kill myself."

"You don't like me."

"Really, Crisco? What was your first clue?"

63

"Say we saw them, right here, right now, coming down to finish us off. What would you do?"

"I don't know. Ask them to kill you first. What's the point, Crisco?"

"Are you a virgin?" he asked suddenly.

I stared at him. He was totally serious. But most thirteen-year-old boys are when it comes to hormonal issues.

"Screw you," I said, and brushed past him, heading back toward the camp.

Bad choice of words. He trotted after me and not one strand of plastered-down hair moved as he ran. It was like a shiny black helmet.

"I'm serious, Cassie," he puffed. "These are the times when any night could be your last night."

"Dork, it was that way before they came, too."

He grabbed my wrist. Tugged me around. Pushed his wide, greasy face close to mine. I had an inch on him, but he had twenty pounds on me.

"Do you really want to die without knowing what it's like?"

"How do you know I don't?" I said, yanking free. "Don't ever touch me again." Changing the subject.

"Nobody's gonna know," he said. "I won't tell anyone."

He tried to grab me again. I slapped his hand away with my left and popped him hard in the nose with the open palm of my right. It opened up a faucet of bright red blood. It ran into his mouth, and he gagged.

"Bitch," he gasped. "At least you've got someone. At least everybody you ever frigging knew in your life isn't dead."

He busted out in tears. Fell onto the path and gave in to it, the bigness of it, the big Buick that's parked over you, the horrible feeling that, as bad as it's been, it's going to get worse.

Ah, crap.

I sat on the path next to him. Told him to lean his head back. He complained that made the blood run down his throat.

"Don't tell anybody," he begged. "I'll lose my cred."

I laughed. I couldn't help it.

"Where'd you learn to do that?" he asked.

"Girl Scouts."

"There's badges for that?"

"There's badges for everything."

Actually, it was seven years of karate classes. I dropped karate last year. Don't remember my reasons now. They seemed like good ones at the time.

"I'm one, too," he said.

"What?"

He spat a wad of blood and mucus into the dirt. "A virgin."

What a shock.

"What makes you think I'm a virgin?" I asked.

"You wouldn't have hit me if you weren't."

14

ON OUR SIXTH DAY in camp, I saw a drone for the first time.

Glittering gray in the bright afternoon sky.

There was a lot of shouting and running around, people grabbing guns, waving their hats and shirts or just spazzing in general: crying, jumping, hugging, high-fiving one another. They thought they were rescued. Hutchfield and Brogden tried to calm everybody down, but weren't very successful. The drone zipped across the sky, disappeared behind the trees, then came back, slower this time. From the ground, it looked like a blimp. Hutchfield and Dad huddled in the doorway of the barracks, watching it, swapping a pair of binoculars back and forth.

"No wings. No markings. And did you see that first pass? Mach 2 at least. Unless we've launched some kind of classified aircraft, no way this thing is terrestrial." As he spoke, Hutchfield was popping his fist up and down in the dirt, beating out a rhythm to match the words.

Dad agreed. We were herded into the barracks. Dad and Hutchfield hovered in the doorway, still swapping the binoculars back and forth.

"Is it the aliens?" Sammy asked. "Are they coming, Cassie?"

"Shhh."

I looked over and saw Crisco watching me. *Twenty minutes,* he mouthed.

"If they come, I'm going to beat them up," Sammy whispered. "I'm going to karate kick them and I'm going to kill them all!"

"That's right," I said, nervously running my hand over his hair.

"I'm not going to run," he said. "I'm going to kill them for killing Mommy."

The drone vanished—straight up, Dad told me later. If you blinked, you missed it.

We reacted to the drone the way anyone would react.

We freaked.

Some people ran. Grabbed whatever they could carry and raced into the woods. Some just took off with the clothes on their backs and the fear in their guts. Nothing Hutchfield said could stop them.

The rest of us huddled in the barracks until night came on, then we took the freakout party to the next level. Had they spotted us? Were the Stormtroopers or clone army or robot walkers next? Were we about to be fried by laser cannons? It was pitch-black. We couldn't see a foot in front of our noses, because we didn't dare light the kerosene lamps. Frantic whispers. Muffled crying. Huddled on our cots, jumping at every little sound. Hutchfield assigned the best marksmen to the night watch. If it moved, shoot it. No one was allowed outside without permission. And Hutchfield never gave permission.

That night lasted a thousand years.

Dad came up to me in the dark and pressed something into my hands.

A loaded semiautomatic Luger.

"You don't believe in guns," I whispered.

"I used to not believe in a lot of things."

A lady started to recite the Lord's Prayer. We called her Mother Teresa. Big legs. Skinny arms. A faded blue dress. Wispy gray hair. Somewhere along the way she had lost her dentures. She was always working her beads and talking to Jesus. A few others joined her. Then some more. "'Forgive us our trespasses, as we forgive those who trespass against us.'" At which point her arch nemesis, the sole atheist in Camp Ashpit's foxhole, a college professor named Dawkins, shouted out, "Particularly those of extraterrestrial origin!"

"You're going to hell!" a voice yelled at him in the dark.

"How will I know the difference?" Dawkins hollered back.

"Quiet!" Hutchfield called softly from his spot in the doorway. "Stow that praying, people!"

"His judgment has come upon us," Mother Teresa wailed.

Sammy scooted closer to me on the cot. I shoved the gun between my legs. I was afraid he might grab it and accidently blow my head off.

"Shut up, all of you!" I said. "You're scaring my brother."

"I'm not scared," Sammy said. His little fist twisting in my shirt. "Are you scared, Cassie?"

"Yes," I said. I kissed the top of his head. His hair smelled a little sour. I decided to wash it in the morning.

If we were still there in the morning.

"No, you're not," he said. "You're never scared."

"I'm so scared right now, I could pee my pants."

He giggled. His face felt warm in the crook of my arm. Did he have a fever? That's how it starts. I told myself I was being paranoid. He'd been exposed a hundred times. And the Red Tsunami roars in fast once you're exposed, unless you have immunity. And Sammy had to have it. If he didn't, he'd already be dead.

"You better put on a diaper," he teased me.

"Maybe I will."

"'Though I walk through the valley of the shadow of death . . .'" She wasn't going to stop. I could hear her beads clicking in the dark. Dawkins was humming loudly to drown her out. "Three Blind Mice." I couldn't decide who was more annoying, the fanatic or the cynic.

"Mommy said they might be angels," Sammy said suddenly.

"Who?" I asked.

"The aliens. When they first came, I asked if they came to kill us, and she said maybe they weren't aliens at all. Maybe they were angels from heaven, like in the Bible when the angels talk to Abraham and to Mary and to Jesus and everybody."

"They sure talked a lot more to us back then," I said.

"But then they did kill us. They killed Mommy."

He started to cry.

"'Thou prepared a table for me in the presence of my enemies.'"

I kissed the top of his head and rubbed his arms.

"'Thou anointed my head with oil.'"

"Cassie, does God hate us?"

"No. I don't know."

"Does he hate Mommy?"

"Of course not. Mommy was a good person."

"Then why did he let her die?"

I shook my head. I felt heavy all over, like I weighed twenty thousand tons.

"'My cup runneth over.'"

"Why did he let the aliens come and kill us? Why doesn't God stop them?"

"Maybe," I whispered slowly. Even my tongue felt heavy. "Maybe he will."

"'Surely goodness and mercy will follow me all the days of my life.'"

"Don't let them get me, Cassie. Don't let me die."

"You're not going to die, Sams."

"Promise?"

I promised.

15

THE NEXT DAY, the drone came back.

Or a different drone, identical to the first. The Others probably hadn't traveled all the way from another planet with just one in the hold.

It moved slowly across the sky. Silent. No growl of an engine.

No hum. Just gliding soundlessly, like a fishing lure drawn through still water. We hustled into the barracks. No one had to tell us. I found myself sitting on a cot next to Crisco.

"I know what they're going to do," he whispered.

"Don't talk," I whispered back.

He nodded, and said, "Sonic bombs. You know what happens when you're blasted with two hundred decibels? Your eardrums shatter. Your lungs bust open and air gets into your bloodstream, and then your heart collapses."

"Where do you come up with this crap, Crisco?"

Dad and Hutchfield were crouched by the open door again. They watched the same spot for several minutes. Apparently, the drone had frozen in the sky.

"Here, I got you something," Crisco said. It was a diamond pendant necklace. Body booty from the ash pit.

"That's disgusting," I told him.

"Why? It's not like I stole it or anything." He pouted. "I know what it is. I'm not stupid. It's not the necklace. It's me. You'd take it in a heartbeat if you thought I was hot."

I wondered if he was right. If Ben Parish had dug the necklace out of the pit, would I have taken the gift?

"Not that I think *you* are," Crisco added.

Bummer. Crisco the grave robber didn't think I was hot.

"Then why do you want to give it to me?"

"I was a douche that night in the woods. I don't want you to hate me. Think I'm a creeper."

A little late for that.

"I don't want dead people's jewelry," I said.

"Neither do they," he said, meaning dead people.

He wasn't going to leave me alone. I scooted up to sit behind

Dad. Over his shoulder, I saw a tiny gray dot, a silvery freckle on the unblemished skin of the sky.

"What's happening?" I whispered.

Right when I said that, the dot disappeared. Moved so fast, it seemed to wink out.

"Reconnaissance flights," Hutchfield breathed. "Has to be."

"We had satellites that could read someone's watch from orbit," Dad said quietly. "If we could do that with our primitive technology, why would they need to leave their ship to spy on us?"

"You got a better theory?" Hutchfield didn't like his decisions being questioned.

"They may have nothing to do with us," Dad pointed out. "These things might be atmospheric probes or devices used to measure something they can't calibrate from space. Or they're looking for something that can't be detected until we're mostly neutralized."

Then Dad sighed. I knew that sigh. It meant he believed something was true that he didn't want to be true.

"It comes down to a simple question, Hutchfield: Why are they here? Not to rape the planet for our resources—there's plenty of those spread evenly throughout the universe, so you don't have to travel hundreds of light-years to get them. Not to kill us, though killing us—or most of us—is necessary. They're like a landlord who kicks out a deadbeat renter so he can get the house cleaned up for the new tenant; I think this has always been about getting the place ready."

"Ready? Ready for what?"

Dad smiled humorlessly.

"Moving day."

16

AN HOUR BEFORE DAWN. Our last day at Camp Ashpit. A Sunday.

Sammy beside me. Little kid snuggly warm, hand on his bear, other hand on my chest, curled-up pudgy baby-fist.

The best part of the day.

Those few seconds when you're awake but empty. You forget where you are. What you are now, what you were before. It's all breath and heartbeat and blood moving. Like being in your mother's womb again. The peace of the void.

That's what I thought the sound was at first. My own heartbeat.

Thumpa-thumpa-thumpa. Faint, then louder, then really loud, loud enough to feel the beat on your skin. A glow sprang up in the room, grew brighter. People were stumbling around, yanking on clothes, fumbling for guns. The bright glow faded, came back. Shadows jumped across the floor, raced up the ceiling. Hutchfield was yelling at everyone to stay calm. It wasn't working. Everyone recognized the sound. And everyone knew what that sound meant.

Rescue!

Hutchfield tried to block off the doorway with his body.

"Stay inside!" he hollered. "We don't want to—"

He was shoved out of the way. *Oh yes, we do.* We poured out the doorway and stood in the yard and waved at the helicopter, a Black Hawk, as it made another sweep of the compound, black against the lightening dark of the predawn sky. The spotlight stabbed down, blinding us, but most of us were already blinded by tears. We jumped, we shouted, we hugged one another. A couple of people were waving little American flags, and I remember wondering where the hell they got those.

Hutchfield was furiously screaming at us to get back inside. Nobody listened. He wasn't the boss of us anymore. The People in Charge had arrived.

And then, just as unexpectedly as it had come, the helicopter made one last turn and thundered out of sight. The sound of its rotors faded. A heavy silence flooded in after it. We were confused, stunned, frightened. They must have seen us. Why didn't they land?

We waited for the helicopter to come back. All morning we waited. People packed up their things. Speculated about where they would take us, what it would be like, how many others would be there. A Black Hawk helicopter! What else had survived the 1st Wave? We dreamed of electric lights and hot showers.

No one doubted we'd be rescued now that the People in Charge knew about us. Help was on its way.

Dad, being Dad, of course, wasn't so sure.

"They may not come back," he said.

"They wouldn't just leave us here, Dad," I said. Sometimes you had to talk to him like he was Sammy's age. "How does that make sense?"

"It may not have been a search and rescue. They might have been looking for something else."

"The drone?"

The one that had crashed a week earlier. He nodded.

"Still, they know we're here now," I said. "They'll do something."

He nodded again. Absently, like he was thinking about something else.

"They will," he said. He looked hard at me. "Do you still have the gun?"

I patted my back pocket. He threw his arm around me and led me to the storehouse. He pulled aside an old tarp lying in a corner. Underneath it was an M16 semiautomatic assault rifle. The same rifle that would become my bestie after everyone else was gone.

He picked it up and turned it in his hands, inspecting the rifle with that same absentminded professor look in his eyes.

"What do you think?" he whispered.

"About that? It's totally badass."

He didn't jump on me for the language. Instead, he gave a little laugh.

He showed me how it worked. How to hold it. How to aim. How to switch out a clip.

"Here, you try."

He held it toward me.

I think he was pleasantly surprised by what a quick study I was. And my coordination was pretty good, thanks to the karate lessons. Dance classes have nothing on karate when it comes to developing grace.

"Keep it," he said when I tried to hand it back. "I hid it in here for you."

"Why?" I asked. Not that I minded having it, but he was freaking me out a little. While everyone else was celebrating, my father was giving me training in firearms.

"Do you know how to tell who the enemy is in wartime, Cassie?" His eyes darted around the shack. Why couldn't he look at me?

"The guy who's shooting at you—that's how you tell. Don't forget that." He nodded toward the gun. "Don't walk around with it. Keep it close, but keep it hidden. Not in here and not in the barracks. Okay?"

Shoulder pat. Shoulder pat not quite enough. Big hug.

"From now on, never let Sam out of your sight. Understand, Cassie? Never. Now go find him. I've got to see Hutchfield. And Cassie? If someone tries to take that rifle from you, you tell them to bring it up with me. And if they still try to take it, shoot them."

He smiled. Not with his eyes, though. His eyes were as hard and blank and cold as a shark's.

He was lucky, my dad. All of us were. Luck had carried us through the first three waves. But even the best gambler will tell you that luck only lasts so long. I think my dad had a feeling that day. Not that our luck had run out. No one could know that. But I think he knew in the end it wouldn't be the lucky ones left standing.

It would be the hardcore. The ones who tell Lady Luck to go screw herself. The ones with hearts of stone. The ones who could let a hundred die so one might live. The ones who see the wisdom in torching a village in order to save it.

The world was FUBAR now.

And if you're not okay with that, you're just a corpse waiting to happen.

I took the M16 and hid it behind a tree bordering the path to the ash pit.

17

THE LAST REMNANT of the world I knew ripped apart on a sunny, warm Sunday afternoon.

Heralded by the growl of diesel engines, the rumble and squeak of axles, the whine of air brakes. Our sentries spotted the convoy long before it reached the compound. Saw the bright sunlight glinting off windows and the plumes of dust trailing the huge tires like contrails. We didn't rush out to greet them with flowers and kisses. We stayed back while Hutchfield, Dad, and our four best shooters went out to meet them. Everyone was feeling a little spooked. And a lot less enthusiastic than we'd been just a few hours before.

Everything we'd expected to happen since the Arrival didn't. Everything we hadn't did. It took two whole weeks into the 3rd Wave for us to realize that the deadly flu was part of their plan. Still, you tend to believe what you always believed, think what you always thought, expect what you always expected, so it was never "Will we be rescued?" It was "When will we be rescued?"

And when we saw exactly what we wanted to see, what we expected to see—the big flatbed loaded with soldiers, the Humvees bristling with machine gun turrets and surface-to-air launchers—we still held back.

Then the school buses pulled into view.

Three of them, bumper to bumper.

Packed with kids.

Nobody expected that. Like I said, it was so weirdly normal, so shockingly surreal. Some of us actually laughed. A yellow freaking school bus! Where the hell is the school?

After a few tense minutes, where all we could hear was the throaty snarl of engines and the faint laughter and calls of the children on the buses, Dad left Hutchfield talking to the commander and came over to me and Sammy. A knot of people gathered around us to listen in.

"They're from Wright-Patterson," Dad said. He sounded out of breath. "And apparently a lot more of our military has survived than we thought."

"Why are they wearing gas masks?" I asked.

"It's precautionary," he answered. "They've been in lockdown since the plague hit. We've all been exposed; we could be carriers."

He looked down at Sammy, who was pressed up against me, his arms wrapped around my leg.

"They've come for the children," Dad said.

"Why?" I asked.

"What about us?" Mother Teresa demanded. "Aren't they going to take us, too?"

"He says they're coming back for us. Right now there's only room for the children."

Looking at Sammy.

"They're not splitting us up," I said to Dad.

"Of course not." He turned away and abruptly marched into the barracks. Came out again, carrying my backpack and Sammy's bear. "You're going with him."

He didn't get it.

"I'm not going without you," I said. What was it about guys like my father? Somebody in charge shows up and they check their brains at the door.

"You heard what he said!" Mother Teresa cried shrilly, shaking her beads. "Just the children! If anyone else goes, it should be me . . . women. That's how it's done. Women and children first! Women and children."

Dad ignored her. There went the hand on my shoulder. I shrugged his hand away.

"Cassie, they have to get the most vulnerable to safety first. I'll be just a few hours behind you—"

"No!" I shouted. "We all stay or we all go, Dad. Tell them we'll be fine here until they get back. I can take care of him. I've been taking care of him."

"And you will take care of him, Cassie, because you're going, too."

"Not without you. I won't leave you here, Dad."

He smiled like I had said something kiddy-cute.

"I can take care of myself."

I couldn't put it into words, this feeling like a hot coal in my gut, that splitting up what was left of our family would be the end of our family. That if I left him behind I would never see him again. Maybe it wasn't rational, but the world I lived in wasn't rational anymore.

Dad pried Sammy from my leg, slung him onto his hip, grabbed my elbow with his free hand, and marched us toward the buses. You couldn't see the soldiers' faces through the buggy-looking gas masks. But you could read the names stitched onto their green camouflage.

GREENE.

WALTERS.

PARKER.

Good, solid, all-American names. And the American flags on their sleeves.

And the way they held themselves, erect but loose, alert but relaxed. Coiled springs.

The way you expect soldiers to look.

78

We reached the last bus in the line. The children inside shouted and waved at us. It was all one big adventure.

The burly soldier at the door raised his hand. His name patch said BRANCH.

"Children only," he said, his voice muffled by the mask.

"I understand, Corporal," Dad said.

"Cassie, why are you crying?" Sammy said. His little hand reached for my face.

Daddy lowered him to the ground. Knelt to bring his face close to Sammy's.

"You're going on a trip, Sam," Dad said. "These nice army men are taking you to a place where you'll be safe."

"Aren't you coming, Daddy?" Tugging on Dad's shirt with his tiny hands.

"Yes. Yes, Daddy's coming, just not yet. Soon, though. Very soon."

He pulled Sammy into his arms. Last hug. "You be good now. You do what the nice army men tell you. Okay?"

Sammy nodded. Slipped his hand into mine.

"Come'n, Cassie. We're going to ride a bus!"

The black mask whipped around. A gloved hand went up.

"Just the boy."

I started to tell him to stuff it. I wasn't happy about leaving Dad behind, but Sammy wasn't going anywhere without me.

The corporal cut me off. "Only the boy."

"She's his sister," Dad tried. He was being reasonable. "And she's a child, too. She's only sixteen."

"She'll have to stay here," the corporal said.

"Then he's not getting on," I said, wrapping both arms around Sammy's chest. He'd have to pull my damn arms off to take my little brother.

There was this awful moment when the corporal didn't say anything. I had the urge to rip the mask off his head and spit in his face. The sun glinted off the visor, a hateful ball of light.

"You want him to stay?"

"I want him to stay with *me*," I corrected him. "On the bus. Off the bus. Whatever. With me."

"No, Cassie," Dad said.

Sammy started to cry. He got it: It was Daddy and the soldier against me and him, and there was no winning that battle. He got it before I did.

"He can stay," the soldier said. "But we can't guarantee his safety."

"Oh, really?" I shouted into his bug-face. "You think? Whose safety *can* you guarantee?"

"Cassie . . . ," Dad started.

"You can't guarantee shit," I yelled.

The corporal ignored me. "It's your call, sir," he said to Dad.

"Dad," I said. "You heard him. He can stay with us."

Dad chewed on his bottom lip. He lifted his head and scratched under his chin, and his eyes regarded the empty sky. He was thinking about the drones, about what he knew and what he didn't know. He was remembering what he'd learned. He was weighing odds and calculating probabilities and ignoring the little voice piping up from the deepest part of him: *Don't let him go.*

So of course he did the most reasonable thing. He was a responsible adult, and that's what responsible adults do.

The reasonable thing.

"You're right, Cassie," he said finally. "They can't guarantee our safety—no one can. But some places are safer than others." He grabbed Sammy's hand. "Come on, sport."

"No!" Sammy screamed, tears streaming down bright red cheeks. "Not without Cassie!"

"Cassie's going," Dad said. "We're both going. We'll be right behind you."

"I'll protect him, I'll watch him, I won't let anything happen to him," I pleaded. "They're coming back for the rest of us, right? We'll just wait for them to come back." I pulled on his shirt and put on my best pleading face. The one that usually got me what I wanted. "Please, Daddy, don't do this. It isn't right. We have to stay together, *we have to.*"

It wasn't going to work. He had that hard look in his eyes again: cold, clamped down, remorseless.

"Cassie," he said. "Tell your brother it's okay."

And I did. After I told myself it was okay. I told myself to trust Dad, trust the People in Charge, trust the Others not to incinerate the school buses full of children, trust that trust itself hadn't gone the way of computers and microwavable popcorn and the Hollywood movie where the slimeballs from Planet Xercon are defeated in the final ten minutes.

I knelt on the dusty ground in front of my little brother.

"You need to go, Sams," I said. His fat lower lip bobbed up and down. Clutching the bear to his chest.

"But, Cassie, who's going to hold you when you're scared?" He was being totally serious. He looked so much like Dad with that concerned little frown that I almost laughed.

"I'm not scared anymore. And you shouldn't be scared, either. The soldiers are here now, and they're going to make us safe."

I looked up at Corporal Branch. "Isn't that right?"

"That's right."

"He looks like Darth Vader," Sammy whispered. "Sounds like him, too."

"Right, and remember what happens? He turns into a good guy at the end."

"Only after he blows up a whole planet and kills a lot of people."

I couldn't help it—I laughed. God, he was smart. Sometimes I thought he was smarter than me and Dad combined.

"You're going to come later, Cassie?"

"You bet I am."

"Promise?"

I promised. Whatever happened. No. Matter. What.

That was all he needed to hear. He pushed the teddy bear into my chest.

"Sam?"

"For when you're scared. But don't leave him." He held up a tiny finger to emphasize his point. "Don't forget."

He stuck out his hand to the corporal. "Lead on, Vader!" Gloved hand engulfed pudgy hand. The first step was almost too high for his little legs. The kids inside squealed and clapped when he turned the corner and hit the center aisle.

Sammy was the last to board. The door closed. Dad tried to put his arm around me. I stepped away. The engine revved. The air brakes hissed.

And there was his face against the smudged glass and his smile as he rocketed across a galaxy far, far away in his yellow X-wing starfighter, jumping to warp speed, until the dusty yellow space-ship was swallowed by dust.

18

"THIS WAY, SIR," the corporal said politely, and we followed him back to the compound. Two Humvees had left to escort the buses back to Wright-Patterson. The remaining Humvees sat facing the barracks and the storage shed, the barrels of their mounted machine guns pointing at the ground, like the dipped heads of some metallic creatures dozing.

The compound was empty. Everybody—including the soldiers—had gone inside the barracks.

Everybody except one.

As we walked up, Hutchfield came out of the storage shed. I don't know what was beaming brighter, his shaved head or his smile.

"Outstanding, Sullivan!" he boomed at Dad. "And you wanted to bug out after that first drone."

"Looks like I was wrong," Dad said with a tight smile.

"Briefing by Colonel Vosch in five minutes. But first I need your ordnance."

"My what?"

"Your weapon. Colonel's orders."

Dad glanced at the soldier standing beside us. The blank, black eyes of the mask stared back at him.

"Why?" Dad asked.

"You need an explanation?" Hutchfield's smile stayed put, but his eyes narrowed.

"I would like one, yes."

"It's SOP, Sullivan, standard operating procedure. You can't have a bunch of untrained, inexperienced civilians packing heat in wartime." Talking down to him, like he was a moron.

He held out his hand. Dad pulled the rifle slowly from his shoulder. Hutchfield snatched the rifle from Dad and disappeared into the storehouse.

Dad turned to the corporal. "Has anyone made contact with the . . ." He searched for the right word. "The Others?"

One word, spoken in a raspy monotone: "No."

Hutchfield came out and smartly saluted the corporal. He was neck-deep in his element now, back with his brothers in arms. He was bursting all over with excitement, like any second he would pee himself.

"All weapons accounted for and secured, Corporal."

All except two, I thought. I looked at Dad. He didn't move a muscle, except the ones around his eyes. Flick to the right, flick to the left. *No.*

There was only one reason I could think of that he'd do that. And when I think about it, if I think too much about it, I start to hate my father. Hate him for distrusting his own instincts. Hate him for ignoring the little voice that must have been whispering, *This is wrong. Something about this is wrong.*

I hate him right now. If he were here right now, I'd punch him in the face for being such an ignorant dweeb.

The corporal motioned toward the barracks. It was time for Colonel Vosch's briefing.

Time for the world to end.

19

I PICKED OUT Vosch right away.

Standing just inside the door, very tall, the only guy in fatigues not cradling a rifle against his chest.

He nodded to Hutchfield when we stepped inside the old hospital/charnel house. Then Corporal Branch gave a salute and squeezed into the line of soldiers that ringed the walls.

That's how it was: soldiers standing along three of the four walls, refugees in the middle.

Dad's hand sought out mine. Sammy's teddy in one hand, the other hanging on to his.

How about it, Dad? Did that little voice get louder when you saw the men with guns against the walls? Is that why you grabbed my hand?

"All right, now can we get some answers?" someone shouted when we stepped inside.

Everybody started to talk at once—everyone except the soldiers—shouting out questions.

"Have they landed?"

"What do they look like?"

"What are they?"

"What are those gray ships we keep seeing in the sky?"

"When do the rest of us get to leave?"

"How many survivors have you found?"

Vosch held up his hand for quiet. It only half worked.

Hutchfield gave him a smart salute. "All present and accounted for, sir!"

I did a quick head count. "No," I said. I raised my voice to be heard over the din. "No!" I looked at Dad. "Crisco's not here."

Hutchfield frowned. "Who's Crisco?"

"He's this cree—this kid—"

"Kid? Then he left on the buses with the others."

The others. It's kind of funny when I think about it now. Funny in a sickening way.

"We need everyone in this building," Vosch said from behind his mask. His voice was very deep, a subterranean rumble.

"He probably had a freakout," I said. "He's kind of a wuss."

"Where would he go?" Vosch asked.

I shook my head. I had no clue. Then I did, more than a clue. I knew where Crisco had gone.

"The ash pit."

"Where is the ash pit?"

"Cassie," Dad spoke up. He was squeezing my hand hard. "Why don't you go get Crisco for us so the colonel can start our briefing?"

"Me?"

I didn't get it. I think Dad's little voice was screaming by this point, but I couldn't hear it, and he couldn't say it. All he could do was try to telegraph it with his eyes. Maybe it was this: *Do you know how to tell who the enemy is, Cassie?*

I don't know why he didn't volunteer to go with me. Maybe he thought they wouldn't suspect a kid of anything, and one of us would make it—or at least have a chance to make it.

Maybe.

"All right," Vosch said. He flicked his finger at Corporal Branch: *Go with her.*

"She'll be okay alone," Dad said. "She knows those woods like

86

the back of her hand. Five minutes, right, Cassie?" He looked at Vosch and smiled. "Five minutes."

"Don't be a dumbass, Sullivan," Hutchfield said. "She can't go out there without an escort."

"Sure," Dad said. "Right. You're right, of course."

He leaned over and gave me a hug. Not too tight, not too long. A quick hug. Squeeze. Release. Anything more would seem like a good-bye.

Good-bye, Cassie.

Branch turned to his commander and said, "First priority, sir?" And Vosch nodded. "First priority."

We stepped into the bright sunshine, the man in the gas mask and the girl with the teddy bear. Straight ahead a couple of soldiers were leaning against a Humvee. I hadn't seen them when we passed the Humvees before. They straightened at the sight of us. Corporal Branch gave them a thumbs-up and then held up his index finger. *First priority.*

"How far is it?" he asked me.

"Not far," I answered. My voice sounded very small to me. Maybe it was Sammy's teddy, tugging me back to childhood.

He followed me down the trail that snaked into the dense woods behind the compound, rifle held in front of him, barrel down. The dry ground crunched in protest under his brown boots.

The day was warm, but it was cooler under the trees, their leaves a rich, late-summer green. We passed the tree where I'd stashed the M16. I didn't look back at it. I kept walking toward the clearing.

And there he was, the little shit, up to his ankles in bones and dust, clawing through the broken remains for that last, useless, priceless trinket, one more for the road so whenever he got to where the road ended he'd be the Man.

His head came around when we stepped inside the ring of trees. Glistening with sweat and the crap he slopped in his hair. Streaks of black soot stained his cheeks. He looked like some sorry-ass excuse of a football player. When he saw us, his hand whipped behind his back. Something silver flashed in the sun.

"Hey! Cassie? Hey, there you are. I came back here looking for you because you weren't in the barracks, and then I saw . . . there was this—"

"Is he the one?" the soldier asked me. He slung the rifle over his shoulder and took a step toward the pit.

It was me, the soldier in the middle, and Crisco in the pit of ash and bone.

"Yeah," I said. "That's Crisco."

"That's not my name," he squeaked. "My real name is—"

I'll never know Crisco's real name.

I didn't see the gun or hear the report of the soldier's sidearm. I didn't see the soldier draw it from his holster, but I wasn't looking at the soldier, I was looking at Crisco. His head snapped back, like someone had yanked on his greasy locks, and he sort of folded up as he went down, clutching the treasures of the dead in his hand.

20

MY TURN.

The girl wearing the backpack and carrying the ridiculous teddy bear, standing just a couple of yards behind him.

The soldier pivoted, arm extended. My memory's a little fuzzy about this next part. I don't remember dropping the bear or yanking the gun from my back pocket. I don't even remember pulling the trigger.

The next clear memory I have is of the black visor shattering.

And the soldier falling to his knees in front of me.

And seeing his eyes.

His three eyes.

Well, of course I realized later he didn't really have three eyes. The one in the middle was the blackened entry wound of the bullet.

It must have shocked him to turn around and see a gun pointed at his face. It made him hesitate. How long? A second? Less than a second? But in that millisecond, eternity coiled on itself like a giant anaconda. If you've ever been through a traumatic accident, you know what I'm talking about. How long does a car crash last? Ten seconds? Five? It doesn't feel that short if you're in it. It feels like a lifetime.

He pitched over face-first into the dirt. There was no question I'd wasted him. My bullet had blasted a pie plate–sized hole in the back of his head.

But I didn't lower the gun. I kept it pointed at his half head as I backed toward the trail.

Then I turned and ran like hell.

In the wrong direction.

Toward the compound.

Not smart. But I wasn't thinking at that point. I'm only sixteen, and this was the first person I'd shot point-blank in the face. I was having trouble dealing.

I just wanted to get back to Dad.

Dad would fix this.

Because that's what dads do. They fix things.

My mind didn't register the sounds at first. The woods echoed with the staccato bursts of automatic weapons and people screaming, but it wasn't computing, like Crisco's head snapping back and the way he flopped into the gray dust like every bone in his body had suddenly turned into Jell-O, the way his killer had swung around in a perfectly executed pirouette with the barrel of the gun flashing in the sunlight.

The world was ripping apart. And pieces of the wreckage were raining all around me.

It was the beginning of the 4th Wave.

I skittered to a stop before reaching the compound. The hot smell of gunpowder. Wisps of smoke curling out of the barrack windows. There was a person crawling toward the storage shed.

It was my father.

His back was arched. His face was covered in dirt and blood. The ground behind my father was pockmarked with my father's blood.

He looked over as I came out of the trees.

No, Cassie, he mouthed. Then his arms gave out. He toppled over, lay still.

A soldier emerged from the barracks. He strolled over to my father. Easy, catlike grace, shoulders relaxed, arms loose at his sides.

I backed into the trees. I raised the gun. But I was over a hundred feet away. If I missed . . .

It was Vosch. He seemed even taller standing over the crumpled form of my father. Dad wasn't moving. I think he was playing dead.

It didn't matter.

Vosch shot him anyway.

I don't remember making any noise when he pulled the trigger. But I must have done something to set off Vosch's Spidey sense. The black mask whipped around, sunlight flashing off the visor. He held up his index finger toward two soldiers coming out of the barracks, then jabbed his thumb in my direction.

First priority.

21

THEY TOOK OFF toward me like a couple of cheetahs. That's how fast they seemed to move. I'd never seen anyone run that fast in my life. The only thing that comes close is a scared-shitless girl who's just seen her father murdered in the dirt.

Leaf, branch, vine, bramble. The rush of air in my ears. The rapid-fire *scuffscuffscuff* of my shoes on the trail.

Shards of blue sky through the canopy, blades of sunlight impaling the shattered earth. The ripped-apart world careened.

I slowed as I neared the spot where I'd hidden my father's last present to me. Mistake. The high-caliber rounds smacked into the tree trunk two inches from my ear. The impact sent fragments of pulverized wood into my face. Tiny, hair-thin slivers embedded themselves in my cheek.

Do you know how to tell who the enemy is, Cassie?

I couldn't outrun them.

I couldn't outgun them.

Maybe I could outsmart them.

22

THEY ENTERED THE CLEARING, and the first thing they saw was the body of Corporal Branch, or whatever it was that called itself Corporal Branch.

"There's one over there," I heard one say.

The crunch of heavy boots in a bowlful of brittle bones.

"Dead."

The cackle of a static frequency, then: "Colonel, we've got Branch and one unidentified civilian. That's a negative, sir. Branch is KIA, repeat Branch is KIA." Now he spoke to his buddy, the one standing by Crisco. "Vosch wants us back ASAP."

Crunch-crunch said the bones as he heaved himself out of the pit.

"She ditched this."

My backpack. I tried to throw it into the woods, as far away from the pit as I could. But it hit a tree and landed just inside the far edge of the clearing.

"Strange," the voice said.

"It's okay," his buddy said. "The Eye will take care of her."

The Eye?

Their voices faded. The sound of the woods at peace returned. A whisper of wind. The warble of birds. Somewhere in the brush a squirrel fussed.

Still, I didn't move. Each time the urge to run started to rise up in me, I squashed it down.

No hurry now, Cassie. They've done what they've come to do. You have to stay here till dark. Don't move!

So I didn't. I lay still inside the bed of dust and bones, covered by the ashes of their victims, the Others' bitter harvest.

And I tried not to think about it.

What I was covered in.

Then I thought, *These bones were people, and these people saved my life,* and then I didn't feel so creeped.

They were just people. They didn't ask to be there any more than I did. But they were there and I was there, so I lay still.

It's weird, but it was almost like I felt their arms, warm and soft, enfolding me.

I don't know how long I lay there, with the arms of dead people holding me. It felt like hours. When I finally stood up, the sunlight had aged to a golden sheen and the air had turned a little cooler. I was covered head to toe in gray ash. I must have looked like a Mayan warrior.

The Eye will take care of her.

Was he talking about the drones, an eye-in-the-sky thing? And if he was talking about the drones, then this wasn't some rogue unit scouring the countryside to waste possible carriers of the 3rd Wave so the unexposed wouldn't be infected.

That would definitely be bad.

But the alternative would be much, much worse.

I trotted over to my backpack. The deep woods called to me. The more distance I put between myself and them, the better it was gonna be. Then I remembered my father's gift, far up the path, practically within spitting distance of the compound. Crap, why hadn't I stashed it in the ash pit?

It sure might prove more useful than a handgun.

I didn't hear anything. Even the birds had gone mum. Just wind. Its fingers trailed through the mounds of ash, flicking it into the air, where it danced fitfully in the golden light.

They were gone. It was safe.

But I hadn't heard them leave. Wouldn't I have heard the roar of the flatbed motor, the growl of the Humvees as they left?

Then I remembered Branch stepping toward Crisco.

Is he the one?

Swinging the rifle behind his shoulder.

The rifle. I crept over to the body. My footfalls sounded like thunder. My own breath like mini explosions.

He had fallen facedown at my feet. Now he was faceup, though that face was still mostly hidden by the gas mask.

His sidearm and rifle were gone. They must have taken them. For a second I didn't move. And moving was a very good idea at that juncture of the battle.

This wasn't part of the 3rd Wave. This was something completely different. It was the beginning of the 4th, definitely. And maybe the 4th Wave was a sick version of *Close Encounters of the Third Kind.* Maybe Branch wasn't human and that's why he was wearing a mask.

I knelt beside the dead soldier. Grasped the top of the mask firmly, and pulled until I could see his eyes, very human-looking brown eyes, staring sightlessly into my face. I kept pulling.

Stopped.

I wanted to see and I didn't want to see. I wanted to know but I didn't want to know.

Just go. It doesn't matter, Cassie. Does it matter? No. It doesn't matter.

Sometimes you say things to your fear—things like *It doesn't matter*, the words acting like pats on the head of a hyper dog.

I stood up. No, it really didn't matter if the soldier had a mouth like a lobster or looked like Justin Bieber's twin brother.

I grabbed Sammy's teddy from the dirt and headed for the far side of the clearing.

Something stopped me, though. I didn't head off into the woods. I didn't rush off to embrace the one thing with the best chance to save me: distance.

It might have been the teddy bear that did it. When I picked it up, I saw my brother's face pressed against the back window of the bus, heard his little voice inside my head.

For when you're scared. But don't leave him. Don't forget.

I almost did forget. If I hadn't walked over to check Branch for weapons, I would have. Branch had fallen practically on top of poor teddy.

Don't leave him.

I didn't actually see any bodies back there. Just Dad's. What if someone had survived those three minutes of eternity in the barracks? They could have been wounded, still alive, left for dead.

Unless I didn't leave. If there was someone still alive back there and the faux soldiers had gone, then I would be the one leaving them for dead.

Ah, crap.

You know how sometimes you tell yourself that you have a choice, but really you don't have a choice? Just because there are alternatives doesn't mean they apply to you.

I turned around and headed back, stepping around the body of Branch as I went, and dove into the dusky tunnel of the trail.

--- **23** ---

I DIDN'T FORGET the assault rifle the third time around. I shoved the Luger into my belt, but I couldn't very well expect to fire an assault rifle with a teddy bear in one hand, so I had to leave him on the trail.

"It's okay. I won't forget you," I whispered to Sammy's bear.

I stepped off the path and wove quietly through the trees. When I got close to the compound, I dropped and crawled the rest of the way to the edge.

Well, that's why you didn't hear them leave.

Vosch was talking to a couple of soldiers at the doorway to the storehouse. Another group was messing around by one of the Humvees. I counted seven in all, which left five more I couldn't see. Were they off in the woods somewhere, looking for me? Dad's body was gone—maybe the others had pulled disposal duty. There were forty-two of us, not counting the kids who had left on the buses. That's a lot of disposing.

Turns out I was right: It was a disposal operation.

It's just that Silencers don't dispose of bodies the way we do.

Vosch had taken off his mask. So had the two guys who were with him. They didn't have lobster mouths or tentacles growing out of their chins. They looked like perfectly ordinary human beings, at least from a distance.

They didn't need the masks anymore. Why not? The masks must have been part of the act. We would expect them to protect themselves from infection.

Two of the soldiers came over from the Humvee carrying what looked like a bowl or globe the same dull gray metallic color as the drones. Vosch pointed at a spot midway between the storehouse and the barracks, the same spot, it looked like, where my father had fallen.

Then everybody left, except one female soldier, who was kneeling now beside the gray globe.

The Humvees roared to life. Another engine joined the duet: the flatbed troop carrier, parked at the head of the compound out of sight. I'd forgotten about that. The rest of the soldiers must have already loaded up and were waiting. Waiting for what?

The remaining soldier stood up and trotted back to the Humvee. I watched him climb aboard. Watched the Humvee spin out in a boiling cloud of dust. Watched the dust swirl and settle. The stillness of summer at dusk settled with it. The silence pounded in my ears.

And then the gray globe began to glow.

That was a good thing, a bad thing, or a thing that was neither good nor bad, but whatever it was, good, bad, or neither, depended on your point of view.

They had put the globe there, so to them it was a good thing.

The glow was getting brighter. A sickly yellowish green. Pulsing slightly. Like a . . . A what? A beacon?

I peered into the darkening sky. The first stars had begun to come out. I didn't see any drones.

If it was a good thing from their point of view, that meant it was probably a bad thing from mine.

Well, not probably. Leaning more toward definitely.

The interval between pulses shortened every few seconds. The pulse became a flash. The flash became a blink.

Pulse . . . Pulse . . . Pulse . . .

Flash, flash, flash.

Blinkblinkblink.

In the gloom, the globe reminded me of an eye, a pale greenish-yellow eyeball winking at me.

The Eye will take care of her.

My memory has preserved what happened next as a series of snapshots, like freeze-frame stills from an art house movie, with those jerky, handheld camera angles.

SHOT 1: On my butt, doing a crab-crawl away from the compound.

SHOT 2: On my feet. Running. The foliage a blur of green and brown and mossy gray.

SHOT 3: Sammy's bear. The chewed-up little arm gummed and gnawed since he was a baby slipping from my fingers.

SHOT 4: Me on my second attempt to pick up that damned bear.

SHOT 5: The ash pit in the foreground. I'm halfway between Crisco's body and Branch's. Clutching Sammy's bear to my chest.

SHOTS 6–10: More woods, more me running. If you look closely, you can see the ravine in the left-hand corner of the tenth frame.

SHOT 11: The final frame. I'm suspended in midair above the shadow-filled ravine, taken right after I launched myself off the edge.

The green wave roared over my curled-up body at the bottom,

carrying along tons of debris, a rocketing mass of trees, dirt, the bodies of birds and squirrels and woodchucks and insects, the contents of the ash pit, shards of the pulverized barracks and storehouse—plywood, concrete, nails, tin—and the first couple of inches of soil in a hundred-yard radius of the blast. I felt the shock wave before I hit the muddy bottom of the ravine. An intense, bone-rattling pressure over every inch of my body. My eardrums popped, and I remembered Crisco saying, *You know what happens when you're blasted with two hundred decibels?*

No, Crisco, I don't.

But I've got an idea.

24

I CAN'T STOP thinking about the soldier behind the coolers and the crucifix in his hand. The soldier and the crucifix. I'm thinking maybe that's why I pulled the trigger. Not because I thought the crucifix was another gun. I pulled the trigger because he was a soldier, or at least he was dressed like a soldier.

He wasn't Branch or Vosch or any of the soldiers I saw that day my father died.

He wasn't and he was.

Not any of them, and all of them.

Not my fault. That's what I tell myself. It's their fault. *They're the ones, not me,* I tell the dead soldier. *You want to blame somebody, blame the Others, and get off my back.*

Run = die. Stay = die. Sort of the theme of this party.

Beneath the Buick, I slipped into a warm and dreamy twilight. My makeshift tourniquet had stopped most of the bleeding, but the wound throbbed with each slowing beat of my heart.

It's not so bad, I remember thinking. *This whole dying thing isn't so bad at all.*

And then I saw Sammy's face pressed against the back window of the yellow school bus. He was smiling. He was happy. He felt safe surrounded by those other kids, and besides, the soldiers were there now, the soldiers would protect him and take care of him and make sure everything was okay.

It had been bugging me for weeks. Keeping me up at night. Hitting me when I least expected it, when I was reading or foraging or just lying in my little tent in the woods thinking about my life before the Others came.

What was the point?

Why did they play that giant charade of soldiers arriving in the nick of time to save us? The gas masks, the uniforms, the "briefing" in the barracks. What was the point to all that when they could have just dropped one of their blinky eyeballs from a drone and blown us all to hell?

On that cold autumn day while I lay bleeding to death beneath the Buick, the answer hit me. Hit me harder than the bullet that had just torn through my leg.

Sammy.

They wanted Sammy. No, not just Sammy. They wanted all the kids. And to get the kids, they had to make us trust them. *Make the humans trust us, get the kids, and then we blow them all to hell.*

But why bother saving the children? Billions had died in the first three waves; it wasn't like the Others had a soft spot for kids. Why did the Others take Sammy?

I raised my head without thinking and whacked it into the Buick's undercarriage. I barely noticed.

I didn't know if Sammy was alive. For all I knew, I was the last person on Earth. But I had made a promise.

The cool asphalt scraping against my back.

The warm sun on my cold cheek.

My numb fingers clawing at the door handle, using it to pull my sorry, self-pitying butt off the ground.

I can't put any weight on my wounded leg. I lean against the car for a second, then push myself upright. On one leg, but upright.

I might be wrong about them wanting to keep Sammy alive. I'd been wrong about practically everything since the Arrival. I still could be the last human being on Earth.

I might be—no, I probably am—doomed.

But if I'm it, the last of my kind, the last page of human history, like hell I'm going to let the story end this way.

I may be the last one, but I am the one still standing. I am the one turning to face the faceless hunter in the woods on an abandoned highway. I am the one not running, not staying, but facing.

Because if I am the last one, then I am humanity.

And if this is humanity's last war, then I am the battlefield.

II

WONDERLAND

25

CALL ME ZOMBIE.

Head, hands, feet, back, stomach, legs, arms, chest—everything hurts. Even blinking hurts. So I try not to move and I try not to think too much about the pain. I try not to think too much period. I've seen enough of the plague over the past three months to know what's coming: total system meltdown, starting with your brain. The Red Death turns your brain to mashed potatoes before your other organs liquefy. You don't know where you are, who you are, what you are. You become a zombie, the walking dead—if you had the strength to walk, which you don't.

I'm dying. I know that. Seventeen years old and the party's over. Short party.

Six months ago my biggest worries were passing AP Chemistry and finding a summer job that paid enough for me to finish rebuilding the engine on my '69 Corvette. And when the mothership first appeared, sure, that took up some of my thoughts, but after a while it faded to a distant fourth. I watched the news like everybody else and spent way too much time sharing funny YouTube videos about it, but I never thought it would affect me personally. Seeing all the demonstrations and marches and riots on TV leading up to the first attack was like watching a movie or news footage from a foreign country. It didn't seem like any of it was happening to me.

Dying isn't so different from that. You don't feel like it's going to happen to you . . . until it happens to you.

I know I'm dying. Nobody has to tell me.

Chris, the guy who shared this tent with me before I got sick, tells me anyway: "Dude, I think you're dying," he says, squatting outside the tent's opening, his eyes wide and unblinking above the filthy rag that he presses against his nose.

Chris has come by to check up on me. He's about ten years older, and I think he looks at me like a little brother. Or maybe he's come to see if I'm still alive; he's in charge of disposal for this part of the camp. The fires burn day and night. By day the refugee camp ringing Wright-Patterson swims in a dense, choking fog. At night the firelight turns the smoke a deep crimson, like the air itself is bleeding.

I ignore his remark and ask him what he's heard from Wright-Patterson. The base has been on full lockdown since the tent city sprang up after the attack on the coasts. No one allowed in or out. They're trying to contain the Red Death, that's what they tell us. Occasionally some well-armed soldiers well-wrapped in hazmat suits roll out the main gates with water and rations, tell us everything will be okay, and then hightail it back inside, leaving us to fend for ourselves. We need medicine. They tell us there's no cure for the plague. We need sanitation. They give us shovels to dig a trench. We need information. *What the hell is going on?* They tell us they don't know.

"They don't know anything," Chris says to me. He's on the thin side, balding, an accountant before the attacks made accounting obsolete. "Nobody knows anything. Just a bunch of rumors that everybody treats like news." He cuts his eyes at me, then looks away. Like looking at me hurts. "You want to hear the latest?"

Not really. "Sure." To keep him there. I've only known the guy for a month, but he's the only guy left who I know. I lie here on this old camping bed with a sliver of sky for a view. Vague, people-shaped forms drift by in the smoke, like figures out of a horror movie, and sometimes I can hear screaming or crying, but I haven't spoken to another person in days.

"The plague isn't theirs, it's ours," Chris says. "Escaped from some top-secret government facility after the power failed."

I cough. He flinches, but he doesn't leave. He waits for the fit to subside. Somewhere along the way he lost one of the lenses to his glasses. His left eye is stuck in a perpetual squint. He rocks from foot to foot in the muddy ground. He wants to leave; he doesn't want to leave. I know the feeling.

"Wouldn't that be ironic?" I gasp. I can taste blood.

He shrugs. Irony? There is no irony anymore. Or maybe there's just so much of it that you can't call it irony. "It's not ours. Think about it. The first two attacks drive the survivors inland to take shelter in camps just like this one. That concentrates the population, creating the perfect breeding ground for the virus. Millions of pounds of fresh meat all conveniently located in one spot. It's genius."

"Gotta hand it to 'em," I say, trying to be ironic. I don't want him to leave, but I also don't want him to talk. He has a habit of going off on rants, one of those guys who has an opinion about everything. But something happens when every person you meet dies within days of your meeting them: You start being a lot less picky about who you hang out with. You can overlook a lot of flaws. And you let go of a lot of personal hang-ups, like the big lie that having your insides turn to soup doesn't scare the living shit out of you.

"They know how we think," he says.

"How the hell do you know what they know?" I'm getting

pissed. I'm not sure why. Maybe I'm jealous. We shared the tent, same water, same food, and I'm the one who's dying. What makes him so special?

"I don't," he answers quickly. "The only thing I know is I don't know anything anymore."

In the distance, a gun fires. Chris barely reacts. Gunfire is pretty common in the camp. Potshots at birds. Warning shots at the gangs coming for your stash. Some shots signal a suicide, a person in the final stages who decides to show the plague who's boss. When I first came to the camp, I heard a story about a mom who took out her three kids and then did herself rather than face the Fourth Horseman. I couldn't decide whether she was brave or stupid. And then I stopped worrying about it. Who cares what she *was* when what she is now is dead?

He doesn't have much more to say, so he says it quickly to get the hell away. Like a lot of the uninfected, Chris has a bad case of the twitchies, always waiting for the other shoe to drop. Scratchy throat—from the smoke or . . . ? Headache—from lack of sleep or hunger or . . . ? It's the moment you're passed the ball and out of the corner of your eye you see the two-hundred-and-fifty-pound linebacker bearing down at full speed—only the moment never ends.

"I'll come back tomorrow," he says. "You need anything?"

"Water." Though I can't keep it down.

"You got it, dude."

He stands up. All I can see now is his mud-stained pants and mud-caked boots. I don't know how I know, but I know it's the last I'll see of Chris. He won't come back, or if he does, I won't realize it. We don't say good-bye. Nobody says good-bye anymore. The word has taken on a whole new meaning since the Big Green Eye in the Sky showed up.

I watch the smoke swirl in his passing. Then I pull out the silver chain from beneath the blanket. I run my thumb over the smooth surface of the heart-shaped locket, holding it close to my eyes in the fading light. The clasp broke on the night I yanked it free from her neck, but I managed to fix it using a pair of fingernail clippers.

I look toward the tent opening and see her standing there, and I know it isn't really her, it's the virus showing her to me, because she's wearing the same locket I'm holding in my hand. The bug has been showing me all kinds of things. Things I want to see and things I don't. The little girl in the opening is both.

Bubby, why did you leave me?

I open my mouth. I taste blood. "Go away."

Her image begins to shimmer. I rub my eyes, and my knuckles come away wet with blood.

You ran away. Bubby, why did you run?

And then the smoke pulls her apart, splinters her, smashes her body into nothing. I call out to her. Crueler than seeing her is the not seeing her. I'm clutching the silver chain so tight that the links cut into my palm.

Reaching for her. Running from her.

Reaching. Running.

Outside the tent, the red smoke of funeral pyres. Inside, the red fog of plague.

You're the lucky one, I tell Sissy. *You left before things got really messy.*

Gunfire erupts in the distance. Only this time it's not the sporadic *pop-pop* of some desperate refugee firing at shadows, but big guns that go off with an eardrum-thumping *puh-DOOM*. The high-pitched screeching of tracer fire. The rapid reports of automatic weapons.

Wright-Patterson is under attack.

Part of me is relieved. It's like a release, the final cracking open of the storm after the long wait. The other part of me, the one that still thinks I might survive the plague, is ready to wet his pants. Too weak to move off the cot and too scared to do it even if I wasn't. I close my eyes and whisper a prayer for the men and women of Wright-Patterson to waste an invader or two for me and Sissy. But mostly for Sissy.

Explosions now. Big explosions. Explosions that make the ground tremble, that vibrate against your skin, that press hard against your temples and push on your chest and squeeze. It sounds as if the world is being ripped apart, which in a way it is.

The little tent is choking with smoke, and the opening glows like a triangular eye, a burning ember of bright hellish red. *This is it,* I'm thinking. *I'm not going to die of the plague after all. I'm going to live long enough to be wasted by an actual alien invader. A better way to go, quicker anyway.* Trying to put a positive spin on my impending demise.

A gunshot rings out. Very close, judging by the sound of it, maybe two or three tents down. I hear a woman screaming incoherently, another shot, and then the woman isn't screaming anymore. Then silence. Then two more shots. The smoke swirls, the red eye glows. I can hear him now, coming toward me, hear his boots squishing in the wet earth. I fumble under the wad of clothing and jumble of empty water bottles beside the cot for my gun, a revolver Chris had given me on the day he invited me to be his tentmate. *Where's your gun?* he asked. He was shocked to learn I wasn't packing. *You have to have a gun, pal,* he said. *Even the kids have guns.* Never mind that I can't hit the broad side of a barn or that the odds are very good I'll shoot off my own foot; in the post-human age, Chris is a firm believer in the Second Amendment.

I wait for him to appear in the opening, Sissy's silver locket in one hand, Chris's revolver in the other. In one hand, the past. In the other, the future. That's one way to look at it.

Maybe if I play possum he—or it—will move on. I watch the opening through slits for eyes.

And then he's here, a thick, black pupil in the crimson eye, swaying unsteadily as he leans inside the tent, three, maybe four feet away, and I can't see his face, but I can hear him gasping for breath. I'm trying to control my own breathing, but no matter how shallowly I do it, the rattle of the infection in my chest sounds louder than the explosions of the battle. I can't make out exactly what he's wearing, except his pants seem to be tucked into his tall boots. A soldier? Must be. He's holding a rifle.

I'm saved. I raise the hand holding the locket and call out weakly. He stumbles forward. Now I can see his face. He's young, just a little older than I am, and his neck is shiny with blood, and so are the hands that hold the rifle. He goes to one knee beside the cot, then recoils when he sees my face, the sallow skin, the swollen lips, and the sunken bloodshot eyes that are the telltale signs of the plague.

Unlike mine, the soldier's eyes are clear—and wide with terror.

"We had it wrong, all wrong!" he whispers. "They're already here—been here—right here—inside us—the whole time—inside us."

Two large shapes leap through the opening. One grabs the soldier by the collar and drags him outside. I raise the old revolver— or try to, because it slips from my hand before I can lift it two inches above the blanket. Then the second one is on me, knocking the revolver away, yanking me upright. The aftershock of pain blinds me for a second. He yells over his shoulder at his buddy, who has just ducked back inside. "Scan him!" A large metal disk is pressed against my forehead.

"He's clean."

"And sick." Both men are dressed in fatigues—the same fatigues worn by the soldier they took away.

"What's your name, buddy?" one of them asks. I shake my head. I'm not getting this. My mouth opens, but no intelligible sound comes out.

"He's gone zombie," his partner says. "Leave him."

The other one nods, rubbing his chin, looking down at me. Then he says, "The commander ordered retrieval of all uninfected civilians."

He tucks the blanket around me, and with one fluid motion heaves me out of the bunk and over his shoulder. As a definitively infected civilian, I'm pretty shocked.

"Chill, zombie," he tells me. "You're going to a better place now."

I believe him. And for a second I let myself believe I'm not going to die after all.

26

THEY TAKE ME to a quarantined floor at the base hospital reserved for plague victims, nicknamed the Zombie Ward, where I get an armful of morphine and a powerful cocktail of antiviral drugs. I'm treated by a woman who introduces herself as Dr. Pam. She has soft eyes, a calm voice, and very cold hands. She wears her hair in a tight bun. And she smells like hospital disinfectant mingled with a hint of perfume. The two smells don't go well together.

I have a one-in-ten chance of survival, she tells me. I start to laugh. I must be a little delirious from the drugs. One in ten? And here I was thinking the plague was a death sentence. I couldn't be happier.

Over the next two days, my fever soars to a hundred and four. I break into a cold sweat, and even my sweat is flecked with blood. I float in and out of a delirious twilight sleep while they throw everything at the infection. There is no cure for the Red Death. All they can do is keep me doped up and comfortable until the bug decides whether it likes the way I taste.

The past shoves its way in. Sometimes Dad is sitting next to me, sometimes Mom, but most of the time it's Sissy. The room turns red. I see the world through a diaphanous curtain of blood. The ward recedes behind the red curtain. It's just me and the invader inside me and the dead—not just my family, but all the dead, all however-many-billion of them, reaching for me as I run. Reaching. Running. And it occurs to me that there's no real difference between us, the living and the dead; it's just a matter of tense: past-dead and future-dead.

On the third day, the fever breaks. By the fifth, I'm holding down liquids and my eyes and lungs have begun to clear. The red curtain pulls back, and I can see the ward, the gowned and masked doctors and nurses and orderlies, the patients in various stages of death, past and future, floating on the gentle sea of morphine or being wheeled out of the room with their faces covered, the present-dead.

On the sixth day, Dr. Pam declares the worst over. She orders me off all meds, which kind of bums me out; I'm going to miss my morphine.

"Not my call," she tells me. "You're being moved into the convalescent ward till you can get back on your feet. We're going to need you."

"Need me?"

"For the war."

The war. I remember the firefight, the explosions, the soldier bursting into the tent and *they're inside us!*

"What's going on?" I ask. "What happened here?"

She's already turned away, handing my chart to an orderly and telling him in a quiet voice, but not so quiet I can't hear, "Bring him to the exam room at fifteen hundred hours, after he's clear of the meds. Let's tag and bag him."

27

I'M TAKEN TO a large hangar near the entrance to the base. Everywhere I look, there're signs of the recent battle. Burned-out vehicles, the rubble of demolished buildings, stubborn little fires smoldering, pockmarked asphalt, and three-foot-wide craters from mortar fire. But the security fence has been repaired, and beyond it I can see a no-man's-land of blackened earth where Tent City used to be.

Inside the hangar, soldiers are painting huge red circles on the shiny concrete floor. There are no planes. I'm wheeled through a door in the back, into an examination room, where I'm heaved onto the table and left alone for a few minutes, shivering in my thin hospital gown under the bright fluorescent lights. What's with the big red circles? And how did they get the power back on?

And what did she mean by "Let's tag and bag him"? I can't keep my thoughts from flying in every direction. What happened here? If the aliens attacked the base, where are the dead aliens? Where's their downed spacecraft? How did we manage to defend ourselves against an intelligence thousands of years more advanced than ours—and defeat it?

The inner door opens, and Dr. Pam comes in. She shines a bright light in my eyes. Listens to my heart, my lungs, thumps on a couple places. She shows me a silver-gray pellet about the size of a grain of rice.

"What's that?" I ask. I half expect her to say it's an alien spaceship: We've discovered they're the size of an amoeba.

Instead, she says the pellet is a tracking device, hooked into the base's mainframe. Highly classified, been used by the military for years. The idea is to implant all surviving personnel. Each pellet transmits its own unique signal, a signature that can be picked up by detectors as far as a mile away. To keep track of us, she tells me. To keep us safe.

She gives me a shot in the back of my neck to numb me, then inserts the pellet under my skin, near the base of my skull. She bandages the insertion point, then helps me back into the wheelchair and takes me into the adjoining room. It's much smaller than the first room. A white reclining chair that reminds me of a dentist's. A computer and monitor. She helps me into the chair and proceeds to tie me down: straps across my wrists, straps across my ankles. Her face is very close to mine. The perfume has a slight edge today over the disinfectant in the Odor Wars. She doesn't miss my expression. "Don't be scared," she says. "It isn't painful."

Scared, I whisper, "What isn't?"

She steps over to the monitor and starts punching in commands.

"It's a program we found on a laptop that belonged to one of the infested," Dr. Pam explains. Before I can ask what the hell an infested is, she rolls on: "We're not sure what the infesteds had been using it for, but we know it's perfectly safe. Its code name is Wonderland."

"What's it do?" I ask. I'm not sure what she's telling me, but it sounds like she's telling me that the aliens had somehow infiltrated Wright-Patterson and hacked into its computer systems. I can't get the word *infested* out of my head. Or the bloody face of the soldier bursting into my tent. *They're inside us.*

"It's a mapping program," she answers. Which really isn't an answer.

"What does it map?"

She looks at me for one long, uncomfortable moment, as if she's deciding whether to tell the truth. "It maps you. Close your eyes, big, deep breath. Counting down from three . . . two . . . one . . ."

And the universe implodes.

Suddenly I'm there, three years old, holding on to the sides of my crib, jumping up and down and screaming like someone's murdering me. I'm not remembering that day; I'm experiencing it.

Now I'm six, swinging my plastic baseball bat. The one I loved; the one I forgot I had.

Ten now, riding home from the pet store with a bag of goldfish in my lap and debating names with my mom. She's wearing a bright yellow dress.

Thirteen, it's a Friday night, I'm playing pee-wee football, and the crowd is cheering. Going deep.

The reel begins to slow. I feel like I'm drowning—drowning in the dream of my life. My legs kick helplessly against the restraints, strapped in tight, running.

Running.

First kiss. Her name is Lacey. My ninth-grade algebra teacher and her horrible handwriting. Getting my driver's license. Everything there, no blank spaces, all of it pouring out of me while I'm pouring into Wonderland.

All of it.

Green blob in the night sky.

Holding the boards while Dad nails them over the living room windows. The sound of gunfire down the street, glass shattering, people screaming. And the hammer falling: *bam, bam, BAM.*

"Blow out the candles": Mom's hysterical whisper. "Can't you hear them? They're coming!"

And my father, calmly, in the pitch black: "If anything happens to me, take care of your mother and baby sister."

I'm in free fall. Terminal velocity. There's no escaping it. I won't just remember that night. I'll live it all over again.

It has chased me all the way to Tent City. The thing I ran from, that I'm still running from, the thing that's never let me go.

What I reach for. What I run from.

Take care of your mother. Take care of your baby sister.

The front door crashes open. Dad fires point-blank into the chest of the first intruder. The guy must be high on something, because he just keeps coming. I see a sawed-off shotgun in my father's face, and that's the last I see of my father's face.

The room fills with shadows, and one of the shadows is my mother, and then more shadows and hoarse shouts and I'm tearing up the stairs cradling Sissy in my arms, realizing too late I'm running toward a dead end.

A hand catches my shirt and flings me backward, and I tumble back down the stairs, shielding Sissy with my body, smacking down headfirst at the bottom.

Then shadows, huge shadows, and a swarm of fingers, pulling her out of my arms. And Sissy, screaming, *Bubby, Bubby, Bubby, Bubby!*

I reach for her in the dark. My fingers hook on the locket around her neck and tear the silver chain free.

Then, like the day the lights blinked out forever, my sister's voice abruptly dies.

Then the punks are on me. Three of them, jacked up on dope or desperate to find some, kicking, punching, a furious rain of blows into my back, my stomach, and as I bring up my hands to shield my face, I see the silhouette of Dad's hammer rising over my head.

It whistles down. I roll away. The head of the hammer grazes my temple, its momentum carrying it right into the guy's shin. He falls to his knees with an agonized howl.

On my feet now, running down the hall to the kitchen, and the thunder of footsteps as they come after me.

Take care of your baby sister.

Tripping on something in the backyard, probably the garden hose or one of Sissy's stupid toys. Falling face-first in the wet grass under a star-stuffed sky, and the glowing green orb, the circling Eye, coldly staring down at me, the one with the silver locket clutched in his bleeding hand, the one who lived, the one who did not go back, the one who ran.

28

I'VE FALLEN SO DEEP, nothing can reach me. For the first time in weeks, I feel numb. I don't even feel like *me*. There's no place where I end and the nothingness begins.

Her voice comes into the darkness, and I grab on to it, a lifeline to pull me out of the bottomless well.

"It's over. It's all right. It's over . . ."

I break the surface into the real world, gasping for air, crying uncontrollably like a complete pansy, and I'm thinking, *You're wrong, Doc. It's never over. It just goes on and on and on.* Her face swims into view, and my arm jerks against the restraint as I try to grab her. She needs to make this stop.

"What the hell was that?" I ask in a croaky whisper. My throat is burning, my mouth dry. I feel like I weigh about five pounds, like all the flesh has been torn from my bones. And I thought the plague was bad!

"It's a way for us to see inside you, to look at what's really going on," she says gently. She runs her hand over my forehead. The gesture reminds me of my mother, which reminds me of losing my mother in the dark, of running from her in the night, which reminds me I shouldn't be strapped down in this white chair. I should be with them. I should have stayed and faced what they faced. *Take care of your little sister.*

"That's my next question," I say, fighting to stay focused. "What's going on?"

"They're inside us," she answers. "We were attacked from the inside, by infected personnel who'd been embedded in the military."

She gives me a few minutes to process this while she wipes the tears from my face with a cool, moist cloth. It's maddening, how motherly she is, and the soothing coolness of the cloth, a pleasant torture.

She sets aside the cloth and looks deeply into my eyes. "Using the ratio of infected to clean here at the base, we estimate that one out of every three surviving human beings on Earth is one of them."

She loosens the straps. I'm insubstantial as a cloud, light as a balloon. When the final strap comes free, I expect to fly out of the chair and smack the ceiling.

"Would you like to see one?" she asks.

Holding out her hand.

29

SHE WHEELS ME down a hallway to an elevator. It's a one-way express that carries us several hundred feet below the surface. The doors open into a long corridor with white cinder-block walls. Dr. Pam tells me we're in the bomb shelter complex that's nearly as large as the base above us, built to withstand a fifty-megaton nuclear blast. I tell her I'm feeling safer already. She laughs like she thinks that's very funny. I'm rolling past side tunnels and unmarked doors and, though the floor is level, I feel as if I'm being taken to the very bottom of the world, to the hole where the devil sits. There are soldiers hurrying up and down the corridor; they avert their eyes and stop talking as I'm wheeled past them.

Would you like to see one?

Yes. Hell no.

She stops at one of the unmarked doors and swipes a key card through the locking mechanism. The red light turns green. She rolls me into the room, stopping the chair in front of a long mirror, and my mouth falls open and I drop my chin and close my eyes, because whatever is sitting in that wheelchair isn't me, it can't be me.

When the mothership first appeared, I was one hundred and ninety pounds, most of it muscle. Forty pounds of that muscle is gone. The stranger in that mirror looked back at me with the eyes of the starving: huge, sunken, ringed in puffy, black bags. The virus has taken a knife to my face, carving away my cheeks, sharpening my chin, thinning my nose. My hair is stringy, dry, falling out in places.

He's gone zombie.

Dr. Pam nods at the mirror. "Don't worry. He won't be able to see us."

He? Who's she talking about?

She hits a button, and the lights in the room on the other side of the mirror flood on. My image turns ghostlike. I can see through myself to the person on the other side.

It's Chris.

He's strapped to a chair identical to the one in the Wonderland room. Wires run from his head to a large console with blinking red lights behind him. He's having trouble keeping his head up, like a kid nodding off in class.

She notices my stiffening at the sight of him and asks, "What? Do you know him?"

"His name is Chris. He's my . . . I met him in the refugee camp. He offered to share his tent and he helped me when I got sick."

"He's your friend?" She seems surprised.

"Yes. No. Yes, he's my friend."

"He's not what you think he is."

She touches a button, and the monitor pops to life. I tear my eyes away from Chris, from the outside of him to the inside, from apparent to hidden, because on the screen I can see his brain encased in translucent bone, glowing a sickly yellowish green.

"What is that?" I whisper.

"The infestation," Dr. Pam says. She presses a button and zooms in on the front part of Chris's brain. The pukish color intensifies, glowing neon bright. "This is the prefrontal cortex, the thinking part of the brain—the part that makes us human."

She zooms in tight on an area no larger than the head of a pin, and then I see it. My stomach does a slow roll. Embedded in the soft tissue is a pulsing egg-shaped growth, anchored by thousands of rootlike tendrils fanning out in all directions, digging into every crease and crevice of his brain.

"We don't know how they did it," Dr. Pam says. "We don't even know if the infected are aware of their presence, or if they've been puppets their entire lives."

The thing entangling itself in Chris's brain, pulsing.

"Take it out of him." I can barely form words.

"We've tried," Dr. Pam says. "Drugs, radiation, electroshock, surgery. Nothing works. The only way to kill them is to kill the host."

She slides the keyboard in front of me. "He won't feel anything."

Confused, I shake my head. I don't get it.

"It lasts less than a second," Dr. Pam assures me. "And it's completely painless. This button right here."

I look down at the button. It has a label: EXECUTE.

"You're not killing Chris. You're destroying the thing inside him that would kill you."

"He had his chance to kill me," I argue. Shaking my head. It's too much. I can't deal. "And he didn't. He kept me alive."

"Because it wasn't time yet. He left you before the attack, didn't he?"

I nod. I'm looking at him again through the two-way mirror, through the indistinct frame of my see-through self.

"You're killing the things that are responsible for this." She presses something into my hand.

Sissy's locket.

Her locket, the button, and Chris. And the thing inside Chris.

And me. Or what's left of me. What's left of me? What do I have left? The metal links of Sissy's necklace cut into my palm.

"It's how we stop them," Dr. Pam urges me. "Before there's no one left to stop them."

Chris in the chair. The locket in my hand. How long have I been running? Running, running, running. Christ, I'm sick of running. I should have stayed. I should have faced it. If I had faced it then, I wouldn't be facing it now, but sooner or later you have to choose between running and facing the thing you thought you could not face.

I bring my finger down as hard as I can.

30

I LIKE THE CONVALESCENT WING a lot more than the Zombie Ward. It smells better, for one thing, and you get your own room. You're not stuck out on the floor with a hundred other people. The room is quiet and private, and it's easy to pretend the world is what it was before the attacks. For the first time in weeks, I'm able to eat solid food and make it to the bathroom by myself—though I avoid looking in the mirror. The days seem brighter, but the nights are bad: Every time I close my eyes, I see my skeletal self in the execution room, Chris strapped down in the room on the other side, and my bony finger coming down.

Chris is gone. Well, according to Dr. Pam, Chris never was. There was the thing inside Chris controlling him that had embedded itself into his brain (they don't know how) sometime in the past (they don't know when). No aliens descended from the mothership to attack Wright-Patterson. The attack came from within, with infested soldiers turning their guns on their comrades. Which meant they had been hiding inside us for a long time, waiting for the first three waves to whittle our population down to a manageable number before revealing themselves.

What did Chris say? *They know how we think.*

They knew we'd seek safety in numbers. Knew we'd take shelter with the guys who had guns. So, Mr. Alien, how do you overcome that? It's simple, because you know how we think, don't you? You embed sleeper units where the guns are. Even if your troops fail in the initial assault, like they did at Wright-Patterson, you succeed in your ultimate goal of blowing society apart. If the enemy looks just like you, how do you fight him?

At that point, it's game over. Starvation, disease, wild animals: It's only a matter of time before the last, isolated survivors are dead.

From my window six stories up I can see the front gates. Around dusk, a convoy of old yellow school buses rolls out, escorted by Humvees. The buses return several hours later loaded down with people, mostly kids—though it's hard to tell in the dark—who are taken into the hangar to be tagged and bagged, the "infested" winnowed out and destroyed. That's what my nurses tell me, anyway. To me, the whole thing seems crazy, given what we know about the attacks. How did they kill so many of us so quickly? Oh yeah, because humans herd like sheep! And now here we are, clustering again. Right in plain sight. We might as well paint a big red bull's-eye on the base. *Here we are! Fire when ready!*

And I can't take it anymore.

Even as my body grows stronger, my spirit begins to crumple.

I really don't get it. What's the point? Not their point; that's been pretty damn clear from the beginning.

I mean what's the point of us anymore? I'm sure if we didn't cluster again, they'd have another plan, even if that plan were using infested assassins to take us out one stupid, isolated human at a time.

There's no winning. If I had somehow saved my sister, it wouldn't have mattered. I would have bought her another month or two tops.

We're the dead. There's no one else now. There's the past-dead and the future-dead. Corpses and corpses-to-be.

Somewhere between the basement room and this room, I lost

Sissy's locket. I wake up in the middle of the night, my hand clutching empty air, and I hear her screaming my name like she's standing two feet away, and I'm furious, I'm pissed as hell, and I tell her to shut up, I lost it, it's gone. I'm dead like her, doesn't she get it? A zombie, that's me.

I stop eating. I refuse my meds. I lie in bed for hours, staring at the ceiling, waiting for it to be over, waiting to join my sister and the seven billion other lucky ones. The virus that was eating me has been replaced by a different disease that's even more hungry. A disease with a kill rate of 100 percent. And I tell myself, *Don't let them do it, man! This is part of their plan, too,* but it doesn't do any good. I can give myself pep talks all day long; it doesn't change the fact that the moment the mothership appeared in the sky, it was game over. Not a matter of if, but when.

And right when I reach the point of no return, when the last part of me able to fight is about to die, as if he's been waiting all this time for me to reach that point, my savior appears.

The door opens and his shadow fills the space—tall, lean, hard-edged, as if his shadow were cut from a slab of black marble. That shadow falls over me as he walks toward the bed. I want to look away, but I can't. His eyes—cold and blue as a mountain lake—pin me down. He comes into the light, and I can see his short-cropped sandy hair and his sharp nose and his thin lips drawn tight in a humorless smile. Crisp uniform. Shiny black boots. The officer insignia on his collar.

He looks down at me in silence for a long, uncomfortable moment. Why can't I look away from those ice-blue eyes? His face is so chiseled it looks unreal, like a wood carving of a human face.

"Do you know who I am?" he asks. His voice is deep, very deep,

126

a voice-over-on-a-movie-preview deep. I shake my head. How the hell could I know that? I'd never seen him before in my life.

"I'm Lieutenant Colonel Alexander Vosch, the commander of this base."

He doesn't offer me his hand. He just stares at me. Steps around to the end of the bed, looks at my chart. My heart is pounding hard. It feels like I've been called to the principal's office.

"Lungs good. Heart rate, blood pressure. Everything's good." He hangs the chart back on the hook. "Only everything isn't good, is it? In fact, everything is pretty damn bad."

He pulls a chair close to the bed and sits down. The motion is seamless, smooth, uncomplicated, like he's practiced it for hours and gotten sitting down to an exact science. He adjusts the crease in his pants into a perfectly straight line before he goes on.

"I've seen your Wonderland profile. Very interesting. And very instructive."

He reaches into his pocket, again with so much grace that it's more like a dance move than a gesture, and pulls out Sissy's silver locket.

"I believe this is yours."

He drops it on the bed next to my hand. Waits for me to grab it. I force myself to lie still, I'm not sure why.

His hand returns to his breast pocket. He tosses a wallet-size photo into my lap. I pick it up. There's a little blond kid around six, maybe seven. With Vosch's eyes. Being held in the arms of a pretty lady around Vosch's age.

"You know who they are?"

Not a hard question. I nod. For some reason, the picture bothers me. I hold it out for him to take back. He doesn't.

"They're my silver chain," he says.

"I'm sorry," I say, because I don't know what else to say.

"They didn't have to do it this way, you know. Have you thought about that? They could have taken their own sweet time killing us—so why did they decide to kill us so quickly? Why send down a plague that kills nine out of every ten people? Why not seven out of ten? Why not five? In other words, what's their damn hurry? I have a theory about that. Would you like to hear it?"

No, I think. I wouldn't. Who is this guy, and why is he here talking to me?

"There's a quote from Stalin," he says. "'A single death is a tragedy; a million is a statistic.' Can you imagine seven billion of anything? I have trouble doing it. It pushes the limits of our ability to comprehend. And that's exactly why they did it. Like running up the score in football. You played football, right? It isn't about destroying our capability to fight so much as crushing our will to fight."

He takes the photograph and slips it back into his pocket. "So I don't think about the 6.98 billion people. I think about just two."

He nods toward Sissy's locket. "You left her. When she needed you, you ran. And you're still running. Don't you think it's time you stop running and fight for her?"

I open my mouth, and whatever I meant to say comes out as, "She's dead."

He waves his hand in the air. I'm being stupid. "We're all dead, son. Some of us are just a little further along than others. You're wondering who the hell I am and why I'm here. Well, I told you who I am, and now I'm going to tell you why I'm here."

"Good," I whisper. Maybe after he tells me, he'll leave me alone. He's weirding me out. Something about the way he looks at me with that icy stare, the—there's no other word for it—hardness of him, like he's a statue come to life.

"I'm here because they've killed almost all of us, but not all of us. And that's their mistake, son. That's the flaw in their plan. Because if you don't kill all of us all at once, whoever's left are not going to be the weak ones. The strong ones—and only the strong ones—will survive. The bent but unbroken, if you know what I mean. People like me. And people like you."

I'm shaking my head. "I'm not strong."

"Well, that's where you and I will have to disagree. You see, Wonderland doesn't just map out your experiences; it maps out *you*. It tells us not just who you are, but what you are. Your past and your potential. And your potential, I kid you not, is off the charts. You are exactly what we need at exactly the time we need it."

He stands up. Towering over me. "Get up."

Not a request. His voice is as rock hard as his features. I heave myself onto the floor. He brings his face close to mine and says in a low, dangerous voice, "What do you want? Be honest."

"I want you to leave."

"No." Shaking his head sharply. "What do you want?"

I feel my lower lip poking out, like a tiny kid about to collapse completely. My eyes are burning. I bite down hard on the edges of my tongue and force myself not to look away from the cold fire in his eyes.

"Do you want to die?"

Do I nod? I can't remember. Maybe I did, because he says, "I'm not going to let you. So now what?"

"So I guess I'm going to live."

"No, you're not. You're going to die. You're going to die, and there's nothing you or I or anyone else can do to stop it. You, me, everyone left on this big, beautiful blue planet is going to die and make way for them."

He's cut right to the heart of it. It's the perfect thing to say at the perfect moment, and what he's been trying to get out of me suddenly explodes.

"Then what's the point, huh?" I shout into his face. "What's the fucking point? You have all the answers, so you tell me, because I have no idea anymore why I should give a damn!"

He grabs me by the arm and slings me toward the window. He's beside me in two seconds and flings open the curtain. I see the school buses idling beside the hangar and a line of children waiting to go inside.

"You're asking the wrong person," he snarls. "Ask them why you should give a damn. Tell them there's no point. Tell them you want to die."

He grabs my shoulders and whirls me around to face him. Slaps me hard in the chest.

"They've flipped the natural order on us, boy. Better to die than live. Better to give up than fight. Better to hide than face. They know the way to break us is to kill us first here." Slapping my chest again. "The final battle for this planet will not be fought over any plain or mountain or jungle or desert or ocean. It will happen here." Popping me again. Hard. *Pop, pop, pop.*

And I'm totally gone by this point, giving in to everything I've bottled up inside since the night my sister died, sobbing like I've never cried before, like crying is something new to me and I like the way it feels.

"You are the human clay," Vosch whispers fiercely in my ear. "And I am Michelangelo. I am the master builder, and you will be my masterpiece." Pale blue fire in his eyes, burning to the bottom of my soul. "God doesn't call the equipped, son. God equips the called. And you have been called."

He leaves me with a promise. The words burn so hot in my mind, the promise follows me into the deepest hours of the night and into the days that follow.

I will teach you to love death. I will empty you of grief and guilt and self-pity and fill you up with hate and cunning and the spirit of vengeance. I will make my final stand here, Benjamin Thomas Parish.

Slapping my chest over and over until my skin burns, my heart on fire. *And you will be my battlefield.*

III
SILENCER

31

IT SHOULD have been easy. All he had to do was wait.

He was very good at waiting. He could crouch for hours, motionless, silent, he and his rifle one body, one mind, the line fuzzy between where he ended and the weapon began. Even the fired bullet seemed connected to him, bound by an invisible cord to his heart, until the bullet wedded bone.

The first shot dropped her, and he quickly fired again, missing entirely. A third shot as she dived to the ground beside the car, and the back window of the Buick exploded in a cloud of pulverized shatterproof glass.

She'd gone under the car. Her only option, really, which left him two: wait for her to come out or leave his position in the woods bordering the highway and end it. The option with the least risk was staying put. If she crawled out, he would kill her. If she didn't, time would.

He reloaded slowly, with the deliberateness of someone who knows he has all the time in the world. After days of stalking her, he guessed she wasn't going anywhere. She was too smart for that. Three shots had failed to take her down, but she understood the odds of a fourth missing. What had she written in her diary?

In the end it wouldn't be the lucky ones left standing.

She would play the odds. Crawling out had zero chance of success. She couldn't run, and even if she could, she didn't know in which direction safety lay. Her only hope was for him to abandon his hiding place and force the issue. Then anything was possible. She might even get lucky and shoot him first.

If there was a confrontation, he didn't doubt she would refuse to go down quietly. He had seen what she did to the soldier in the convenience store. She may have been terrified at the time, and killing him may have bothered her afterward, but her fear and guilt didn't stop her from filling his body with lead. Fear didn't paralyze Cassie Sullivan, like it did some humans. Fear crystallized her reason, hardened her will, clarified her options. Fear would keep her under the car, not because she was afraid of coming out, but because staying there was her only hope of staying alive.

So he would wait. He had hours before nightfall. By then, she would have either bled to death or be so weak from blood loss and dehydration that finishing her would be easy.

Finishing her. Finishing Cassie. Not Cassie for Cassandra. Or Cassie for Cassidy. Cassie for Cassiopeia, the girl in the woods who slept with a teddy bear in one hand and a rifle in the other. The girl with the strawberry blond curls who stood a little over five feet four in her bare feet, so young-looking he was surprised to learn she was sixteen. The girl who sobbed in the pitch black of the deep woods, terrified one moment, defiant the next, wondering if she was the last person on Earth, while he, the hunter, hunkered a dozen feet away, listening to her cry until exhaustion carried her down into a restless sleep. The perfect time to slip silently into her camp, put the gun to her head, and finish her. Because that's what he did. That's what he was: a finisher.

He had been finishing humans since the advent of the plague. For four years now, since he was fourteen, when he awakened inside the human body chosen for him, he had known what he was. Finisher. Hunter. Assassin. The name didn't matter. Cassie's name for him, Silencer, was as good as any. It described his purpose: to snuff out the human noise.

But he didn't that night. Or the nights that followed. And each night, creeping a little closer to the tent, inching his way over the woodland blanket of decaying leaves and moist loamy soil until his shadow rose in the narrow opening of the tent and fell over her, and the tent was filled with her smell, and there would be the sleeping girl clutching the teddy bear and the hunter holding his gun, one dreaming of the life that was taken from her, the other thinking of the life he'd take. The girl sleeping and the finisher, willing himself to finish her.

Why didn't he finish her?

Why couldn't he finish her?

He told himself it was unwise. She couldn't stay in these woods indefinitely. He could use her to lead him to others of her kind. Humans are social animals. They cluster like bees. The attacks relied on this critical adaptation. The evolutionary imperative that drove them to live in groups was the opportunity to kill them by the billions. What was the saying? Strength in numbers.

And then he found the notebooks and discovered there was no plan, no real goal except to survive to the next day. She had nowhere to go and no one left to go to. She was alone. Or thought she was.

He didn't return to her camp that night. He waited until the afternoon of the following day, not telling himself he was giving her time to pack up and leave. Not letting himself think about her silent, desperate cry: *Sometimes I think I might be the last human on Earth.*

Now, as the last human's last minutes spun out beneath the car on the highway, the tension in his shoulders began to fade. She wasn't going anywhere. He lowered the rifle and squatted at the base of the tree, rolling his head from side to side to ease the stiffness in his neck. He was tired. Hadn't been sleeping well lately. Or eating. He'd dropped some pounds since the 4th Wave rolled out. He wasn't too concerned. They'd anticipated some psychological and physical blowback at the beginning of the 4th Wave. The first kill would be the hardest, but the next would be easier, and the one after that easier still, because it's true: Even the most sensitive person can get used to even the most insensitive thing.

Cruelty isn't a personality trait. Cruelty is a habit.

He pushed that thought away. To call what he was doing cruel implied he had a choice. Choosing between your kind and another species wasn't cruel. It was necessary. Not easy, especially when you've lived the last four years of your life pretending to be no different from them, but necessary.

Which raised the troubling question: Why didn't he finish her that first day? When he heard the shots inside the convenience store and followed her back to the campsite, why didn't he finish her then, while she lay crying in the dark?

He could explain away the three missed shots on the highway. Fatigue, lack of sleep, the shock of seeing her again. He had assumed she would head north, if she ever left her camp at all, not head back south. He had felt a sudden rush of adrenaline, as if he'd turned a street corner and run into a long-lost friend. That must have been what threw off that first shot. The second and third he could chalk up to luck—her luck, not his.

But what about all those days that he followed her, sneaking into her camp while she was away foraging, doing a bit of foraging himself through her belongings, including the diary in which she had written, *Sometimes in my tent, late at night, I think I can hear the stars scraping against the sky?* What about those predawn mornings when he slid silently through the woods to where she slept, determined to finish it this time, to do what he had prepared all his life to do? She wasn't his first kill. She wouldn't be his last.

It should have been easy.

He rubbed his slick palms against his thighs. It was cool in the trees, but he was dripping with sweat. He scrubbed his sleeve across his eyes. The wind on the highway: a lonely sound. A squirrel scampered down the tree next to him, unconcerned by his presence. Below him, the highway disappeared over the horizon in both directions, and nothing moved except the trash and the grass bowing in the lonely wind. The buzzards had found the three bodies lying in the median; three fat birds waddled in for a closer look while the rest of the flock circled in the updrafts high overhead. The buzzards and other scavengers were enjoying a population explosion. Buzzards, crows, feral cats, packs of hungry dogs. He'd stumbled upon more than one desiccated corpse that had clearly been someone's dinner.

Buzzards. Crows. Aunt Millie's tabby. Uncle Herman's Chihuahua. Blowflies and other insects. Worms. Time and the elements clean up the rest. If she didn't come out, Cassie would die beneath the car. Within minutes of her last breath, the first fly would arrive to lay eggs in her.

He pushed the distasteful image away. It was a human thought. It had been only four years since his Awakening, and he still fought against seeing the world through human eyes. On the day of his Awakening, when he saw the face of his human mother for the first time, he burst into tears: He had never seen anything so beautiful—or so ugly.

It had been a painful integration for him. Not seamless or

139

quick, like some Awakenings he'd heard of. He supposed his had been more difficult than others because the childhood of his host body had been a happy one. A well-adjusted, healthy human psyche was the hardest to absorb. It had been—still was—a daily struggle. His host body wasn't something apart from him that he manipulated like a puppet on a string. It *was* him. The eyes he used to see the world, they were his eyes. This brain he used to interpret, analyze, sense, and remember the world, it was his brain, wired by thousands of years of evolution. Human evolution. He wasn't trapped inside it and didn't ride about in it, guiding it like a jockey on a horse. He was this human body, and it was him. And if something should happen to it—if, for example, it died— he would perish with it.

It was the price of survival. The cost of his people's last, desperate gamble:

To rid his new home of humanity, he had to become human.

And being human, he had to overcome his humanity.

He stood up. He didn't know what he was waiting for. Cassie for Cassiopeia was doomed, a breathing corpse. She was badly injured. Run or stay, there was no hope. She had no way to treat her wound and no one for miles who could help her. She had a small tube of antibiotic cream in her backpack, but no suture kit and no bandages. In a few days, the wound would become infected, gangrene would set in, and she would die, assuming another finisher didn't come along in the interim.

He was wasting time.

So the hunter in the woods stood up, startling the squirrel. It rocketed up the tree with an angry hiss. He swung his rifle to his shoulder and brought the Buick into the sight, swinging the red crosshairs back and forth and up and down its body. What if he blew out the tires? The car would collapse onto its rims, perhaps pinning her beneath its two-thousand-pound frame. There'd be no running then.

The Silencer lowered his rifle and turned his back on the highway.

The buzzards feeding in the median heaved their cumbersome bodies into the air.

The lonely wind died.

And then his hunter's instinct whispered, *Turn around.*

A bloody hand emerged from the undercarriage. An arm followed. Then a leg.

He swung his rifle into position. Sighted her in the crosshairs. Holding his breath, sweat coursing down his face, stinging his eyes. She was going to do it. She was going to run. He was relieved and anxious at the same time.

He couldn't miss with this fourth shot. He spread his legs wide and squared his shoulders and waited for her to make her move. The direction wouldn't matter. Once she was out in the open, there was nowhere to hide. Still, part of him hoped she would run in the opposite direction, so he wouldn't have to place the bullet in her face.

Cassie hauled herself upright, collapsed for a moment against the car, then righted herself, balancing precariously on her wounded leg, clutching the handgun. He placed the red cross in the middle of her forehead. His finger tightened on the trigger.

Now, Cassie. Run.

She pushed away from the car. Brought up the handgun. Pointed it at a spot fifty yards to his right. Swung it ninety degrees, swung it back. Her voice came to him shrill and small in the deadened air.

"Here I am! Come and get me, you son of a bitch!"

I'm coming, he thought, for the rifle and the bullet were a part of him, and when the round wed bone, he would be there, too, inside her, the instant she died.

Not yet. Not yet, he told himself. *Wait till she runs.*

But Cassie Sullivan didn't run. Her face, speckled with dirt and grease and blood from the cut on her cheek, seemed just inches away through the scope, so close he could count the freckles on her nose. He could see the familiar look of fear in her eyes, a look he had seen a hundred times, the look we give back to death when death looks at us.

But there was something else in her eyes, too. Something that warred with her fear, strove against it, shouted it down, kept her still and the gun moving. Not hiding, not running, but facing.

Her face blurred in the crosshairs: Sweat was dripping into his eyes.

Run, Cassie. Please run.

A moment comes in war when the last line must be crossed. The line that separates what you hold dear from what total war demands. If he couldn't cross that line, the battle was over, and he was lost.

His heart, the war.

Her face, the battlefield.

With a cry only he could hear, the hunter turned.

And ran.

IV

MAYFLY

32

AS WAYS TO DIE GO, freezing to death isn't such a bad one.

That's what I'm thinking as I freeze to death.

You feel warm all over. There's no pain, none at all. You're all floaty, like you just chugged a whole bottle of cough syrup. The white world wraps its white arms around you and carries you downward into a frosty white sea.

And the silence so—shit—silent, that the beating of your heart is the only sound in the universe. So quiet, your thoughts make a whispery noise in the dull, freezing air.

Waist-deep in a drift, under a cloudless sky, the snowpack holding you upright because your legs can't anymore.

And you're going, *I'm alive, I'm dead, I'm alive, I'm dead.*

And there's that damn bear with its big, brown, blank, creepy eyes staring at you from its perch in the backpack, going, *You lousy shit, you promised.*

So cold your tears freeze against your cheeks.

"It's not my fault," I told Bear. "I don't make the weather. You got a beef, take it up with God."

That's what I've been doing a lot lately: taking it up with God. Like: *God, WTF?*

Spared from the Eye so I could kill the Crucifix Soldier. Saved from the Silencer so my leg could get infected, making every step a journey over hell's highway. Kept me going until the blizzard came in for two solid days, trapping me in this waist-high drift so I could die of hypothermia under a gloriously blue sky.

Thanks, God.

Spared, saved, kept, the bear says. *Thanks, God.*

It doesn't really matter, I'm thinking. I was all over Dad for getting so fangirly about the Others, and for spinning the facts to make things seem less bleak, but I wasn't actually much better than he was. It was just as hard for me to swallow the idea that I had gone to bed a human being and woken up a cockroach. Being a disgusting, disease-carrying bug with a brain the size of a pinhead isn't something you deal with easily. It takes time to adjust to the idea.

And the bear goes, *Did you know a cockroach can live up to a week without its head?*

Yeah. Learned that in bio. So your point is I'm a little worse off than a cockroach. Thanks. I'll work on exactly what kind of disease-carrying pest I am.

It hits me then. Maybe that's why the Silencer on the highway let me live: spritz the bug, walk away. Do you really need to stick around while it flips on its back and claws the air with its six spindly legs?

Stay under the Buick, run, stand your ground—what did it matter? Stay, run, stand, whatever; the damage was done. My leg wasn't going to heal on its own. The first shot was a death sentence, so why waste any more bullets?

I rode out the blizzard in the rear compartment of an Explorer. Folded down the seat, made myself a cozy metal hut in which to watch the world turn white, unable to crack the power windows to let in fresh air, so the SUV quickly filled up with the smell of blood and my festering wound.

I used up all the pain pills from my stash in the first ten hours. Ate up the rest of my rations by the end of day one in the SUV. When I got thirsty, I popped the hatch a crack and scooped up handfuls of snow. Left the hatch popped up to get some fresh air—until my teeth were chattering and my breath turned into blocks of ice in front of my eyes.

By the afternoon of day two, the snow was three feet deep and my little metal hut began to feel less like a refuge than a sarcophagus. The days were only two watts brighter than the nights, and the nights were the negation of light—not dark, but lightlessness absolute. *So,* I thought, *this is how dead people see the world.*

I stopped worrying about why the Silencer had let me live. Stopped worrying about the very weird feeling of having two hearts, one in my chest and a smaller one, a mini heart, in my knee. Stopped caring whether the snow stopped before my two hearts did.

I didn't exactly sleep. I floated in that space in between, hugging Bear to my chest, Bear who kept his eyes open when I could not. Bear, who kept Sammy's promise to me, being there for me in the space between.

Um, speaking of promises, Cassie . . .

I must have apologized to him a thousand times during those two snowbound days. *I'm sorry, Sams. I said no matter what, but what you're too young to understand is there's more than one kind of bullshit. There's the bullshit you know that you know; the bullshit you don't know and know you don't know; and the bullshit you just think you know but really don't. Making a promise in the middle of an alien black op falls under the last category. So . . . sorry!*

So sorry.

One day later now, waist-deep in a snowbank, Cassie the ice maiden, with a jaunty little cap made out of snow and frozen hair and ice-encrusted eyelashes, all warm and floaty, dying by inches, but at least dying on her feet trying to keep a promise she had no prayer of keeping.

So sorry, Sams, so sorry.

No more bullshit.

I'm not coming.

33

THIS PLACE CAN'T BE HEAVEN. It doesn't have the right vibe.

I'm walking in a dense fog of white lifeless nothingness. Dead space. No sound. Not even the sound of my own breath. In fact, I can't even tell if I'm breathing. That's number one on the "How do I know if I'm alive?" checklist.

I know someone is here with me. I don't see him or hear him, touch or smell him, but I know he's here. I don't know how I know he's a he, but I do know, and he's watching me. He's staying still while I move through the thick white fog, but somehow he's always the same distance away. It doesn't freak me that he's there, watching. It doesn't exactly comfort me, either. He's another fact, like the fact of the fog. There's the fog and un-breathing me and the person with me, always close, always watching.

But there's no one there when the fog clears, and I find myself in a four-poster bed beneath three layers of quilts that smell faintly of cedar. The white nothing fades and is replaced by the warm yellow glow of a kerosene lamp sitting on the small table beside the bed. Lifting my head a little, I can see a rocking chair, a freestanding full-length mirror, and the slatted doors of a bedroom closet. A plastic tube is attached to my arm, and the other end is attached to a bag of clear fluid hanging from a metal hook.

It takes a few minutes to absorb my new surroundings, the fact that I'm numb from the waist down, and the ultra-mega-confusing fact that I'm definitely not dead.

I reach down, and my fingers find thick bandages wrapped around my knee. I'd also like to feel my calf and toes, because there's no sensation and I'm kind of concerned I don't *have* a calf or toes or anything else below the big wad of bandages. But I can't reach that far without sitting up, and sitting up isn't an option. It seems like the only working parts are my arms. I use those to throw the covers off, exposing the upper half of my body to the chilly air. I'm wearing a floral-print cotton nightie. And then I'm like, *What's with the cotton nightie?* Beneath which, I am naked. Which means, of course, that at some point between the removal of my clothes and donning of the nightie I was completely naked, which means I was *completely naked.*

Okay, ultra-mega-confusing fact number two.

I turn my head to the left: dresser, table, lamp. To the right: window, chair, table. And there's Bear, reclining on the pillow beside me, staring thoughtfully at the ceiling, not a care in the world.

Where the hell are we, Bear?

The floorboards rattle as below me someone slams a door. The *kulump, kulump* of heavy boots on bare wood. Then silence. A very heavy silence, if you don't count my heart knocking against my ribs, which you probably should since it sounds as loud as one of Crisco's sonic bombs.

Thunk-thunk-thunk. Growing louder with each *thunk.*

Someone is coming up the stairs.

I try to sit up. Not a smart idea. I get about four inches off the pillow and that's it. Where's my rifle? Where's my Luger? Someone is just outside the door now, and I can't move, and even if I could all I have is this damned stuffed toy. What was I going to do with that? Snuggle the dude to death?

When you're out of options, the best option is to do nothing. Play dead. The possum option.

I watch the door swing open through slits for eyes. I see a red plaid shirt, a wide brown belt, blue jeans. A pair of large, strong hands and very nicely trimmed fingernails. I keep my breath nice and even while he stands right beside me, by the metal pole, checking my drip, I guess. Then he turns and there's his butt and then he turns again and his face lowers into view as he sits in the rocker by the mirror. I can see his face, and I can see my face in the mirror. *Breathe, Cassie, breathe. He has a good face, not the face of someone who wants to hurt you. If he wanted to hurt you, he wouldn't have brought you here and stuck an IV in you to keep you hydrated, and the sheets feel nice and clean, and so what, he took your clothes and dressed you in this cotton nightie, what did you expect him to do? Your clothes were filthy, like you, only you're not anymore, and your skin smells a little like lilacs, which means holy Christ he* bathed *you.*

Trying to keep my breath steady and not doing a very good job at it.

Then the owner of the good face says, "I know you're awake."

When I don't say anything, he goes, "And I know you're watching me, Cassie."

"How do you know my name?" I croak. My throat feels like it's lined with sandpaper. I open up my eyes. I can see him clearer now. I wasn't wrong about the face. It's good in a clean-cut, Clark Kent kind of way. I'm guessing eighteen or nineteen, broad through the shoulders, nice arms, and those hands with the perfect cuticles. *Well,* I tell myself, *it could be worse. You could have been rescued by some fifty-year-old perv sporting a spare tire the size of a monster truck's who keeps his dead mother in the attic.*

"Driver's license," he says. He doesn't get up. He stays in the chair with his elbows resting on his knees and his head lowered, which strikes me as more shy than menacing. I watch his dangling hands and imagine them running a warm, wet cloth over every inch of my body. My completely naked body.

"I'm Evan," he says next. "Evan Walker."

"Hi," I say.

He gives a little laugh like I said something funny.

"Hi," he says.

"Where the hell am I, Evan Walker?"

"My sister's bedroom." His deep-set eyes are a chocolate brown, like his hair, and a little mournful and questioning, like a puppy's.

"Is she . . . ?"

He nods. Rubbing his hands together slowly. "Whole family. How about you?"

"Everyone except my baby brother. That's, um, his bear, not mine."

He smiles. It's a good smile, like his face. "It's a very nice bear."

"He's looked better."

"Like most things."

153

I assume he's talking about the world in general, not my body. "How did you find me?" I ask.

He looks away. Looks back at me. Chocolate-colored, lost-puppy eyes. "The birds."

"What birds?"

"Buzzards. When I see them circling, I always check it out. You know. In case—"

"Sure, okay." I didn't want him to elaborate. "So you brought me here to your house, stuck me with an IV—where'd you get the IV, anyway? And then you took off all my . . . and then you cleaned me up . . ."

"I honestly couldn't believe you were alive, and then I couldn't believe you'd stay alive." He's rubbing his hands together. Is he cold? Nervous? I'm both. "The IV was already here. It came in handy during the plague. I shouldn't say this, I guess, but every day I came home I honestly expected you to be dead. You were in pretty bad shape."

He reaches into his shirt pocket, and for some reason I flinch, which he notices, and then smiles reassuringly. He holds out a chunk of knotty-looking metal the size of a thimble.

"If this had hit you practically anyplace else, you *would* be dead." He rolls the slug between his index finger and thumb. "Where'd it come from?"

I roll my eyes. Can't help it. But I leave out the *duh*. "A rifle."

He shakes his head. He thinks I don't understand the question. Sarcasm doesn't appear to work on him. If that's true, I'm in trouble: It's my normal mode of communication.

"Whose rifle?"

"I don't know—the Others. A troop of them pretending to be soldiers wasted my father and everybody in our refugee camp. I

154

was the only one who made it out alive. Well, not counting Sammy and the rest of the kids."

He's looking at me like I'm completely whacked. "What happened to the kids?"

"They took them. In school buses."

"School buses . . . ?" He's shaking his head. Aliens in school buses? He looks like he's about to smile. I must have looked a little too long at his lips, because he rubs them self-consciously with the back of his hand. "Took them where?"

"I don't know. They told us Wright-Patterson, but—"

"Wright-Patterson. The air force base? I heard it was abandoned."

"Well, I'm not sure you can trust anything they tell you. They *are* the enemy." I swallow. My throat's parched.

Evan Walker must be one of those people who notices everything, because he says, "You want something to drink?"

"I'm not thirsty," I lie. Now, why did I lie about something like that? To show him how tough I am? Or to keep him in that chair because he's the first person I've talked to in weeks, if you didn't count the bear, which you shouldn't.

"Why did they take the kids?" His eyes are big and round now, like Bear's. It's hard to decide his best feature. Those soft, chocolaty eyes or the lean jaw? Maybe the thick hair, the way it falls over his forehead when he leans toward me.

"I don't know the real reason, but I figure it's a very good one to them and a very bad one to us."

"Do you think . . . ?" He can't finish the question—or won't, to spare me having to answer it. He's looking at Sam's bear leaning on the pillow beside me.

"What? That my little brother's dead? No. I think he's alive. Mostly because it doesn't make sense that they'd pull out the kids, then kill everybody else. They blew up the whole camp with some kind of green bomb—"

"Wait a minute," he says, holding up one of his large hands. "A green bomb?"

"I'm not making this up."

"Why green, though?"

"Because green is the color of money, grass, oak leaves, and alien bombs. How the hell would I know why it was green?"

He's laughing. A quiet, held-in kind of laugh. When he smiles, the right side of his mouth goes slightly higher than the left. Then I'm like, *Cassie, why are you staring at his mouth anyway?*

Somehow the fact that I was rescued by a very good-looking guy with a lopsided grin and large, strong hands is the most unnerving thing that has happened to me since the Others arrived.

Thinking about what happened at the camp is giving me the heebie-jeebies, so I decide to change the subject. I peer down at the quilt covering me. It looks homemade. The image of an old woman sewing it flashes through my mind and, for some reason, I suddenly feel like crying.

"How long have I been here?" I ask weakly.

"It'll be a week tomorrow."

"Did you have to cut . . . ?" I don't know how to put the question.

Thankfully, I don't have to. "Amputate? No. The bullet just missed your knee, so I think you'll be able to walk, but there could be nerve damage."

"Oh," I said. "I'm getting used to that."

34

HE LEAVES ME for a little while and returns with some clear broth, not chicken- or beef-based, but some kind of meat, deer maybe, and while I clutch the edges of the quilt he helps me sit up so I can sip, holding the warm cup in both hands. He's staring at me, not a creeper stare, but the way you look at a sick person, feeling a little sick yourself and not knowing how to make it better. Or maybe, I think, it *is* a creeper stare and the concerned look is just a clever cover. Are pervs only pervs if you don't find them attractive? I called Crisco a sicko for trying to give me a corpse's jewelry, and he said I wouldn't think that if he were Ben Parish–hot.

Remembering Crisco kills my appetite. Evan sees me staring at the cup in my lap and gently pulls it from my hands and places it on the table.

"I could have done that," I say, more sharply than I meant to.

"Tell me about these soldiers," he says. "How do you know they weren't . . . human?"

I tell him about them showing up not long after the drones, the way they loaded up the kids, then gathered everybody into the barracks and mowed them down. But the clincher was the Eye. Clearly extraterrestrial.

"They're human," he decides after I'm done. "They must be working with the visitors."

"Oh God, please don't call them that." I hate that name for them. The talking heads used it before the 1st Wave—all the You-Tubers, everyone in the Twitterverse, even the president during news briefings.

"What should I call them?" he asks. He's smiling. I get the feeling he'd call them turnips if I wanted him to.

"Dad and I called them the Others, as in not us, not human."

"That's what I mean," he says, nodding seriously. "The odds of their looking exactly like us are astronomically slim."

He sounds just like my dad on one of his speculative rants, and suddenly I'm annoyed, I'm not sure why.

"Well, that's terrific, isn't it? A two-front war. Us-versus-them and us-versus-us-and-them."

He shakes his head ruefully. "It wouldn't be the first time people have changed sides once the victor is obvious."

"So the traitors grab the kids out of the camp because they're willing to help wipe out the human race, but they draw the line at anyone under eighteen?"

He shrugs. "What do you think?"

"I think we're seriously screwed when the men with guns decide to help the bad guys."

"I could be wrong," he says, but he doesn't sound like he thinks he is. "Maybe they are visi—Others, I don't know, disguised as humans, or maybe even some kind of clones . . ."

I'm nodding. I've heard this before, too, during one of Dad's endless ruminations about what the Others might look like.

It's not a question of why couldn't they, but why wouldn't they? We've known about their existence for five months. They must have known about ours for years. Hundreds, maybe thousands of years. Plenty of time to extract DNA and "grow" as many copies as they needed. In fact, they might have to wage the ground war with copies of us. In a thousand ways, our planet might not be viable for their bodies. Remember *War of the Worlds*?

Maybe that's the source of my current snippiness. Evan is going all-out Oliver Sullivan on me. And that puts Oliver Sullivan dying in the dirt right in front of me when all I want to do is look away.

"Or maybe they're like cyborgs, Terminators," I say, only half joking. I've seen a dead one up close, the soldier I shot point-blank at the ash pit. I didn't check his pulse or anything, but he sure seemed dead to me, and the blood looked real enough.

Remembering the camp and what happened there never fails to freak me, so I start to freak.

"We can't stay here," I say urgently.

He looks at me like I've lost my mind. "What do you mean?"

"They'll find us!" I grab the kerosene lamp, yank off the glass top, and blow hard at the dancing flame. It hisses at me, stays lit. He pulls the glass out of my hand and slips it back over the base of the lamp.

"It's thirty-seven degrees outside, and we're miles from the nearest shelter," he says. "If you burn down the house, we're toast." Toast? Maybe that's an attempt at humor, but he isn't smiling. "Besides, you're not well enough to travel. Not for another three or four weeks, at least."

Three or four *weeks*? Who does this teenage version of the Brawny paper-towel guy think he's kidding? We won't last three *days* with lights shining through the windows and smoke curling from the chimney.

He's picked up on my growing distress. "Okay," he says with a sigh. He extinguishes the lamp, and the room plunges into darkness. Can't see him, can't see anything. I can smell him, though, a mixture of wood smoke and something like baby powder, and after a few more minutes, I can *feel* his body displacing the air a few inches away from mine.

"Miles away from the nearest shelter?" I ask. "Where the hell do you live, Evan?"

159

"My family's farm. About sixty miles from Cincinnati."

"How far from Wright-Patterson?"

"I don't know. Seventy, eighty miles? Why?"

"I told you. They took my baby brother."

"You said that's where they *said* they were taking him."

Our voices, wrapping around each other's, entwining, and then tugging free, in the pitch black.

"Well, I have to start somewhere," I say.

"And if he isn't there?"

"Then I go somewhere else." I made a promise. That damned bear will never forgive me if I don't keep it.

I can smell his breath. Chocolate. Chocolate! My mouth starts to water. I can actually feel my saliva glands pumping. I haven't had solid food in weeks, and what does he bring me? Some greasy mystery meat–based broth. He's been holding out on me, this farm boy bastard.

"You realize there's a lot more of them than you, right?" he asks.

"And your point is?"

He doesn't answer. So I say, "Do you believe in God, Evan?"

"Sure I do."

"I don't. I mean, I don't know. I did before the Others came. Or thought I did, when I thought about it at all. And then they came and . . ." I have to stop for a second to collect myself. "Maybe there's a God. Sammy thinks there is. But he also thinks there's a Santa Claus. Still, every night I said his prayer with him, and it didn't have anything to do with me. It was about Sammy and what *he* believed, and if you could have seen him take that fake soldier's hand and follow him onto that bus . . ."

I'm losing it, and it doesn't matter to me much. Crying is always easier in the dark. Suddenly my cold hand is blanketed by

Evan's warmer one, and his palm is as soft and smooth as the pillowcase beneath my cheek.

"It kills me," I sob. "The way he trusted. Like the way *we* trusted before they came and blew the whole goddamned world apart. Trusted that when it got dark there would be light. Trusted that when you wanted a fucking strawberry Frappuccino you could plop your ass in the car, drive down the street, and get yourself a fucking strawberry Frappuccino! *Trusted . . .*"

His other hand finds my cheek, and he wipes away my tears with his thumb. The chocolate scent overwhelms me as he bends over and whispers in my ear, "No, Cassie. No, no, no."

I throw my arm around his neck and press his dry cheek against my wet one. I'm shaking like an epileptic, and for the first time I can feel the weight of the quilts on the top of my toes because the blinding dark sharpens your other senses.

I'm a bubbling stew of random thoughts and feelings. I'm worried my hair might smell. I want some chocolate. This guy holding me—well, it's more like I was holding him—has seen me in all my naked glory. What did he think about my body? What did *I* think about my body? Does God really care about promises? Do I really care about God? Are miracles something like the Red Sea parting or more like Evan Walker finding me locked in a block of ice in a wilderness of white?

"Cassie, it's going to be okay," he whispers into my ear, chocolate breath.

When I wake up the next morning, there's a Hershey's Kiss sitting on the table beside me.

35

HE LEAVES THE OLD FARMHOUSE every night to patrol the grounds and to hunt. He tells me he has plenty of dry goods and his mom was a devoted preserver and canner, but he likes fresh meat. So he leaves me to find edible creatures to kill, and on the fourth day he comes into the room with an honest-to-God hamburger on a hot, homemade bun and a side of roasted potatoes. It's the first real food I've had since escaping Camp Ashpit. It's also a freaking hamburger, which I haven't tasted since the Arrival and which, I think I've pointed out, I was willing to kill for.

"Where'd you get the bread?" I ask midway through the burger, grease rolling down my chin. I haven't had bread, either. It's light and fluffy and slightly sweet.

He could give me any number of snarky replies, since there is only one way he could have gotten it. He doesn't. "I baked it."

After feeding me, he changes the dressing on my leg. I ask if I want to look. He says no, I most definitely do not want to look. I want to get out of bed, take a real bath, be like a person again. He says it's too soon. I tell him I want to wash and comb out my hair. Too soon, he insists. I tell him if he won't help me I'm going to smash the kerosene lamp over his head. So he sets a kitchen chair in the middle of the claw-foot tub in the little bathroom down the hall with its peeling flowery wallpaper and carries me to it, plops me down, leaves, and comes back with a big metal tub filled with steaming water.

The tub must be very heavy. His biceps strain against his sleeves,

162

like he's Bruce Banner mid-Hulkifying, and the veins stand out on his neck. The water smells faintly of rose petals. He uses a lemonade pitcher decorated with smiley-faced suns as a ladle, and I lean my head back for him. He starts to work in the shampoo, and I push his hands away. This part I can do myself.

The water courses from my hair into the gown, plastering the cotton to my body. Evan clears his throat, and when he turns his head his thick hair does this swooshy thing across his dark brow and I'm a little disturbed, but in a pleasant way. I ask for the widest-toothed comb he has, and he digs in the cupboard beneath the sink while I watch him out of the corner of my eye, barely noticing the way his powerful shoulders roll beneath his flannel shirt, or his faded jeans with the frayed back pockets, definitely paying no attention to the roundness of his butt inside those jeans, totally ignoring the way my earlobes burn like fire beneath the lukewarm water dripping from my hair. After a couple eternities, he finds a comb, asks if I need anything before he leaves, and I mumble *no* when what I really want to do is laugh and cry at the same time.

Alone, I force myself to concentrate on my hair, which is a horrible mess. Knots and tangles and bits of leaf and little wads of dirt. I work on the knots until the water goes cold and I start to shiver in my wet nightie. I pause once in the chore when I hear a tiny sound just outside the door.

"Are you standing out there?" I ask. The small, tiled bathroom magnifies sound like an echo chamber.

There's a pause, and then a soft answer: "Yes."

"*Why* are you standing out there?"

"I'm waiting to rinse your hair."

"This is going to take a while," I say.

"That's okay."

"Why don't you go bake a pie or something and come back in about fifteen minutes."

I don't hear an answer. But I don't hear him leave.

"Are you still there?"

The floorboards in the hall creak. "Yes."

I give up after another ten minutes of teasing and pulling. Evan comes back in, sits on the edge of the tub. I rest my head in the palm of his hand while he rinses the suds from my hair.

"I'm surprised you're here," I tell him.

"I live here."

"That you *stayed* here." A lot of young guys left for the nearest police station, National Guard armory, or military base after news of the 2nd Wave started trickling in from survivors fleeing inland. Like after 9/11, only times ten.

"There were eight of us, counting Mom and Dad," he says. "I'm the oldest. After they died, I took care of the kids."

"Slower, Evan," I say as he empties half the pitcher onto my head. "I feel like I'm being waterboarded."

"Sorry." He presses the edge of his hand against my forehead to act as a dam. The water is deliciously warm and tickly. I close my eyes.

"Did you get sick?" I ask.

"Yeah. Then I got better." He ladles more water from the metal tub into the pitcher, and I hold my breath, anticipating the tickly warmth. "My youngest sister, Val, she died two months ago. That's her bedroom you're in. Since then I've been trying to figure out what to do. I know I can't stay here forever, but I've hiked all the way to Cincinnati, and maybe I don't need to explain why I'm never going back."

One hand pours while the other presses the wet hair against my scalp to wring out the excess water. Firmly, not too hard, just right. Like I'm not the first girl whose hair he's washed. A little, hysterical voice inside my head is screaming, *What do you think you're doing? You don't even know this guy!* but that same voice is going, *Great hands; ask him for a scalp massage while he's at it.*

While outside my head, his deep, calm voice is saying, "Now I'm thinking it doesn't make sense to leave until it gets warmer. Maybe Wright-Patterson or Kentucky. Fort Knox is only a hundred and forty miles from here."

"Fort Knox? What, you're going on a heist?"

"It's a fort, as in heavily *fortified.* A logical rallying point." Gathering the ends of my hair in his fist and squeezing, and the *plop-plops* of the water spattering in the claw-foot tub.

"If it were *me*, I wouldn't go anyplace that's a logical rallying point," I say. "Logically those'll be the first points they wipe off the map."

"From what you've told me about the Silencers, it's not logical to rally anywhere."

"Or stay anywhere longer than a few days. Keep your numbers small and keep moving."

"Until . . . ?"

"There is no *until*," I snap at him. "There's just *unless.*"

He dries my hair with a fluffy white towel. There's a fresh nightie lying on the closed toilet seat. I look up into those chocolate-colored eyes and say, "Turn around." He turns around. I reach past the frayed back pockets of the jeans that conform to the butt that I'm not looking at and pick up the dry nightie. "If you try to peek in that mirror, I'll know," I warn the guy who's already seen me naked, but that was *unconsciously* naked, which is not the same thing. He nods, lowers his head, and pinches his lower lip like he's sealing off a smile.

I wiggle out of the wet nightie, slip the dry one over my head, and tell him it's okay to turn around.

He lifts me from the chair and carries me back to his dead sister's bed, and I have one arm around his shoulders, and his arm is tight—though not *too* tight—across my waist. His body feels about twenty degrees warmer than mine. He eases me onto the mattress and pulls the quilts over my bare legs. His cheeks are very smooth, his hair neatly groomed, and his cuticles, as I've pointed out, are impeccable. Which means grooming is very high on his list of priorities in the postapocalyptic era. Why? Who's around to see him?

"So how long has it been since you've seen another person?" I ask. "Besides me."

"I see people practically every day," he says. "The last *living* one before you was Val. Before her, it was Lauren."

"Lauren?"

"My girlfriend." He looks away. "She's dead, too."

I don't know what to say. So I say, "The plague sucks."

"It wasn't the plague," he says. "Well, she had it, but it wasn't the plague that killed her. She did that herself, before it could."

He's standing awkwardly beside the bed. Doesn't want to leave, doesn't have an excuse to stay.

"I just couldn't help but notice how nice . . ." No, not a good intro. "I guess it's hard, when it's just you, to really care about . . ." Nuh-uh.

"Care about what?" he asks. "One person when almost every person is gone?"

"I wasn't talking about me." And then I give up trying to come up with a polite way to say it. "You take a lot of pride in how you look."

"It isn't pride."

"I wasn't accusing you of being stuck-up—"

"I know; you're thinking what's the point now?"

Well, actually, I was hoping the point was *me*. But I don't say anything.

"I'm not sure," he says. "But it's something I can control. It gives structure to my day. It makes me feel more . . ." He shrugs. "More human, I guess."

"And you need help with that? Feeling human?"

He looks at me funny, then gives me something to think about for a long time after he leaves:

"Don't *you*?"

36

HE'S GONE MOST of the nights. During the days he waits on me hand and foot, so I don't know when the guy sleeps. By the second week, I was about to go nuts cooped up in the little upstairs bedroom, and on a day when the temperature climbed above freezing, he helped me into some of Val's clothes, averting his eyes at the appropriate moments, and carried me downstairs to sit on the front porch, throwing a big wool blanket over my lap. He left me there and came back with two steaming mugs of hot chocolate. I can't say much about the view. Brown, lifeless, undulating earth, bare trees, a gray, featureless sky. But the cold air felt good against my cheeks, and the hot chocolate was the perfect temperature.

We don't talk about the Others. We talk about our lives before the Others. He was going to study engineering at Kent State after graduating. He had offered to stay on the farm for a couple years, but his father insisted that he go to college. He had known Lauren since the fourth grade, started dating her in their sophomore year. There was talk of marriage. He noticed I got quiet when Lauren came up. Like I said, Evan is a noticer.

"How about you?" he asked. "Did you have a boyfriend?"

"No. Well, kind of. His name was Ben Parish. I guess you could say he had this thing for me. We dated a couple of times. You know, casually."

I wonder what made me lie to him. He doesn't know Ben Parish from a hole in the ground. Which is kind of the same way Ben knew *me*. I swirled the remains of my hot chocolate and avoided his eyes.

The next morning he showed up at my bedside with a crutch carved from a single piece of wood. Sanded to a glossy finish, lightweight, the perfect height. I took one look at it and demanded that he name three things he *isn't* good at.

"Roller skating, singing, and talking to girls."

"You left out stalking," I told him as he helped me out of the bed. "I can always tell when you're lurking around corners."

"You only asked for three."

I'm not going to lie: My rehab sucked. Every time I put weight on my leg, pain shot up the left side of my body, my knee buckled, and the only things that kept me from falling flat on my ass were Evan's strong arms.

168

But I kept at it during that long day and the long days that followed. I was determined to get strong. Stronger than before the Silencer cut me down and abandoned me to die. Stronger than I was in my little hideout in the woods, rolled up in my sleeping bag, feeling sorry for myself while Sammy was suffering God knows what. Stronger than the days at Camp Ashpit, where I walked around with a huge chip on my shoulder, angry at the world for being what the world was, for what it had always been: a dangerous place that our human noise had made seem a whole lot safer.

Three hours of rehab in the morning. Thirty-minute break for lunch. Then three more hours of rehab in the afternoon. Working on rebuilding my muscles until I felt them melt into a sweaty, jellylike mass.

But I still wasn't done for the day. I asked Evan what happened to my Luger. I had to get over my fear of guns. And my accuracy sucked. He showed me the proper grip, how to use the sight. He set up empty gallon-size paint cans on the fence posts for targets, replacing those with smaller cans as my aim improved. I ask him to take me hunting with him—I need to get used to hitting a moving, breathing target—but he refuses. I'm still pretty weak, I can't even run yet, and what happens if a Silencer spots us?

We take walks at sunset. At first I didn't make it more than half a mile before my leg gave out and Evan had to carry me back to the farmhouse. But each day I was able to go a hundred yards farther than the day before. A half mile became three-quarters became a whole. By the second week I was doing two miles without stopping. Can't run yet, but my pace and stamina have vastly improved.

Evan stays with me through dinner and a couple hours into the night, and then he shoulders his rifle and tells me he'll be back before sunrise. I'm usually asleep when he comes in—and it's usually way past sunrise.

"Where do you go every night?" I asked him one day.

"Hunting." A man of few words, this Evan Walker.

"You must be a lousy hunter," I teased him. "You hardly ever come back with anything."

"I'm actually very good," he said matter-of-factly. Even when he says something that, on paper, sounds like bragging, it isn't. It's the way he says it, casually, like he's talking about the weather.

"You just don't have the heart to kill?"

"I have the heart to do what I have to do." He ran his fingers through his hair and sighed. "In the beginning it was about staying alive. Then it was about protecting my brothers and sisters from the crazies running around after the plague first hit. Then it was about protecting my territory and supplies . . ."

"What's it about now?" I asked quietly. That was the first time I'd seen him even mildly worked up.

"It settles my nerves," he admitted with an embarrassed shrug. "Gives me something to do."

"Like personal hygiene."

"And I have trouble sleeping at night," he went on. Wouldn't look at me. Not looking at anything, really. "Well. Sleeping period. So after a while I gave up trying and started sleeping during the day. Or trying to. The fact is I only sleep two or three hours a day."

"You must be really tired."

He finally looked at me, and there was something sad and desperate in his eyes.

"That's the worst part," he said softly. "I'm not. I'm not tired at all."

I was still uneasy about his disappearing at night, so once I tried to follow him. Bad idea. I lost him after ten minutes, got worried *I'd* get lost, turned to go back, and found myself staring up into his face.

He didn't get mad. Didn't accuse me of not trusting him. He just said, "You shouldn't be out here, Cassie," and escorted me inside.

More out of concern for my mental health than our personal safety (I don't think he was completely sold on the whole Silencer idea), he hung heavy blankets over the windows in the great room downstairs so we could have a fire and light a couple of lamps. I waited there until he returned from his forays in the dark, sleeping on the big leather sofa or reading one of his mom's battered paperback romance novels with the buffed-out, half-naked guys on the covers and the ladies dressed in full-length ball gowns caught in midswoon. Then around three in the morning he would come home, and we'd throw some more wood on the fire and talk. He doesn't like to talk about his family much (when I asked about his mother's taste in books, he just shrugged and said she liked literature). He steers the conversation back to me when things start getting too personal. Mostly he wants to talk about Sammy, as in how I plan to keep my promise to him. Since I have no idea how I'm going to do that, the discussion never ends well. I'm vague; he presses for specifics. I'm defensive; he's insistent. Finally I get mean, and he shuts down.

"So walk me through this again," he says late one night after going around and around for an hour. "You don't know exactly who or what they are, but you know they have lots of heavy artillery and access to alien weaponry. You don't know where they've taken your brother, but you're going there to rescue him. Once you get there, you don't know how you're going to rescue him, but—"

"What is this?" I ask. "Are you trying to help or make me feel stupid?"

We're sitting on the big fluffy rug in front of the fireplace, his rifle on one side, my Luger on the other, and the two of us in between.

He holds up his hands in a fake gesture of surrender. "I'm just trying to understand."

"I'm starting at Camp Ashpit and picking up the trail from there," I say for about the thousandth time. I think I know why he keeps asking the same questions, but he's so damned obtuse, it's hard to pin him down. Of course, he could say the same thing about me. As plans go, mine is more of a general goal pretending to be a plan.

"And if you can't pick up the trail?" he asks.

"I won't give up until I do."

He's nodding a nod that says, *I'm nodding, but I'm not nodding because I think what you're saying makes sense. I'm nodding because I think you're a total fool and I don't want you to go all kung fu on me with a crutch I made with my own hands.*

So I say, "I'm not a total fool. You'd do the same for Val."

He doesn't have a quick reply to that. He wraps his arms around his legs and rests his chin on his knees, staring at the fire.

"You think I'm wasting my time," I accuse his flawless profile. "You think Sammy's dead."

"How could I know that, Cassie?"

"I'm not saying you know that. I'm saying you *think* that."

"Does it matter what I think?"

"No, so shut up."

"I wasn't saying anything. *You* said—"

"Don't . . . say . . . anything."

"I'm not."

"You just did."

"I'll stop."

"But you're not. You say you will, then you just keep going."

He starts to say something, then shuts his mouth so hard, I hear his teeth click.

"I'm hungry," I say.

"I'll get you something."

"Did I ask you to get me anything?" I want to pop him right in that perfectly shaped mouth. Why do I want to hit him? Why am I so mad right now? "I'm perfectly capable of waiting on myself. This is the problem, Evan. I didn't show up here to give your life purpose now that your life's over. That's up to you to figure out."

"I want to help you," he says, and for the first time I see real anger in those puppy-dog eyes. "Why can't saving Sammy be my purpose, too?"

His question follows me into the kitchen. It hangs over my head like a cloud while I slap some cured deer meat onto some flat bread Evan must have baked in his outdoor oven like the Eagle Scout he is. It follows me as I hobble back into the great room and plop down on the sofa directly behind his head. I have this urge to kick him right between his broad shoulders. On the table beside me is a book entitled *Love's Desperate Desire*. Based on the cover, I would have called it *My Spectacular Washboard Abs*.

That's my big problem. That's it! Before the Arrival, guys like Evan Walker never looked twice at me, much less shot wild game for me and washed my hair. They never grabbed me by the back of the neck like the airbrushed model on his mother's paperback, abs a-clenching, pecs a-popping. My eyes have never been looked deeply into, or my chin raised to bring my lips within an inch of theirs. I was the girl in the background, the just-friend, or—worse—the friend of a just-friend, the you-sit-next-to-her-in-geometry-but-can't-remember-her-name girl. It would have been better if some middle-aged collector of Star Wars action figures had found me in that snowbank.

"What?" I ask the back of his head. "Now you're giving me the silent treatment?"

His shoulders jiggle up and down. You know, one of those wry, silent chuckles, accompanied by a rueful shake of the head. *Girls! So silly.*

"I should have asked, I guess," he says. "I shouldn't have assumed."

"What?"

He rotates around on his butt to face me. Me on the sofa, him on the floor, looking up. "That I was going with you."

"*What?* We weren't even talking about that! And why would you want to go with me, Evan? Since you think he's *dead*?"

"I just don't want *you* to be dead, Cassie."

That does it.

I hurl my deer meat at his head. The plate glances off his cheek, and he's up and in my face before I can blink. He leans in close, putting his hands on either side of me, boxing me in with his arms. Tears shine in his eyes.

"You're not the only one," he says through gritted teeth. "My twelve-year-old sister died in my arms. She choked to death on her own blood. And there was nothing I could do. It makes me sick, the way you act as if the worst disaster in human history somehow revolves around *you*. You're not the only one who's lost everything—not the only one who thinks they've found *the one thing* that makes any of this shit make sense. You have your promise to Sammy, and I have *you*."

He stops. He's gone too far, and he knows it.

"You don't 'have' me, Evan," I say.

"You know what I mean." He's looking intently at me, and it's very hard to keep from turning away. "I can't stop you from going. Well, I guess I *could*, but I also can't let you go alone."

"Alone is better. You know that. It's the reason you're still alive!" I poke my finger into his heaving chest.

He pulls away, and I fight the instinct to reach for him. There's a part of me that doesn't want him to pull away.

"But it's not the reason *you* are," he snaps. "You won't last two minutes out there without me."

I explode. I can't help it. It was the perfectly wrong thing to say at the perfectly wrong time.

"Screw you!" I shout. "I don't need you. I don't need anyone! Well, I *guess* if I needed someone to wash my hair or slap a bandage on a boo-boo or bake me a cake, you'd be the guy!"

After two tries, I manage to get on my feet. Time for the angrily-storming-out-of-the-room part of the argument, while the guy folds his arms over his manly chest and pouts. I pause halfway up the stairs, telling myself I'm stopping to catch my breath, not to let him catch up. He's not following me anyway. So I struggle up the remaining steps and into my bedroom.

No, not my bedroom. Val's bedroom. I don't have a bedroom anymore. Probably never will again.

Oh, screw self-pity. The world doesn't revolve around you. And screw guilt. You aren't the one who made Sammy get on that bus. And while you're at it, screw grief. Evan's crying over his baby sister won't bring her back.

I have you. Well, Evan, the truth is it doesn't matter whether there are two of us or two hundred of us. We don't stand a chance.

175

Not against an enemy like the Others. I'm making myself strong for . . . what? So when I go down, at least I go down strong? What difference does that make?

I slap Bear from his perch on the bed with an angry snarl. *What the hell are* you *staring at?* He flops over to his side, arm sticking up in the air like he's raising his hand in class to ask a question.

Behind me, the door creaks on its rusty hinges.

"Get out," I say without turning around.

Another *creeeeak*. Then a *click*. Then silence.

"Evan, are you standing outside that door?"

Pause. "Yes."

"You're kind of a lurker, you know that?"

If he answers, I don't hear him. I'm hugging myself. Rubbing my hands up and down my arms. The little room is freezing. My knee aches like hell, but I bite my lip and remain stubbornly on my feet, my back to the door.

"Are you still there?" I say when I can't take the silence anymore.

"If you leave without me, I'll just follow you. You can't stop me, Cassie. How are you going to stop me?"

I shrug helplessly, fighting back tears. "Shoot you, I guess."

"Like you shot the Crucifix Soldier?"

The words hit me like a bullet between the shoulder blades. I whirl around and fling open the door. He flinches, but stands his ground.

"How do you know about him?" Of course, there's only one way he could know. "You read my diary."

"I didn't think you were going to live."

"Sorry to disappoint you."

"I guess I wanted to know what happened—"

"You're lucky I left the gun downstairs or I *would* shoot you

176

right now. Do you know how *creepy* that makes me feel, knowing you read that? How much did you read?"

He lowers his eyes. A warm red blush spreads across his cheeks. "You read all of it, didn't you?" I'm totally embarrassed. I feel violated and ashamed. It's ten times worse than when I first woke up in Val's bed and realized he had seen me naked. That was just my body. This was my soul.

I punch him in the stomach. There's no give at all; it's like I hit a slab of concrete.

"I can't believe you," I shout. "You sat there—just *sat* there—while I lied about Ben Parish. You knew the truth and you just sat there and let me lie!"

He jams his hands in his pockets, looking at the floor. Like a little boy busted for breaking his mother's antique vase. "I didn't think it mattered that much."

"You didn't think . . . ?" I'm shaking my head. Who *is* this guy? All of a sudden I've got a bad case of the jitters. Something is seriously wrong here. Maybe it's the fact that he lost his whole family and his girlfriend or fiancée or whatever she was and for months he's been living alone pretending that doing really nothing is really doing something. Maybe he's cocooned himself on this isolated patch of Ohio farmland as a way of dealing with all the shit the Others have ladled out, or maybe he's just weird—weird before the Arrival and just as weird after—but whatever it is, something is seriously twisted about this Evan Walker. He's too calm, too rational, too cool for it to be completely, well, cool.

"Why did you shoot him?" he asks quietly. "The soldier in the convenience store."

"You know why," I say. I'm about to burst into tears.

He's nodding. "Because of Sammy."

Now I'm *really* confused. "It had nothing to do with Sammy."

He looks up at me. "Sammy took the soldier's hand. Sammy got on that bus. Sammy *trusted*. And now, even though I saved you, you won't let yourself trust me."

He grabs my hand. Squeezes it hard. "I'm not the Crucifix Soldier, Cassie. And I'm not Vosch. I'm just like you. I'm scared and I'm angry and I'm confused and I don't know what the hell I'm going to do, but I do know you can't have it both ways. You can't say you're human in one breath and a cockroach in the next. You don't believe you're a cockroach. If you believed that, you wouldn't have turned to face the sniper on the highway."

"Oh my God," I whisper. "It was just a *metaphor*."

"You want to compare yourself to an insect, Cassie? If you're an insect, then you're a mayfly. Here for a day and then gone. That doesn't have anything to do with the Others. It's always been that way. We're here, and then we're gone, and it's not about the time we're here, but what we do with the time."

"What you're saying makes absolutely no sense, you know that?" I feel myself leaning toward him, all the fight draining out of me. I can't decide if he's holding me back or holding me up.

"You're the mayfly," he murmurs.

And then Evan Walker kisses me.

Holding my hand against his chest, his other hand sliding across my neck, his touch feathery soft, sending a shiver that travels down my spine into my legs, which are having a hard time keeping me upright. I can feel his heart slamming against my palm and I can smell his breath and feel the stubble on his upper lip, a sandpapery contrast to the softness of his lips, and Evan is looking at me and I'm looking back at him.

I pull back just enough to speak. "Don't kiss me."

He lifts me into his arms. I seem to float upward forever, like when I was a little girl and Daddy flung me into the air, feeling as if I'd just keep going up until I reached the edge of the galaxy.

He lays me on the bed. I say, right before he kisses me again, "If you kiss me again, I'm going to knee you in the balls."

His hands are incredibly soft, like a cloud touching me.

"I won't let you just . . ." He searches for the right word. ". . . fly away from me, Cassie Sullivan."

He blows out the candle beside the bed.

I feel his kiss more intensely now, in the darkness of the room where his sister died. In the quiet of the house where his family died. In the stillness of the world where the life we knew before the Arrival died. He tastes my tears before I can feel them. Where there would be tears, his kiss.

"I didn't save you," he whispers, lips tickling my eyelashes. "You saved me."

He repeats it over and over, until we fall asleep pressed against each other, his voice in my ear, my tears in his mouth.

"You saved me."

V

THE WINNOWING

37

CASSIE, through the smudged window, shrinking.

Cassie, on the road, holding Bear.

Lifting his arm to help him wave good-bye.

Good-bye, Sammy.

Good-bye, Bear.

The road dust boiling up from the big black wheels of the bus, and Cassie shrinking into the brown swirl.

Good-bye, Cassie.

Cassie and Bear getting smaller and smaller, and the hardness of the glass beneath his fingers.

Good-bye, Cassie. Good-bye, Bear.

Until the dust swallows them, and he's alone on the crowded bus, no Mommy no Daddy no Cassie, and maybe he shouldn't have left Bear, because Bear had been with him since before he could remember anything. There had always been Bear. But there had always been Mommy, too. Mommy and Nan-Nan and Grandpa and the rest of his family. And the kids from Ms. Neyman's class and Ms. Neyman and the Majewskis and the nice checkout lady at Kroger who kept the strawberry suckers beneath her counter. They had always been there, too, like Bear, since before he could re- member, and now they weren't. Who had always been there wasn't anymore, and Cassie said they weren't coming back.

Not ever.

The glass remembers it when he takes his hand away. It holds the memory of his hand. Not like a picture, more like a fuzzy shadow, the way his mother's face is fuzzy when he tries to remember it.

Except Daddy's and Cassie's, all the faces he's known since he knew what faces were are fading. Every face is new now, every face a stranger's face.

A soldier walks down the aisle toward him. He's taken off his black mask. His face is round, his nose small and dotted with freckles. He doesn't look much older than Cassie. He's passing out bags of gummy fruit snacks and juice boxes. Dirty fingers claw for the treats. Some of the children haven't had a meal in days. For some, the soldiers are the first adults they've seen since their parents died. Some kids, the quietest ones, were found along the outskirts of town, wandering among the piles of blackened, half-burned bodies, and they stare at everything and everyone as if everything and everyone were something they've never seen before. Others, like Sammy, were rescued from refugee camps or small bands of survivors in search of rescue, and their clothes aren't quite as ragged and their faces not quite as thin and their eyes not quite as vacant as the quiet ones', the ones found wandering among the piles of the dead.

The soldier reaches the back row. He's wearing a white band on his sleeve with a big red cross on it.

"Hey, want a snack?" the soldier asks him.

The juice box and the chewy gooey treats in the shape of dinosaurs. The juice is cold. Cold. He hasn't had a cold drink in forever.

The soldier slides into the seat beside him and stretches his long legs into the aisle. Sammy pushes the thin plastic straw into the juice box and sips, while his eyes fall to the still form of a girl huddled in the seat across from them. Her shorts are torn, her pink top is stained with soot, her shoes caked with mud. She is smiling in her sleep. A good dream.

"Do you know her?" the soldier asks Sammy.

Sammy shakes his head. She had not been in the refugee camp with him.

"Why do you have that big red cross?"

"I'm a medic. I help sick people."

"Why did you take off your mask?"

"Don't need it now," the medic answers. He pops a handful of gummies into his mouth.

"Why not?"

"The plague's back there." The soldier jerks his thumb toward the back window, where the dust boiled up and Cassie shrunk to nothing, holding Bear.

"But Daddy said the plague is everywhere."

The soldier shakes his head. "Not where we're going," he says.

"Where are we going?"

"Camp Haven."

Against the grumbling engine and the whooshing wind through the open windows, it sounded like the soldier said Camp Heaven.

"Where?" Sammy asks.

"You're going to love it." The soldier pats his leg. "We've got it all fixed up for you."

"For me?"

"For everyone."

Cassie on the road, helping Bear wave good-bye.

"Then why didn't you bring everyone?"

"We will."

"When?"

"As soon as you guys are safe." The soldier glances at the girl again. He stands up, pulls off his green jacket, and gently lets it fall over her.

"You're the most important thing," the soldier says, and his boyish face is set and serious. "You're the future."

The narrow dusty road becomes a wider paved road, and then the buses turn onto an even wider road. Their engines rev up to a guttural roar, and they shoot toward the sun on a highway cleared of wrecks and stalled cars. They've been dragged or pushed onto the roadsides to clear the way for the busloads of children.

The freckle-nosed medic comes down the aisle again, and this time he's handing out bottles of water and telling them to close the windows because some of the children are cold and some are scared by the rush of the wind that sounds like a monster roaring. The air in the bus quickly grows stale and the temperature rises, making the children sleepy.

But Sam gave Bear to Cassie to keep her company, and he's never slept without Bear, not ever, not since Bear came to him, anyway. He is tired, but he is also Bearless. The more he tries to forget Bear, the more he remembers him, the more he misses him, and the more he wishes he hadn't left him behind.

The soldier offers him a bottle of water. He sees something is wrong, though Sammy smiles and pretends he doesn't feel so empty and Bearless. The soldier sits beside him again, asks his name, and says his name is Parker.

"How much farther?" Sammy asks. It will be dark soon, and the dark is the worst time. Nobody told him, but he just knows that when they finally come it will be in the dark and it will be without warning, like the other waves, and there will be nothing you can do about it, it will just happen, like the TV winking out and the cars dying and the planes falling and the plague, the Pesky Ants, Cassie and Daddy called it, and his mommy wrapped in bloody sheets.

When the Others first came, his father told him the world had changed and nothing would be like before, and maybe they'd take him inside the mothership, maybe even take him on adventures in outer space. And Sammy couldn't wait to go inside the mothership and blast off into space just like Luke Skywalker in his X-wing starfighter. It made every night feel like Christmas Eve. When morning came, he thought he would wake up and all the wonderful presents the Others had brought would be there.

But the only thing the Others brought was death.

They hadn't come to give him anything. They had come to take everything away.

When would it—when would *they*—stop? Maybe never. Maybe the aliens wouldn't stop until they had taken everything away, until the whole world was like Sammy, empty and alone and Bearless.

So he asks the soldier, "How much farther?"

"Not far at all," the soldier called Parker answers. "You want me to stay here with you?"

"I'm not afraid," Sammy says. *You have to be brave now,* Cassie told him the day his mother died. When he saw the empty bed and knew without asking that she was gone with Nan-Nan and all the others, the ones he knew and the ones he didn't know, the ones they piled up and burned at the edge of town.

"You shouldn't be," the soldier says. "You're perfectly safe now."

That's exactly what Daddy said on a night after the power died, after he boarded the windows and blocked off the doors, when the bad men with guns came out to steal things.

You're perfectly safe.

After Mommy got sick and Daddy slipped the white paper mask over Cassie's and his faces.

Just to be sure, Sam. I think you're perfectly safe.

"And you're gonna love Camp Haven," the soldier says. "Wait till you see it. We fixed it up just for kids like you."

"And they can't find us there?"

Parker smiles. "Well, I don't know about that. But it's probably the most secure place in North America right now. There's even an invisible force field, in case the visitors try anything."

"Force fields aren't real."

"Well, people used to say the same thing about aliens."

"Have you seen one, Parker?"

"Not yet," Parker answers. "Nobody has, at least not in my company, but we're looking forward to it." He smiles a hard soldiery smile, and Sammy's heart quickens. He wishes he were old enough to be a soldier like Parker.

"Who knows?" Parker says. "Maybe they look just like us. Maybe you're looking at one right now." A different kind of smile now. Teasing.

The soldier stands up, and Sammy reaches for his hand. He doesn't want Parker to leave.

"Does Camp Heaven really have a force field?"

"Yep. And manned watchtowers and twenty-four/seven video surveillance and twenty-foot fencing topped with razor wire and big, mean guard dogs that can smell a nonhuman five miles away."

Sammy's nose crinkles. "That doesn't sound like heaven! That sounds like prison!"

"Except a prison keeps the bad guys in and our camp keeps 'em out."

38

NIGHT.

The stars above, bright and cold, and the dark road below, and the humming of the wheels on the dark road beneath the cold stars. The headlamps stabbing the thick dark. The swaying of the bus and the stale warm air.

The girl across the aisle is sitting up now, dark hair matted to the side of her head, cheeks hollow and skin drawn tight across her skull, making her eyes seem owly huge.

Sammy smiles hesitantly at her. She doesn't smile back. Her stare is fixed on the water bottle leaning against his leg. He holds out the bottle. "Want some?" A bony arm shoots across the space between them, and she pulls the bottle from his hand, gulps down the rest of the water in four swallows, then tosses the empty bottle onto the seat beside her.

"I think they have more, if you're still thirsty," Sammy says.

The girl doesn't say anything. She stares at him, hardly blinking.

"And they have gummies, too, if you're hungry."

She just looks at him, not speaking. Legs curled up beneath Parker's green jacket, round eyes unblinking.

"My name's Sam, but everybody calls me Sammy. Except Cassie. Cassie calls me Sams. What's your name?"

The girl raises her voice over the hum of the wheels and the growl of the engine.

"Megan."

Her thin fingers pluck at the green material of the army jacket. "Where did this come from?" she wonders aloud, her voice barely conquering the humming and growling in the background. Sammy gets up and slides into the empty space beside her. She flinches, drawing her legs back as far as she can.

"From Parker," Sammy tells her. "That's him sitting up there by the driver. He's a medic. That means he takes care of sick people. He's really nice."

The thin girl named Megan shakes her head. "I'm not sick."

Eyes cupped in dark circles, lips cracked and peeling, hair matted and entangled with twigs and dead leaves. Her forehead is shiny, and her cheeks are flushed.

"Where are we going?" she wants to know.

"Camp Heaven."

"Camp . . . what?"

"It's a fort," Sammy says. "And not just any fort. The biggest, best, safest fort in the whole world. It even has a force field!"

It's very warm and stuffy on the bus, but Megan can't stop shivering. Sammy tucks Parker's jacket under her chin. She stares at his face with her huge, owly eyes. "Who's Cassie?"

"My sister. She's coming, too. The soldiers are going back for her. For her and Daddy and all the others."

"You mean she's alive?"

Sammy nods, puzzled. Why wouldn't Cassie be alive?

"Your father and your sister are alive?" Her bottom lip quivers. A tear cuts a trail through the soot on her face. The soot from the smoke from the fires from the bodies burning.

Without thinking, Sammy takes her hand. Like when Cassie took his the night she told him what the Others had done.

That was their first night in the refugee camp. The hugeness of what had happened over the past few months hadn't hit him until that night, after the lamps were turned off and he lay curled next to Cassie in the dark. Everything had happened so fast, from the day the power died to the day his father wrapped Mommy in the white sheet to their arrival at the camp. He always thought they'd go home one day and everything would be like it was before they came. Mommy wouldn't come back—he wasn't a baby; he knew Mommy wasn't coming back—but he didn't understand that there was no going back, that what had happened was forever.

Until that night. The night Cassie held his hand and told him Mommy was just one of billions. That almost everybody on Earth was dead. That they would never live in their house again. That he would never go to school again. That all his friends were dead.

"It isn't right," Megan whispers now in the dark of the bus. "It isn't right." She is staring at Sammy's face. "My whole family's gone, and your father *and* your sister? It isn't right!"

Parker has gotten up again. He's stopping at each seat, speaking softly to each child, and then he's touching their foreheads. When he touches them, a light glows in the gloom. Sometimes the light is green. Sometimes it's red. After the light fades away, Parker stamps the child's hand. Red light, red stamp. Green light, green stamp.

"My little brother was around your age," Megan says to Sammy. It sounds like an accusation: *How come you're alive and he isn't?*

"What's his name?" Sammy asks.

"What's that matter? Why do you want to know his name?"

He wishes Cassie were here. Cassie would know what to say to make Megan feel better. She always knew the right thing to say.

"His name was Michael, okay? Michael Joseph, and he was six years old and he never did anything to anybody. Is that okay? Are you happy now? Michael Joseph was my brother's name. You want to know everybody else's?"

She is looking over Sammy's shoulder at Parker, who has stopped at their row.

"Well, hello, sleepyhead," the medic says to Megan.

"She's sick, Parker," Sammy tells him. "You need to make her better."

"We're going to make everybody better," Parker says with a smile.

"I'm not sick," Megan says, then shivers violently beneath Parker's green jacket.

"Heck no," Parker says with a nod and a big grin. "But maybe I should check your temperature, just to make sure. Okay?"

He holds up a quarter-size silver disk. "Anything over a hundred degrees glows green." He leans over Sammy and presses the disk against Megan's forehead. It lights up green. "Uh-oh," Parker says. "Lemme check you, Sam."

The metal is warm against his forehead. Parker's face is bathed for a second in red light. Parker rolls the stamp over the back of Megan's hand. The green ink shines wetly in the dimness. It's a smiley face. Then a red smiley face for Sammy.

"Wait for them to call your color, okay?" Parker says to Megan. "Greens are going straight to the hospital."

"I'm not sick," Megan shouts hoarsely. Her voice cracks. She doubles over, coughing, and Sammy instinctively recoils.

Parker pats him on the shoulder. "It's just a bad cold, Sam," he whispers. "She's gonna be okay."

"I'm not going to the hospital," Megan tells Sammy after Parker returns to the front of the bus. She furiously rubs the back of her hand against the jacket, smearing the ink. The smiley face is now just a green blob.

"You have to," Sammy says. "Don't you want to get better?"

She shakes her head sharply. He doesn't get it. "Hospitals aren't where you go to get better. Hospitals are where you go to die."

After his mother got sick, he asked Daddy, "Aren't you going to take Mommy to the hospital?" And his father said that it wasn't safe. Too many sick people, not enough doctors, and not anything the doctors could do for her, anyway. Cassie told him the hospital was broken, just like the TV and the lights and the cars and everything else.

"Everything's broken?" he asked Cassie. "Everything?"

"No, not everything, Sams," she answered. "Not this."

She took his hand and put it against his chest, and his pounding heart pushed fiercely against his open palm.

"Unbroken," she said.

39

HIS MOTHER WILL only come to him in the in-between space, the gray time between waking and sleeping. She stays away from his dreams, as if she knows not to go there, because dreams are not real but feel more than real when you're dreaming them. She loves him too much to do that.

Sometimes he can see her face, though most of the time he can't, just her shape, a little darker than the gray behind his lids, and he can smell her and touch her hair, feel it trail through his fingers. If he tries too hard to see her face, she fades into the dark. And if he tries to hold her too tightly, she slips away like her hair between his fingers.

The hum of the wheels on the dark road. The stale warm air and the swaying of the bus beneath the cold stars. How much farther to Camp Heaven? It seems like they've been on the dark road beneath the cold stars forever. He waits for his mother in the in-between space, his eyes closed, while Megan watches him with those big, round, owly eyes.

He falls asleep waiting.

He is still asleep when the three school buses pull up to the gates of Camp Haven. High above in the watchtower, the sentry pushes a button, the electronic lock releases, and the gate slides open. The buses pull in and the gate slides shut behind them.

He doesn't wake up until the buses roll to a stop with a final, angry hiss of their brakes. Two soldiers are moving down the aisle, waking the children who have fallen asleep. The soldiers are heavily armed, but they smile and their voices are gentle. *It's okay. Time to get up. You're perfectly safe now.*

Sammy sits up, squinting in the sudden blaze of light flooding through the windows, and looks outside. They have stopped in front of a large airplane hangar. The big bay doors are closed, so he can't see inside. For a moment he isn't worried about being in a strange place without Daddy or Cassie or Bear. He knows what the bright light means: The aliens couldn't kill the power here. It also means Parker told the truth: The camp does have a force field. It has to. They don't care if the Others know about the camp.

They are perfectly safe.

Megan's breath is heavy in his ear, and he turns to look at her. Her eyes are huge in the glare of the floodlights. She grabs his hand.

"Don't leave me," she begs.

A big man heaves himself onto the bus. He stands beside the driver, hands on hips. He has a wide, fleshy face and very small eyes.

"Good morning, boys and girls, and welcome to Camp Haven! My name is Major Bob. I know you're tired and hungry and maybe a little scared . . . Who's a little scared right now? Raise your hand." No hands go up. Twenty-six pairs of eyes stare blankly at him, and Major Bob grins. His teeth are small, like his eyes. "That's outstanding. And you know what? You shouldn't be scared! Our camp is the safest place in the whole ding-dong world right now, I kid you not. You're all perfectly safe." He turns to one of the smiling soldiers, who hands him a clipboard. "Now there are only two rules here at Camp Haven. Rule number one: Remember your colors. Everybody hold up your colors!" Twenty-five fists fly into the air. The twenty-sixth, Megan's, remains in her lap. "Reds, in a couple of minutes you'll be escorted into Hangar Number One for processing. Greens, sit tight, you've got a little farther to go."

"I'm not going," Megan whispers in Sammy's ear.

"Rule number two!" Major Bob booms. "Rule two is two words: Listen and follow. That's easy to remember, right? Rule two, two words. Listen to your group leader. Follow every instruction your group leader gives you. Don't question and don't talk back. They are—we all are—here for one reason and one reason only, and that's to keep you guys safe. And we can't keep you guys safe unless you guys listen and follow all instructions, right away, no questions." He hands the clipboard back to the smiling soldier, claps his pudgy hands, and says, "Any questions?"

"He just said don't ask questions," Megan whispers. "And then he asks if we have any questions."

195

"Outstanding!" Major Bob yells. "Let's get you processed! Reds, your group leader is Corporal Parker. No running, pushing, or shoving, but keep it moving. No breaking line and no talking, and remember to show your stamp at the door. Let's move it, people. The sooner we get you processed, the sooner you can catch some sleep and have some breakfast. I'm not saying the food is the best in the world, but there's plenty of it!"

He lumbers down the steps. The bus rocks with each footfall. Sammy starts to get up, and Megan yanks him back down.

"Don't leave me," she says again.

"But I'm a red," Sammy protests. He feels sorry for Megan, but he's anxious to leave. It feels like he's been on the bus forever. And the sooner the buses are empty, the sooner they can turn around and go back for Cassie and Daddy.

"It's all right, Megan," he tries to comfort her. "You heard Parker. They're going to make everybody better."

He falls into line behind the other reds. Parker is standing at the bottom of the steps, checking stamps. The driver shouts out, "Hey!" and Sammy turns, just as Megan hits the bottom step. She slams into Parker's chest and screams when he grabs her flailing arms.

"Let me go!"

The driver pulls her from Parker's grip and drags her back up the steps, an arm locked around her waist.

"Sammy!" Megan screams. "Sammy, don't leave me! Don't let them—"

The doors slam closed, cutting off her cries. Sammy glances up at Parker, who gives him a reassuring pat on the shoulder.

"She's going to be fine, Sam," the medic says quietly. "Come on."

As he walks to the hangar, he can hear her screaming behind

the yellow metal skin of the bus, over the throaty growl of its engine, the hiss of its brakes letting go. Screaming as if she's dying, as if they're torturing her. And then he steps through a side door into the hangar and he can't hear her anymore.

A soldier is standing just inside the door. He hands Sammy a card with the number forty-nine printed on it.

"Go to the closest red circle," the soldier tells him. "Sit down. Wait for your number to be called."

"I gotta get over to the hospital now," Parker says. "Stay frosty, champ, and remember it's all cool now. There's nothing that can hurt you here." He tousles Sammy's hair, promises he'll see him again soon, and gives him a fist bump before leaving.

There are no planes in the huge hangar, much to Sammy's disappointment. He'd never seen a fighter jet up close, though he has piloted one a thousand times since the Arrival. While his mother lay dying down the hall, he was in the cockpit of a Fighting Falcon, soaring at the edge of the atmosphere at three times the speed of sound, heading straight toward the alien mothership. Sure, its gray hull bristled with gun turrets and ray cannons and its force field glowed a fiendish, sickly green, but there was a weakness in the field, a hole only two inches wider than his fighter, that if he hit just right . . . And he'd have to hit it just right, because the whole squadron had been wiped out, he was down to his last missile, and there was no one left to defend the Earth from the alien horde but him, Sammy "the Viper" Sullivan.

Three large red circles have been painted on the floor. Sam joins the other children in the one closest to the door and sits down. He can't get Megan's terrified screams out of his head. Her huge eyes and the way her skin shimmered with sweat and the sick-smell of her breath. Cassie told him the Pesky Ants was over, that it had killed all the people it was going to kill because some people couldn't catch it, like Cassie and Daddy and him and everyone else at Camp Ashpit. They were immune, Cassie said.

But what if Cassie's wrong? Maybe the disease took longer to kill some people. Maybe it's killing Megan right now.

Or maybe, he thinks, the Others have unleashed a second plague, one even worse than the Pesky Ants, one that will kill everyone who survived the first one.

He pushes the thought away. Since the death of his mother, he's become good at pushing bad thoughts away.

There are over a hundred kids gathered into the three circles, but the hangar is very quiet. The boy sitting next to Sammy is so exhausted, he lies down on his side on the cold concrete, curls into a ball, and falls asleep. The boy is older than Sammy, maybe ten or eleven, and he sleeps with his thumb tucked firmly between his lips.

A bell rings, and then a lady's voice blares over a loudspeaker. First in English, then in Spanish.

"WELCOME, CHILDREN, TO CAMP HAVEN! WE ARE SO HAPPY TO SEE ALL OF YOU! WE KNOW YOU'RE TIRED AND HUNGRY AND SOME OF YOU AREN'T FEELING VERY WELL, BUT EVERYTHING WILL BE FINE NOW. STAY IN YOUR CIRCLE AND LISTEN CAREFULLY FOR YOUR NUMBER TO BE CALLED. DON'T LEAVE YOUR CIRCLE FOR ANY REASON. WE DON'T WANT TO LOSE ANY OF YOU! STAY QUIET AND CALM AND REMEMBER THAT WE'RE HERE TO TAKE CARE OF YOU! YOU'RE PERFECTLY SAFE."

A moment later, the first number is called out. The child rises from his red circle and is escorted by a soldier to a door painted the same color at the far end of the hangar. The soldier takes the card from him and opens the door. The child goes in alone. The soldier closes the door and returns to his station beside a red circle. Each circle has two soldiers, both heavily armed, but they smile. All the soldiers smile. They never stop smiling.

One by one the children's numbers are called. They leave their circle, cross the hangar floor, and disappear behind the red door. They don't come back.

It takes almost an hour for the lady to call Sammy's number. Morning comes, and sunlight breaks through the high windows, filling the hangar with golden light. He's very tired, ravenously hungry, and a little stiff from sitting so long, but he leaps up when he hears it—"FORTY-NINE! PROCEED TO THE RED DOOR, PLEASE! NUMBER FORTY-NINE!"—and in his hurry nearly trips over the sleeping boy beside him.

A nurse is waiting for him on the other side of the door. He knows she's a nurse because she's wearing green scrubs and soft-soled sneakers like Nurse Rachel from his doctor's office. Her smile is warm like Nurse Rachel's, too, and she takes his hand and leads him into a small room. There's a hamper overflowing with dirty clothing and paper robes hanging from hooks next to a white curtain.

"Okay, champ," the nurse says. "How long has it been since you've had a bath?"

She laughs at his startled expression. Then the nurse whips back the white curtain to reveal a shower stall.

"Everything comes off and into the hamper. Yes, even the underwear. We love children here, but not lice or ticks or anything with more than two legs!"

Though he protests, the nurse insists on doing the chore herself. He stands with his arms folded in front of him while she squirts a stream of foul-smelling shampoo into his hair and sudses his entire body, from his head to his toes. "Keep your eyes closed tight or it'll burn," the nurse gently instructs him.

She lets him dry himself off, and then tells him to put on one of the paper robes.

"Go through that door over there." She points at the door at the other end of the room.

The robe is much too big for him. The bottom of it trails the floor as he goes to the next room. Another nurse is waiting there for him. She's heavier than the first one, older, and not quite so friendly. She has Sammy step onto the scale, writes down his weight on a clipboard beside his number, and then has him hop onto the examination table. She places a metal disk—the same kind Parker used on the bus—against his forehead.

"I'm taking your temperature," she explains.

He nods. "I know. Parker told me. Red means normal."

"You're red, all right," the nurse says. Her cold fingers press on his wrist, taking his pulse.

Sammy shivers. He's goose-bumpy cold in the flimsy robe and a little scared. He never liked going to the doctor, and he's worried they might give him a shot. The nurse sits down in front of him and says she needs to ask some questions. He's supposed to listen carefully and answer as honestly as he can. If he doesn't know the answer, that's okay. Does he understand?

What's his full name? How old is he? What town is he from? Did he have any brothers or sisters? Are they alive?

"Cassie," Sammy says. "Cassie's alive."

The nurse writes down Cassie's name. "How old is Cassie?"

"Cassie is sixteen. They're going back to get her," Sammy tells the nurse.

"Who is?"

"The soldiers. The soldiers said there wasn't room for her, but they were going back to get her and Daddy."

"Daddy? So your father is alive, too? What about your mother?"

Sammy shakes his head. Bites his lower lip. He shudders violently. So cold. He remembers two empty seats on the bus, the one Parker sat next to him in and the one he sat in next to Megan. He blurts out, "They said there was no room on the bus, but there *was* room. Daddy and Cassie could have come, too. Why didn't the soldiers let them come?"

The nurse answers, "Because you're the first priority, Samuel."

"But they're going to bring them, too, right?"

"Eventually, yes."

More questions. How did his mother die? What happened after that?

The nurse's pen flies over the page. She gets up and pats his bare knee. "Don't be scared," she tells him before she leaves. "You're perfectly safe here." Her voice sounds flat to Sammy, like she's repeating something she's said a thousand times. "Sit tight. The doctor will be here in a minute."

It feels much longer than a minute to Sammy. He wraps his thin arms around his chest, trying to hold in his body heat. His eyes restlessly roam the little room. A sink and cabinet. The chair the nurse sat in. A rolling stool in one corner and, mounted from the ceiling directly above the stool, a camera, its gleaming black eye aimed directly at the examination table.

The nurse comes back in, followed by the doctor. Dr. Pam is as tall and thin as the nurse is short and round. Immediately, Sammy feels calmer. There is something about the tall doctor lady that reminds him of his mother. Maybe it's the way she talks to him, looking directly into his eyes, her voice warm and gentle. Her hands are warm, too. She doesn't wear gloves to touch him like the nurse did.

She does what he expects, the doctor stuff he's used to. Shines a light in his eyes, in his ears, down his throat. Listens to him breathe through the stethoscope. Rubs just beneath his jaw, but not too hard, all the while humming softly under her breath.

"Lie all the way back, Sam."

Firm fingers pressing on his belly.

"Any pain when I do this?"

She has him stand up, bend over, reach for his toes, while she runs her hands up and down along his spine.

"Okay, sport, hop back on the table."

He jumps back quickly onto the crinkly paper, sensing the visit is almost over. There won't be a shot. Maybe they'll prick his finger, and that's no fun, but at least there won't be a shot.

"Hold out your hand for me."

Dr. Pam places a tiny gray tube no larger than a grain of rice into his palm.

"Know what this is? It's called a microchip. Did you ever have a pet, a dog or a cat, Sammy?"

No. His father is allergic. He always wanted a dog, though.

"Well, some owners put a device very much like this one into their pets in case they run away or get lost. This one's a little different, though. It puts out a signal that we can track."

It goes just underneath the skin, the doctor explains, and no matter where Sammy is, they'll be able to find him. Just in case something happens. It's very safe here at Camp Haven, but just a few months ago everyone thought the world was safe from an alien attack, so now we have to be careful, we have to take every precaution . . .

He stops listening after the words *underneath the skin*. They're going to inject that gray tube into him? Fear begins to gnaw anew around the edges of his heart.

"It won't hurt," the doctor says, sensing the nibbling fear. "We give you a little shot to numb you first, and then you'll have just a small sore spot for a day or two."

The doctor is very kind. He can see that she understands how much he hates shots and she really doesn't want to do it. She has to do it. She shows him the needle used for the shot to numb him. It's very tiny, hardly wider than a human hair. Like a mosquito bite, the doctor says. That isn't so bad. He's been bitten by mosquitoes lots of times. And Dr. Pam promises he won't feel the gray tube go in. He won't feel anything at all after the numbing shot.

He lies on his tummy, tucking his face into the crook of his elbow. The room is cold, and the swipe of the alcohol at the base of his neck makes him shudder violently. The nurse tells him to relax. "The more you tense up, the sorer you'll be," she tells him. He tries to think of something nice, something that will take his mind off what's about to happen. He sees Cassie's face in his mind's eye, and he's surprised. He expected to see his mother's face.

Cassie is smiling. He smiles back at her, into the crook of his arm. A mosquito that must be the size of a bird bites down hard on the back of his neck. He doesn't move, but whimpers softly against his skin. In less than a minute, it's over.

Number forty-nine has been tagged.

40

AFTER THE DOCTOR bandages the insertion point, she makes a note in his chart, hands the chart to the nurse, and tells Sammy there's just one more test.

He follows the doctor into the next room. It's much smaller than the examination room, hardly larger than a closet. In the middle of the room is a chair that reminds Sammy of the one at his dentist's, narrow and high-backed, thin armrests on either side.

The doctor tells him to have a seat. "Lean all the way back, head back, too, that's right. Stay relaxed."

Whirrr. The back of the chair lowers, the front rises, bringing up his legs until he is almost fully reclined. The doctor's face comes into view. Smiling.

"Okay, Sam, you've been very patient with us, and this is the last test, I promise. It doesn't last long and it doesn't hurt, but sometimes it can be a little, well, intense. It's a test of the implant we just put in. To make sure it's working okay. It takes a few minutes to run, and you have to keep very, very still. That can be hard to do, can't it? You can't wiggle or squirm or even scratch your nose, or it will ruin the test. Think you can do that?"

Sammy nods. He is returning the doctor's warm smile. "I've played freeze tag before," he assures her. "I'm really good at it."

"Good! But just in case, I'm going to put these straps around your wrists and ankles, not very tight, but just in case your nose does start to itch. The straps will remind you to keep still. Would that be okay?"

Sammy nods. When he's strapped in, she says, "Okay, I'm going to step over to the computer now. The computer is going to send a signal to calibrate the transponder, and the transponder is going to send a signal back. It doesn't take more than a few seconds, but it may feel longer—maybe a lot longer. Different people react in different ways. Ready to give it a try?"

"Okay."

"Good! Close your eyes. Keep them closed until I say you can open them. Take big, deep breaths. Here we go. Keep those eyes closed now. Counting down from three . . . two . . . one . . ."

A blinding white fireball explodes inside Sammy Sullivan's head. His body stiffens; his legs strain against the restraints; his tiny fingers lock on to the chair arms. He hears the doctor's soothing voice on the other side of the blinding light, saying, "It's all right, Sammy. Don't be afraid. Just a few more seconds, I promise . . ."

He sees his crib. And there's Bear lying next to him in the crib, and then there's the mobile of stars and planets spinning lazily over his bed. He sees his mother, leaning over him, holding a spoonful of medicine and telling him he has to take it. There's Cassie in the backyard, and it's summer and he's toddling around in a pair of Pull-Ups, and Cassie is spraying water from the hose high into the air so a rainbow springs up out of nothing. She whips the hose back and forth, laughing as he chases it, the fleeting, uncatchable colors, shimmering splinters of the golden light. "Catch the rainbow, Sammy! Catch the rainbow!"

The images and memories pour out of him, like water rushing down a drain. In no more than ninety seconds, the entirety of Sammy's life roars out of him and into the mainframe, an avalanche of touch and smell and taste and sound, before fading into the white nothingness. His mind is laid bare in the blinding white, all that he has experienced, all that he remembers, and even those

205

things that he can't remember; everything that makes up the personality of Sammy Sullivan is pulled and sorted and transmitted by the device at the base of his neck into Dr. Pam's computer.

Number forty-nine has been mapped.

41

DR. PAM UNDOES the straps and helps him out of the chair. Sammy's knees give out. She holds on to his arms to keep him from falling. His stomach heaves, and he vomits on the white floor. Everywhere he looks, black blobs jiggle and bounce. The big, unsmiling nurse takes him back to the examination room, puts him on the table, tells him everything is fine, asks if she can bring him anything.

"I want my bear!" he screams. "I want my daddy and my Cassie and I want to go home!"

Dr. Pam appears beside him. Her kind eyes glow with understanding. She knows what he's feeling. She tells him how brave he is, how brave and lucky and smart to have come this far. He passed the final test with flying colors. He's perfectly healthy and perfectly safe. The worst is over.

"That's what my daddy said every time something bad happened, and every time it just got worse," Sammy says, choking back tears.

They bring him a white jumpsuit to put on. It reminds him of a fighter pilot's outfit, zippered in the front, the material slick to the touch. The suit is too big for him. The sleeves keep falling over his hands.

"Do you know why you're so important to us, Sammy?" Dr. Pam asks. "Because you're the future. Without you and all those other children, we won't stand a chance against them. That's why we searched for you and brought you here and why we're doing all this. You know some of the things they've done to us, and they're terrible. Terrible, awful things, but that isn't the worst part, that isn't everything they've done."

"What else have they done?" Sammy whispers.

"Do you really want to know? I can show you, but only if you want to know."

In the white room, he had just relived his mother's death, smelled her coppery blood, watched his father wash it from his hands. But those weren't the worst things the Others had done, the doctor said. Did he really want to know?

"I want to know," he says.

The doctor holds up the small silver disk the nurse had used to take his temperature, the same device Parker had pressed against his and Megan's foreheads on the bus.

"This isn't a thermometer, Sammy," Dr. Pam says. "It does detect something, but it isn't your temperature. It tells us who you are. Or maybe I should say *what* you are. Tell me something, Sam. Have you seen one of them yet? Have you seen an alien?"

He shakes his head no. Shivering inside the white suit. Curled up on the little examination table. Sick to his stomach, head pounding, weak from hunger and exhaustion. Something in him wants her to stop. He nearly shouts out, *Stop! I don't want to know!* But he bites his lip. He doesn't want to know; he *has* to know.

207

"I'm very sorry to say you have seen one," Dr. Pam says in a soft, sad voice. "We all have. We've been waiting for them to come since the Arrival, but the truth is they've been here, right under our noses, for a very long time."

He is shaking his head over and over. Dr. Pam is wrong. He's never seen one. For hours he listened to Daddy speculating about what they might look like. Heard his father say they might never know what they look like. There had been no messages from them, no landers, no signs of their existence except the grayish-green mothership in high orbit and the unmanned drones. How could Dr. Pam be saying he had seen one?

She holds out her hand. "If you want to see, I can show you."

VI

THE HUMAN CLAY

42

BEN PARISH IS DEAD.

I don't miss him. Ben was a wuss, a crybaby, a thumb-sucker. Not Zombie.

Zombie is everything Ben wasn't. Zombie is hardcore. Zombie is badass. Zombie is stone-cold.

Zombie was born on the morning I left the convalescent ward. Traded in my flimsy gown for a blue jumpsuit. Assigned a bunk in Barracks 10. Whipped back into shape by three squares a day and brutal physical training, but most of all by Reznik, the regiment's senior drill instructor, the man who smashed Ben Parish into a million pieces, then reconstructed him into the merciless zombie killing machine that he is today.

Don't get me wrong: Reznik is a cruel, unfeeling, sadistic bastard, and I fall asleep every night fantasizing about ways to kill him. From day one he's made it his mission to make my life as miserable as possible, and he's pretty much succeeded. I've been slapped, punched, pushed, kicked, and spat on. I've been ridiculed, mocked, and screamed at until my ears rang. Forced to stand for hours in the freezing rain, scrub the entire barracks floor with a toothbrush, disassemble and reassemble my rifle until my fingers bled, run until my legs turned to jelly . . . you get the idea.

I didn't get it, though. Not at first. Was he training me to be a soldier or trying to kill me? I was pretty sure it was the latter. Then I realized it was both: He really was training me to be a soldier— by trying to kill me.

I'll give you just one example. One's enough.

Morning calisthenics in the yard, every squad in the regiment, over three hundred troops, and Reznik picks this time to publicly humiliate me. Looming over me, his legs spread wide, hands on knees, his fleshy, pockmarked face close to mine as I dipped into push-up number seventy-nine.

"Private Zombie, did your mother have any children that lived?"

"Sir! Yes, sir!"

"I bet when you were born she took one look at you and tried to shove you back in!"

Jamming the heel of his black boot into my ass to force me down. My squad is doing knuckle push-ups on the asphalt trail that rings the yard, because the ground is frozen solid and asphalt absorbs blood; you don't slip around as much. He wants to make me fail before I reach one hundred. I push against his heel: No way I'm starting over. Not in front of the entire regiment. I can feel my fellow recruits watching me. Waiting for my inevitable collapse. Waiting for Reznik to win. Reznik always wins.

"Private Zombie, do you think I'm mean?"

"Sir! No, sir!"

My muscles burn. My knuckles are scraped raw. I've gained back some of the weight, but have I gotten back the heart?

Eighty-eight. Eighty-nine. Almost there.

"Do you hate my guts?"

"Sir! No, sir!"

Ninety-three. Ninety-four. Someone from another squad whispers,

"Who is that guy?" And someone else, a girl's voice, says, "His name is Zombie."

"Are you a killer, Private Zombie?"

"Sir! Yes, sir!"

"Do you eat alien brains for breakfast?"

"Sir! Yes, sir!"

Ninety-five. Ninety-six. The yard is funeral-quiet. I'm not the only recruit who loathes Reznik. One of these days, somebody's going to beat him at his own game, that's the prayer, that's what's on my shoulders as I fight to one hundred.

"Bullshit! I hear you're a coward. I hear you run from a fight."

"Sir! No, sir!"

Ninety-seven. Ninety-eight. Two more and I've won. I hear the same girl—she must be standing close by—whisper, "Come on."

On the ninety-ninth push-up, Reznik shoves me down with his heel. I fall hard on my chest, roll my cheek against the asphalt, and there's his puffy face and tiny pale eyes an inch from mine.

Ninety-nine; one short. The bastard.

"Private Zombie, you are a disgrace to the species. I've hacked up lugies tougher than you. You make me think the enemy was right about the human race. You should be ground up for slop and passed out a hog's shithole! Well, what are you waiting for, you stinking bag of regurgitated puke, an effing invitation?"

My head rolls to one side. *An invitation would be nice, thank you, sir.* I see a girl around my age standing with her squad, her arms folded across her chest, shaking her head at me. *Poor Zombie.* She isn't smiling. Dark eyes, dark hair, skin so fair it seems to be glowing in the early-morning light. I have the feeling I know her from somewhere, though this is the first time I remember seeing her. There are hundreds of kids being trained for war and hundreds more arriving every day, handed blue jumpsuits, assigned to squads, packed into the barracks ringing the yard. But she has the kind of face you remember.

"Get up, you maggot! Get up and give me a hundred more. One hundred more, or by God I will rip out your eyeballs and hang them from my rearview like a pair of fuzzy dice!"

I'm totally spent. I don't think I've got enough left for even one more.

Reznik doesn't give a crap about what I think. That's the other thing it took me a while to understand: They not only don't care what I think—they don't *want* me to think.

His face is so close to mine, I can smell his breath. It smells like spearmint.

"What is it, sweetheart? Are you tired? Do you want nappy-time?"

Do I have at least one push-up left in me? If I can do just one more, I won't be a total loser. I press my forehead against the asphalt and close my eyes. There is a place I go, a space I found inside me after Commander Vosch showed me the final battle-field, a center of complete stillness that isn't touched by fatigue or hopelessness or anger or anything brought on by the coming of the Big Green Eye in the Sky. In that place, I have no name. I'm not Ben or Zombie—I just am. Whole, untouchable, unbroken. The last living person in the universe who contains all human potential—including the potential to give the biggest asshole on Earth just one more.

And I do.

43

NOT THAT THERE'S ANYTHING special about me.

Reznik is an equal-opportunity sadist. He treats the six other recruits of Squad 53 with the same savage indecency. Flintstone, who's my age, with his big head and bushy unibrow; Tank, the skinny, quick-tempered farm boy; Dumbo, the twelve-year-old with the big ears and quick smile that disappeared quickly during the first week of basic; Poundcake, the eight-year-old who never talks, but who's our best shot by far; Oompa, the chubby kid with the crooked teeth who's last in every drill but first in chow line; and finally the youngest, Teacup, the meanest seven-year-old you'll ever meet, the most gung ho of all of us, who worships the ground Reznik walks on, no matter how much she's screamed at or kicked around.

I don't know their real names. We don't talk about who we were before or how we came to the camp or what happened to our families. None of that matters. Like Ben Parish, those guys—the pre-Flintstone, pre-Tank, pre-Dumbo, etc.—they're dead. Tagged, bagged, and told we are the last, best hope for humanity, we are the new wine poured into old skins. We bonded through hatred— hatred of the infesteds and their alien masters, sure, but also our fierce, uncompromising, unadulterated hatred of Sergeant Reznik, our rage made all the more intense by the fact that we could never express it.

Then the kid named Nugget was assigned to Barracks 10, and one of us, like an idiot, couldn't hold it inside any longer, and all the bottled-up fury exploded free.

217

I'll give you one guess who that idiot was.

I couldn't believe it when that kid showed up at roll call. Five years old tops, lost in his white jumpsuit, shivering in the cold morning air of the yard, looking like he was going to be sick, obviously scared out of his mind. And here comes Reznik with his hat pulled low over his beady eyes and his boots shined to a mirror finish and his voice perpetually hoarse from screaming, shoving his pasty, pockmarked grill down into the poor kid's face. I don't know how the little squirt kept from soiling himself.

Reznik always starts out slow and soft and builds to a big finish, the better to lull you into thinking he might be an actual human being.

"Well, what do we have here? What have they sent us from central casting—is this a hobbit? Are you a magical creature from a storybook realm come to enchant me with your dark magic?"

Reznik was just getting warmed up, and already the kid was fighting back tears. Fresh off the bus after going through God-knows-what on the outside, and here's this crazy middle-aged man pouncing on him. I wondered how he was processing Reznik—or any of this craziness they call Camp Haven. I'm still trying to deal, and I'm a lot older than five.

"Oh, this is cute. This is so precious, I think I might cry! Dear God, I've dunked chicken nuggets bigger than you in my little plastic cup of spicy barbecue sauce!"

Ratcheting up the volume as he brought his face closer to the kid's. And the kid holding up surprisingly well, flinching, eyes darting back and forth, but not moving an inch when I knew he must be thinking about taking off across the yard, just running until he couldn't run anymore.

"What's your story, Private Nugget? Have you lost your

mommy? Do you want to go home? *I know!* Let's close our eyes and make a wish and maybe Mommy will come and take us all home! Wouldn't that be nice, Private Nugget?"

And the kid nodded eagerly, like Reznik had asked the question he'd been waiting to hear. Finally, somebody got to the point! Lifting up his big teddy-bear eyes into the drill sergeant's beady ones . . . it was enough to break your heart. It was enough to make you scream.

But you don't scream. You stand perfectly still, eyes forward, hands at your sides, chest out, heart breaking, watching it out of the corner of your eye while something comes loose inside you, uncoiling like a rattlesnake striking. Something you've been holding in for a long time as the pressure built. You don't know when it's going to blow, you can't predict it, and when it happens there's nothing you can do to stop it.

"Leave him alone."

Reznik whipped around. No one made a sound, but you could hear the inward gasp. On the other side of the line, Flintstone's eyes were wide; he couldn't believe what I just did. I couldn't, either.

"Who said that? Which one of you scum-sucking maggots just signed his own death warrant?"

Striding down the line, face red with fury, hands clinched into fists, knuckles bone white.

"Nobody, huh? Well, I'm going to fall on my knees and cover my head, because the Lord God his holy self has spoken to me from on high!"

He stopped in front of Tank, who was sweating through his jumpsuit though it was about forty degrees outside. "Was it you, puckerhole? I will tear your arms off!" He brought his fist back to punch Tank in the groin.

Cue the idiot.

"Sir, I said it, sir!" I shouted.

Reznik's about-face was slow this time. His journey over to me took a thousand years. In the distance, a crow's harsh call, but that was the only sound I heard.

He stopped just inside my range of vision, not directly in front of me, and that wasn't good. I couldn't turn toward him. I had to keep my eyes forward. Worst of all, I couldn't see his hands; I wouldn't know when—or where—the blow would land, which meant I wouldn't know when to brace for it.

"So Private Zombie is giving the orders now," Reznik said, so softly I could barely hear him. "Private Zombie is Squad Fifty-three's very own catcher in the fucking rye. Private Zombie, I think I have a crush on you. You make me weak in the knees. You make me hate my own mother for giving birth to a male child, so now it's impossible for me to have your babies."

Where was it going to land? My knees? My crotch? Probably the stomach; Reznik has a soft spot for stomachs.

Nope. It was a chop to my Adam's apple with the side of his hand. I staggered backward, fighting to stay upright, fighting to keep my hands at my sides, not going to give him the satisfaction, not going to give him an excuse to hit me again. The yard and the barracks were ringing, then jiggled and melted a little as my eyes filled with tears—of pain, sure, but of something else, too.

"Sir, he's just a little kid, sir," I choked out.

"Private Zombie, you have two seconds, exactly two seconds, to seal that sewer pipe posing as a mouth, or I will incinerate your ass with the rest of the infested alien sons of bitches!"

He took a deep breath, revving up for the next verbal barrage.

Having completely lost my mind, I opened my mouth and let the words come out. I'll be honest: Part of me was filled with relief and something that felt a hell of a lot like joy. I had kept the hate inside for too long.

"Then the senior drill instructor should do it, sir! The private really doesn't care, sir! Just—just leave the kid alone."

Total silence. Even the crow stopped fussing. The rest of the squad had stopped breathing. I knew what they were thinking. We'd all heard the story about the lippy recruit and the "accident" on the obstacle course that put him in the hospital for three weeks. And the other story about the quiet ten-year-old who they found in the showers strung up with an extension cord. Suicide, the doctor said. A lot of people weren't so sure.

Reznik didn't move. "Private Zombie, who is your squad leader?"

"Sir, the private's squad leader is Private Flintstone, sir!"

"Private Flintstone, front and center!" Reznik barked. Flint took one step forward and snapped off a salute. His unibrow jiggled with tension. "Private Flintstone, you're fired. Private Zombie is now squad leader. Private Zombie is ignorant and ugly, but he is not soft." I could feel Reznik's eyes boring into my face. "Private Zombie, what happened to your baby sister?"

I blinked. Twice. Trying not to show anything. My voice cracked a little when I answered, though. "Sir, the private's sister is dead, sir!"

"Because you ran like a chickenshit!"

"Sir, the private ran like a chickenshit, sir!"

"But you're not running now, are you, Private Zombie? Are you?"

"Sir, no, sir!"

He stepped back. Something flashed across his face. An expression I'd never seen before. It couldn't be, of course, but it looked a lot like respect.

"Private Nugget, front and center!"

The newbie didn't move until Poundcake gave him a poke in the back. He was crying. He didn't want to, he was trying to choke it back, but dear Jesus, what little kid wouldn't be crying by that point? Your old life barfs you out and this is where you land?

"Private Nugget, Private Zombie is your squad leader, and you will bunk with him. You will learn from him. He will teach you how to walk. He will teach you how to talk. He will teach you how to think. He will be the big brother you never had. Do you read me, Private Nugget?"

"Sir, yes, sir!" The tiny voice shrill and squeaky, but he got the rules down, and quickly.

And that's how it began.

44

HERE'S A TYPICAL day in the atypical new reality of Camp Haven.

5:00 A.M.: Reveille and wash up. Dress and prep bunks for inspection.

5:10 A.M.: Fall in. Reznik inspects our billets. Finds a wrinkle in someone's sheet. Screams for twenty minutes. Then picks another recruit at random and screams for another twenty for no real reason. Then three laps around the yard freezing our asses off, me urging Oompa and Nugget to keep up or I get to run another lap as the last man to finish. The frozen ground beneath our boots. Our breaths frosting in the air. The twin columns of black smoke from the power plant rising beyond the airfield and the rumble of buses pulling out of the main gate.

6:30 A.M.: Chow in the crowded mess hall that smells faintly like soured milk, reminding me of the plague and the fact that once upon a time I thought about just three things—cars, football, and girls, in that order. I help Nugget with his tray, urging him to eat because, if he doesn't eat, boot camp will kill him. Those are my exact words: *Boot camp will kill you.* Tank and Flintstone laugh at me mothering Nugget. Already calling me Nugget's Nanna. Screw them. After chow we check out the leaderboard. Every morning the scores from the previous day are posted on a big board outside the mess hall. Points for marksmanship. Points for best times on the obstacle course, the air raid drills, the two-mile runs. The top four squads will graduate at the end of November, and the competition is fierce. Our squad's been stuck in tenth place for weeks. Tenth isn't bad, but it's not good enough.

7:30 A.M.: Training. Weapons. Hand-to-hand. Basic wilderness survival. Basic urban survival. Recon. Communications. My favorite is survival training. That memorable session where we had to drink our own urine.

12:00 P.M.: Noon chow. Some mystery meat between hard crusts of bread. Dumbo, whose jokes are as tasteless as his ears are big, cracks that we're not incinerating the infested bodies but grinding them up to feed the troops. I have to pull Teacup off him before she smacks his head with a tray. Nugget stares at his burger like it might jump off his plate and bite his face. Thanks, Dumbo. The kid's skinny enough as it is.

1:00 P.M.: More training. Mostly on the firing range. Nugget is issued a stick for a rifle and fires pretend rounds while we fire real ones into life-size plywood cutouts. The crack of the M16s. The screech of plywood being shredded. Poundcake earns a perfect score; I'm the worst shot in the squad. I pretend the cutout is Reznik, hoping that will improve my aim. It doesn't.

5:00 P.M.: Evening chow. Canned meat, canned peas, canned fruit. Nugget pushes his food around and then bursts into tears. The squad glares at me. Nugget is my responsibility. If Reznik comes down on us for conduct unbefitting, there's hell to pay, and I'm picking up the tab. Extra push-ups, reduced rations—he could even deduct some points. Nothing matters but getting through basic with enough points to graduate, get out into the field, rid ourselves of Reznik. Across the table, Flintstone is glowering at me from beneath the unibrow. He's pissed at Nugget, but more pissed at me for taking his job. Not that I asked for squad leader. He came at me after that day and growled, "I don't care what you are now, I'm gonna make sergeant when we graduate." And I'm like, "More power to you, Flint." The idea of my leading a unit into combat is ludicrous. Meanwhile, nothing I say calms Nugget down. He keeps going on about his sister. About how she promised to come for him. I wonder why the commander would stick a little kid who can't even lift a rifle into our squad. If Wonderland winnowed out the best fighters, what sort of profile did this little guy produce?

6:00 P.M.: Drill instructor Q&A in the barracks, my favorite part of the day, where I get to spend some quality time with my

224

favorite person in the whole wide world. After informing us what worthless piles of desiccated rat feces we are, Reznik opens the floor for questions and concerns.

Most of our questions have to do with the competition. Rules, procedures in case of a tie, rumors about this or that squad cheating. Making the grade is all we can think about. Graduation means active duty, real fighting—a chance to show the ones who died that we had not survived in vain.

Other topics: the status of the rescue and winnowing operation (code name Li'l Bo Peep; I'm not kidding). What news from the outside? When will we hunker full-time in the underground bunker, because obviously the enemy can see what we're doing down here and it's only a matter of time before they vaporize us. For that we get the standard-issue reply: Commander Vosch knows what he's doing. Our job isn't to worry about strategy and logistics. Our job is to kill the enemy.

8:30 P.M.: Personal time. Free of Reznik at last. We wash our jumpsuits, shine our boots, scrub the barracks floor and the latrine, clean our rifles, pass around dirty magazines, and swap other contraband like candy and chewing gum. We play cards and bust each other's nuts and complain about Reznik. We share the day's rumors and tell bad jokes and push back against the silence inside our own heads, the place where the never-ending voiceless scream rises like the superheated air above a lava flow. Inevitably an argument erupts and stops just short of a fistfight. It's tearing away at us. We know too much. We don't know enough. Why is our regiment composed entirely of kids like us, no one over the age of eighteen? What happened to all the adults? Are they being taken somewhere else and, if they are, where and why? Are the Teds the final wave, or is there another one coming, a fifth wave that will make the first four pale in comparison? Thinking about a fifth wave shuts down the conversation.

9:30 P.M.: Lights-out. Time to lie awake and think of a wholly new and creative way to waste Sergeant Reznik. After a while I get tired of that and think about the girls I've dated, shuffling them around in various orders. Hottest. Smartest. Funniest. Blondes. Brunettes. Which base I got to. They start to blend together into one girl, the Girl Who Is No More, and in her eyes Ben Parish, high school hallway god, lives again. From its hiding place under my bunk, I pull out Sissy's locket and press it against my heart. No more guilt. No more grief. I will trade my self-pity for hate. My guilt for cunning. My grief for the spirit of vengeance.

"Zombie?" It's Nugget in the bunk next to me.

"No talking after lights-out," I whisper back.

"I can't sleep."

"Close your eyes and think of something nice."

"Can we pray? Is that against the rules?"

"Sure you can pray. Just not out loud."

I can hear him breathing, the creak of the metal frame as he flips and flops around on the bunk.

"Cassie always said my prayer with me," he confesses.

"Who's Cassie?"

"I told you."

"I forgot."

"Cassie's my sister. She's coming for me."

"Oh, sure." I don't tell him that if she hasn't shown up by now, she's probably dead. It isn't up to me to break his heart; that's time's job.

"She's promised. Promised."

226

A tiny hiccup of a sob. Great. Nobody knows for sure, but we accept it as fact that the barracks are bugged, that every second Reznik is spying on us, waiting for us to break one of the rules so he can bring the hammer down. Violating the no-talking rule at lights-out will earn all of us a week of kitchen patrol.

"Hey, it's all right, Nugget . . ."

Reaching my hand out to comfort him, finding the top of his freshly shaved head, running my fingertips over his scalp. Sissy liked for me to rub her head when she felt bad—maybe Nugget likes it, too.

"Hey, stow that over there!" Flintstone calls out softly.

"Yeah," Tank says. "You wanna get us busted, Zombie?"

"Come here," I whisper to Nugget, scooting over and patting the mattress. "I'll say your prayer with you, and then you can go to sleep, okay?"

The mattress gives with his added weight. Oh God, what am I doing? If Reznik pops in for a surprise inspection, I'll be peeling potatoes for a month. Nugget lies on his side facing me, and his fists rub against my arm as he brings them up to his chin.

"What prayer does she say with you?" I ask.

"'Now I lay me,'" he whispers.

"Somebody put a pillow over that nugget's face," Dumbo says from his bunk.

I can see the ambient light shining in his big brown eyes. Sissy's locket pressed against my chest and Nugget's eyes, glittering like twin beacons in the dark. Prayers and promises. The one his sister made to him. The unspoken one I made to my sister. Prayers are promises, too, and these are the days of broken promises. All of a sudden I want to put my fist through the wall.

"'Now I lay me down to sleep, I pray the Lord my soul to keep.'"

He joins in on the next line.

"'When in the morning light I wake, teach me the path of love to take.'"

The hisses and shushes pick up on the next stanza. Somebody hurls a pillow at us, but we keep praying.

"'Now I lay me down to sleep, I pray the Lord my soul to keep. Your angels watch me through the night, and keep me safe till morning's light.'"

On *angels watch me*, the hissing and shushing stops. A profound stillness settles over the barracks.

Our voices slow on the last stanza. Like we're reluctant to finish because on the other side of a prayer is the nothingness of another exhausted sleep and then another day waiting for the last day, the day we will die. Even Teacup knows she probably won't live to see her eighth birthday. But we'll get up and put ourselves through seventeen hours of hell anyway. Because we will die, but at least we will die unbroken.

"'And if I should die before I wake, I pray the Lord my soul to take.'"

45

THE NEXT MORNING I'm in Reznik's office with a special request. I know what his answer's going to be, but I'm asking anyway.

"Sir, the squad leader requests that the senior drill instructor grant Private Nugget a special exemption from this morning's detail."

"Private Nugget is a member of this squad," Reznik reminds me. "And as a member of this squad, he is expected to perform all duties assigned by Central Command. All duties, Private."

"Sir, the squad leader requests that the senior drill instructor reconsider his decision based on Private Nugget's age and—"

Reznik dismisses the point with a wave of his hand. "The boy didn't drop out of the damned sky, Private. If he didn't pass his prelims, he wouldn't have been assigned to your squad. But the fact of the matter is he *did* pass his prelims, he *was* assigned to your squad, and he *will* perform all duties of your squad as assigned by Central Command, including P and D. Are we clear, Private?"

Well, Nugget, I tried.

"What's P and D?" he asks at morning chow.

"Processing and disposal," I answer, cutting my eyes away from him.

Across from us, Dumbo groans and pushes his tray away. "Great. The only way I can get through breakfast is by not thinking about it!"

"Churn and burn, baby," Tank says, glancing at Flintstone for approval. Those two are tight. On the day Reznik gave me the job, Tank told me he didn't care who was squad leader, he'd only listen to Flint. I shrugged. Whatever. Once we graduated—if we ever graduated—one of us would be promoted to sergeant, and I knew that someone would not be me.

"Dr. Pam showed you a Ted," I say to Nugget. He nods. From his expression, I can tell it isn't a pleasant memory. "You hit the button." Another nod. Slower than the first one. "What do you think happens to the person on the other side of the glass after you hit the button?"

Nugget whispers, "They die."

"And the sick people they bring in from the outside, ones that don't make it once they get here—what do you think happens to them?"

"Oh, come on, Zombie, just tell him!" Oompa says. He's pushed away his food, too. A first for him. Oompa is the only one in the squad who ever goes back for seconds. To put it in the nicest way, the food in camp sucks.

"It isn't something we like to do, but it has to be done," I say, echoing the company line. "Because this is war, you know? It's war."

I look down the table for support. The only one who will make eye contact with me is Teacup, who is nodding happily.

"War," she says. Happily.

Outside the mess hall and across the yard, where several squads are drilling under the watchful eyes of their drill sergeants, Nugget trots along beside me. Zombie's dog, the squad calls him behind his back. Cutting between Barracks 3 and 4 to the road that leads to the power plant and the processing hangars. The day is cold and cloudy; it feels like it might snow. In the distance, the sound of a Black Hawk taking off and the sharp *tat-tat-tat* of automatic weapons' fire. Directly in front of us the twin towers of the plant belching black and gray smoke. The gray smoke fades into the clouds. The black lingers.

A large white tent has been set up outside the entrance to the hangar, the staging area festooned with red-and-white biohazard warning signs. Here we suit up for processing. Once I'm dressed, I help Nugget with his orange suit, the boots, the rubber gloves, the mask, and the hood. I give him the lecture about never, ever taking off any part of his suit inside the hangar, under any circumstances, ever. He has to ask permission before handling anything and, if he has to leave the building for any reason, he has to decon and pass inspection before reentering.

"Just stick with me," I tell him. "It'll be okay."

He nods and his hood bounces back and forth, the faceplate smacking him in the forehead. He's trying to hold it together, and it's not going well. So I say, "They're just people, Nugget. Just people."

Inside the processing hangar, the bodies of the just-people are sorted, the infected from the clean—or, as we call them, the Ted from the unTed. Teds are marked with bright green circles on their foreheads, but you rarely need to look; the Teds are always the freshest bodies.

They've been stacked against the back wall, waiting for their turn to be laid out on the long metal tables that run the length of the hangar. The bodies are in various stages of decay. Some are months old. Some look fresh enough to sit up and wave hello.

It takes three squads to work the line. One squad carts the bodies over to the metal tables. Another processes. A third carries the processed corpses to the front and stacks them for pickup. You rotate the duties to help break up the monotony.

Processing is the most interesting, and where our squad begins. I tell Nugget not to touch, just watch me until he gets the idea.

Empty the pockets. Separate the contents. Trash goes in one bin, electronics in another, precious metals in a third, all other metals in a fourth. Wallets, purses, paper, cash—all trash. Some of the squads can't help themselves—old habits die hard—and walk around with wads of useless hundred-dollar bills stuffed in their pockets.

Photographs, IDs, any little memento that isn't made of ceramic—trash. Almost without exception, from the oldest to the youngest, the pockets of the dead are filled to the brim with the strangest things only the owners could understand the value for.

Nugget doesn't say a word. He watches me work down the line, keeping right beside me as I sidestep to the next body. The hangar is ventilated, but the smell is overpowering. Like any omnipresent smell—or rather, like anything omnipresent—you get used to it; you stop smelling it after a while.

Same is true for your other senses. And your soul. After you've seen your five hundredth dead baby, how can you be shocked or sickened or feel anything at all?

Beside me, Nugget is silent, watching.

"Tell me if you're going to be sick," I tell him sternly. It's horrible throwing up in your suit.

The overhead speakers pop to life, and the tunes begin. Most of the guys prefer rap while they process; I like to mix it up with a little heavy metal and some R&B. Nugget wants something to do, so I have him carry the ruined clothes to the laundry bins. They'll be burned with the processed corpses later that night. Disposal happens next door, in the power plant incinerator. They say the black smoke is from the coal and the gray smoke is from the bodies. I don't know if that's true.

It's the hardest processing I've done. I've got Nugget, my own bodies to process, and the rest of the squad to keep an eye on, because there's no drill sergeants or any adult period inside the processing hangar, except the dead ones. Just kids, and sometimes it's like at school when the teacher is suddenly called out of the room. Things can get crazy.

There's little interaction among the squads outside P&D. The competition for the top slots on the leaderboard is too intense, and there's nothing friendly about the rivalry.

So when I see the fair-skinned, dark-haired girl wheeling corpses from Poundcake's table to the disposal area, I don't go over and introduce myself and I don't grab one of her team members to ask her name. I just watch her while I dig my fingers through the pockets of dead people. I notice she's directing traffic at the door; she must be the squad leader. At the midmorning break, I pull Poundcake aside. He's a sweet kid, quiet, but not in a weird way. Dumbo has a theory that one day the cork will pop and Pound-cake won't stop talking for a week.

"You know that girl from Squad Nineteen working at your table?" I ask him. He nods. "Know anything about her?" He shakes his head. "Why am I asking you this, Cake?" He shrugs. "Okay," I say. "But don't tell anyone I asked."

By the fourth hour on the line, Nugget's not too steady on his feet. He needs a break, so I take him outside for a few minutes, where we sit against the hangar door and watch the black and gray smoke billowing beneath the clouds.

Nugget yanks off his hood and leans his head against the cold metal door, his round face shiny with sweat.

"They're just people," I say again, basically because I don't know what else to say. "It gets easier," I go on. "Every time you do it, you feel it a little less. Until it's like—I don't know—like making your bunk or brushing your teeth."

I'm all tense, waiting for him to lose it. Cry. Run. Explode. Something. But there's just this blank, faraway look in his eyes, and suddenly I'm the one about to explode. Not at him. Or at Reznik for making me bring him. At them. At the bastards who did this to us. Forget about my life—I know how that ends. What about Nugget's? Five frigging years old, and what's he got to look forward to? And why the hell did Commander Vosch assign him

233

to a combat unit? Seriously, he can't even lift a rifle. Maybe the idea is to catch 'em young, train 'em from the ground up. So by the time he's my age you don't have a stone-cold killer, but an ice-cold one. One with liquid nitrogen for blood.

I hear his voice before I feel his hand on my forearm. "Zombie, are you okay?"

"Sure, I'm fine." Here's a strange turn of events, him worried about me.

A large flatbed pulls up to the hangar door, and Squad 19 begins loading bodies, tossing them onto the truck like relief workers heaving sacks of grain. There's the dark-haired girl again, straining at the front end of a very fat corpse. She glances our way before going back inside for the next body. Great. She'll probably report us for goofing off to knock a few points off our score.

"Cassie says it won't matter what they do," Nugget says. "They can't kill all of us."

"Why can't they?" Because, kid, I'd really, really like to know.

"Because we're too hard to kill. We're invista . . . investra . . . invinta . . ."

"Invincible?"

"That's it!" With a reassuring pat on my arm. "Invincible."

Black smoke, gray smoke. And the cold biting our cheeks and the heat from our bodies trapped inside our suits, Zombie and Nugget and the brooding clouds above us and, hidden above them, the mothership that gave birth to the gray smoke and, in a way, to us. Us too.

46

EVERY NIGHT NOW Nugget crawls into my bunk after lights-out to say his prayer, and I let him stay until he falls asleep. Then I carry him back to his bunk. Tank threatens to turn me in, usually after I give him an order he doesn't like. But he doesn't. I think he secretly looks forward to prayer time.

It amazes me how quickly Nugget has adjusted to camp life. Kids are like that, though. They can get used to practically anything. He can't lift a rifle to his shoulder, but he does everything else, and sometimes better than the older kids. He's faster than Oompa on the obstacle course and a quicker study than Flintstone. The one squad member who can't stand him is Teacup. I guess it's jealousy: Before Nugget came, Teacup was the baby of the family.

Nugget did have a mini freakout during his first air raid drill. Like the rest of us, he had no idea it was coming, but unlike the rest of us, he had no idea what the hell was going on.

It happens once a month and always in the middle of the night. The sirens scream so loud, you can feel the floor shaking under your bare feet as you stumble around in the dark, yanking on jumpsuit and boots, grabbing your M16, racing outside as all the barracks empty out, hundreds of recruits pouring across the yard toward the access tunnels that lead underground.

I was a couple of minutes behind the squad because Nugget was hollering his head off and clinging to me like a monkey to his momma, thinking any minute the alien warships would start dropping their payloads.

I shouted at him to calm down and follow my lead. It was a

235

waste of breath. Finally I just picked him up and slung him over my shoulder, rifle clutched in one hand, Nugget's butt in the other. As I sprinted outside, I thought of another night and another screaming kid. The memory made me run harder.

Into the stairwell, down the four flights of stairs awash in yellow emergency light, Nugget's head popping against my back, then through the steel-reinforced door at the bottom, down a short passageway, through the second reinforced door, and into the complex. The heavy door clanged shut behind us, sealing us inside. By now he had decided he might not be vaporized after all, and I could set him down.

The shelter is a confusing maze of dimly lit intersecting corridors, but we've been drilled so much, I could find my way to our station with my eyes closed. I yelled over the siren for Nugget to follow me and I took off. A squad heading in the opposite direction thundered past us.

Right, left, right, right, left, into the final passageway, my free hand gripping the back of Nugget's neck to keep him from falling back. I could see my squad kneeling twenty yards from the back wall of the dead-end tunnel, their rifles trained at the metal grate that covers the airshaft leading to the surface.

And Reznik standing behind them, holding a stopwatch.

Crap.

We missed our time by forty-eight seconds. Forty-eight seconds that would cost us three days of free time. Forty-eight seconds that would drop us another place on the leaderboard. Forty-eight seconds that meant God knows how many more days of Reznik.

Back in the barracks now, we're all too hyped up to sleep. Half the squad is pissed at me, the other half is pissed at Nugget. Tank, of course, blames me.

236

"You should have left him behind," he says. His thin face is flushed with rage.

"There's a reason we drill, Tank," I remind him. "What if this had been the real thing?"

"Then I guess he'd be dead."

"He's a member of this squad, same as the rest of us."

"You still don't get it, do you, Zombie? It's freakin' nature. Whoever's too sick or weak has to go." He yanks off his boots, hurls them into his locker at the foot of the bunk. "If it was up to me, we'd throw all of 'em into the incinerator with the Teds."

"Killing humans—isn't that the aliens' job?"

His face is beet red. He pounds the air with his fist. Flintstone makes a move to calm him down, but Tank waves him away.

"Whoever's too weak, too sick, too old, too slow, too stupid, or too little—they GO!" Tank yells. "Anybody and everybody who can't fight or support the fight—they'll just drag us down."

"They're expendable," I shoot back sarcastically.

"The chain is only as strong as the weakest link," Tank roars. "It's frickin' nature, Zombie. Only the strong survive!"

"Hey, come on, man," Flintstone says to him. "Zombie's right. Nugget's one of the crew."

"You get off my case, Flint," Tank shouts. "All of you! Like it's my fault. Like I'm responsible for this shit!"

"Zombie, do something," Dumbo begs me. "He's going Dorothy."

Dumbo's referring to the recruit who snapped on the rifle range one day, turning her weapon on her own squad members. Two people were killed and three seriously injured before the drill sergeant popped her in the back of the head with his sidearm. Every week there's a story about someone "going Dorothy," or sometimes we say "off to see the wizard." The pressure gets to be too much, and you break. Sometimes you turn on others. Sometimes you turn on yourself. Sometimes I question the wisdom of Central Command, putting high-powered automatic weapons into the hands of some seriously effed-up children.

"Oh, go screw yourself," Tank snarls at Dumbo. "Like you know anything. Like anybody knows anything. What the hell are we doing here? You want to tell me, Dumbo? How about you, squad leader? Can you tell me? Somebody better tell me and they better tell me right now, or I'm taking this place out. I'm taking all of it and all of you out, because this is seriously messed up, man. We're going to take them on, the things that killed seven billion of us? With what? With what?" Pointing the end of his rifle at Nugget, who's clinging to my leg. "With that?" Laughing hysterically.

Everybody goes stiff when the gun comes up. I hold up my empty hands and say as calmly as I can, "Private, lower that weapon right now."

"You're not the boss of me! Nobody's the boss of me!" Standing beside his bunk, the rifle at his hip. On the yellow brick road, all right.

My eyes slide over to Flintstone, who's the closest to Tank, standing a couple of feet to his right. Flint answers with the tiniest of nods.

"Don't you dumbasses ever wonder why they haven't hit us yet?" Tank says. He's not laughing now. He's crying. "You know they can. You know they know we're here, and you know they know what we're doing here, so why are they letting us do it?"

"I don't know, Tank," I say evenly. "Why?"

"Because it doesn't matter anymore what the hell we do! It's over, man. It's done!" Swinging his gun around wildly. If it goes off . . . "And you and me and everybody else on this damn base are history! We're—"

238

Flint's on him, ripping the rifle from his hand and shoving him down hard. Tank's head catches the edge of his bunk when he falls. He curls into a ball, holding his head in both hands, screaming at the top of his lungs, and when his lungs are empty, he fills them and lets loose again. Somehow it's worse than waving around the loaded M16. Poundcake races into the latrine to hide in one of the stalls. Dumbo covers his big ears and scoots to the head of his bunk. Oompa has sidled closer to me, right next to Nugget, who's holding on to my legs with both hands now and peeking around my hip at Tank writhing on the barracks floor. The only one unaffected by Tank's meltdown is Teacup, the seven-year-old. She's sitting on her bunk staring stoically at him, like every night Tank falls to the floor and screams as if he's being murdered.

And it hits me: This *is* murder, what they're doing to us. A very slow, very cruel murder, killing us from our souls outward, and I remember the commander's words: *It isn't about destroying our capability to fight so much as crushing our will to fight.*

It is hopeless. It is crazy. Tank is the sane one because he sees it clearly.

Which is why he has to go.

47

THE SENIOR DRILL INSTRUCTOR agrees with me, and the next morning Tank is gone, taken to the hospital for a full psych eval. His bunk remains empty for a week, while our squad, one man short, falls further and further behind in points. We'll never graduate, never trade in our blue jumpsuits for real uniforms, never venture beyond the electric fence and razor wire to prove ourselves, to pay back a fraction of what we've lost.

We don't talk about Tank. It's as if Tank never existed. We have to believe the system is perfect, and Tank is a flaw in the system.

Then one morning in the P&D hangar, Dumbo motions me over to his table. Dumbo is training to be the squad medic, so he has to dissect designated corpses, usually Teds, to learn about human anatomy. When I come over, he doesn't say anything, but nods at the body lying in front of him.

It's Tank.

We stare at his face for a long moment. His eyes are open, staring sightlessly at the ceiling. He's so fresh, it's unnerving. Dumbo glances around the hangar to make sure no one can overhear us, and then whispers, "Don't tell Flint."

I nod. "What happened?"

Dumbo shakes his head. He's sweating badly under the protective hood. "That's the really freaky thing, Zombie. I can't find anything."

I look back down at Tank. He isn't pale. His skin is slightly pink without a mark on it. How did Tank die? Did he go Dorothy in the psych ward, maybe overdose himself on some drugs?

"What if you cut him open?" I ask.

"I'm not cutting Tank open," he says. He's looking at me as if I just told him to jump off a cliff.

I nod. Stupid idea. Dumbo is no doctor; he's a twelve-year-old kid. I glance around the hangar again. "Get him off this table," I say. "I don't want anyone else to see him." Including me.

Tank's body is stacked with the others by the hangar doors to be disposed. He's loaded onto the transport for the final leg of his journey to the incinerators, where he will be consumed in fire, his ashes mixing with the gray smoke and carried aloft in a column of superheated air, eventually to settle over us in particles too fine to see or feel. He'll stay with us—on us—until we shower that night, washing what's left of Tank into the drains connected to the pipes connected to the septic tanks, where he will mix with our excrement before leaching into the ground.

48

TANK'S REPLACEMENT ARRIVES two days later. We know he's coming, because the night before Reznik announces it during Q&A. He won't tell us anything about him, except the name: Ringer. After he leaves, everybody in the squad is jacked up; Reznik must have named him Ringer for a reason.

Nugget comes over to my bunk and asks, "What's a ringer?"

"Someone who you slip into a team to give it an edge," I explain. "Somebody who's really good."

"Marksmanship," Flintstone guesses. "That's where we're weakest. Poundcake's our best, and I'm okay, but you and Dumbo and Teacup suck. And Nugget can't even shoot."

"Come over here and say I suck," Teacup shouts. Always looking for a fight. If I were in charge, I'd give Teacup a rifle and a couple of clips and let her loose on every Ted in a hundred-mile radius.

After the prayer, Nugget twists and squirms against my back until I can't take it anymore and hiss at him to go back to his bunk.

"Zombie, it's her."

"What's her?"

"Ringer! Cassie is Ringer!"

It takes me a couple of seconds to remember who Cassie is. *Oh, God, not this shit again.*

"I don't think Ringer is your sister."

"You don't know she isn't, either."

It almost comes out of me: *Don't be a dumbass, kid. Your sister isn't coming for you because she's dead.* But I hold it in. Cassie is Nugget's silver locket. What he clings to because if he lets go, there's nothing to keep the tornado from taking him off to Oz like the other Dorothys in camp. It's why a kid army makes sense. Adults don't waste their time on magical thinking. They dwell on the same inconvenient truths that landed Tank on the dissection table.

Ringer isn't at roll call the next morning. And he isn't on the morning run or at chow. We gear up for the range, check our weapons, head out across the yard. It's a clear day, but very cold. Nobody says much. We're all wondering where the new kid is.

Nugget sees Ringer first, standing off in the distance on the firing range, and right away we can see Flintstone was right: Ringer is a hell of a marksman. The target pops out of the tall brown grass and *pop-pop!* the head of the target explodes. Then a different target, but the same result. Reznik is standing off to one side, operating the controls on the targets. He sees us coming and starts hitting buttons fast. The targets rocket out of the grass, one right after the other, and this Ringer kid takes them out before they can get upright with one shot. Beside me, Flintstone gives a long, appreciative whistle.

"He's good."

Nugget gets it before the rest of us. Something about the shoulders or maybe the hips, but he goes, "It's not a he," before he takes off across the field toward the solitary figure cradling the rifle that smokes in the freezing air.

She turns before he reaches her, and Nugget pulls up, first confused, then disappointed. Apparently, Ringer is not his sister.

Weird that she looked taller from a distance. Around Dumbo's height, but thinner than Dumbo—and older. I'm guessing fifteen or sixteen, with a pixie face and dark, deep-set eyes, flawless pale skin, and straight black hair. It's the eyes that get you first. The kind of eyes you search to find something there and you come away with only two possibilities: Either what's there is so deep you can't see it, or there's nothing there at all.

It's the girl from the yard, the one who caught me outside the P&D hangar with Nugget.

"Ringer is a girl," Teacup whispers, wrinkling her nose like she's caught a whiff of something rotten. Not only is she not the baby of the squad anymore, now she's not the only girl.

"What're we going to do with her?" Dumbo is on the edge of panic.

I'm grinning. Can't help it. "We're going to be the first squad to graduate," I say.

And I'm right.

49

RINGER'S FIRST NIGHT in Barracks 10 in one word: awkward.

No banter. No dirty jokes. No macho bluster. We count the minutes ticking down to lights-out like a bunch of nervous geeks on a first date. Other squads might have girls her age; we have Teacup. Ringer seems oblivious to our discomfort. She sits on the edge of Tank's old bunk, disassembling and cleaning her rifle. Ringer likes her rifle. A lot. You can tell by the way she lovingly runs the oily rag up and down the length of its barrel, shining it until the cold metal gleams under the fluorescents. We are trying so hard not to stare at her, it's painful. She reassembles her weapon, places it carefully in the locker beside the bed, and comes over to my bunk. I feel something tighten in my chest. I haven't spoken to a girl my age since . . . when? Before the plague. And I don't think about my life before the plague. That was Ben's life, not Zombie's.

"You're the squad leader," she says. Her voice is flat, no emotion, like her eyes. "Why?"

I answer the challenge in her question with one of my own. "Why not?"

Stripped down to her skivvies and the standard-issue sleeveless T-shirt, her bangs stopping just short of her dark eyebrows, looking down at me. Dumbo and Oompa stop their card game to watch. Teacup is smiling, sensing a fight brewing. Flintstone, who's been folding laundry, drops a clean jumpsuit on top of the pile.

"You're a terrible shot," Ringer says.

"I have other skills," I say, crossing my arms over my chest. "You should see me with a potato peeler."

"You've got a good body." Somebody laughs under his breath; I think it's Flint. "Are you an athlete?"

"I used to be."

She's standing over me with her fists on her hips, bare feet planted firmly on the floor. It's her eyes that get to me. The deep dark of them. Is nothing there—or nearly everything? "Football."

"Good guess."

"And baseball, probably."

"When I was younger."

She changes the subject abruptly. "The guy I replaced went Dorothy."

"That's right."

"Why?"

I shrug. "Does it matter?"

She nods. It doesn't. "I was the leader of my squad."

"No doubt."

"Just because you're leader doesn't mean you'll make sergeant after graduation."

"I sure hope that's true."

"I know it's true. I asked."

She turns on her bare heel and goes back to her bunk. I look down at my feet and notice my nails need trimming. Ringer's feet are very small, with nubby-type toes. When I look up again, she's heading for the showers with a towel thrown over her shoulder. She pauses at the door. "If anybody in this squad touches me, I'll kill them."

There's nothing menacing or funny about the way she says it. As if she's stating a fact, like it's cold outside.

"I'll spread the word," I say.

"And when I'm in the shower, off limits. Total privacy."

"Roger that. Anything else?"

She pauses, staring at me from across the room. I feel myself tense up. What next? "I like to play chess. Do you play?"

I shake my head. Holler at the boys, "Any of you pervs play chess?"

"No," Flint calls back. "But if she's in the mood for some strip poker—"

It happens before I can get two inches off the mattress: Flint on the ground, holding his throat, kicking his legs like a stomped-on bug, Ringer standing over him.

"Also, no demeaning, sexist, pseudo-macho remarks."

"You're cool!" Teacup blurts out, and she means it. Maybe she needs to rethink this whole Ringer thing. Might not be such a bad arrangement having another girl around.

"That's ten days half rations for what you just did," I tell her. Maybe Flint had it coming, but I'm still the boss when Reznik's not around, and Ringer needs to know it.

"Are you writing me up?" No fear in her voice. No anger. No anything.

"I'm giving you a warning."

She nods, steps away from Flint, brushes past me on the way to fetch her toiletry kit. She smells—well, she smells like a girl, and for a second I'm a little light-headed.

"I'll remember you going easy on me," she says with a flip of her bangs, "when they make me Fifty-three's new squad leader."

50

A WEEK AFTER Ringer arrived, Squad 53 moved up from tenth to seventh place. By week three, we had edged past Squad 19 to take fifth. Then, with only two weeks to go, we hit a wall, falling sixteen points back from fourth place, a nearly insurmountable deficit.

Poundcake, who isn't much for words but is a boss with numbers, breaks down the spread. In every category except one, there's very little room for improvement: We're second in obstacle course, third in air raid and the run, and first in "other duties as assigned," a catchall that includes points for morning inspection and "conduct befitting a unit of the armed forces." Our downfall is marksmanship, where we rank sixteenth, despite kickass shooters like Ringer and Poundcake. Unless we can pull up that score in the next two weeks, we're doomed.

Of course, you don't have to be a boss with numbers to know why our score is so low. The squad leader sucks at shooting. So the sucky-shooting squad leader goes to the senior drill instructor and requests extra practice time, but his scores don't budge. My technique isn't bad; I do all the right things in the right order; still, if I score one head shot out of a thirty-round clip, I'm lucky. Ringer agrees it's just dumb luck. She says even Nugget could score one out of thirty. She tries hard not to show it, but my ineptitude with a gun pisses her off. Her former squad ranks second. If she hadn't been reassigned, she'd be guaranteed to graduate with the first class and be first in line for a pair of sergeant stripes.

"I've got a proposition for you," she says one morning as we hit the yard for the morning run. She's wearing a headband to hold back her silky bangs. Not that I notice their silkiness. "I'll help you, on one condition."

"Does it have anything to do with chess?"

"Resign as squad leader."

I glance at her. The cold has painted her ivory cheeks a bright red. Ringer is a quiet person—not Poundcake quiet, but quiet in an intense, unnerving way, with eyes that seem to dissect you with the sharpness of one of Dumbo's surgical knives.

"You didn't ask for it, you don't care about it, why not let me have it?" she asks, keeping her eyes on the path.

"Why do you want it so bad?"

"Giving the orders is my best chance to stay alive."

I laugh. I want to tell her what I've learned. Vosch said it; I knew it to the bottom of my soul: *You're going to die.* This wasn't about survival. It was about payback.

Following the path that snakes out of the yard and across the hospital parking lot to the airfield access road. In front of us now the power plant barfing its black and gray smoke.

"How 'bout this," I suggest. "You help me, we win, I step down."

It's a meaningless offer. We're recruits. It isn't our call who's squad leader; it's Reznik's. And I know this really isn't about who's squad leader anyway. It's about who makes sergeant when we're activated for field duty. Being squad leader doesn't guarantee a promotion, but it can't hurt.

A Black Hawk thunders overhead, returning from night patrol.

"Ever wonder how they did it?" she asks, watching the chopper swing off to our right toward the landing zone. "Got everything running again after the EMP strike?"

"No," I answer honestly. "What do you think?"

Her breaths tiny white explosions in the frigid air. "Underground bunkers, it has to be. That or . . ."

"Or what?"

She shakes her head, puffing out her cold-pinched cheeks, and her black hair swings back and forth as she runs, kissed by the bright morning sun.

"Too crazy, Zombie," she says finally. "Come on, let's see what you've got, football star."

I'm four inches taller than she is. For every one stride I take, she has to take two. So I beat her.

Barely.

That afternoon we hit the range, bringing Oompa along to operate the targets. Ringer watches me fire off a few rounds, then offers her expert opinion: "You're horrible."

"That's the problem. My horribleness." I give her my best smile. Before the alien Armageddon happened, I was known for my smile. Not bragging too much, but I had to be careful never to smile while I drove: It had the capacity to blind oncoming traffic. But it has absolutely no effect on Ringer. She doesn't squint in its overwhelming luminescence. She doesn't even blink.

"Your technique is good. What's going on when you shoot?"

"Generally speaking, I miss."

She shakes her head. Speaking of smiles, I've yet to see so much as a thin-lipped grin from her. I decide to make it my mission to coax one out of her. More a Ben thought than a Zombie one, but old habits die hard.

"I mean between you and the target," she says.

Huh? "Well, when it pops up—"

"No. I'm talking about what happens between here," fingertips on my right hand, "and there," pointing at the target twenty yards away.

"You've lost me, Ringer."

"You have to think of your weapon as a part of you. Not the M16 firing; *you* firing. It's like blowing on a dandelion. You breathe the bullet out."

She swings her rifle off her shoulder and nods to Oompa. She doesn't know where it'll pop up, but the head of the target explodes in a shower of splinters before it even gets upright.

"It's like there's no space, nothing that isn't you. The rifle is you. The bullet is you. The target is you. There's nothing that's not you."

"So basically what you're saying is I'm blowing my own head off."

I almost got a smile with that one. The left corner of her mouth twitches.

"That's very Zenlike," I try again.

Her eyebrows come together. Strike three. "It's more like quantum mechanics."

I nod seriously. "Oh, sure. That's what I meant to say. Quantum mechanics."

She turns her head away. To hide a smile? So I don't see an exasperated eye roll? When she turns back, all I get is that intense, stomach-tightening stare.

"Do you want to graduate?"

"I want to get the hell away from Reznik."

"That isn't enough." She points across the field at one of the cutouts. The wind plays with her bangs. "What do you see when you sight a target?"

"I see a plywood cutout of a person."

"Okay, but who do you see?"

"I know what you meant. Sometimes I picture Reznik's face."

"Does it help?"

"You tell me."

"It's about connection," she says. She motions for me to sit down. She sits in front of me, takes my hands. Hers are freezing, cold as the bodies in P&D. "Close your eyes. Oh, come on, Zombie. How's your way been working for you? Good. Okay, remember, it's not you and the target. It's not what's between you, but what connects you. Think about the lion and the gazelle. What connects them?"

"Um. Hunger?"

"That's the lion. I'm asking what they share."

This is heavy stuff. Maybe it was a bad idea, accepting her offer. Not only do I have her thoroughly convinced I'm a lousy soldier, now there's a real possibility that I'm also a moron.

"Fear," she whispers in my ear, as if she's sharing a secret. "For the gazelle, fear of being eaten. For the lion, fear of starvation. Fear is the chain that binds them together."

The chain. I carry one in my pocket attached to a silver locket. The night my sister died was a thousand years ago; that night was last night. It's over. It's never over. It isn't a line from that night to this day; it's a circle. My fingers tighten around hers.

"I don't know what your chain is," she goes on, warm breath in my ear. "It's different for everyone. They know. Wonderland tells them. It's the thing that made them put a gun in your hand, and it's the same thing that chains you to the target." Then, as if she's read my mind: "It isn't a line, Zombie. It's a circle."

I open my eyes. The setting sun creates a halo of golden light around her. "There is no distance."

She nods and urges me to my feet. "It's almost dark."

I bring up my rifle and tuck the butt against my shoulder. You

251

don't know where the target will rise—you only know that it will. Ringer signals Oompa, and the tall, dead grass rustles to my right a millisecond before the target pops, but that's more than enough time; it's an eternity.

There is no distance. Nothing between me and the not-me.

The target's head disintegrates with a satisfying *crack!* Oompa gives a shout and pumps his fist in the air. I forget myself and grab Ringer around the waist, swinging her off the ground and twirling her around. I'm one very dangerous second away from kissing her. When I set her down, she takes a couple of steps back and tucks her hair carefully behind her ears.

"That was out of line," I say. I don't know who's more embarrassed. We're both trying to catch our breaths. Maybe for different reasons.

"Do it again," she says.

"Shoot or twirl, which one?"

Her mouth twitches. Oh, I'm so close.

"The one that means something."

51

GRADUATION DAY.

Our new uniforms were waiting for us when we returned from morning chow, pressed and starched and neatly folded on our bunks. And an extra special bonus surprise: headbands equipped with the latest in alien detection technology, a clear, quarter-size disk that slips over your left eye. Infested humans will light up through the lens. Or so we're told. Later that day, when I asked the tech exactly how it worked, his answer was simple: Unclean glows green. When I politely asked for a brief demo, he laughed. "You'll get your demo in the field, soldier."

For the first time since coming to Camp Haven—and probably for the last time in our lives—we are kids again. Whooping it up and jumping from bunk to bunk, throwing high fives. Ringer's the only one who ducks into the latrine to change. The rest of us strip where we stand, throwing the hated blue jumpsuits into a pile in the middle of the floor. Teacup has the bright idea to set them on fire and would have if Dumbo didn't snatch the lit match from her hand at the last second.

The only one without a uniform is sitting on his bunk in his white jumpsuit, legs swinging back and forth, arms folded over his chest, bottom lip stuck out a mile. I'm not oblivious. I get it. After I'm dressed, I sit beside him and slap him on the leg.

"You'll get your turn, Private. Hang in there."

"Two years, Zombie."

"So? Think what a hardass you'll be in two years. Put all of us to shame."

Nugget's being assigned to another training squad after we deploy. I promised him he could bunk with me whenever I'm on base, though I have no idea when—or if—I'm ever coming back. Our mission is still top secret, known only to Central Command. I'm not sure even Reznik knows where we're going. I don't really care, as long as Reznik stays here.

"Come on, soldier. You're supposed to be happy for me," I tease him.

"You're not coming back." He says it with so much angry conviction that I don't know what to say. "I'll never see you again."

253

"Of course you're going to see me again, Nugget. I promise."

He hits me as hard as he can. Again and again, right over my heart. I grab his wrist, and he lays into me with his other hand. I grab that one and order him to stand down.

"Don't promise, don't promise, don't promise! Don't promise anything ever, ever, ever!" His little face screwed up with rage.

"Hey, Nugget, hey." I fold his arms over his chest and bend down to look him in the eye. "Some things you don't have to promise. You just do."

I reach into my pocket and pull out Sissy's locket. Undo the clasp. I haven't done that since I fixed it at Tent City. Circle broken. I draw it around his neck and hook the ends together. Circle complete.

"No matter what happens out there, I'll come back for you," I promise him.

Over his shoulder, I see Ringer come out of the bathroom, tucking her hair beneath her new cap. I stand at attention and snap off a salute.

"Private Zombie reporting for duty, squad leader!"

"My one day of glory," she says, returning the salute. "Everybody knows who's making sergeant."

I shrug modestly. "I don't listen to rumors."

"You made a promise you knew you couldn't keep," she says matter-of-factly—which is pretty much the way she says everything. The unfortunate thing is she says it right in front of Nugget. "Sure you don't want to take up chess, Zombie? You'd be very good at it."

Since laughing seems like the least dangerous thing to do at that moment, I laugh.

The door flies open, and Dumbo shouts, "Sir! Good morning, sir!"

We rush to the ends of our bunks and stand at attention as Reznik moves down the line for what will be our final inspection. He's subdued, for Reznik. He doesn't call us maggots or scumbags. He's nitpicky as ever, though. Flintstone's shirt is untucked on one side. Oompa's hat is crooked. He brushes off a speck of lint that only he can see from Teacup's collar. He lingers over Teacup for a long moment, staring down into her face, almost comical in its seriousness.

"Well, Private. Are you ready to die?"

"Sir, yes, sir!" Teacup shouts in her loudest warrior voice.

Reznik turns to the rest of us. "How about you? Are you ready?"

Our voices thunder as one: "Sir! Yes, *sir!*"

Before he leaves, Reznik orders me front and center. "Come with me, Private." A final salute to the troops, then: "See you at the party, children."

On my way out, Ringer gives me a knowing look, as if to say, *Told you so.*

I follow two paces behind the drill sergeant as he marches across the yard. Blue-suited recruits are putting the finishing touches on the speaker's platform, hanging bunting, setting up chairs for the high brass, unrolling a red carpet. A huge banner has been hung across the barracks on the far side: WE ARE HUMANITY. And on the opposite side: WE ARE ONE.

Into a nondescript one-story building on the western side of the compound, passing through a security door marked AUTHORIZED PERSONNEL ONLY. Through a metal detector manned by heavily armed, stone-faced soldiers. Into an elevator that carries us four stories beneath the earth. Reznik doesn't talk. He doesn't even look at me. I have a pretty good idea where we're going, but no idea why. I nervously pick at the front of my new uniform.

Down a long corridor awash in fluorescent lighting. Passing through another security checkpoint. More stone-faced, heavily armed soldiers. Reznik stops at an unmarked door and swipes his key card through the lock. We step inside a small room. A man in a lieutenant's uniform greets us at the door, and we follow him down another hallway and into a large private office. A man sits behind the desk, leafing through a stack of computer printouts.

Vosch.

He dismisses Reznik and the lieutenant, and we're alone.

"At ease, Private."

I spread my feet, put my hands behind my back, right hand loosely gripping my left wrist. Standing in front of the big desk, eyes forward, chest out. He is the supreme commander. I'm a private, a lowly recruit, not even a real soldier yet. My heart is threatening to pop the buttons on my brand-new shirt.

"So, Ben, how are you?"

He's smiling warmly at me. I don't even know how to begin to answer his question. Plus I'm thrown by his calling me Ben. It sounds strange to my own ears after being Zombie for so many months.

He's expecting an answer, and for some stupid reason I blurt out the first thing that pops into my head. "Sir! The private is ready to die, sir!"

He nods, still smiling, and then he gets up, comes around the desk, and says, "Let's speak freely, soldier to soldier. After all, that's what you are now, Sergeant Parish."

I see them then: the sergeant's stripes in his hand. So Ringer was right. I snap back to attention while he pins them on my collar. He claps me on the shoulder, his blue eyes boring into mine.

Hard to look him in the eye. The way he looks at you makes you feel naked, totally exposed.

"You lost a man," he says.

"Yes, sir."

"Terrible thing."

"Yes, sir."

He leans back against the desk, crosses his arms. "His profile was excellent. Not as good as yours, but . . . The lesson here, Ben, is that we all have a breaking point. We're all human, yes?"

"Yes, sir."

He's smiling. Why is he smiling? It's cool in the underground bunker, but I'm beginning to sweat.

"You may ask," he says with an inviting wave of his hand.

"Sir?"

"The question you must be thinking. The one you've had since Tank showed up in processing and disposal."

"How did he die?"

"Overdose, as you no doubt suspected. One day after being taken off suicide watch." He motions to the chair beside me. "Have a seat, Ben. There's something I want to discuss with you."

I sink into the chair, sitting on its edge, back straight, chin up. If it's possible to be at attention while seated, I'm doing it.

"We all have our breaking points," he says, blue eyes bearing down on me. "I'll tell you about mine. Two weeks after the 4th Wave, gathering survivors at a refugee camp about six kilometers from here. Well, not every survivor. Just the children. Although we hadn't detected the infestations yet, we were fairly confident whatever was going on didn't involve children. Since we couldn't know who was the enemy and who wasn't, it was command's decision to terminate any and all personnel over the age of fifteen."

257

His face goes dark. His eyes cut away. Leaning back on the desk, gripping its edge so hard, his knuckles turn white.

"I mean, my decision." Deep breath. "We killed them, Ben. After we loaded up the children, we killed every single one of them. And after we were done, we incinerated their camp. Wiped it off the face of the Earth."

He looks back at me. Incredibly, I see tears in his eyes. "That was my breaking point. Afterward I realized, to my horror, that I was falling into their trap. I was an instrument for the enemy. For every infested person I murdered, three innocent people died. I will have to live with that—because I have to live. Do you understand what I mean?"

I nod. He smiles sadly. "Of course you do. We both have the blood of innocents on our hands, don't we?"

He pushes himself upright, all business now. The tears are gone.

"Sergeant Parish, today we will graduate the top four squads of your battalion. As commander of the winning squad, you have first pick of assignments. Two squads will be deployed as perimeter patrols to protect this base. The other two will be deployed into enemy territory."

This takes me a couple minutes to absorb. He lets me have them. He picks up one of the computer printouts and holds it in front of me. There's a lot of numbers and squiggly lines and strange symbols that mean absolutely nothing to me.

"I don't expect you to be able to read it," he says. "But would you like to guess what this is?"

"That's all it would be, sir," I answer. "A guess."

"It's the Wonderland analytics of an infested human being."

I nod. Why the hell am I nodding? It's not like I understand: *Ah, yes, Commander, an analytic! Please, go on.*

"We've been running them through Wonderland, of course, but we haven't been able to untangle the infestation's map from the victim's—or clone or whatever it is. Until now." He holds up the readout. "This, Sergeant Parish, is what an alien consciousness looks like."

Again, I'm nodding. But this time because I'm starting to get it. "You know what they're thinking."

"Exactly!" Beaming at me, the star pupil. "The key to winning this war isn't tactics or strategy or even imbalances in technology. The real key to winning this war, or any war, is understanding how your enemy thinks. And now we do."

I wait for him to break it to me gently. How does the enemy think?

"Much of what we assumed is correct. They have been watching us for some time. Infestations were embedded in key individuals around the world, sleeper agents, if you will, waiting for the signal to launch a coordinated attack after our population had been whittled down to a manageable number. We know how that attack turned out here at Camp Haven, and we strongly suspect that other military installations were not as fortunate."

He slaps the paper on his thigh. I must have flinched, because he gives me a reassuring smile.

"A third of the surviving population. Planted here to eradicate those who survived the first three waves. You. Me. Your team members. All of us. If you have any fear, as poor Tank did, that a fifth wave is coming, you can put it aside. There will be no fifth wave. They have no intention of leaving their mothership until the human race is exterminated."

"Is that why they haven't . . . ?"

"Attacked us again? We think so. It seems their foremost desire

259

is to preserve the planet for colonization. Now we are in a war of attrition. Our resources are limited; they can't last forever. We know it. They know it. Cut off from supplies, with no means to marshal any significant fighting force, eventually this camp—and any others out there like it—will wither and die, like a vine cut off from its roots."

Weird. He's still smiling. Like something about this doomsday scenario turns him on.

"So what do we do?" I ask.

"The only thing we can do, Sergeant. We take the battle to them."

The way he says it: no doubt, no fear, no hopelessness. *We take the battle to them.* That's why he's the commander. Standing over me, smiling, confident, his chiseled features reminding me of some ancient statue, noble, wise, strong. He is the rock against which the alien waves crash, and he is unbroken. *We are humanity,* the banner read. Wrong. We're pale reflections of it, weak shadows, distant echoes. *He* is humanity, the beating, unbeaten, invincible heart of it. In that moment, if Commander Vosch had told me to put a bullet through my head for the cause, I would have. I would have without a second thought.

"Which brings us back to your assignment," he says quietly. "Our recon flights have identified significant pockets of infested combatants clustered in and around Dayton. A squad will be dropped in—and for the next four hours, it will be on its own. The odds of making it out alive are roughly one in four."

I clear my throat. "And two squads stay here."

He nods. Blue eyes boring deep—to the marrow deep. "Your call."

That same small, secretive smile. He knows what I'm going to say. He knew before I walked through the door. Maybe my Wonderland profile told him, but I don't think so. He knows me.

I rise from the chair to full attention.

And tell him what he already knows.

52

AT 0900 the entire battalion musters in the yard, creating a sea of blue jumpsuits headed by the top four squads in their crisp new fatigues. Over a thousand recruits standing in perfect formation, facing east, the direction of new beginnings, toward the speakers' platform erected the day before. Flags snap in the icy breeze, but we don't feel the cold. We are lit from within by a fire hotter than the one that turned Tank into ash. The brass of Central Command moves down the first line—the winning line—shaking our hands and congratulating us for a job well done. Then a personal word of gratitude from the drill instructors. I've been dreaming of what to say to Reznik when he shakes my hand. *Thanks for making my life a living hell . . . Oh, die. Just die, you son of a bitch . . .* Or my favorite, short and sweet and to the point: *Eff you.* But when he salutes and offers me his hand, I almost lose it. I want to hit him in the face and hug him at the same time.

"Congratulations, Ben," he says, which totally throws me off. I had no idea he even knew my name. He gives me a wink and continues down the line.

There're a couple of short speeches by officers I've never seen before. Then the supreme commander is introduced and the troops go crazy, waving our hats, pumping our fists. Our cheers echo off the buildings encircling the yard, making the roar twice as loud and us seem twice as many. Commander Vosch raises his hand very slowly and deliberately to his forehead, and it's as if he hit a switch: The noise cuts off as we raise our own hands in salute. I can hear quiet snuffling all around me. It's too much. After what brought us here and what we went through here, after all the blood and death and fire, after being shown the ugly mirror of the past through Wonderland and facing the uglier truth of the future in the execution room, after months of brutal training that pushed some of us past the point of no return, we have arrived. We have survived the death of our childhood. We are soldiers now, maybe the last soldiers who will ever fight, the Earth's final and only hope, united as one in the spirit of vengeance.

I don't hear a word of Vosch's speech. I watch the sun rising over his shoulder, framed between the twin towers of the power plant, its light glinting off the mothership in orbit, the sole imperfection in the otherwise perfect sky. So small, so insignificant. I feel like I can reach up and pluck it from the sky, throw it to the ground, grind it to dust beneath my heel. The fire in my chest grows white-hot, spreads over every inch of my body. It melts my bones; it incinerates my skin; I am the sun gone supernova.

I was wrong about Ben Parish dying on the day he left the convalescent ward. I've been carrying his stinking corpse inside me all through basic. Now the last of him is burned away as I stare up at the solitary figure who lit that fire. The man who showed me the true battlefield. Who emptied me so I might be filled. Who killed me so I might live. And I swear I can see him staring back at me with those icy blue eyes that see down to the bottom of my soul, and I know—I know—what he's thinking.

We are one, you and I. Brothers in hate, brothers in cunning, brothers in the spirit of vengeance.

VII
THE HEART TO KILL

53

YOU SAVED ME.

Lying in his arms that night with those words in my ears, and I'm thinking, *Idiot, idiot, idiot. You can't do this. You can't, you can't, you can't.*

The first rule: Trust no one. Which leads to the second rule: The only way to stay alive as long as possible is to stay alone as long as possible.

Now I've broken both.

Oh, they're so clever. The harder survival becomes, the more you want to pull together. And the more you want to pull together, the harder survival becomes.

The point is I had my chance and I didn't do so well on my own. In fact, I sucked. I would have died if Evan hadn't found me.

His body is pressed against my back, his arm is wrapped protectively around my waist, his breath a delicious tickle against my neck. The room is very cold; it would be nice to climb under the covers, but I don't want to move. I don't want him to move. I run my fingers along his bare forearm, remembering the warmth of his lips, the silkiness of his hair between my fingers. The boy who never sleeps, sleeping. Coming to rest upon the Cassiopeian shore, an island in the middle of a sea of blood. *You have your promise, and I have you.*

I can't trust him. I have to trust him.

I can't stay with him. I can't leave him behind.

You can't trust luck anymore. The Others have taught me that. But can you still trust love?

Not that I love him. I don't even know what love feels like. I know how Ben Parish made me feel, which can't be put into words, or at least any words I know.

Evan stirs behind me. "It's late," he murmurs. "You'd better get some sleep."

How did he know I'm awake? "What about you?"

He rolls off the bed and pads toward the door. I sit up, my heart racing, not sure exactly why. "Where are you going?"

"Going to look around a little. I won't be long."

After he leaves, I strip off my clothes and slip on one of his plaid lumberjack shirts. Val had been into the frilly sleepwear. Not my style.

I climb back into bed and pull the covers up to my chin. Dang, it's cold. I listen to the quiet. Of the Evanless house, that is. Outside are the sounds of nature unleashed. The distant barking of wild dogs. The howl of a wolf. The screech of owls. It's winter, the time of year when nature whispers. I expect a symphony of wild things once spring arrives.

I wait for him to come back. An hour goes by. Then two.

I hear the telltale creak again and hold my breath. I usually hear him come in at night. The kitchen door slamming. The heavy tread of his boots coming up the stairs. Now I hear nothing but the creaking on the other side of the door.

I reach over and pick up the Luger from the bedside table. I always keep it near me.

He's dead was my first thought. *It isn't Evan outside that door; it's a Silencer.*

I slide out of bed and tiptoe to the door. Press my ear against the wood. Close my eyes to focus. Holding the gun in the proper two-handed grip, the way he taught me. Rehearsing every step in my head, like he taught me.

Left hand on knob. Turn, pull, two steps back, gun up. Turn, pull, two steps back, gun up . . .

Creeaaaaaak.

Okay, that's it.

I fling open the door, take just one step back—so much for rehearsal—and bring up the gun. Evan jumps back and smacks against the wall, his hands flying up reflexively when he sees the muzzle glinting in front of his face.

"Hey!" he shouts. Eyes wide, hands up, like he's been jumped by a mugger.

"What the hell are you doing?" I'm shaking with anger.

"I was coming back to—to check on you. Can you put the gun down, please?"

"You know I didn't have to open it," I snarl at him, lowering the gun. "I could have shot you through the door."

"Next time I'll definitely knock." He gives me his trademark lopsided smile.

"Let's establish a code for when you want to go all creeper on me. One knock means you'd like to come in. Two means you're just stopping by to spy on me while I sleep." His eyes travel from my face to my shirt (which happens to be his shirt) to my bare legs, lingering a breath too long before returning to my face. His gaze is warm. My legs are cold.

Then he knocks once on the jamb. But it's the smile that gets him in.

We sit on the bed. I try to ignore the fact that I'm wearing his shirt and that shirt smells like him and he's sitting about a foot

269

away also smelling like him and also that there's a hard little knot in the pit of my stomach like a smoldering lump of coal.

I want him to touch me again. I want to feel his hands, as soft as clouds. But I'm afraid if he touches me, all seven billion billion billion atoms that make up my body will blow apart and scatter across the universe.

"Is he alive?" he whispers. That sad, desperate look is back. What happened out there? Why is he thinking about Sams?

I shrug. How can I know the answer to that?

"I knew when Lauren was. I mean, I knew when she wasn't." Picking at the quilt, running his fingers over the stitching, tracing the borders of the patches like he's tracing the path on a treasure map. "I felt it. It was just me and Val then. Val was pretty sick, and I knew she didn't have much time. I knew the timing, almost down to the hour: I'd been through it six times."

It takes him a minute to go on. Something's really spooked him. His eyes won't stay still. They dart about the room, as if trying to find something to distract him—or maybe the opposite, something to ground him in the moment. This moment with me. Not the moment he can't stop thinking about.

"One day I was outside," he says, "hanging up some sheets to dry on the clothesline, and this weird feeling came over me. Like something had popped me in the chest. I mean, it was totally physical, not mental, not a little voice inside my head telling me . . . telling me that Lauren was gone. It felt like someone had punched me hard. And I knew. So I dropped the sheet and hauled ass to her house . . ."

He shakes his head. I touch his knee, then pull my hand back quickly. After the first touch, touching becomes too easy.

"How'd she do it?" I ask. I don't want to make him go

someplace he's not ready to go. So far he's been an emotional ice-berg, two-thirds hidden beneath the surface, listening more than he talks, asking more than he answers.

"Hung herself," he says. "I took her down." He looks away. Here with me, there with her. "Then I buried her."

I don't know what to say. So I don't say anything. Too many people say something when they really have nothing to say.

"I think that's the way it is," he says after a minute. "When you love someone. Something happens to them, and it's a punch in the heart. Not *like* a punch in the heart; a *real* punch in the heart." He shrugs and laughs softly to himself. "Anyway, that's what I felt."

"And you think since I haven't felt it, Sammy must be alive?"

"I know." He shrugs and gives an embarrassed laugh. "It's stu-pid. I'm sorry I brought it up."

"You really loved her, didn't you?"

"We grew up together." His eyes glow at the memory. "She was over here or I was over at her house. Then we got older and she was *always* over here or I was *always* over there. When I could sneak away. I was supposed to be helping my dad on the farm."

"That's where you went tonight, isn't it? Lauren's house."

A tear falls onto his cheek. I wipe it away with my thumb, the way he wiped my tears away on the night I asked him if he be-lieved in God.

He leans forward suddenly and kisses me. Just like that.

"Why did you kiss me, Evan?" Talking about Lauren, then kissing me. It feels weird.

"I don't know." He ducks his head. There's enigmatic Evan, taciturn Evan, passionate Evan, and now shy little boy Evan.

"The next time you better have a good reason," I tease him.

"Okay." He kisses me again.

"Reason?" I ask softly.

"Um. You're really pretty?"

"That's a good one. I don't know if it's true, but it's good."

He cups my face in his soft hands, and then leans in for a third kiss that lingers, igniting the simmering lump in my belly, making the hairs on the back of my neck stand up and do a little happy dance.

"It is true," he whispers, our lips brushing.

We fall asleep in the same spooning position we were in a few hours before, the palm of his hand pressing just below my neck. I wake in the dead hours of the night, and for a second I'm back in the woods inside my sleeping bag, just me, my teddy bear, and my M16—and some stranger pressing his body into mine.

No, it's okay, Cassie. It's Evan, the one who saved you, the one who nursed you back to health, and the one who's willing to risk his life so you can keep some ridiculous promise. Evan, the noticer who noticed you. Evan, the simple farm boy of the warm, gentle, soft hands.

My heart skips a beat. What kind of farm boy has soft hands?

I ease his hand away from my chest. He stirs, sighing against my neck. Now the hairs tickled by his lips dance a different kind of jig. I lightly brush my fingertips over his palm. Soft as a baby's bottom.

Okay, don't panic. It's been a few months since he did any farm work. And you know how nice his cuticles are . . . but can years of calluses be wiped away by a few months off hunting in the woods?

Hunting in the woods . . .

I dip my head slightly to sniff his fingers. It's probably my overactive imagination, but do I detect the acrid, metallic smell of gunpowder? When did he fire a gun? He hadn't gone hunting tonight, just to visit Lauren's grave.

Lying wide awake in his arms as dawn breaks, feeling his heart beating against my back while my own heart pushes against his hand.

You must be a lousy hunter. You hardly ever come back with anything.

I'm actually very good.

You just don't have the heart to kill?

I have the heart to do what I have to do.

What do you have the heart to do, Evan Walker?

54

THE NEXT DAY is agony.

I know I can't confront him. Way too risky. What if the worst is true? That there is no Evan Walker farm boy, only Evan Walker human traitor—or the unthinkable (one word that pretty much sums up this alien invasion): Evan Walker, Silencer. I tell myself this last possibility is ridiculous. A Silencer wouldn't nurse me back to health—much less give me nicknames and play snuggles in the dark. A Silencer would just—well, silence me.

Once I take that irreversible step of confronting him, it's pretty much game over. If he isn't who he claims to be, I'd be giving him no choice. Whatever his reason for keeping me alive, I don't think I'd stay alive very long if he thought I knew the truth.

Go slow. Work it out. Don't tear through it like you always do,

Sullivan. Not your style, but you gotta be methodical for once in your life.

So I pretend nothing's wrong. Over breakfast, though, I work the conversation around to his pre-Arrival days. What kind of work did he do around the farm? Name it, he says. Drove the tractor, baled hay, fed the animals, repaired equipment, strung barbed wire. My eyes on his hands while my mind makes excuses for him. He always wore gloves is the best one, but I can't think of a natural-sounding way to ask. *So, Evan, you have such soft hands to have grown up on a farm. You must have worn gloves all the time and been even more into hand lotion than most guys, huh?*

He doesn't want to talk about the past; it's the future he's worried about. He wants details about the mission. Like every footstep between the farmhouse and Wright-Patterson has to be mapped out, every contingency considered. What if we don't wait till spring and another blizzard hits? What if we find the base abandoned? How do we pick up Sammy's trail then? When do we say enough is enough and give up?

"I'll never give up," I tell him.

I wait for nightfall. I was never very good at waiting, and he notices my restlessness.

"You're going to be okay?" Standing by the kitchen door, rifle dangling from his shoulder. Cupping my face tenderly in those soft hands. And me gazing upward into those puppy-dog eyes, brave Cassie, trusting Cassie, mayfly Cassie. *Sure, I'll be fine. You go out and bag a few people, and I'll pop some corn.*

Then locking the door behind him. Watching him step lightly off the back porch and trot toward the trees, heading west, toward the highway, where, as everyone knows, fresh game like deer and rabbit and *Homo sapiens* like to congregate.

I tear through every room. Four weeks locked up inside it like someone under house arrest, you think I would have poked around a little.

What do I find? Nothing. And a lot.

Family photo albums. There's baby Evan in the hospital wearing the striped newborn hat. Toddler Evan pushing a plastic lawnmower. Five-year-old Evan sitting on a pony. Ten-year-old Evan on the tractor. Twelve-year-old Evan in a baseball uniform . . .

And the rest of his family, including Val—I pick her out right away, and seeing the face of the girl who died in his arms and whose clothes I've taken brings the whole shitty thing back to me, and suddenly I'm like the lowest person left on Earth. Seeing his family in front of the Christmas tree, gathered around birthday cakes, hiking along a mountain trail, forces it down my throat: the end of Christmas trees and birthday cakes and family vacations and the ten thousand other taken-for-granted things. Each photograph the tolling of a bell, a timer clicking down to the end of normal.

And she's in some of the pictures, too. Lauren. Tall. Athletic. Oh, and blond. Of course, she would have to be. They make a very attractive couple. And in more than half the pictures, she isn't looking at the camera; she's looking at him. Not the way I would look at Ben Parish, all squishy around the eyes. She looks at Evan fiercely, like, *This here? It's mine.*

I put the albums away. My paranoia is fading. *So he has soft hands, so what? Soft hands are a nice thing.* I build a roaring fire to heat up the room and push back the shadows that crowd in on me. *So his fingers smell like gunpowder after visiting her grave, so what? There are wild animals running around everywhere. And it wasn't the kind of moment where you go,* Yeah, I went to her grave. Had to shoot a rabid dog coming back, by the way. *Ever since he found you, he's taken care of you, kept you safe, been there for you.*

But no matter how much I lecture myself, I can't calm down. I'm missing something. Something important. I pace back and forth in front of the fireplace, shivering despite the roaring flames. It's like having an itch you can't scratch. But what could it be? I know in my gut I'm not going to find anything incriminating, even if I tear through every inch of the house.

But you haven't searched everywhere, Cassie. You haven't looked in the one place he wouldn't expect you to look.

I limp into the kitchen. Not much time now. Grab a heavy jacket from the hook by the door and a flashlight from the cupboard, tuck the Luger into my waistband, and step outside into the bitter cold. Clear sky, the yard bathed in starlight. I try not to think about the mothership a few hundred miles over my head as I shuffle toward the barn. I don't click on the light until I step inside.

The smell of old manure and mildewed hay. The scampering of rats' feet on the rotting boards over my head. I swing the light around, over the empty stalls and across the dirt floor, into the hayloft. I don't know exactly what I'm looking for, but I keep looking. In every creepy movie ever made, the barn is the prime nesting ground for the things you don't know you're looking for and always regret finding.

I find what I'm not looking for under a pile of ratty blankets heaped against the back wall. Something long and dark glinting in the circle of light. I don't touch it. I reveal it, tossing aside three blankets to reach its resting place.

It's my M16.

I know it's mine. I can see my initials in the stock: C.S., scratched there one afternoon while I hid in the little tent in the woods. *C.S.* for *Completely Stupid.*

I'd lost it on the median when the Silencer struck from the woods. Left it there in my panic. Decided I couldn't go back for it. Now here it is, in Evan Walker's barn. My bestie had found its way back to me.

Do you know how to tell who the enemy is in wartime, Cassie?

I back away from it. Back away from the message it sends. Back all the way to the door while I keep the light shining on its glossy black barrel.

Then I turn and run smack into his rock-hard chest.

55

"CASSIE?" HE SAYS, grabbing my arms to keep me from falling straight back onto my butt. "What are you doing out here?" He glances over my shoulder into the barn.

"I thought I heard a noise." Dumb! Now he might decide to investigate. But it's the first thing that pops into my head. Blurting out first thoughts is something I really should work on—if I live past the next five minutes. My heart is pounding so hard, I can feel my ears ringing.

"You thought you . . . ? Cassie, you shouldn't come out here at night."

I nod and force myself to look into his eyes. Evan Walker is a noticer. "I know, it was stupid. But you'd been gone a long time."

"I was stalking some deer." He's a big, Evan-shaped shadow

in front of me, a shadow with a high-powered rifle against the backdrop of a million suns.

I bet you were. "Let's go inside, okay? I'm freezing to death."

He doesn't move. He's looking into the barn.

"I checked it out," I say, trying to keep my voice steady. "Rats."

"Rats?"

"Yeah. Rats."

"You heard rats? In the barn? From inside the house?"

"No. How could I hear rats from there?" An exasperated roll of the eyes would be good right about now. Not the nervous laugh that escapes instead. "I came out on the porch for some fresh air."

"And you heard them from the porch?"

"They were very big rats." *Flirty smile!* I whip out what I hope passes for one of those, then I hook my arm through his and pull him toward the house. It's like trying to move a concrete pole. If he goes inside the barn and sees the exposed rifle, it's over. Why the hell didn't I cover up the rifle?

"Evan, it's nothing. I got spooked, that's all."

"Okay."

He shoves the barn door closed, and we head back to the farmhouse, his arm draped protectively over my shoulders. He lets the arm fall when we reach the door.

Now, Cassie. Quick side step to the right, Luger from your waistband, proper two-handed grip, knees slightly bent, squeeze, don't pull. Now.

We step inside the warm kitchen. The opportunity passes.

"So I take it you didn't bag any deer," I say casually.

"No." He leans the rifle against the wall, shrugs out of his coat. His cheeks are bright red from the cold.

"Maybe you shot at something else," I say. "Maybe that's what I heard."

He shakes his head. "I didn't shoot at anything." He blows on his hands. I follow him into the great room, where he bends in front of the fireplace to warm his hands. I'm standing behind the sofa a few feet away.

My second chance to take him down. Hitting him from this close would not be a challenge. Or it wouldn't be if his head resembled an empty can of creamed corn, the only kind of target I was used to.

I pull the gun from my waistband.

Finding my rifle in his barn didn't leave me with many options. It was like being under that car on the highway: hide or face. Doing nothing about it, pretending everything was fine between us, accomplished nothing. Shooting him in the back of the head would accomplish something—it would kill him—but after the Crucifix Soldier, it had become one of my priorities never to kill another innocent person. Better to show my hand now while that hand holds a gun.

"There's something I should tell you," I say. My voice is shaking. "I lied about the rats."

"You found the rifle." Not a question.

He turns. With his back to the fire, his face is in shadow; I can't read his expression, but his tone is casual. "I found it a couple of days ago off the highway—remembered you said you dropped one when you ran—then I saw those initials and I figured it had to be yours."

For a minute I don't say anything. His explanation makes perfect sense. I just didn't expect him to jump right into it like that.

"Why didn't you tell me?" I finally ask.

He shrugs. "I was going to. Guess I forgot. What are you doing with that gun, Cassie?"

Oh, I was thinking about blowing your head off, that's all. Thought you might be a Silencer or maybe a traitor to your species or something along those lines. Ha-ha!

I follow his eyes to the weapon in my hand, and suddenly I feel like bursting into tears.

"We have to trust each other," I whisper. "Don't we?"

"Yes," he says, moving toward me now. "We do."

"But how . . . how do you make yourself trust someone?" I say. He's beside me now. He doesn't reach for the gun. He's reaching for me with his eyes. And I want him to catch me before I fall too far away from the Evan-I-thought-I-knew, who saved me to save himself from falling. He's all I've got now. He's my itty-bitty bush growing out of the cliff that I cling to. *Help me, Evan. Don't let me fall. Don't let me lose the part of me that makes me human.*

"You can't make yourself believe anything," he answers softly. "But you can let yourself believe. You can allow yourself to trust."

I nod, looking up into his eyes. So chocolaty warm. So melty and sad. Damn it, why does he have to be so damn beautiful? And why do I have to be so damn aware of it? And how is my trusting him any different from Sammy's taking the soldier's hand before climbing onto that bus? The weird thing is his eyes remind me of Sammy's—filled with a longing to know if everything will be all right. The Others answered that question with an unequivocal no. So what does that make me if I give Evan the same answer? "I want to. Really, really bad."

I don't know how it happened, but my gun is now in his hand. He takes my hand and leads me around to the sofa. Sets the gun on top of *Love's Desperate Desire*, sits close to me, but not too close, and rests his elbows on his knees. He rubs his large hands together as if they're still cold. They're not; I had just held one.

"I don't want to leave here," he confesses. "For a lot of reasons that seemed very good until I found you." He claps his hands together softly in frustration; it isn't coming out right. "I know you didn't ask to be my reason for going on with . . . with everything. But from the moment I found you . . ." He turns and grabs my hands in his, and suddenly I'm a little scared. His grip is hard, his eyes swim with tears. It's like I'm holding him back from tumbling over the edge of a cliff.

"I had it all wrong," he says. "Before I found you, I thought the only way to hold on was to find something to live for. It isn't. To hold on, you have to find something you're willing to die for."

VIII

THE SPIRIT OF VENGEANCE

56

THE WORLD IS SCREAMING.

Just the icy wind racing through the open hatch of the Black Hawk, but that's what it sounds like. At the height of the plague, when people were dying by the hundreds every day, the panicky residents of Tent City would sometimes toss an unconscious person into the fire by mistake, and you didn't just hear their screams as they were burned alive, you felt them like a punch to your heart.

Some things you can never leave behind. They don't belong to the past. They belong to you.

The world is screaming. The world is being burned alive.

Through the chopper windows, you can see the fires dotting the dark landscape, amber blotches against the inky backdrop, multiplying as you near the outskirts of the city. These aren't funeral pyres. Lightning from summer storms started them, and the autumn winds carried the smoldering embers to new feeding grounds, because there was so much to eat, the pantry was stuffed. The world will burn for years. It will burn until I'm my father's age—if I live that long.

We're skimming ten feet above treetop level, the rotors muffled by some kind of stealth technology, approaching downtown Dayton from the north. A light snow is falling; it shimmers around the fires below like golden halos, shedding light, illuminating nothing.

I turn from the window and see Ringer across the aisle, staring at me. She holds up two fingers. I nod. Two minutes to the drop. I

285

pull the headband down to position the lens of the eyepiece over my left eye and adjust the strap.

Ringer is pointing at Teacup, who's in the chair next to me. Her eyepiece keeps slipping. I tighten the strap; she gives me a thumbs-up, and something sour rises in my throat. Seven years old. Dear Jesus. I lean over and shout in her ear, "You stay right next to me, understand?"

Teacup smiles, shakes her head, points at Ringer. *I'm staying with her!* I laugh. Teacup's no dummy.

Over the river now, the Black Hawk skimming only a few feet above the water. Ringer is checking her weapon for the thousandth time. Beside her, Flintstone is tapping his foot nervously, staring forward, looking at nothing.

There's Dumbo inventorying his med kit, and Oompa bending his head in an attempt to keep us from seeing him stuff one last candy bar into his mouth.

Finally, Poundcake with his head down, hands folded in his lap. Reznik named him Poundcake because he said he was soft and sweet. He doesn't strike me as either, especially on the firing range. Ringer's a better marksman overall, but I've seen Poundcake take out six targets in six seconds.

Yeah, Zombie. Targets. Plywood cutouts of human beings. When it comes down to the real deal, how will his aim be then? Or any of ours?

Unbelievable. We're the vanguard. Seven kids who just six months ago were, well, just kids; we're the counterpunch to attacks that left seven billion dead.

There's Ringer, staring at me again. As the chopper begins to descend, she unbuckles her harness and steps across the aisle.

Places her hands on my shoulders and shouts in my face, "Remember the circle! We're not going to die!"

We dive into the drop zone fast and steep. The chopper doesn't land; it hovers a few inches above the frozen turf while the squad hops out. From the open hatchway, I look over and see Teacup struggling with her harness. Then she's loose and jumps out ahead of me. I'm the last to go. In the cockpit, the pilot looks over his shoulder, gives me a thumbs-up. I return the signal.

The Black Hawk rockets into the night sky, turning hard north, its black hull blending quickly into the dark clouds until they swallow it, and it's gone.

The air in the little park by the river has been blasted clear of snow by the rotors. After the chopper leaves, the snow returns, spinning angrily around us. The sudden quiet that follows the screaming wind is deafening. Straight ahead a huge human shadow looms: the statue of a Korean War veteran. To the statue's left is the bridge. Across the bridge and ten blocks southwest is the old courthouse where several infesteds have amassed a small arsenal of automatic weapons and grenade launchers, as well as FIM-92 Stinger missiles, according to the Wonderland profile of one infested captured in Operation Li'l Bo Peep. It's the Stingers that brought us here. Our air capability has been devastated by the attacks; it's imperative we protect the few resources we have left.

Our mission is twofold: Destroy or capture all enemy ordnance and terminate all infested personnel.

Terminate with extreme prejudice.

Ringer's on the point; she has the best eyes. We follow her past the stern-faced statue onto the bridge; Flint, Dumbo, Oompa, Poundcake, and Teacup, with me covering our rear. Weaving

287

through the stalled cars that seem to pop through a white curtain, covered in three seasons' worth of debris. Some have had their windows smashed, decorated with graffiti, looted for any valuables, but what's valuable anymore? Teacup scurrying along in front of me on baby feet—she's valuable. There's my big takeaway from the Arrival. By killing us, they showed us the idiocy of stuff. The guy who owned this BMW? He's in the same place as the woman who owned that Kia.

We pull up just shy of Patterson Boulevard, at the southern end of the bridge. Hunker down beside the smashed front bumper of an SUV and survey the road ahead. The snow cuts down our visibility to about half a block. This might take a while. I look at my watch. Four hours till pickup back at the park.

A tanker truck has stalled out in the middle of the intersection twenty yards away, blocking our view of the left-hand side of the street. I can't see it, but I know from the mission briefing there's a four-story building on that side, a prime sentry point if they wanted to keep an eye on the bridge. I motion for Ringer to keep to the right as we leave the bridge, putting the truck between us and the building.

She pulls up sharply at the truck's front bumper and drops to the ground. The squad follows her lead, and I belly-scoot forward to join her.

"What do you see?" I whisper.

"Three of them, two o'clock."

I squint through my eyepiece toward the building on the other side of the street. Through the cottony fuzz of the snow, I see three green blobs of light bobbing along the sidewalk, growing larger as they approach the intersection. My first thought is, *Holy crap, these lenses actually work.* My second thought: *Holy crap, Teds, and they're coming straight at us.*

"Patrol?" I ask Ringer.

She shrugs. "Probably marked the chopper and they're coming to check it out." She's lying on her belly, holding them in her sights, waiting for the order to fire. The green blobs grow larger; they've reached the opposite corner. I can barely make out their bodies beneath the green beacons on top of their shoulders. It's a weird, jarring effect, as if their heads are engulfed in a spinning, iridescent green fire.

Not yet. If they start to cross, give the order.

Beside me, Ringer takes a deep breath, holds it, waits for my order patiently, like she could wait for a thousand years. Snow settles on her shoulders, clings to her dark hair. The tip of her nose is bright red. The moment drags out. What if there's more than three? If we announce our presence, it could bring a hundred of them down on us from a dozen different hiding places. Engage or wait? I chew on my bottom lip, working through the options.

"I've got them," she says, misreading my hesitation.

Across the street, the green blobs of light are stationary, clustered together as if locked in conversation. I can't tell if they're even facing this way, but I'm sure they don't know we're here. If they did, they'd rush us, open fire, take cover, do something. We have the element of surprise. And we have Ringer. Even if she misses with the first shot, the follow-ups won't. It's an easy call, really.

So what's stopping me from making it?

Ringer must be wondering the same thing, because she glances over at me and whispers, "Zombie? What's the call?"

There's my orders: *Terminate all infested personnel.* There's my gut instinct: *Don't rush. Don't force the issue. Let it play out.* And there's me, squeezed in the middle.

A heartbeat before our ears register the high-powered rifle's report, the pavement two feet in front of us disintegrates in a spray of dirty snow and pulverized concrete. That resolves my dilemma fast. The words fly out as if snatched from my lungs by the icy wind: "Take them."

Ringer's bullet smashes into one of the bobbing green lights, and the light winks out. One light takes off to our right. Ringer swings the barrel toward my face. I duck as she fires again, and the second light winks out. The third seems to shrink as he tears up the street, heading back the way he came.

I jump to my feet. Can't let him get away to sound the alarm. Ringer grabs my wrist and yanks hard to bring me back down.

"Damn it, Ringer, what are you do—"

"It's a trap." She points at the six-inch scar in the concrete. "Didn't you hear it? It didn't come from them. It came from over there." She jerks her head toward the building on the opposite side of the street. "From our left. And judging by the angle, from high up, maybe the roof."

I shake my head. A fourth infested on the roof? How did he know we were here—and why didn't he warn the others? We're hidden behind the truck, which means he must have spotted us on the bridge—spotted us and held his fire until we were blocked from view and there was no way he could hit us. It didn't make sense.

And Ringer goes, like she's read my mind, "I guess this is what they meant by 'the fog of war.'"

I nod. Things are getting way too complicated way too fast.

"How'd he see us cross?" I ask.

She shakes her head. "Night vision, has to be."

"Then we're screwed." Pinned down. Beside several thousands of gallons of gasoline. "He'll take out the truck."

Ringer shrugs. "Not with a bullet, he won't. That only works in the movies, Zombie." She looks at me. Waiting for my call.

Along with the rest of the squad. I glance behind me. Their eyes look back at me, big and bug-eyed in the snowy dark. Teacup is either freezing to death or shaking with complete terror. Flint is scowling, and the only one to speak up and let me know what the rest are thinking: "Trapped. We abort now, right?"

Tempting, but suicidal. If the sniper on the roof doesn't take us down on the retreat, the reinforcements that must be coming will.

Retreating is not an option. Advancing is not an option. Staying put is not an option. There are no options.

Run = die. Stay = die.

"Speaking of night vision," Ringer growls, "they might have thought of that before dropping us on a night mission. We're totally blind out here."

I stare at her. *Totally blind. Bless you, Ringer.* I order the squad to close ranks around me and whisper, "Next block, right-hand side, attached to the back side of the office building, there's a parking garage." Or at least there should be, according to the map. "Get up to the third floor. Buddy system: Flint with Ringer, Poundcake with Oompa, Dumbo with Teacup."

"What about you?" Ringer asks. "Where's your buddy?"

"I don't need a buddy," I answer. "I'm a freaking zombie."

Here comes the smile. Wait for it.

57

I POINT OUT the embankment leading down to the water's edge. "All the way down to that walking trail," I say to Ringer. "And don't wait for me." She shakes her head, frowning. I lean in, keeping my expression as serious as I can. "I thought I had you with the zombie remark. One of these days, I'm going to get a smile out of you, Private."

Very much not smiling. "I don't think so, sir."

"You have something against smiling?"

"It was the first thing to go." Then the snow and the dark swallow her. The rest of the squad follows. I can hear Teacup whimpering beneath her breath as Dumbo leads her off, going, "Run hard when it goes, Cup, okay?"

I squat beside the truck's fuel tank and grab hold of the metal cap, praying one of those counterintuitive prayers that this bad boy is topped off—or better, half-full, since fumes will give us the biggest bang for the buck. I don't dare ignite the cargo, but the few gallons of diesel contained beneath it should set it off. I hope.

The cap is frozen. I beat on it with the butt of my rifle, wrap both hands around it, and give it everything I've got. It pops loose with a very pungent, very satisfying hiss. I'll have ten seconds. Should I count? Naw, screw it. I pull the pin on the grenade, drop it in the hole, and take off down the hill. The snow whips fitfully in my wake. My toe catches on something and I tumble the rest of the way, landing on my back at the bottom, hitting my head on the asphalt of the paved walking trail. I see snow spinning around my head and I can smell the river, and then I hear a soft *wuh-wuumph* and the tanker jumps about two feet into the air, followed by a gorgeous blossoming fireball that reflects off the falling snow, a mini universe of tiny suns shimmering, and now I'm up and chugging up the hill, my team nowhere in sight, and I can feel the heat against my left cheek as I come even with the truck, which is still in one piece, the tank intact. Dropping the grenade inside the fuel tank didn't ignite the cargo. Do I throw another? Do I keep running? Blinded by the explosion, the sniper would rip off his night vision goggles. He won't be blind for long.

I'm through the intersection and onto the curb when the gasoline ignites. The blast throws me forward, over the body of the first Ted dropped by Ringer, right into the glass doors of the office building. I hear something crack and hope it's the doors and not some important part of me. Huge jagged shards of metal rain down, pieces of the tank torn apart by the blast hurled a hundred yards in every direction at bullet speeds. I hear someone screaming as I fold my arms over my head and curl myself into the tiniest ball possible. The heat is incredible. It's like I've been swallowed by the sun.

The glass behind me shatters—from a high-caliber bullet, not the explosion. *Half a block from the garage—go, Zombie.* And I'm going hard until I come across Oompa crumpled on the sidewalk, Poundcake kneeling beside him, tugging on his shoulder, his face twisted in a soundless cry. It was Oompa I heard screaming after the tanker blew, and it takes me only a half second to see why: A piece of metal the size of a Frisbee juts out of his lower back.

I push Poundcake toward the garage—"Go!"—and heave Oompa's round little body over my shoulder. I hear the report of the rifle this time, two beats after the shooter across the street fires, and a chunk of concrete breaks free of the wall behind me.

The first level of the garage is separated from the sidewalk by a waist-high concrete wall. I ease Oompa over the wall, then hop over and duck down. *Ka-thunk:* A fist-size chunk of the wall blows back toward me. Kneeling beside Oompa, I look up to see Poundcake hoofing it toward the stairwell. Now, as long as there isn't another sniper's nest in this building, and as long as the infested who got away hasn't taken refuge here, too . . .

A quick check of Oompa's injury isn't encouraging. The sooner I can get him upstairs to Dumbo, the better.

"Private Oompa," I breathe in his ear. "You do not have permission to die, understood?"

He nods, sucking in the freezing air, blowing it out again, warm from the center of his body. But he's as white as the snow billowing in the golden light. I throw him back onto my shoulder and trot to the stairs, keeping as low as I can without losing my balance.

I take the stairs two at a time till I reach the third level, where I find the unit crouched behind the first line of cars, several feet back from the wall that faces the sniper's building. Dumbo is kneeling beside Teacup, working on her leg. Her fatigues are ripped, and I can see an ugly red gash where a bullet tore across her calf. Dumbo slaps a dressing over the wound, hands her off to Ringer, then rushes over to Oompa. Flintstone is shaking his head at me.

"Told you we should abort," Flint says. His eyes glitter with malice. "Now look."

I ignore him. Turn to Dumbo. "Well?"

"It's not good, Sarge."

"Then make it good." I look over at Teacup, who's buried her head into Ringer's chest, whimpering softly.

"It's superficial," Ringer tells me. "She can move."

294

I nod. Oompa down. Teacup shot. Flint ready to mutiny. A sniper across the street and a hundred or so of his best friends on their way to the party. I've got to come up with something brilliant and come up with it quickly. "He knows where we are, which means we can't camp here long. See if you can take him."

She nods, but she can't peel Teacup off her. I hold out my hands wet with Oompa's blood: *Give her to me.* Delivered, Teacup squirms against my shirt. She doesn't want me. I jerk my head toward the street and turn to Poundcake, "Cake, go with Ringer. Take the SOB out."

Ringer and Poundcake duck between two cars and disappear. I stroke Teacup's bare head—somewhere along the way she lost her cap—and watch Dumbo gingerly pull on the fragment in Oompa's back. Oompa howls in agony, his fingers clawing at the ground. Unsure, Dumbo looks up at me. I nod. It's gotta come out. "Quick, Dumbo. Slow makes it worse." So he yanks.

Oompa folds in on himself, and the echoes of his screams rocket around the garage. Dumbo tosses the jagged piece of metal to one side and shines his light on the gaping wound.

Grimacing, he rolls Oompa onto his back. His shirtfront is soaked. Dumbo rips the shirt open, exposing the exit wound: The shrapnel had entered through his back and slammed through to the other side.

Flint turns away, crawls a couple feet, and his back arches as he vomits. Teacup gets very still watching all this. She's going into shock. Teacup, the one who screamed the loudest during mock charges in the yard. Teacup, the bloodthirstiest, the one who sang the loudest in P&D. I'm losing her.

And I'm losing Oompa. As Dumbo presses wadding against the wound in Oompa's gut, trying to stem the flow, his eyes seek out mine.

"What are your orders, Private?" I ask him.

"I—I am not to—to . . ."

Dumbo tosses the blood-soaked dressing away and presses a fresh patch against Oompa's stomach. Looking into my face. Doesn't have to say anything. Not to me. Not to Oompa.

I ease Teacup from my lap and kneel beside Oompa. His breath smells like blood and chocolate.

"It's because I'm fat," he chokes out. He starts to cry.

"Stow that shit," I tell him sternly.

He whispers something. I bring my ear close to his mouth. "My name is Kenny." Like it's a terrible secret he's been afraid to share.

His eyes roll toward the ceiling. Then he's gone.

58

TEACUP'S LOST IT. Hugging her legs, forehead pressed against her upraised knees. I call over to Flint to keep an eye on her. I'm worried about Ringer and Poundcake. Flint looks like he wants to kill me with his bare hands.

"You're the one who gave the order," he snarls. "You watch her."

Dumbo is cleaning his hands of Oompa's—no, Kenny's—blood. "I got it, Sarge," he says calmly, but his hands are shaking.

"Sarge," Flint spits out. "That's right. What now, Sarge?"

I ignore him and scramble toward the wall, where I find Poundcake squatting beside Ringer. She's on her knees, peeking over the edge of the wall toward the building across the street. I lower myself beside her, avoiding Poundcake's questioning look.

"Oompa's not screaming anymore," Ringer says without taking her eyes off the building.

"His name was Kenny," I say. Ringer nods; she gets it, but it takes Poundcake a minute or two more. He scoots away, putting distance between us, and presses both hands against the concrete, takes a deep, shuddering breath.

"You had to, Zombie," Ringer says. "If you hadn't, we might all be Kenny."

That sounds really good. It sounded good when I said it to myself. Looking up at her profile, I wonder what Vosch was thinking, pinning the stripes on my collar. The commander promoted the wrong squad member.

"Well?" I ask her.

She nods across the street. "Pop goes the weasel."

I slowly rise up. In the light of the dying fire, I can see the building: a facade of broken windows, peeling white paint, and the roof one story higher than us. A vague shadow that might be a water tower up there, but that's all I see.

"Where?" I whisper.

"He just ducked down again. Been doing that. Up, down, up, down, like a jack-in-the-box."

"Just one?"

"Only one I've seen."

"Does he light up?"

Ringer shakes her head. "Negative, Zombie. He doesn't read infested."

I chew on my bottom lip. "Poundcake see him, too?"

She nods. "No green." Watching me with those dark eyes like knives cutting deep.

"Maybe he's not the shooter . . . ," I try.

297

"Saw his weapon," she says. "Sniper rifle."

So why doesn't he glow green? The ones on the street lit up, and they were farther away than he is. Then I think it doesn't matter if he glows green or purple or nothing at all: He's trying to kill us, and we can't move until he's neutralized. And we have to move before the one who got away comes back with reinforcements.

"Aren't they smart?" Ringer mutters, like she's read my mind. "Put on a human face so no human face can be trusted. The only answer: Kill everyone or risk being killed by anyone."

"He thinks we're one of them?"

"Or decided it doesn't matter. Only way to be safe."

"But he fired on us—not on the three right below him. Why would he ignore the easy shots to take the impossible one?"

Like me, she doesn't have an answer to that question. Unlike me, it's not high on her list of problems to be resolved. "Only way to be safe," she repeats pointedly. I look over at Poundcake, who's looking back at me. Waiting for my decision, but there really isn't a decision to make.

"Can you take him from here?" I ask Ringer.

She shakes her head. "Too far away. I'd just give away our position."

I scoot over to Poundcake. "Stay here. In ten minutes, open up on him to cover our crossing." Staring up at me all doe-eyed and trusting. "You know, Private, it's customary to acknowledge an order from your commanding officer." Poundcake nods. I try again: "With a 'yes, sir.'" He nods again. "Like, out loud. With words." Another nod.

Okay, at least I tried.

When Ringer and I join the others, Oompa's body is gone.

They stashed him in one of the cars. Flint's idea. Very similar to his idea for the rest of us.

"We've got good cover in here. I say we hunker down in the cars until pickup."

"Only one person's vote counts in this unit, Flint," I tell him.

"Yeah, and how's that working out for us?" he says, thrusting his chin toward me, mouth curled into a sneer. "Oh, I know. Let's ask Oompa!"

"Flintstone," Ringer says. "At ease. Zombie's right."

"Until you two walk into an ambush, and then I guess he's wrong."

"At which point you're the C.O., and you can make the call," I snap. "Dumbo, you've got Teacup duty." If we can pry her off Ringer. She's pasted herself back onto Ringer's leg. "If we're not back in thirty minutes, we're not coming back."

And then Ringer says, because she's Ringer, "We're coming back."

59

THE TANKER'S BURNED down to its tires. Crouching in the pedestrian entrance to the garage, I point at the building across the street glowing orange in the firelight.

"That's our entry point. Third window from the left-hand corner, completely busted out, see it?"

Ringer nods absently. Something's on her mind. She keeps fiddling with the eyepiece, pulling it away from her eye, pushing it back again. The certainty she showed in front of the squad is gone.

"The impossible shot . . . ," she whispers. Then she turns to me. "How do you know when you're going Dorothy?"

I shake my head. Where's this coming from? "You're not going Dorothy," I tell her, and punctuate it with a pat on the arm.

"How can you be sure?" Eyes darting back and forth, restless, looking for somewhere to light. The way Tank's eyes danced before he popped. "Crazy people—they never think they're crazy. Their craziness makes perfect sense to them."

There's a desperate, very un-Ringerlike look in her eyes.

"You're not crazy. Trust me."

Wrong thing to say.

"Why should I?" she shoots back. It's the first time I've heard any emotion out of her. "Why should I trust you, and why should you trust me? How do you know I'm not one of them, Zombie?"

Finally, an easy question. "Because we've been screened. And we don't light up in each other's eyepieces."

She looks at me for a very long moment, then she murmurs, "God, I wish you played chess."

Our ten minutes are up. Above us, Poundcake opens up on the rooftop across the street; the sniper immediately returns fire; and we go. We're barely off the curb when the asphalt explodes in front of us. We split up, Ringer zipping off to the right, me to the left, and I hear the whine of the bullet, a high-pitched sandpapery sound, about a month before it tears open the sleeve of my jacket. The instinct burned into me from months of drilling to return fire is very hard to resist. I leap onto the curb and in two strides I'm pressed hard against the comforting cold concrete of the building. That's when I see Ringer slip on a patch of ice and fall face-first toward the curb. She waves me back. "No!" A round bites off a piece of the curbing that rakes across her neck. Screw her *no*. I bound over to her, grab her arm, and sling her toward the building. Another round whizzes past my head as I backpedal to safety.

She's bleeding. The wound shimmers black in the firelight. She waves me on, *Go, go*. We trot along the side of the building to the broken window and dive inside.

Took less than a minute to cross. Felt like two hours.

We're inside what used to be an upscale boutique. Looted several times over, full of empty racks and broken hangers, creepy headless mannequins and posters of overly serious fashion models on the walls. A sign on the service counter reads, GOING OUT OF BUSINESS SALE.

Ringer's scrunched into a corner of the room with good angles on the windows and the door coming in from the lobby. A hand on her neck, and that hand is gloved in blood. I have to look. She doesn't want me to look. I'm like, "Don't be stupid, I have to look." So she lets me look. It's superficial, between a cut and a gouge. I find a scarf lying on a display table and she wads it up and presses it against her neck. Nods at my torn sleeve.

"Are you hit?"

I shake my head and ease down on the floor beside her. We're both pulling hard for air. My head swims with adrenaline. "Not to be judgmental, but as a sniper, this guy sucks."

"Three shots, three misses. Makes you wish this was baseball."

"A lot more than three," I correct her. Multiple tries at the targets, and the only true hit a superficial wound to Teacup's leg.

"Amateur."

"He probably is."

"Probably." She bites off the word.

301

"He didn't light up and he's no pro. A loner defending his turf, maybe hiding from the same guys we came after. Scared shitless." I don't add *like us*. I'm only sure about one of us.

Outside, Poundcake continues to occupy the sniper. *Pop-pop-pop*, a heavy quiet, then *pop-pop-pop*. The sniper responds each time.

"Then this should be easy," Ringer says, her mouth set in a grim line.

I'm a little taken aback. "He didn't light up, Ringer. We don't have authorization to—"

"I do." Pulling her rifle into her lap. "Right here."

"Um. I thought our mission was to save humanity."

She looks at me out of the side of her uncovered eye. "Chess, Zombie: defending yourself from the move that hasn't happened yet. Does it matter that he doesn't light up through our eyepieces? That he missed us when he could have taken us down? If two possibilities are equally probable but mutually exclusive, which one matters the most? Which one do you bet your life on?"

I'm nodding at her, but not following her at all. "You're saying he still could be infested," I guess.

"I'm saying the safe bet is to proceed as if he is."

She pulls her combat knife from its sheath. I flinch, remembering her Dorothy remark. Why did Ringer pull out her knife?

"What matters," she says thoughtfully. There's a terrible stillness to her now, a thunderhead about to crack, a steaming volcano about to blow. "What matters, Zombie? I was always pretty good at figuring that out. Got a lot better at it after the attacks. What really matters? My mom died first. That was bad—but what really mattered was I still had my dad, my brother, and baby sister. Then I lost them, and what mattered was I still had *me*. And there wasn't much that mattered when it came to me. Food. Water. Shelter. What else do you need? What else matters?"

This is bad, halfway down the road to being really bad. I have no idea where she's going with this, but if Ringer goes Dorothy on me now, I'm screwed. Maybe the rest of my crew with me. I need to bring her back into the present. Best way is by touch, but I'm afraid if I touch her she'll gut me with that ten-inch blade.

"Does it matter, Zombie?" She cranes her neck to look up at me, turning the knife slowly in her hands. "That he shot at us and not the three Teds right in front of him? Or that when he shot at us he missed every time?" Turning the knife slowly, the tip denting her finger. "Does it matter that they got everything up and running after the EMP attack? That they're operating right underneath the mothership, gathering up survivors, killing infesteds and burning their bodies by the hundreds, arming and training us and sending us out to kill the rest? Tell me that those things don't matter. Tell me the odds are insignificant that they aren't really *them*. Tell me what possibility I should bet my life on."

I'm nodding again, but this time I do follow her, and that path ends in a very dark place. I squat down beside her and look her dead in the eye. "I don't know what this guy's story is and I don't know about the EMP, but the commander told me why they're leaving us alone. They think we're no longer a threat to them."

She flips back her bangs and snaps, "How does the commander know what they think?"

"Wonderland. We were able to profile a—"

"Wonderland," she echoes. Nodding sharply. Eyes cutting from my face to the snowy street outside and back again. "Wonderland is an alien program."

"Right." Stay with her, but gently try to lead her back. "It is,

Ringer. Remember? After we took back the base, we found it hidden—"

"Unless we didn't. Zombie, *unless we didn't.*" She jabs the knife toward me. "It's a possibility, equally valid, and possibilities matter. Trust me, Zombie; I'm an expert on what matters. Up to now, I've been playing blind man's bluff. Time for some chess." She flips the knife around and shoves the handle toward me. "Cut it out of me."

I don't know what to say. I stare dumbly at the knife in her hand.

"The implants, Zombie." Poking me in the chest now. "We have to take them out. You do me and I'll do you."

I clear my throat. "Ringer, we can't cut them out." I scramble for a second for the best argument, but all I can come up with is, "If we can't make it back to the rendezvous point, how're they going to find us?"

"Damn it, Zombie, haven't you been listening to anything I've said? What if they aren't *us*? What if they're *them*? What if this whole thing has been a lie?"

I'm about to lose it. Okay, not about to. "Oh, for Christ's sake, Ringer! Do you know how cra—stupid that sounds? The enemy rescuing us, training us, giving us weapons? Come on, let's cut the crap; we've got a job to do. You may not be happy about it, but I am your C.O. . . ."

"All right." Very calm now. As cool as I'm hot. "I'll do it myself."

She whips the blade around to the back of her neck, bowing her head low. I yank the knife from her hand. Enough.

"Stand down, Private." I hurl her knife into the deep shadows across the room and get up. I'm shaking, every part of me, voice too. "You want to play the odds, that's cool. Stay here until I get back. Better yet, just waste me now. Maybe my alien masters have figured out a way to hide my infestation from you. And after you've done me, go back across the street and kill them all, put a bullet in Teacup's head. She could be the enemy, right? So blow her frigging head off! It's the only answer, right? Kill everyone or risk being killed by anyone."

Ringer doesn't move. Doesn't say anything, either, for a very long time. Snow whips through the broken window, the flakes a deep crimson color, reflecting the smoldering crumbs of the tanker.

"Are you sure you don't play chess?" she asks. She pulls the rifle back into her lap, runs her index finger along the trigger. "Turn your back on me, Zombie."

We're at the end of the dark path now, and it's a dead end. I'm out of anything that passes for a cogent argument, so I come back with the first thing that pops into my head.

"My name is Ben."

She doesn't miss a beat. "Sucky name. Zombie's better."

"What's your name?" Keeping at it.

"That's one of the things that doesn't matter. Hasn't for a long time, Zombie." Finger caressing the trigger slowly. Very slowly. It's hypnotic, dizzying.

"How about this?" Searching for a way out. "I cut out the tracker, and you promise not to waste me." This way I keep her on my side, because I'd rather take on a dozen snipers than one Dorothied Ringer. In my mind's eye, I can see my head shattering like one of those plywood people on the firing range.

She cocks her head, and the side of her mouth twitches in an almost-but-not-quite smile. "Check."

I give her back an honest-to-goodness smile, the old Ben Parish smile, the one that got me practically everything I wanted. Well, not practically; I'm being modest.

"Is that *check* as in *yes*, or are you giving me a chess lesson?"

She sets her gun aside and turns her back to me. Bows her head. Pulls her silky black hair away from her neck.

"Both."

Pop-pop-pop goes Poundcake's gun. And the sniper answers. Their jam plays in the background as I kneel behind Ringer with my knife. Part of me more than willing to humor her if it keeps me—and the rest of the unit—alive. The other part screaming silently, *Aren't you, like, giving a mouse a cookie? What will she demand next—a physical inspection of my cerebral cortex?*

"Relax, Zombie," she says, quiet and calm, the old Ringer again. "If the trackers aren't ours, it's probably not a good idea to have them inside us. If they are ours, Dr. Pam can always implant us again when we get back. Agreed?"

"Checkmate."

"Check and mate," she corrects me.

Her neck is long and graceful and very cold beneath my fingers as I explore the area beneath the scar for the lump. My hand shakes. *Just humor her. It probably means a court-martial and the rest of your life peeling potatoes, but at least you'll be alive.*

"Be gentle," she whispers.

I take a deep breath and draw the tip of the blade along the tiny scar. Her blood wells up bright red, shockingly red against her pearly skin. She doesn't even flinch, but I have to ask: "Am I hurting you?"

"No, I like it a lot."

I tease the implant from her neck with the tip of the blade. She grunts softly. The pellet clings to the metal, sealed within a droplet of blood.

"So," she says, turning around. The almost-smile is almost there. "How was it for you?"

I don't answer. I can't. I've lost the ability to talk. The knife falls from my hand. I'm two feet away looking right at her, but her face is gone. I can't see it through my eyepiece.

Ringer's entire head is lit up in a blinding green fire.

60

MY FIRST REACTION is to yank off the hardware, but I don't. I'm paralyzed with shock. A shudder of revulsion next. Then panic. Followed closely by confusion. Ringer's head has lit up like a Christmas tree, bright enough to be seen a mile away. The green fire sparks and swirls, so intense it burns an afterimage in my left eye.

"What is it?" she demands. "What happened?"

"You lit up. As soon as I pulled out the tracker."

We stare at each other for a long couple of minutes. Then she says, "Unclean glows green."

I'm already on my feet, M16 in my hands, backing toward the door. And outside, beneath the sound-deadening snowfall, Pound-cake and the sniper, trading barbs. Unclean glows green. Ringer doesn't make a move for the rifle lying next to her. Through my right eye, she's normal. Through the left, she burns like a Roman candle.

"Think this through, Zombie," she says. "Think this through." Holding up her empty hands, scratched and scuffed from her fall, one caked in dried blood. "I lit up after you pulled out the implant. The eyepieces don't pick up infestations. They react when there's no implant."

"Excuse me, Ringer, but that makes no freaking sense. They lit up on those three infesteds. Why would the eyepieces light up if they weren't?"

"You know why. You just can't admit it to yourself. They lit up because those people weren't infested. They're just like us, the only difference being they don't have implants."

She stands up. God, she looks so small, like a kid . . . But she is a kid, right? Through one eye normal. Through the other a green fireball. Which is she? *What* is she?

"Take us in." She steps toward me. I bring up the gun. She stops. "Tag and bag us. Train us to kill." Another step. I swing the muzzle toward her. Not at her. But toward her: *Stay away.* "Anyone who isn't tagged will glow green, and when they defend themselves or challenge us, shoot at us like that sniper up there— well, that just proves they're the enemy, doesn't it?" Another step. Now I'm aiming right at her heart.

"Don't," I beg her. "Please, Ringer." One face pure. One face in fire.

"Until we've killed everyone who isn't tagged." Another step. Right in front of me now. The end of the gun pressing lightly against her chest. "It's the 5th Wave, Ben."

I'm shaking my head. "No fifth wave. No fifth wave! The commander said—"

"The commander lied."

She reaches up with bloody hands and pulls the rifle from my grip. I feel myself falling into a completely different kind of wonderland, where up is down and true is false and the enemy has two faces, my face and his, the one who saved me from drowning, who took my heart and made it a battlefield.

She gathers her hands into mine and pronounces me dead: "Ben, *we're* the 5th Wave."

61

WE ARE HUMANITY.

It's a lie. Wonderland. Camp Haven. The war itself.

How easy it was. How incredibly easy, even after all that we'd been through. Or maybe it was easy *because* of all we'd been through.

They gathered us in. They emptied us out. They filled us up with hate and cunning and the spirit of vengeance.

So they could send us out again.

To kill what's left of the rest of us.

Check and mate.

I'm going to be sick. Ringer hangs on to my shoulder while I heave all over a poster that fell off the wall: FALL INTO FASHION!

There's Chris, behind the two-way glass. And there's the button marked EXECUTE. And there's my finger, slamming down. How easy it was to make me kill another human being.

When I'm done, I rock back on my heels. I feel Ringer's cool fingers rubbing my neck. Hear her voice telling me it's going to be okay. I yank off the eyepiece, killing the green fire and giving Ringer back her face. She's Ringer and I'm me, only I'm not sure what *me* means anymore. I'm not what I thought I was. The world is not what I thought it was. Maybe that's the point:

It's their world now, and we're the aliens.

"We can't go back," I choke out. And there's her deep-cutting eyes and her cool fingers massaging my neck.

"No, we can't. But we can go forward." She picks up my rifle and pushes it against my chest. "And we can start with that son of a bitch upstairs."

Not before taking out my implant. It hurts more than I expect, less than I deserve.

"Don't beat yourself up," Ringer tells me while she digs it out. "They fooled all of us."

"And the ones they couldn't, they called Dorothys and killed."

"Not the only ones," she says bitterly. And then it hits me like a punch in the heart: the P&D hangar. The twin stacks spewing black and gray smoke. The trucks loaded with bodies—hundreds of bodies every day. Thousands every week. And the buses pulling in all night, every night, filled with refugees, filled with the walking dead.

"Camp Haven isn't a military base," I whisper as blood trickles down my neck.

She shakes her head. "Or a refugee camp."

I nod. Swallow back the bile rising in my throat. I can tell she's waiting for me to say it out loud. Sometimes you have to speak the truth aloud or it doesn't seem real. "It's a death camp."

There's an old saying about the truth setting you free. Don't buy it. Sometimes the truth slams the cell door shut and throws a thousand bolts.

"Are you ready?" Ringer asks. She seems anxious to get it over with.

"We don't kill him," I say. Ringer gives me a look like *WTF?* But I'm thinking of Chris strapped to a chair behind a two-way mirror. Thinking of heaving bodies onto the conveyor belt that carried its human cargo into the hot, hungry mouth of the incinerator. I've been their tool long enough. "Neutralize and disarm, that's the order. Understood?"

She hesitates, then nods. I can't read her expression—not unusual. Is she playing chess again? We can still hear Poundcake firing from across the street. He has to be getting low on ammo. It's time.

Stepping into the lobby is a dive into total darkness. We advance shoulder-to-shoulder, trailing our fingers along the walls to keep our bearings in the dark, trying every door, looking for the one to the stairs. The only sounds are our breath in the stale, cold air and the sloshing of our boots through an inch of sour-smelling, freezing cold water; a pipe must have burst. I push open a door at the end of the hall and feel a rush of fresh air. Stairwell.

We pause on the fourth-floor landing, at the bottom of the narrow steps that lead up to the roof. The door is cracked open; we can hear the sharp report of the sniper's rifle, but can't see him. Hand signals are useless in the dark, so I pull Ringer close and press my lips against her ear.

"Sounds like he's straight ahead." She nods. Her hair tickles my nose. "We go in hard."

She's the better shooter; Ringer will go first. I'll take the second shot if she misses or goes down. We've drilled this a hundred times, but we always practiced eliminating the target, not disabling it. And the target never fired back at us. She steps up to the door. I'm standing right behind her, hand on her shoulder.

The wind whistles through the crack like the mewling of a dying animal. Ringer waits for my signal with her head bowed, breathing evenly and deeply, and I wonder if she's praying and, if she is, if she prays to the same God I do. Somehow I don't think so. I pat her once on the shoulder and she kicks open the door and it's like she's been shot out of a cannon, disappearing in the swirl of snow before I'm two steps onto the roof, and I hear the sharp *pop-pop-pop* of her weapon before I almost trip over her kneeling in the wet, white carpet of snow. Ten feet in front of her, the sniper lies on his side, clutching his leg with one hand while he reaches for his rifle with the other. It must have flown from his grip when she popped him. Ringer fires again, this time at the reaching hand. It's three inches across, and she scores a direct hit. In the murky dark. Through heavy snow. He pulls his hand back to his chest with a startled scream. I tap Ringer on the top of her head and signal her to pull up.

"Lie still!" I yell at him. "Don't move!"

He sits up, pressing his shattered hand against his chest, facing the street, hunched over, and we can't see what his other hand is doing, but I see a flash of silver and hear him growl, "Maggots," and something inside me goes cold. I know that voice.

It has screamed at me, mocked me, belittled me, threatened me, cursed me. It followed me from the minute I woke to the minute I went to bed. It's hissed, hollered, snarled, and spat at me, at all of us.

Reznik.

We both hear it. And it nails down our feet. It stops our breath. It freezes our thoughts.

And it buys him time.

Time that grinds down as he comes up, slowing as if the

universal clock set in motion by the big bang is running out of steam.

Pushing himself to his feet. That takes about seven or eight minutes.

Turning to face us. That takes at least ten.

Holding something in his good hand. Punching at it with his bloody one. That lasts a good twenty minutes.

And then Ringer comes alive. The round slams into his chest. Reznik falls to his knees. His mouth comes open. He pitches forward and lands facedown in front of us.

The clock resets. No one moves. No one says anything.

Snow. Wind. Like we're standing alone on the summit of an icy mountaintop. Ringer goes over to him, rolls him onto his back. Pulls the silver device from his hand. I'm looking down at that pasty, pockmarked, rat-eyed face, and somehow I'm surprised and not surprised.

"Spend months training us so he can kill us," I say.

Ringer shakes her head. She's looking at the display of the silver device. Its light shines on her face, playing up the contrast between her fair skin and jet-black hair. She looks beautiful in its light, not angelic-beautiful, more like avenging angel–beautiful.

"He wasn't going to kill us, Zombie. Until we surprised him and gave him no choice. And then not with the rifle." She holds up the device so I can see the display. "I think he was going to kill us with this."

A grid occupies the top half of the display. There's a cluster of green dots on the far left-hand corner. Another green dot closer to the middle.

"The squad," I say.

"And this lone dot here must be Poundcake."

"Which means if we hadn't cut out our implants—"

"He'd have known exactly where we were," Ringer says. "He'd be waiting for us, and we'd be screwed."

She points out the two highlighted numbers on the bottom of the screen. One of them is the number I was assigned when Dr. Pam tagged and bagged me. I'm guessing the other one is Ringer's. Beneath the numbers is a flashing green button.

"What happens if you press that button?" I ask.

"My guess is nothing." And she presses it.

I flinch, but her guess is right.

"It's a kill switch," she says. "Has to be. Linked to our implants."

He could have fried all of us anytime he wanted. Killing us wasn't the goal, so what was? Ringer sees the question in my eyes. "The three 'infesteds'—that's why he fired the opening shot," she says. "We're the first squad out of the camp. It makes sense they'd monitor us closely to see how we perform in actual combat. Or what we think is actual combat. To make sure we react to the green bait like good little rats. They must have dropped him in before us—to pull the trigger in case we didn't. And when we didn't, he gave us a little incentive."

"And he kept firing at us because . . . ?"

"Kept us hyped and ready to blow away any damn green shiny thing that glowed."

In the snow, it's as if she's looking at me through a gauzy white curtain. Flakes dust her eyebrows, sparkle in her hair.

"Awful big risk to take," I point out.

"Not really. He had us on this little radar. Worst-case scenario, all he had to do was hit the button. He just didn't consider the worst-worst case."

"That we'd cut out the implants."

314

Ringer nods. She wipes away the snow clinging to her face. "I don't think the dumb bastard expected us to turn and fight."

She hands the device to me. I close the cover, slip it into my pocket.

"It's our move, Sergeant," she says quietly, or maybe it's the snow tamping down her voice. "What's the call?"

I suck down a lungful of air, let it out slowly. "Get back to the squad. Pull everyone's implant . . ."

"And?"

"Hope like hell there isn't a battalion of Rezniks on its way right now."

I turn to go. She grabs my arm. "Wait! We can't go back without implants."

It takes me a second to get it. Then I nod, rubbing the back of my hand across my numb lips. We'll light up in their eyepieces without the implants. "Poundcake will drop us before we're halfway across the street."

"Hold them in our mouths?"

I shake my head. What if we accidently swallow them? "We have to stick them back where they came from, bandage the wounds up tight, and . . . ."

"Hope like hell they don't fall out?"

"And hope pulling them out didn't deactivate them . . . What?" I ask. "Too much hope?"

The side of her mouth twitches. "Maybe that's our secret weapon."

62

"THIS IS SERIOUSLY, seriously messed up," Flintstone says to me. "Reznik was sniping us?"

We're sitting against the concrete half wall of the garage, Ringer and Poundcake on the flanks, watching the street below. Dumbo is on one side of me, Flint on the other, Teacup between them, pressing her head against my chest.

"Reznik is a Ted," I tell him for the third time. "Camp Haven is theirs. They've been using us to—"

"Stow it, Zombie! That's the craziest, most paranoid load of crap I've ever heard!" Flintstone's wide face is beet red. His unibrow jumps and twitches. "You wasted our drill instructor! Who was trying to waste us! On a mission to waste Teds! You guys can do what you want, but this is it for me. This is it."

He pushes himself to his feet and shakes his fist at me. "I'm going back to the rendezvous point to wait for the evac. This is . . ." He searches for the right word, then settles for, "Bullshit."

"Flint," I say, keeping my voice low and steady. "Stand down."

"Unbelievable. You've gone Dorothy. Dumbo, Cake, are you buying this? You can't be buying this."

I pull the silver device from my pocket. Flip it open. Shove it toward his face. "See that green dot right there? That's you." I scroll down to his number and highlight with a jab of my thumb. The green button flashes. "Know what happens when you hit the green button?"

It's one of those things you lie awake at night for the rest of your life and wish you could take back.

Flintstone jumps forward and snatches the device from my hand. I might have gotten to him in time, but Teacup's in my lap and it slows me down. All that happens before he hits the button is my shout of "No!"

Flintstone's head snaps back violently as if someone has smacked him hard in the forehead. His mouth flies open, his eyes roll toward the ceiling.

Then he drops, straight down and loose-limbed, like a puppet whose strings have lost their tension.

Teacup is screaming. Ringer pulls her off me, and I kneel beside Flint. Though I do it anyway, I don't have to check his pulse to know he's dead. All I have to do is look at the display of the device clutched in his hand, at the red dot where the green one used to be.

"Guess you were right, Ringer," I say over my shoulder.

I ease the control pad out of Flintstone's lifeless hand. My own hand is shaking. Panic. Confusion. But mostly anger: I'm furious at Flint. I am seriously tempted to smash my fist into his big, fat face.

Behind me, Dumbo says, "What are we going to do now, Sarge?" He's panicking, too.

"Right now you're going to cut out Poundcake's and Teacup's implants."

His voice goes up an octave. "Me?"

Mine goes down one. "You're the medic, right? Ringer will do yours."

"Okay, but then what are we going to do? We can't go back. We can't—where're we supposed to go now?"

Ringer is looking at me. I'm getting better at reading her expressions. That slight downturn of her mouth means she's bracing herself, like she already knows what I'm about to say. Who knows? She probably does.

"You're not going back, Dumbo."

"You mean *we* aren't going back," Ringer corrects me. "*We,* Zombie."

I stand up. It seems to take me forever to get upright. I step over to her. The wind whips her hair to one side, a black banner flying.

"We left one behind," I say.

She shakes her head sharply. Her bangs swing back and forth in a pleasant way. "Nugget? Zombie, you can't go back for him. It's suicide."

"I can't leave him. I made a promise." I start to explain it, but I don't even know how to begin. How do I put it into words? It isn't possible. It's like locating the starting point of a circle.

Or finding the first link in a silver chain.

"I ran one time," I finally say. "I'm not running again."

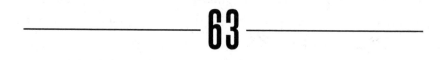

63

THERE IS THE SNOW, tiny pinpricks of white, spinning down.

There is the river reeking of human waste and human remains, black and swift and silent beneath the clouds that hide the glowing green eye of the mothership.

And there's the seventeen-year-old high school football jock dressed up like a soldier with a high-powered semiautomatic rifle that the ones from the glowing green eye gave him, crouching by the statue of a real soldier who fought and died with clear mind and clean heart, uncorrupted by the lies of an enemy who knows how he thinks, who twists everything good in him to evil, who uses his hope and trust to turn him into a weapon against his own kind. The kid who didn't go back when he should have and now goes back when he shouldn't. The kid called Zombie, who made a promise, and if he breaks that promise, the war is over—not the big war, but the war that matters, the one in the battlefield of his heart.

Because promises matter. They matter now more than ever.

In the park by the river in the snow spinning down.

I feel the chopper before I hear it. A change in pressure, a thrumming against my exposed skin. Then the rhythmic percussion of the blades, and I rise unsteadily, pressing my hand into the bullet wound in my side.

"Where should I shoot you?" Ringer asked.

"I don't know, but it can't be the legs or the arms."

And Dumbo, who had plenty of experience with human anatomy from processing duty: "Shoot him in the side. Close range. And angled this way, or you'll puncture his intestines."

And Ringer: "What do we do if I puncture your intestines?"

"Bury me, because I'll be dead."

A smile? No. Damn.

And afterward, as Dumbo examined the wound, she asked, "How long do we wait for you?"

"No more than a day."

"A day?"

"Okay. Two days. If we aren't back in forty-eight hours, we aren't coming back."

She didn't argue with me. But she said, "If you aren't back in forty-eight hours, I'm coming back for you."

"Dumb move, chess player."

"This isn't chess."

Black shadow roaring over the bare branches of the trees ringing the park, and the heavy pulsing beat of the rotors like an enormous racing heart, and the icy wind blasting down, pressing on my shoulders as I hoof it toward the open hatch.

The pilot whips his head around as I dive inside. "Where's your unit?"

Falling into the empty seat. "Go! Go!"

And the pilot: "Soldier, where's your unit?"

From the trees my unit answers, opening up a barrage of continuous fire, and the rounds slam and pop into the reinforced hull of the Black Hawk, and I'm shouting at the top of my lungs, "Go, go, go!" Which costs me: With every "Go!" blood is forced through the wound and dribbles through my fingers.

The pilot lifts off, shoots forward, then banks hard to the left. I close my eyes. *Go, Ringer. Go.*

The Black Hawk lays down strafing fire, pulverizing the trees, and the pilot is shouting something at the copilot, and the chopper is over the trees now, but Ringer and my crew should be long gone, down on the walking trail that borders the dark banks of the river. We circle the trees several times, firing until the trees are shattered stubs of their former selves. The pilot glances into the hold, sees me lying across two seats, holding my bloody side. He pulls up and hits the gas. The chopper shoots toward the clouds; the park is swallowed up by the white nothing of the snow.

I'm losing consciousness. Too much blood. Too much. There's Ringer's face, and damn if she isn't just smiling, she's laughing, and good for me, good for me that I made her laugh.

And there's Nugget, and he definitely isn't smiling.

Don't promise, don't promise, don't promise! Don't promise anything ever, ever, ever!

"I'm coming. I promise."

64

I WAKE UP where it began, in a hospital bed, bandaged up and floating on a sea of painkillers, circle complete.

It takes me several minutes to realize I'm not alone. There's someone sitting in the chair on the other side of the IV drip. I turn my head and see his boots first, black, shined to a mirror finish. The faultless uniform, starched and pressed. The chiseled face, the piercing blue eyes that bore down to the bottom of me.

"And so here you are," Vosch says softly. "Safe if not entirely sound. The doctors tell me you're extraordinarily lucky to have survived. No major damage; the bullet passed clean through. Amazing, really, given that you were shot at such close range."

What are you going to tell him?

I'm going to tell him the truth.

"It was Ringer," I tell him. *You bastard. You son of a bitch.* For months I saw him as my savior—as *humanity's* savior, even. His promises gave me the cruelest gift: hope.

He cocks his head to one side, reminding me of some bright-eyed bird eyeing a tasty morsel.

"And why did Private Ringer shoot you, Ben?"

You can't tell him the truth.

Okay. Screw the truth. I'll give him facts instead.

"Because of Reznik."

"Reznik?"

"Sir, Private Ringer shot me because I defended Reznik's being there."

"And why would you need to defend Reznik's being there, Sergeant?" Crossing his legs and cupping his upraised knee with his hands. It's hard to maintain eye contact with him for more than three or four seconds at a time.

"They turned on us, sir. Well, not all of them. Flintstone and Ringer—and Teacup, but only because Ringer did. They said Reznik's being there proved that this was all a lie, and that you—"

He holds up a hand. "'This'?"

"The camp, the infesteds. That we weren't being trained to kill the aliens. The aliens were training us to kill one another."

He doesn't say anything at first. I almost wish he would laugh or smile or shake his head. If he did anything like that, I might have some doubt; I might rethink the whole this-is-an-alien-head-fake thing and conclude I am suffering from paranoia and battle-induced hysteria.

Instead he just stares back at me with no expression, with those bird-bright eyes.

"And you wanted no part of their little conspiracy theory?"

I nod. A good, strong, confident nod—I hope. "They went Dorothy on me, sir. Turned the whole squad against me." I smile. A grim, tough, soldiery grin—I hope. "But not before I took care of Flint."

"We recovered his body," Vosch tells me. "Like you, he was shot

322

at very close range. Unlike you, the target was a little higher up in the anatomy."

Are you sure about this, Zombie? Why do you need to shoot him in the head?

They can't know he's been zapped. Maybe if I do enough damage, it'll destroy the evidence. Stand back, Ringer. You know I don't have the best aim in the world.

"I would have wasted the rest of them, but I was outnumbered, sir. I decided the best thing to do was get my ass back to base and report."

Again he doesn't move, doesn't say anything for a long time. Just stares. *What are you?* I wonder. *Are you human? Are you a Ted? Or are you . . . something else? What the hell* are *you?*

"They've vanished, you know," he finally says. Then waits for my answer. Luckily, I've thought of one. Or Ringer did. Credit where credit is due.

"They cut out their trackers."

"Yours too," he points out. And waits. Over his shoulder, I see orderlies in their green scrubs moving along the row of beds and hear the squeak of their shoes along the linoleum floor. Just another day in the hospital of the damned.

I'm ready for his question. "I was playing along. Waiting for an opening. Dumbo did Ringer next, after me, and that's when I made my move."

"Shooting Flintstone . . ."

"And then Ringer shot me."

"And then . . ." Arms crossed over his chest now. Chin lowered. Studying me with hooded eyes. The way a bird of prey might its supper.

"And then I ran. Sir."

So I'm able to take Reznik down in the dark in the middle of a snowstorm, but I can't pop you from two feet away? He won't buy it, Zombie.

I don't need him to buy it. Just rent it for a few hours.

He clears his throat. Scratches beneath his chin. Studies the ceiling tiles for a little while before looking back at me. "How fortunate for you, Ben, that you made it to the evac point before bleeding to death."

Oh, you bet, you whatever-you-are. Fortunate as hell.

A silence slams down. Blue eyes. Tight mouth. Folded arms.

"You haven't told me everything."

"Sir?"

"You're leaving something out."

I slowly shake my head. The room sways like a ship in a storm. How much painkiller did they give me?

"Your former drill sergeant. Someone in your unit must have searched him. And found one of these in his possession." Holding up a silver device identical to Reznik's. "At which point someone—I would think you, being the ranking officer—would wonder what Reznik was doing with a mechanism capable of terminating your lives with a touch of a button."

I'm nodding. Ringer and I figured he'd go there, and I'm ready with an answer. Whether he buys it or not, that's the question.

"There's only one explanation that makes any sense, sir. It was our first mission, our first real combat. We needed to be monitored. And you needed a fail-safe in case any of us went Dorothy—turned on the others . . ."

I trail off, out of breath and glad that I am, because I don't trust myself on the dope. My thinking isn't crystal clear. I'm walking through a minefield in some very dense fog. Ringer anticipated this. She made me practice this part over and over as we waited in the park for the chopper to return, right before she pressed her sidearm against my stomach and pulled the trigger.

The chair scrapes against the floor, and suddenly Vosch's lean, hard face fills my vision.

"It really is extraordinary, Ben. For you to resist the group dynamics of combat, the enormous pressure to follow the herd. It's almost—well, inhuman, for lack of a better word."

"I'm human," I whisper, heart beating in my chest so hard, for a second I'm sure he can see it beating through my thin gown.

"Are you? Because that's the crux of it, isn't it, Ben? That's the whole ballgame! Who is human—and who is not. Have we not eyes, Ben? Hands, organs, dimensions, senses, affections, passions? If you prick us, do we not bleed? And if you wrong us, shall we not revenge?"

The hard angle of the jaw. The severity of the blue eyes. The thin lips pale against the flushed face.

"Shakespeare. *The Merchant of Venice.* Spoken by a member of a despised and persecuted race. Like our race, Ben. The human race."

"I don't think they hate us, sir." Trying to keep my cool in this strange and unexpected turn in the minefield. My head is spinning. Gut-shot, doped up, discussing Shakespeare with the commandant of one of the most efficient death camps in the history of the world.

"They have a strange way of showing their affection."

"They don't love or hate us. We're just in the way. Maybe to them, we're the infestation."

"*Periplaneta americana* to their *Homo sapiens*? In that contest, I'll take the cockroach. Very difficult to eradicate."

325

He pats me on the shoulder. Gets very serious. We've come to the real meat of it, do or die time, pass or fail; I can feel it. He's turning the sleek silver device over and over in his hand.

Your plan sucks, Zombie. You know that.

Okay. Let's hear yours.

We stay together. Take our chances with whoever's holed up in the courthouse.

And Nugget?

They won't hurt him. Why are you so worried about Nugget? God, Zombie, there are hundreds of kids—

Yeah, there are. But I made a promise to one.

"This is a very grave development, Ben. Very grave. Ringer's delusion will drive her to seek shelter with the very things she was tasked to destroy. She will share with them everything she knows about our operations. We've dispatched three more squads to pre-empt her, but I'm afraid it may be too late. If it *is* too late, we'll have no choice but to execute the option of last resort."

His eyes burn with their own pale blue fire. I actually shiver when he turns away, cold all of a sudden, and very, very scared.

What is the option of last resort?

He may not have bought it, but he did rent it. I'm still alive. And as long as I'm alive, Nugget has a chance.

He turns back as if he's just remembered something.

Crap. Here it comes.

"Oh, one more thing. Sorry to be the bearer of bad tidings, but we're pulling you off the pain meds so we can run a full debriefing on you."

"Debriefing, sir?"

"Combat is a funny thing, Ben. It plays tricks on your memory.

And we've found that the meds interfere with the program. It should take about six hours for your system to be clear."

I still don't get it, Zombie. Why do I have to shoot you? Why can't the story be you gave us the slip? It's a little over-the-top, if you ask me.

I have to be injured, Ringer.

Why?

So they'll put me on meds.

Why?

To buy me time. So they don't take me straight there from the chopper.

Take you where?

So I don't have to ask what Vosch is talking about, but I ask anyway: "You're plugging me in to Wonderland?"

He crooks his finger at an orderly, who comes forward holding a tray. A tray with a syringe and a tiny silver pellet.

"We're plugging you in to Wonderland."

IX

A FLOWER
TO THE RAIN

65

WE FELL ASLEEP last night in front of the fireplace, and this morning I woke up in our bed—no, not our bed. My bed. Val's bed? The bed, and I don't remember climbing the stairs, so he must have carried me up and tucked me in, only he isn't in bed with me now. I'm a little panicky when I realize he's not here. It's a lot easier to push down my doubt when he's with me. When I can see those eyes the color of melted chocolate and hear his deep voice that falls over me like a warm blanket on a cold night. *Oh, you're such a hopeless case, Cassie. Such a train wreck.*

I dress quickly in the weak light of dawn and go downstairs. He's not there, either, but my M16 is, cleaned and loaded and leaning against the mantel. I call out his name. Silence answers.

I pick up the gun. The last time I fired it was on Crucifix Soldier Day.

Not your fault, Cassie. And not his fault.

I close my eyes and see my father lying gut-shot in the dirt, telling me, *No, Cassie,* right before Vosch walked over and silenced him.

His fault. Not yours. Not the Crucifix Soldier's. His.

I have a very vivid image of ramming the end of the rifle against Vosch's temple and blowing his head off his shoulders.

First I have to find him. And then politely ask him to stand still so I can ram the end of my rifle against his temple and blow his head off his shoulders.

I find myself on the sofa next to Bear, and I cradle them both, Bear in one arm, my rifle in the other, like I'm back in the woods in my tent under the trees that were under the sky that was under the baleful eye of the mothership that was beneath the explosion of stars of which ours is just one—and what are the freaking odds that the Others would pick our star out of the 100 sextillion in the universe to set up shop?

It's too much for me to handle. I can't defeat the Others. I'm a cockroach. Okay, I'll go with Evan's mayfly metaphor; mayflies are prettier, and at least they can fly. But I can take out a few of the bastards before my single day on Earth is over. And I plan to start with Vosch.

A hand falls on my shoulder. "Cassie, why are you crying?"

"I'm not. It's my allergies. This damn bear is full of dust."

He sits down next to me, on the bear side, not the gun side.

"Where were you?" I ask to change the subject.

"Checking out the weather."

"And?" *Full sentences, please. I'm cold and I need your warm-blanky voice to keep me safe.* I draw my knees up to my chest, resting my heels on the edge of the sofa cushion.

"I think we're good for tonight." The morning light sneaks through a crack in the sheets hung over the window and paints his face golden. The light shimmers in his dark hair, sparkles in his eyes.

"Good." I snuffle loudly.

"Cassie." He touches my knee. His hand is warm; I feel its heat through my jeans. "I had this weird idea."

"All of this is just a really bad dream?"

He shakes his head, laughs nervously. "I don't want you to take this the wrong way, so hear me out before you say anything, okay? I've been thinking a lot about this, and I wouldn't even mention it if I didn't think—"

"Tell me, Evan. Just—tell—me." *Oh God, what's he going to tell me?* My body tightens up. *Never mind, Evan. Don't tell me.*

"Let me go."

I shake my head, confused. Is this a joke? I look down at his hand on my knee, fingers gently squeezing. "I thought you *were* going."

"I mean, let *me* go." Giving my knee a tiny shake to get me to look at him.

Then I get it. "Let you go by yourself. I stay here, and you go find my brother."

"Okay, now, you promised to hear me out—"

"I didn't promise you anything." I push his hand off my knee. The thought of his leaving me behind isn't just offensive—it's terrifying. "My promise was to Sammy, so drop it."

He doesn't. "But you don't know what's out there."

"And you do?"

"Better than you."

He reaches for me; I put my hand against his chest. *Oh no, buddy.* "Then tell me what's out there."

He throws up his hands. "Think about who has a better chance of living long enough to keep your promise. I'm not saying it's because you're a girl or because I'm stronger or tougher or whatever. I'm saying if just one of us goes, then the other one would still have a chance of finding him in case the worst happens."

"Well, you're probably right about that last part. But it shouldn't be you who tries first. He's *my* brother. Like hell I'm going to wait around here for a Silencer to knock on the door and ask to borrow a cup of sugar. I'll just go by myself."

333

I push myself off the sofa like I'm heading out at that very second. He grabs my arm; I yank it back.

"Stop it, Evan. You keep forgetting that I'm letting you go with me, not the other way around."

He drops his head. "I know. I know that." Then a rueful laugh. "I also knew what your answer would be, but I had to ask."

"Because you think I can't take care of myself?"

"Because I don't want you to die."

66

WE'VE BEEN PREPARING for weeks. On this last day, there wasn't much left to do except wait for nightfall. We're traveling light; Evan thought we could reach Wright-Patterson in two or three nights, barring an unexpected delay like another blizzard or one of us getting killed—or both of us getting killed, which would delay the operation indefinitely.

Despite keeping my supplies to a bare minimum, I have trouble getting Bear to fit into the backpack. Maybe I should cut off his legs and tell Sammy they were blown off by the Eye that took out Camp Ashpit.

The Eye. That would be better, I decided: not a bullet to Vosch's brain, but an alien bomb jammed down his pants.

"Maybe you shouldn't take him," Evan says.

"Maybe you should shut up," I mutter, pushing Bear's head down into his stomach and tugging the zipper closed. "There."

Evan is smiling. "You know, when I first saw you in the woods, I thought he was your bear."

"Woods?"

His smile fades.

"You didn't find me in the woods," I remind him. Suddenly the room feels about ten degrees colder. "You found me in the middle of a snowbank."

"I meant I was in the woods, not you," he says. "I saw you from the woods a half mile away."

I'm nodding. Not because I believe him. I'm nodding because I know I'm right not to.

"You're not out of those woods yet, Evan. You're sweet and you have incredible cuticles, but I'm still not sure why your hands are so soft, or why you smelled like gunpowder the night you supposedly visited your girlfriend's grave."

"I told you last night, I haven't helped around the farm in two years, and I was cleaning my gun earlier that day. I don't know what else I can—"

I cut him off. "I'm only trusting you because you're handy with a rifle and haven't killed me with it, even though you've had about a thousand opportunities. Don't take this personally, but there's something I don't get about you and this whole situation, but that doesn't mean I'm never going to get it. I'll figure it out, and if the truth is something that puts you on the other side of me, then I will do what I have to do."

"What?" Smiling that damned lopsided, sexy grin, shoulders up, hands stuffed deep in his pockets with a sort of aw-shucks attitude, which I guess is meant to drive me the good kind of crazy. What is it about him that makes me want to slap him and kiss

335

him, run from him and to him, throw my arms around him and knee him in the balls, all at the same time? I'd like to blame the Arrival for the effect he has on me, but something tells me guys have been doing this to us for a lot longer than a few months.

"What I have to do," I tell him.

I head upstairs. Thinking about what I have to do reminded me of something I meant to do before we left.

In the bathroom, I poke around in the drawers until I find a pair of scissors, and then proceed to lop off six inches of my hair. The floorboards creak behind me, and I shout, "Stop lurking!" without turning around. A second later, Evan sticks his head into the room.

"What are you doing?" he asks.

"Symbolically cutting my hair. What are *you* doing? Oh, that's right. Following me, lurking in doorways. One of these days maybe you'll work up the courage to step over the threshold, Evan."

"It looks like you're actually cutting your hair."

"I've decided to get rid of all the things that bug me." Giving him a look in the mirror.

"Why does it bug you?"

"Why are you asking?" Looking at my reflection now, but he's there in the corner of my eye. Damn it, more symbolism.

He wisely makes an exit. *Snip, snip, snip,* and the sink fills up with my curls. I hear him clumping around downstairs, then the kitchen door slamming. I guess I was supposed to ask his permission first. Like he owns me. Like I'm a puppy he found lost in the snow.

I step back to examine my handiwork. With the short cut and no makeup, I look about twelve years old. Okay, no older than fourteen. But with the right attitude and the right prop, someone

336

might mistake me for a tween. Maybe even offer me a ride to safety on their friendly yellow school bus.

That afternoon a gray sheet of clouds draws itself across the sky, bringing an early dusk. Evan disappears again and comes back a few minutes later carrying two five-gallon containers of gasoline. I give him a look, and he says, "I was thinking a diversion might help."

It takes me a minute to process. "You're going to burn down your house?"

He nods. He seems kind of excited about the prospect.

"I'm going to burn down my house."

He lugs one of the containers upstairs to douse the bedrooms. I go out onto the porch to escape the fumes. A big black crow is hopping across the yard, and he stops and gives me a beady-eyed look. I consider pulling out my gun and shooting him.

I don't think I'd miss. I'm a pretty good shot now, thanks to Evan, and also I really hate birds.

The door opens behind me and a wave of nauseating fumes roars out. I step off the porch and the crow takes off, screeching. Evan splashes down the porch, then tosses the empty can against the side of the house.

"The barn," I say. "If you wanted to create a diversion, you should have burned down the barn. That way the house would still be here when we get back." *Because I'd like to believe we're coming back, Evan. You, me, and Sammy, one big happy family.*

"You know we're not coming back," he says, and lights the match.

67

TWENTY-FOUR HOURS LATER and I've completed the circle that connects me and Sammy as if by a silver cord, returning to the place where I made my promise.

Camp Ashpit is exactly how I left it, which means there is no Camp Ashpit, just a dirt road cutting through woods interrupted by a mile-wide emptiness where Camp Ashpit used to be, the ground harder than steel and bare of everything, even the tiniest weed or blade of grass or dead leaf. Of course, it's winter, but somehow I don't think when springtime comes this Other-made clearing will blossom like a meadow.

I point to a spot on our right. "That's where the barracks was. I think. It's hard to tell without any point of reference except the road. Over there the storage shed. Back that way the ash pit, and farther back the ravine."

Evan is shaking his head with wonder. "There's nothing left." He stamps his foot on the rock-hard ground.

"Oh yeah, there is. I'm left."

He sighs. "You know what I mean."

"I'm being too intense," I say.

"Hmmm. Not really like you." He tries out a smile, but his smile isn't working that well lately. He's been very quiet since we left his house burning in the middle of farm country. In the waning daylight, he kneels on the hard ground, pulls out the map, and points at our location with his flashlight.

"The dirt road over there isn't on the map, but it must connect

338

with this road, maybe around here? We can follow it to 675, and then it's a straight shot to Wright-Patterson."

"How far?" I ask, peering over his shoulder.

"About twenty-five or thirty miles. Another day if we push it."

"We'll push it."

I sit down beside him and dig through his pack for something to eat. I find some cured mystery meat wrapped in wax paper and a couple of hard biscuits. I offer one to Evan. He shakes his head no.

"You need to eat," I scold him. "Stop worrying so much."

He's afraid we'll run out of food. He has his rifle, of course, but there'll be no hunting during this phase of the rescue operation. We have to pass quietly through the countryside—not that the countryside has been particularly quiet. The first night, we heard gunfire. Sometimes the echo of a single gun going off, sometimes more than one. Always in the distance, though, never close enough to freak us out. Maybe lone hunters like Evan, living off the land. Maybe roving gangs of Twigs. Who knew? Maybe there are other sixteen-year-old girls with M16s stupid enough to think they are humanity's last representatives on Earth.

He gives in and takes one of the biscuits. Gnaws off a hunk. Chews thoughtfully, looking around the wasteland as the light dies. "What if they've stopped running buses?" he asks for the hundredth time. "How do we get in?"

"We come up with something else." Cassie Sullivan: expert strategic planner.

He gives me a look. "Professional soldiers. Humvees. And Black Hawks. And this—what did you call it?—green-eyed bomb. We better come up with something good."

He jams the map into his pocket and stands up, adjusting the rifle over his shoulder. He's on the verge of something. I'm not sure what. Tears? Screams? Laughter?

Me too. All three. And maybe not for the same reasons. I've decided to trust him, but like somebody once said, you can't force yourself to trust. So you put all your doubts in a little box and bury it deep and then try to forget where you buried it. My problem is that buried box is like a scab I can't stop picking at.

"We better go," he says tightly, glancing up at the sky. The clouds that moved in the day before still linger, hiding the stars. "We're exposed here."

Suddenly, Evan snaps his head to the left and goes all statuelike.

"What is it?" I whisper.

He holds up his hand. Gives a sharp shake of his head. Peers into the near perfect darkness. I don't see anything. Don't hear anything. But I'm not a hunter like Evan.

"A damned flashlight," he murmurs. He presses his lips to my ear. "What's closer, the woods on the other side of the road or the ravine?"

I shake my head. I really don't know. "The ravine, I guess."

He doesn't hesitate. He grabs my hand, and we take off in a quick trot toward where I hoped the ravine was. I don't know how far we ran till we came to it. Probably not as far as it seemed, because it seemed like we ran forever. Evan lowers me down the rocky face to the bottom, then jumps in beside me.

"Evan?"

He presses his finger to his lips. Scoots up the side to peek over the edge. He motions to his pack, and I fish around until I find his binoculars. I tug on his pant leg—*What's going on?*—but he shakes off my hand. He taps his fingers against his thigh, thumb tucked. Four of them? Is that what he meant? Or is he using some kind of hunter's code, like, *Get down on all fours!*

He doesn't move for a long time. Finally he shimmies back down and puts his lips to my ear again.

"They're coming this way." He squints in the gloom toward the opposite wall of the ravine, which is much steeper than the one we came down, but there are woods on the other side, or what's left of them: shattered stumps of trees, tangles of broken branches and vines. Good cover. Or at least better cover than being totally exposed in a gully where the bad guys can pick you off like fish in a barrel. He bites his lip, weighing the odds. Do we have time to scale the other side before being spotted?

"Stay down."

He swings his rifle off his shoulder and braces his boots against the unsteady surface, resting his elbows on the ground above. I'm standing directly beneath him, cradling the M16. Yeah, he told me to stay down, I know. But I'm not about to huddle in a heap waiting for the end. I've been there before, and I'm never going back.

Evan fires; the twilight stillness shatters. The kickback of the rifle knocks him off balance, his foot slips, and he falls straight down. Luckily, there's a moron directly beneath him to break his fall. Lucky for him. Not so lucky for the moron.

He rolls off me, yanks me to my feet, and shoves me toward the opposite side. But it's kind of difficult to move fast when you can't breathe.

A flare drops into the ravine, ripping apart the dark with a hellish red glare. Evan slides his hands under my arms and hurls me toward the top. I catch hold of the edge with my fingertips and furiously dig into the wall with my toes, like some crazy bicyclist.

341

Then Evan's hands on my butt for the final heave-ho, and I'm on the other side.

I swing around to help him up, but he shouts for me to run—no reason to be quiet now—as a small, pineapple-shaped object plops into the ravine behind him.

I scream, "Grenade!" which gives Evan an entire second to take cover.

That's not quite enough time.

The blast drops him, and at that moment a figure wearing fatigues appears on the opposite side of the ravine. I open up with my M16, screaming incoherently at the top of my lungs. The figure scrambles backward, but I keep firing at the spot where he stood. I don't think he was expecting Cassie Sullivan's answer to his invitation to party down post–alien apocalypse style.

I empty my clip, slap home a fresh one. Count to ten. Make myself look down, sure of what I'm going to see when I do. Evan's body at the bottom of the ravine, ripped to shreds, all because I was the one thing he found worth dying for. Me, the girl who let him kiss her but never kissed him first. The girl who never thanked him for saving her life but paid him back with sarcasm and accusations. I know what I'm going to see when I look down, but that's not what I see.

Evan is gone.

The little voice inside my head whose job it is to keep me alive shouts, *Run!*

So I run.

Leaping over fallen trees and winter dry scrub, and now the familiar *pop-pop-pop* of rapid-arms fire.

Grenades. Flares. Assault weapons. These aren't Twigs after us. These are pros.

Outside the fiendish glow of the flare, I hit a wall of dark, then run smack into a tree. The impact knocks me off my feet. I don't know how far I ran, but it must be a good distance, because I can't see the ravine, can't hear anything but my own heartbeat roaring in my ears.

I scuttle forward to a fallen pine tree and huddle behind it, waiting for the breath I left back at the ravine to catch up with me. Waiting for another flare to drop into the woods in front of me. Waiting for the Silencers to come crashing through the underbrush.

A rifle pops in the distance, followed by a high-pitched scream. Then an answering barrage of automatic weapons and another grenade explosion, and then silence.

Well, it isn't me they're shooting at, so it must be Evan, I think. Which makes me feel better and a whole lot worse, because he's out there alone against pros, and where am I? Hiding behind a tree like a girl.

But what about Sams? I can run back into a fight I'll probably lose, or stay down to stay alive long enough to keep my promise.

It's an either/or world.

Another *crack!* of a rifle. Another girly scream.

More silence.

He's picking them off one by one. A farm boy with no combat experience against a squad of professional soldiers. Outnumbered. Outgunned. Cutting them down with the same brutal efficiency as the Silencer on the interstate, the hunter in the woods who chased me under a car and then mysteriously disappeared.

Crack!

Scream.

Silence.

I don't move. I wait behind my log, terrified. Over the past

343

ten minutes, it's become such a dear friend, I consider naming it: Howard, my pet log.

You know, when I first saw you in the woods, I thought he was your bear.

The snap and crunch of dead leaves and twigs underfoot. A darker shadow against the dark of the woods. The soft call of the Silencer. My Silencer.

"Cassie? Cassie, it's safe now."

I heave myself upright and point my rifle directly at Evan Walker's face.

68

HE PULLS UP QUICKLY, but the look of confusion comes slowly.

"Cassie, it's me."

"I know it's you. I just don't know who you are."

His jaw tightens. His voice is strained. Anger? Frustration? I can't tell. "Lower the gun, Cassie."

"Who are you, Evan? If that's evan your name. *Even* your name."

He smiles wanly. And then he falls to his knees, sways, topples over, and lies still.

I wait, the gun trained on the back of his head. He doesn't move. I hop over Howard and poke him with my toe. He still doesn't move. I kneel beside him, resting the butt of my rifle on my thigh, and press my fingers against his neck, feeling for a pulse. He's alive. His pants are shredded from the thighs down. Wet to the touch. I smell my fingertips. Blood.

I lean my M16 against the fallen tree and roll Evan onto his back. His eyelids flutter. He reaches up and touches my cheek with his bloody palm.

"Cassie," he whispers. "Cassie for Cassiopeia."

"Stop it," I say. I notice his rifle lying next to him and kick it out of his reach. "How bad are you hurt?"

"I think pretty bad."

"How many were there?"

"Four."

"They never had a chance, did they?"

Long sigh. His eyes lift up to mine. I don't need him to speak; I can see the answer in his eyes. "Not much, no."

"Because you don't have the heart to kill, but you have the heart to do what you have to do." I hold my breath. He must know where I'm going with this.

He hesitates. Nods. I can see the pain in his eyes. I look away so he can't see the pain in mine. *But you started down this road, Cassie. No turning back now.*

"And you're very good at what you have the heart to do, aren't you?"

Well, that's the question, isn't it? Yours, too: What do you have the heart to do, Cassie?

He saved my life. How could he also be the one who tried to take it? It doesn't make sense.

Do I have the heart to let him bleed to death because now I know he lied to me—that he isn't gentle Evan Walker the reluctant hunter, the grieving son and brother and lover, but something that might not even be human? Do I have what it takes to follow the first rule down to its final, brutal, unforgiving conclusion and put a bullet through his finely sculpted forehead?

Oh, crap, who are you kidding?

I start to unbutton his shirt. "Got to get these clothes off," I mutter.

"You don't know how long I've waited to hear you say that." Smile. Lopsided. Sexy.

"You're not charming your way out of this one, buddy. Can you sit up a little? A little more. Here, take these." A couple of pain pills from the first aid kit. He swallows them with two long gulps of water from a bottle I hand him.

I pull off his shirt. He's looking up into my face; I avoid his gaze. While I tug off his boots, he unbuckles his belt and pulls down the zipper. He lifts his butt, but I can't get his pants off—they're plastered to his body with tacky blood.

"Rip them," he says. He rolls over onto his stomach. I try, but the material keeps slipping through my fingers when I pull.

"Here, use this." He holds up a bloody knife. I don't ask him where the blood came from.

I cut from hole to hole slowly; I'm terrified of cutting him. Then I strip the pants away from each leg, like peeling a banana. That's it, the perfect metaphor: peeling a banana. I have to know what the truth is, and you can't get to the tasty fruit without stripping off the outer layer.

Speaking of fruit, I'm down—I mean, he's down—to his underwear.

Confronted with them, I ask, "Do I need to look at your butt?"

"I've been wondering about your opinion."

"Enough with the lame attempts at humor." I slice the material at both hips and peel back the underwear, exposing him. His butt is bad. I mean bad as in peppered with shrapnel wounds. Otherwise, it's pretty good.

I dab at the blood with some gauze from the kit, fighting back hysterical giggles. I blame it on the unbearable stress, not on the fact that I'm wiping Evan Walker's ass.

"God, you're a mess."

He's gasping for air. "Just try to stop the bleeding for now."

I pack the wounds on this side of him the best I can. "Can you roll back over?" I ask.

"I'd rather not."

"I need to see the front." *Oh my God. The front?*

"The front's okay. Really."

I sit back, exhausted. Guess that's one thing I'll take his word for. "Tell me what happened."

"After I got you out of the ravine, I ran. Found a shallow spot to climb out. Circled around them. The rest you probably heard."

"I heard three shots. You said there were four guys."

"Knife."

"This knife?"

"That knife. This is his blood on my hands, not mine."

"Oh, thanks." I scrub my cheek where he touched me. I decide to just come out with the worst explanation for what's going on. "You're a Silencer, aren't you?"

Silence. How ironic.

"Or are you human?" I whisper. *Say human, Evan. And when you say it, say it perfectly so there's no doubt. Please, Evan, I really need you to take the doubt away. I know you said you can't make yourself trust—so, damn it, make somebody else trust. Make me trust. Say it. Say you're human.*

"Cassie . . ."

"Are you human?"

"Of course I'm human."

I take a deep breath. He said it, but not perfectly. I can't see his face; it's tucked beneath his elbow. Maybe if I could see his face that would make it perfect and I could let this awful thought go. I pick up some sterile wipes and begin to clean his blood—or whoever's—from my hands.

"If you're human, why have you been lying to me?"

"I haven't lied to you about everything."

"Just the parts that matter."

"Those are the parts I haven't lied about."

"Did you kill those three people on the interstate?"

"Yes."

I flinch. I didn't expect him to say yes. I expected an *Are you kidding? Stop being so paranoid.* Instead I get a soft, simple answer, as if I asked him if he ever skinny-dipped.

Next question is the hardest yet: "Did you shoot me in the leg?"

"Yes."

I shudder and drop the bloody wipe between my legs. "Why did you shoot me in the leg, Evan?"

"Because I couldn't shoot you in the head."

Well. There you have it.

I pull out the Luger and hold it in my lap. His head is about a foot from my knee. The one thing that puzzles me is the person with the gun is shaking like a leaf and the one at her mercy is perfectly calm.

"I'm going now," I tell him. "I'm going to leave you to bleed to death the way you left me under that car."

I wait for him to say something.

"You're not leaving," he points out.

"I'm waiting to hear what you have to say."

"This is complicated."

348

"No, Evan. Lies are complicated. The truth is simple. Why were you shooting people on the highway?"

"Because I was afraid."

"Afraid of what?" I ask.

"Afraid they weren't people."

I sigh and fish out a bottle of water from my backpack, lean back against the fallen tree, and take a deep drink.

"You shot those people on the highway—and me, and God knows who else; I know you weren't going out every night hunting animals—because you already knew about the 4th Wave. I'm your Crucifix Soldier."

He nods into the crook of his elbow. Muffled voice: "If you want to put it that way."

"If you wanted me dead, why did you pull me out of the snow instead of letting me freeze to death?"

"I didn't want you dead."

"After shooting me in the leg and leaving me to bleed to death under a car."

"No, you were on your feet when I ran."

"You ran? Why did you run?" I'm having trouble picturing it.

"I was afraid."

"You shot those people because you were afraid. You shot me because you were afraid. You ran because you were afraid."

"I might have some issues with fear."

"Then you find me and bring me to the farmhouse, nurse me back to health, cook me a hamburger and wash my hair and teach me how to shoot and make out with me for the purpose of . . . what?"

He rolls his head around to look at me with one eye. "You know, Cassie, this is a little unfair of you."

My mouth drops open. "Unfair of me?"

"Grilling me while I'm shot up with shrapnel."

"That isn't my fault," I snap. "You're the one who insisted on coming." A thrill of fear rockets down my spine. "Why did you come, Evan? Is this some kind of trick? Are you using me for something?"

"Rescuing Sammy was your idea," he points out. "I tried to talk you out of it. I even offered to go myself."

He's shivering. He's naked and it's forty degrees. I drape his jacket over his back and cover the rest of him the best I can with his denim shirt.

"I'm sorry, Cassie."

"For which part?"

"All the parts." His words are slurring: the pain pills kicking in.

I'm gripping the gun hard now with both hands. Shaking like him, but not from the cold.

"Evan, I killed that soldier because I didn't have a choice—I didn't go looking for people to kill every day. I didn't hide in the woods by the side of the road and take out every person who came along because they might be one of them." I'm nodding to myself. It really is simple. "You can't be who you say you are because who you say you are could not have done what you did!"

I don't care about anything but the truth now. And not being an idiot. And not feeling anything for him, because feeling something for him will make what I have to do that much harder, maybe impossible, and if I want to save my brother, nothing can be impossible.

"What's next?" I say.

"In the morning, we'll have to get the shrapnel out."

"I mean after this wave. Or are you the last wave, Evan?"

He's looking up at me with that one exposed eye and wiggling his head back and forth. "I don't know how I can convince you—"

I press the muzzle of the gun against his temple, right beside the big chocolaty eye staring up at me, and snarl, "1st Wave: lights out. 2nd Wave: surf's up. 3rd Wave: pestilence. 4th Wave: Silencer. What's next, Evan? What is the 5th Wave?"

He doesn't answer. He's passed out.

69

AT DAWN he's still out cold, so I grab my rifle and hike out of the woods to assess his handiwork. Probably not the smartest thing to do. What if our midnight raiders called for backup? I'd be the prize in a turkey shoot. I'm not a bad shot, but I'm no Evan Walker.

Well, even Evan Walker is no Evan Walker.

I don't know what he is. He says he's human, and he looks like a human, talks like a human, bleeds like a human and, okay, kisses like a human. And a rose by any other name, blah, blah, blah. He says the right things, too, like the reason he was sniping people is the same reason I shot the Crucifix Soldier.

The problem is, I don't buy it. And now I can't decide which is better, a dead Evan or a live Evan. Dead Evan can't help me keep my promise. Live Evan can.

Why did he shoot me, then save me? What did he mean when he said that I'd saved him?

It's weird. When he held me in his arms, I felt safe. When he kissed me, I was lost in him. It's like there are two Evans. There

351

is the Evan I know and the Evan I don't. Evan the farm boy with the soft hands who strokes me till I'm purring like a cat. Evan the pretender who is the cold-blooded killer who shot me.

I'm going to assume he's human—at least biologically. Maybe he's a clone grown on board the mothership from harvested DNA. Or maybe something less Star Warsy and more despicable: a traitor to his species. Maybe that's what the Silencers are: human mercenaries.

The Others are giving him something to kill us. Or they threatened him—like kidnapping someone he loves (Lauren? I never actually saw her grave) and offering him a deal. *Kill twenty humans and you get them back.*

The last possibility? That he is what he says he is. Alone, scared, killing before someone can kill him, a firm adherent to the first rule, until he broke it by letting me go and then bringing me back.

It explains what happened as well as the first two possibilities. Everything fits. It could be the truth. Except for one niggling little problem.

The soldiers.

That's why I don't leave him in the woods. I want to see what he did for myself.

Since Camp Ashpit is now more featureless than a salt flat, I have no trouble finding Evan's kills. One by the lip of the ravine. Two more side by side a few hundred yards away. All three head shots. In the dark. While they were shooting at him. The last one is lying near where the barracks used to be, maybe even the exact spot where Vosch murdered my father.

None of them are older than fourteen. All of them are wearing these weird silver eye patches. Some kind of night vision technology? If so, it makes Evan's accomplishment all the more impressive, in a sickening sort of way.

Evan's awake when I get back. Sitting up against the fallen tree. Pale, shivering, eyes sunk back in his head.

"They were kids," I tell him. "They were just kids."

I kick my way into the dead brush behind him and empty out my stomach.

Then I feel better.

I go back to him. I've decided not to kill him. Yet. He's still worth more to me alive. If he is a Silencer, he may know what happened to my brother. So I grab the first aid kit and kneel between his spread legs.

"Okay, time to operate."

I find a pack of sterile wipes in the kit. Silently, he watches me clean his victim's blood off the knife.

I swallow hard, tasting the fresh vomit. "I've never done this before," I say. Kind of obvious thing to say, but it feels like I'm talking to a stranger.

He nods, rolls onto his stomach. I pull the shirt away, exposing his bottom half.

I've never seen a naked guy before. Now here I am kneeling between his legs, though I can't see his total nakedness. Just the back half. Strange, I never thought my first time with a naked guy would be like this. Well, I guess that isn't so strange.

"You want another pain pill?" I ask. "It's cold and my hands are shaking . . ."

"No pill," he grunts, face tucked into the crook of his arm.

I work slowly at first, gingerly poking into the wounds with the tip of the knife, but I quickly learn that isn't the best way to dig metal out of human—or maybe nonhuman—flesh: You just prolong the agony.

His butt takes the longest. Not because I'm lingering. There's just so much shrapnel. He doesn't squirm. He barely flinches. Sometimes he goes, "Oooh!" Sometimes he sighs.

I lift the jacket off his back. Not too many wounds here, and mostly concentrated along the lower part. Stiff fingers, sore wrists, I force myself to be quick—quick but careful.

"Hang in there," I murmur. "Almost done."

"Me too."

"We don't have enough bandages."

"Just get the worst."

"Infection . . . ?"

"There's some penicillin tablets in the kit."

He rolls back over as I dig out the pills. He takes two with a sip of water. I sit back, sweating, though it isn't much above freezing.

"Why kids?" I ask.

"I didn't know they were kids."

"Maybe not, but they were heavily armed and knew what they were doing. Their problem was, so did you. You must have forgotten to mention your commando training."

"Cassie, if we can't trust each other—"

"Evan, we *can't* trust each other." I want to crack him in the head and burst into tears at the same time. I've reached the point of being tired of being tired. "That's the whole problem."

Overhead, the sun has broken free from the clouds, exposing us to a bright blue sky.

"Alien clone children?" I guess. "America scraping the bottom of the conscription barrel? Seriously, why are kids running around with automatic weapons and grenades?"

He shakes his head. Sips some water. Winces. "Maybe I will take another one of those pain pills."

"Vosch said just the kids. They're snatching children to turn them into an army?"

"Maybe Vosch isn't one of them. Maybe the army took the kids."

"Then why did he kill everybody else? Why did he put a bullet in my dad's head? And if he isn't one of them, where'd he get the Eye? Something's wrong here, Evan. And you know what's going on. We both know you do. Why can't you just tell me? You'll trust me with a gun and to pull shrapnel out of your ass, but you won't trust me with the truth?"

He stares at me for a long moment. Then he says, "I wish you hadn't cut your hair."

I would have lost it, but I'm too cold, too nauseated, and too strung out. "I swear to God, Evan Walker," I say in a dead voice, "if I didn't need you, I would kill you right now."

"I'm glad you need me, then."

"And if I find out you're lying to me about the most important part, I will kill you."

"What's the most important part?"

"About being human."

"I'm as human as you are, Cassie."

He pulls my hand into his. Both our hands are stained with blood. Mine with his. His with that of a boy not much older than my brother. How many people has this hand killed?

"Is that what we are?" I ask. I'm about to lose it big-time. I can't trust him. I have to trust him. I can't believe. I have to believe. Is this the Others' ultimate goal, the wave to end all waves, stripping our humanity down to its bare, animalistic bones, until we're nothing but soulless predators doing their dirty work for them, as solitary as sharks and with as much compassion?

He notices the cornered-animal look in my eyes. "What is it?"

"I don't want to be a shark," I whisper.

He looks at me for a long, uncomfortable moment. He could have said, *Shark? Who? What? Huh? Who said you were a shark?* Instead, he begins to nod, like he totally gets it. "You aren't."

You, not *we*. I give his long look back to him. "If the Earth was dying and we had to leave," I say slowly, "and we found a planet but someone was there before us, someone who for some reason we weren't compatible with . . ."

"You'd do whatever was necessary."

"Like sharks."

"Like sharks."

I guess he was trying to be gentle about it. It mattered to him, I guess, that my landing wouldn't be too hard, that the shock wouldn't be too great. He wanted, I think, for me to get it without his having to say it.

I fling his hand away. I'm furious that I ever let him touch me. Furious at myself for staying with him when I knew there were things he wasn't telling me. Furious at my father for letting Sammy get on that bus. Furious at Vosch. Furious at the green eye hovering on the horizon. Furious at myself for breaking the first rule for the first cute guy that came along, and for what? For what? Because his hands were large but gentle and his breath smelled like chocolate?

I pound his chest over and over until I forget why I'm hitting him, until I'm emptied of fury and all that's left inside is the black hole where Cassie used to be.

He grabs at my flailing fists. "Cassie, stop it! Settle down! I'm not your enemy."

"Then whose enemy are you, huh? Because you're somebody's. You weren't out hunting every night—not animals, anyway. And you didn't learn killer ninja moves working on your daddy's farm. You keep saying what you're not, and all I want to know is what you are. What are you, Evan Walker?"

He lets go of my wrists and surprises me by pressing his hand against my face, running his smooth thumb over my cheek, across the bridge of my nose. As if he's touching me for the last time.

"I am a shark, Cassie," he says slowly, drawing the words out, as if he might be speaking to me for the last time. Looking into my eyes with tears in his, as if he's seeing me for the last time. "A shark who dreamed he was a man."

I'm falling faster than the speed of light into the black hole that opened with the Arrival and then devoured everything in its path. The hole my father stared into when my mother died, the one I thought was out there, separate from me, but really never was. It was inside me, and it had been inside me since the beginning, growing, eating up every ounce of hope and trust and love I had, chewing its way through the galaxy of my soul while I clung to a choice—a choice who is looking at me now as if for the last time.

So I do the thing most reasonable people would in my situation.

I run.

Crashing through the woods in the bitter winter air, bare branch, blue sky, withered leaf, then bursting from the tree line into an open field, the frozen ground crunchy beneath my boots, under the dome of the indifferent sky, the brilliant blue curtain drawn over a billion stars that are still there, still looking down at her, the running girl with her short hair bouncing and tears streaming down her cheeks, not running from anything, not running to anything, just running, running like hell, because that's the most logical thing to do when you realize the one person on Earth you've decided to trust isn't from the Earth. Never mind that he saved your ass more times than you can remember, or that he could have killed you a hundred times over, or that there's something about him, something tormented and sad and terribly, terribly lonely, like *he* was the last person on Earth, not the girl shivering in a sleeping bag, hugging a teddy bear in a world gone quiet.

Shut up, shut up, just shut up.

70

HE'S GONE when I come back. And, yes, I came back. Where was I supposed to go, without my gun and especially without that damned bear, my reason for living? I wasn't scared to go back—he'd had ten billion opportunities to kill me; what did one more matter?

There's his rifle. His backpack. The first aid kit. And there's his shredded jeans by Howard the log. Since he didn't pack another pair of pants, my guess is that he's cavorting about the freezing woods in just his hiking boots, like a calendar pinup. No, wait. His shirt and jacket are missing.

"Come on, Bear," I growl, snatching up my backpack. "It's time to get you back to your owner."

I grab my rifle, check the magazine, ditto for the Luger, pull on a pair of black knit gloves because my fingers have gone numb, steal the map and flashlight from his backpack, and head for the ravine. I'll risk the daylight to put distance between me and Sharkman. I don't know where he went, maybe to call in the drone strikes now that his cover's blown, but it doesn't matter. That's what I decided on the way back, after running until I couldn't run anymore: It really doesn't matter who or what Evan Walker is. He kept me from dying. Fed me, bathed me, protected me. He helped me to get strong. He even taught me how to kill. With an enemy like that, who needs friends?

Into the ravine. Ten degrees colder in the shadows. Up and over onto the blasted landscape of Camp Ashpit, running on ground as hard as asphalt, and there's the first body, and I think, *If Evan is one of them, whose team do you play for?* Would Evan kill one of his own kind to keep up the facade with me—or was he forced to kill them because they thought he was human? Thinking that makes me sick with despair: There's no bottom to this crap. The more you dig, the further down it goes.

I pass another body with barely a glance, and then that bare glance registers and I turn back. The kid soldier has no pants on.

It doesn't matter. I keep moving. On the dirt road now, heading north. Still trotting. *Move, Cassie, move, move.* Forgot the food. Forgot the water. Doesn't matter. Doesn't matter. The sky is cloudless, huge, a gigantic blue eye staring down. I run along the edge of the road near the woods abutting the west side. If I see a drone, I'll dive for cover. If I see Evan, I'll shoot first and ask questions later. Well, not just Evan. Anyone.

Nothing matters but the first rule. Nothing matters except getting Sammy. I forgot that for a while.

Silencers: human, semihuman, clone human, or alien-projecting-human holograph? Doesn't matter. The ultimate goal of the Others: eradication, internment, or enslavement? Doesn't matter. My chances of success: one, point one, or point zero zero zero one percent? Doesn't matter.

Follow the road, follow the road, follow the dusty dirt road . . .

After a couple miles it veers to the west, connecting with Highway 35. Another few miles on Highway 35 to the junction of 675. I can take cover at the overpass there and wait for the buses. If the buses still run on Highway 35. If they're still running at all.

At the end of the dirt road, I pause long enough to scan the terrain behind me. Nothing. He's not coming. He's letting me go.

I head a few feet into the trees to catch my breath. The minute I sink to the ground, everything I've been running from catches up to me long before my breath.

I am a shark who dreamed he was a man . . .

Someone is screaming—I can hear her screams echoing through the trees. The sound goes on and on. Let it bring a horde of Silencers down upon me, I don't care. I press my hands against my head and rock back and forth, and I have this weird sensation of floating above my body, and then I'm rocketing into the sky at a thousand miles an hour and watching myself dwindle into a tiny spot before the immensity of the Earth swallows me. It's as if I've been loosed from the Earth. As if there were nothing to hold me down anymore and I'm being sucked into the void. As if I were bound by a silver cord and now that cord has snapped.

I thought I knew what loneliness was before he found me, but I had no clue. You don't know what real loneliness is until you've known the opposite.

"Cassie."

Two seconds: on my feet. Another two and a half: swinging the M16 toward the voice. A shadow darts between the trees on my left and I open up, spraying bullets willy-nilly at tree trunks and branches and empty air.

"Cassie."

In front of me, about two o'clock. I empty the clip. I know I didn't hit him. Know I don't have a prayer of hitting him. He's a Silencer. But if I keep shooting, maybe he'll back off.

"Cassie."

Directly behind me. I take a deep breath, reload, and then deliberately turn and pump some more lead into the innocent trees.

Don't you get it, dummy? He's getting you to use up your ammo.

So I wait, feet wide, shoulders square, gun up, scanning right and left, and I can hear his voice in my head, giving instruction back at the farm: *You have to feel the target. Like it's connected to you. Like you're connected to it . . .*

It happens in the space of time between one second and the next. His arm drops around my chest, he rips the rifle from my hands, then relieves me of the Luger. After another half second, he's locked me in a bear hug, crushing me into his chest and lifting my feet a couple inches off the ground as I kick furiously with my heels, twisting my head back and forth, snapping at his forearm with my teeth.

And the whole time his lips tickling the delicate skin of my ear. "Cassie. Don't. Cassie . . ."

"Let . . . me . . . go."

"That's been the whole problem. I can't."

71

EVAN LETS ME KICK and squirm until I'm exhausted, then he plops me down against a tree and steps back.

"You know what happens if you run," he warns me. His face is flushed. He's having a hard time catching his breath. When he turns to retrieve my weapons, his movements are stiff, deliberate. Catching me—after taking the grenade for me—has cost him. His jacket hangs open, exposing his denim shirt, and the pants he took from the dead kid are two sizes too small, tight in all the wrong places. It looks like he's wearing a pair of capris.

"You'll shoot me in the back of the head," I say.

He tucks my Luger into his belt and swings the M16 over one shoulder.

"I could have done that a long time ago."

I guess he's talking about the first time we met. "You're a Silencer," I say. It takes everything in me not to jump up and tear off through the trees again. Of course, running from him is pointless. Fighting him is pointless. So I have to outsmart him. It's like I'm back under that car on the day we first met. No hiding from it. No running from it.

He sits down a few feet away, resting his rifle across his thighs. He's shivering.

"If your job is to kill us, why didn't you kill me?" I ask.

He answers without hesitating, as if he's decided long before I asked the question what his answer would be.

"Because I'm in love with you."

My head falls back against the rough bark of the tree. The bare branches overhead are hard-edged against the bright blue sky. "Well, this is a tragic love story, isn't it? Alien invader falls for human girl. The hunter for his prey."

"I am human."

"'I am human . . . but.' Finish it, Evan." *Because* I'm *finished now, Evan. You were the last one, my only friend in the world, and now you're gone. I mean, you're here, whatever you are, but Evan, my Evan, he's gone.*

"Not *but*, Cassie. *And*. I am human and I'm not. I'm neither and I'm both. I am Other and I am you."

I look into his eyes, deep-set and very dark in the shadowy air, and say, "You make me want to puke."

"How could I tell you the truth when the truth meant you would leave me and leaving me meant you would die?"

"Don't preach to me about dying, Evan." Wagging my finger at his face. "I watched my mother die. I watched one of you kill my father. I've seen more death in six months than anyone else in human history."

He pushes my hand down and says through gritted teeth, "And if there had been something you could have done to protect your father, to save your mother, wouldn't you have done it? If you knew a lie would save Sammy, wouldn't you lie?"

You bet I would. I would even pretend to trust the enemy to save Sammy. I'm still trying to wrap my mind around *Because I'm in love with you.* Trying to come up with some other reason he betrayed his species.

Doesn't matter, doesn't matter. Only one thing matters. A door slammed closed behind Sammy the day he got on that bus, a door with a thousand locks, and I realize sitting in front of me is the guy with the keys.

"You know what's at Wright-Patterson, don't you?" I say. "You know exactly what happened to Sam."

He doesn't answer. Doesn't nod yes. Doesn't shake his head no. What's he thinking? That it's one thing to spare a single measly random human but something seriously different to give away the master plan? Is this Evan Walker's under-the-Buick moment, when you can't run, can't hide, and your only option is to turn and face?

"Is he alive?" I ask. I lean forward; the rough tree bark is cutting into my spine.

He hesitates for a half breath, then: "He probably is."

"Why did they . . . why did you bring him there?"

"To prepare him."

"To prepare him for what?"

Waits a full breath this time. Then: "The 5th Wave."

I close my eyes. For the first time, looking at that beautiful face is too much to endure. God, I'm tired. So frigging tired, I could sleep for a thousand years. If I slept for a thousand years, maybe I'd wake up and the Others would be gone and there'd be happy children frolicking in these woods. *I am Other and I am you.* What the hell does that mean? I'm too tired to chase the thought.

I open my eyes and force myself to look at him. "You can get us in."

He's shaking his head.

"Why not?" I ask. "You're one of them. You can say you captured me."

"Wright-Patterson isn't a prison camp, Cassie."

"Then what is it?"

"For you?" Leaning toward me; his breath warms my face. "A

death trap. You won't last five seconds. Why do you think I've been trying everything I can think of to keep you from going there?"

"Everything? Really? How about telling me the truth? How about something like, 'Hey, Cass, about this rescue thingy of yours. I'm an alien like the guys who took Sam, so I know what you're doing is absolutely hopeless'?"

"Would it have made a difference if I had?"

"That isn't the point."

"No, the point is your brother is being held at the most important base we—I mean, the Others—have established since the purge began—"

"Since the what? What did you call it? The purge?"

"Or the cleansing." He can't meet my eyes. "Sometimes it's called that."

"Oh, that's what you're doing? Cleaning up the human mess?"

"That's not my word for it, and purging or cleansing or whatever you want to call it wasn't my decision," he protests. "If it makes you feel any better, I never thought we should—"

"I don't want to feel better! The hatred I'm feeling at this moment is all I need, Evan. All I need." *Okay, that was honest, but don't go too far. He's the guy with the keys. Keep him talking.* "Never thought you should do what?"

He takes a long drink from the water flask, offers it to me. I shake my head. "Wright-Patterson isn't just any base—it's *the* base," he says, weighing each word carefully. "And Vosch isn't just any commander—he's *the* commander, the leader of all field operations and the architect of the cleans—the one who designed the attacks."

"Vosch murdered seven billion people." The number sounds weirdly hollow in my ears. After the Arrival, one of Dad's favorite themes was how advanced the Others must be, how high they must have climbed on the evolutionary ladder to reach the stage of intergalactic travel. And this is their solution to the human "problem"?

"There were some of us who didn't think annihilation was the answer," Evan says. "I was one of them, Cassie. My side lost the argument."

"No, Evan, that would be *my* side that lost."

It's more than I can take. I stand up, expecting him to stand, too, but he stays where he is, looking up at me.

"He doesn't see you as some of us do . . . as I do," he says. "To him, you're a disease that will kill its host unless it's wiped out."

"I'm a disease. That's what I am to you."

I can't look at him anymore. If I look at Evan Walker for one more second, I'm going to be sick.

Behind me, his voice is soft, level, almost sad. "Cassie, you're up against something that is way beyond your capacity to fight. Wright-Patterson isn't just another cleansing camp. The complex underneath it is the central coordinating hub for every drone in this hemisphere. It's Vosch's eyes, Cassie; it's how he sees you. Breaking in to rescue Sammy isn't just risky—it's suicidal. For both of us."

"Both of us?" I glance at him out of the corner of my eye. He hasn't moved.

"I can't pretend to take you prisoner. My assignment isn't to capture people—it's to kill them. If I try to walk in with you as my prisoner, they'll kill you. And then they'll kill me for not killing you. And I can't sneak you in. The base is patrolled by drones, protected by a twenty-foot-high electric fence, watchtowers, infrared cameras, motion detectors . . . and a hundred people just like me, and you know what I can do."

"Then I sneak in without you."

He nods. "It's the only possible way—but just because something is possible doesn't mean it isn't suicidal. Everyone they bring in—I mean the people they don't kill right away—is put through a screening program that maps their entire psyche, including their memories. They'll know who you are and why you're there . . . and then they'll kill you."

"There's got to be a scenario that doesn't end with them killing me," I insist.

"There is," he says. "The scenario where we find a safe spot to hide and wait for Sammy to come to us."

My mouth drops open, and I think, *Huh?* Then I say it: "Huh?"

"It might take a couple of years. How old is he, five? The youngest allowed is seven."

"The youngest allowed to do what?"

He looks away. "You saw."

The little kid whose throat he cut at Camp Ashpit, wearing fatigues, toting a rifle almost as big as he was. Now I do want a drink. I walk over to him, and he gets very still while I bend over and pick up the flask. After four big swallows, my mouth is still dry.

"Sam is the 5th Wave," I say. The words taste bad. I take another long drink.

Evan nods. "If he passed his screening, he's alive and being . . ." He searches for the word. "Processed."

"Brainwashed, you mean."

"More like indoctrinated. In the idea that the aliens have been using human bodies, and we—I mean humans—have figured out a way to detect them. And if you can detect them, you can—"

"That isn't fiction," I interrupt. "You are using human bodies."

He shakes his head. "Not the way Sammy thinks we are."

"What does that mean? Either you are or you aren't."

"Sammy thinks we look like some kind of infestation attached to human brains, but—"

"Funny, that's exactly the way I picture you, Evan. An infestation." I can't help myself.

His hand comes up. When I don't slap it away or take off running into the woods, he slowly wraps his fingers around my wrist and gently pulls me to the ground beside him. I'm sweating slightly, though it's bitingly cold. What now?

"There was a boy, a real human boy, named Evan Walker," he says, looking deeply into my eyes. "Just like any kid, with a mom and a dad and brothers and sisters, completely human. Before he was born, I was inserted into him while his mother slept. While we both slept. For thirteen years I slept inside Evan Walker, while he learned to sit up, to eat solid food, to walk and talk and run and ride a bike, I was there, waiting to wake up. Like thousands of Others in thousands of other Evan Walkers around the world. Some of us were already awake, setting up our lives to be where we needed to be when the time came."

I'm nodding, but why am I nodding? He came to a human body? What the hell does that mean?

"The 4th Wave," he says, trying to be helpful. "Silencers. It's a good name for us. We were silent, hiding inside human bodies, hiding inside human lives. We didn't have to pretend to be you. We *were* you. Human and Other. Evan didn't die when I awakened. He was . . . absorbed."

Ever the noticer, Evan notices I'm totally creeped out by this. He reaches out to touch me and flinches when I pull away.

"So what are you, Evan?" I whisper. "Where are you? You said you were . . . what did you say?" My mind's racing a gazillion miles an hour. "Inserted. Inserted where?"

"Maybe *inserted* isn't the best word. I guess the concept that comes closest is *downloaded*. I was downloaded into Evan when his brain was still developing."

I shake my head. For a being centuries more advanced than I am, he sure has a hard time answering a simple question.

"But what are you? What do you look like?"

He frowns. "You know what I look like."

"No! Oh God, sometimes you can be so . . ." *Careful, Cassie, don't go there. Remember what matters.* "Before you became Evan, before you came here, when you were on your way to Earth from wherever it is you came from, what did you look like?"

"Nothing. We haven't had bodies in tens of thousands of years. We had to give them up when we left our home."

"You're lying again. What, you look like a toad or a warthog or a slug or something? Every living thing looks like something."

"We are pure consciousness. Pure being. Abandoning our bodies and downloading our psyches into the mothership's mainframe was the only way we could make the journey." He takes my hand and curls my fingers into a fist. "This is me," he says softly. He covers my fist with his hands, enfolding it. "This is Evan. It's not a perfect analogy, because there's no place where I end and he begins." He smiles shyly. "I'm not doing very well, am I? Do you want me to show you who I am?"

Holy crap! "No. Yes. What do you mean?" I picture him peeling off his face like a creature from a horror movie.

His voice shakes a little. "I can show you what I am."

"It doesn't involve any kind of insertion, does it?"

He laughs softly. "I guess it does. In a way. I'll show you, Cassie, if you want to see."

Of course I want to see. And of course I don't want to see. It's clear he wants to show me—will showing me get me one step closer to Sams? But this isn't totally about Sammy. Maybe if Evan shows me, I'll understand why he saved me when he should have killed me. Why he held me in the dark night after night to keep me safe—and to keep me sane.

He's still smiling at me, probably delighted that I'm not clawing his eyes out or laughing him off, which might hurt worse. My hand is lost in his, gently bound, like the tender heart of a rose within the bud, waiting for the rain.

"What do I have to do?" I whisper.

He lets go of my hand. Reaches toward my face. I flinch. "I would never hurt you, Cassie." I breathe. Nod. Breathe some more. "Close your eyes." He touches my eyelids gently, so gently, a butterfly's wings.

"Relax. Breathe deep. Empty your mind. If you don't, I can't come in. Do you want me to come in, Cassie?"

Yes. No. Dear God, how far do I have to go to keep my promise?

I whisper, "Yes."

It doesn't begin inside my head like I expected. Instead a delicious warmth spreads through my body, expanding from my heart outward, and my bones and muscles and skin dissolve in the warmth that spreads out from me, until the warmth overcomes the Earth and the boundaries of the universe. The warmth is everywhere and everything. My body and everything outside my body belongs to it. Then I feel him; he is in the warmth, too, and there's no separation between us, no spot where I end and he begins, and I open up like a flower to the rain, achingly slow and dizzyingly fast, dissolving in the warmth, dissolving in him and there's nothing to *see*, that's just the convenient word he used because there is no word to describe him, he just *is*.

And I open to him, a flower to the rain.

72

THE FIRST THING I do after I open my eyes is break out in heart-wrenching sobs. I can't help it: I've never felt so abandoned in my life.

"Maybe that was too soon," he says, pulling me into his arms and stroking my hair.

And I let him. I'm too weak, too confused, too empty and forlorn to do anything else but let him hold me.

"I'm sorry I lied to you, Cassie," he murmurs into my hair.

The cold squeezes back down. Now I have just the memory of the warmth.

"You must hate being trapped inside there," I whisper, pressing my hand against his chest. I feel his heart push back.

"It doesn't feel like I'm trapped," he says. "In a way, it feels like I've been freed."

"Freed?"

"To feel something again. To feel this." He kisses me. A different kind of warmth spreads through my body.

Lying in the enemy's arms. What's the matter with me? These

beings burned us alive, crushed us, drowned us, infected us with a plague that made us bleed to death from the inside out. I watched them kill everyone I knew and loved—with one special exception—and here I am, playing sucky-face with one! I let him inside my soul. I shared something with him more precious and intimate than my body.

For Sammy's sake, that's why. A good answer, but complicated. The truth is simple.

"You said you lost the argument over what to do about the human disease," I say. "What was your answer?"

"Coexistence." Talking to me, but addressing the stars above us. "There aren't that many of us, Cassie. Only a few hundred thousand. We could have inserted ourselves in you, lived out our new lives without anyone ever knowing we were here. Not many of my people agreed with me. They saw pretending to be human as beneath them. They were afraid the longer we pretended to be human, the more human we would become."

"And who would want that?"

"I didn't think I would," he admits. "Until I became one."

"When you . . . 'woke up' in Evan?"

He shakes his head and says simply, as if it's the most obvious thing in the world, "When I woke up in *you*, Cassie. I wasn't fully human until I saw myself in your eyes."

And then there are real human tears in his real human eyes, and it's my turn to hold him while his heart breaks. My turn to see myself in his eyes.

Somebody might say that I'm not the only one lying in the enemy's arms.

I am humanity, but who is Evan Walker? Human and Other. Both and neither. By loving me, he belongs to no one.

He doesn't see it that way.

"I'll do whatever you say, Cassie," he says helplessly. His eyes shine brighter than the stars overhead. "I understand why you have to go. If it were you inside that camp, I would go. A hundred thousand Silencers couldn't stop me."

He presses his lips against my ear and whispers low and fierce, as if he's sharing the most important secret in the world, which maybe he is.

"It's hopeless. And it's stupid. It's suicidal. But love is a weapon they have no answer for. They know how you think, but they can't know what you feel."

Not *we*. *They*.

A threshold has been crossed, and he isn't stupid. He knows it's the kind you can't cross back over.

WE SPEND OUR LAST DAY TOGETHER sleeping under the highway overpass like two homeless people, which literally we both are. One person sleeps, the other keeps watch. When it's his turn to rest, he gives my guns back without hesitating and falls asleep instantly, as if it doesn't occur to him I could easily run away or shoot him in the head. I don't know; maybe it does occur to him. Our problem has always been that we don't think like they do. It's why I trusted him in the beginning and why he knew I would trust him. Silencers kill people. Evan didn't kill me. Ergo, Evan couldn't be a Silencer. See? That's logic. Ahem—human logic.

At dusk we finish the rest of our provisions and hike up the embankment to take cover in the trees bordering Highway 35. The buses run only at night, he tells me. And you'll know when they're coming. You can hear the sound of their engines for miles because that's the only sound for miles. First you see the headlights, and then you hear them, and then they're whizzing past like big yellow race cars because the highway's been cleared of wrecks and there aren't speed limits anymore. He doesn't know: Maybe they'll stop, maybe they won't. Maybe they'll just slow down long enough for one of the soldiers on board to put a bullet between my eyes. Maybe they won't come at all.

"You said they were still gathering people," I point out. "Why wouldn't they come?"

He's watching the road beneath us. "At some point the 'rescued' will figure out they've been duped, or the survivors on the outside will. When that happens, they'll shut down the base—or the part of the base that's dedicated to cleansing." He clears his throat. Staring down at the road.

"What does that mean, 'shut down the base'?"

"Shut it down the way they shut down Camp Ashpit."

I think about what he's saying. Like him, looking at the empty road.

"Okay," I say finally. "Then we hope Vosch hasn't pulled the plug yet."

I scoop up a handful of dirt and twigs and dead leaves and rub it over my face. Another handful for my hair. He watches me without saying anything.

"This is the point where you bop me over the head," I say. I smell like the earth, and for some reason I think about my father kneeling in the rose bed and the white sheet. "Or offer to go in my place. Or bop me in the head and then go in my place."

He jumps to his feet. For a second I'm afraid he is going to bop me over the head, he's that upset. Instead, he wraps his arms around himself like he's cold—or he does it to keep himself from bopping me over the head.

"It's suicide," he snaps. "We're both thinking it. One of us might as well say it. Suicide if I go, suicide if you go. Dead or alive, he's lost."

I pull the Luger from my waistband. Put it on the ground at his feet. Then the M16.

"Save these for me," I tell him. "I'm going to need them when I get back. And by the way, somebody should say this: You look ridiculous in those pants." I scooch over to the backpack without getting up. Pull out Bear. No need to dirty him up; he's already rough-looking.

"Are you listening to me?" he demands.

"The problem is you don't listen to yourself," I shoot back. "There's only one way in, and that's the way Sammy took. You can't go. I have to. So don't even open your mouth. If you say anything, I'll slap you."

I stand up, and a weird thing happens: As I rise, Evan seems to shrink. "I'm going to get my little brother, and there's only one way I can do it."

He's looking up at me, nodding. He has been inside me. There has been no place where he ended and I began. He knows what I'm going to say:

Alone.

74

THERE ARE THE STARS, the pinpricks of light stabbing down.

There is the empty road beneath the light stabbing down and the girl on the road with the smudged face and twigs and dead leaves entangled in her short, curly hair, clutching a battered old teddy bear, on the empty road, beneath the stars stabbing down.

There is the growl of engines and then the twin bars of the headlights cutting across the horizon, and the lights grow larger, brighter, like two stars going supernova, bearing down on the girl, who has secrets in her heart and promises to keep, and she faces the lights that bear down on her, she does not run or hide.

The driver sees me with plenty of time to stop. The brakes squeal, the door hisses open, and a soldier steps onto the asphalt. He has a gun but he doesn't point it at me. He looks at me, pinned in the headlights, and I look back at him.

He's wearing a white armband with a red cross on it. His name tag says PARKER. I remember that name. My heart skips a beat. What if he recognizes me? I'm supposed to be dead.

What's my name? Lizbeth. Am I hurt? No. Am I alone? Yes.

Parker does a slow 360, surveying the landscape. He doesn't see the hunter in the woods who is watching this play out, his scope trained on Parker's head. Of course Parker doesn't see him. The hunter in the woods is a Silencer.

Parker takes my arm and helps me onto the bus. It smells like blood and sweat. Half the seats are empty. There are kids. Adults, too. They don't matter, though. Only Parker and the driver and the soldier with the name tag HUDSON matter. I flop into the last seat by the emergency door, the same seat Sam sat in when he pressed his little hand to the glass and watched me shrink until the dust swallowed me.

Parker hands me a bag of smushed gummies and a bottle of water. I don't want either, but I consume both. The gummies have been in his pocket and are warm and gooey, and I'm afraid I'm going to be sick.

The bus picks up speed. Someone near the front is crying. Besides that, there's the hum of the wheels and the high rev of the engine and the cold wind rushing through the cracked windows.

Parker comes back with a silver disk that he presses against my forehead. To take my temperature, he tells me. The disk glows red. I'm good, he says. What's my bear's name?

Sammy, I tell him.

Lights on the horizon. That's Camp Haven, Parker tells me. It's perfectly safe. No more running. No more hiding. I nod. Perfectly safe.

The light grows, seeps slowly through the windshield, then rushes in as we get closer, flooding the bus now, and we're pulling up to the gate and a loud bell goes off and the gate rolls open. The silhouette of a soldier high in the watchtower.

We stop in front of a hangar. A fat man bounds onto the bus, light on the balls of his feet like a lot of fat guys. His name is Major Bob. We shouldn't be afraid, he tells us. We are perfectly safe. There are only two rules to remember. Rule one is remember our colors. Rule two is listen and follow.

I fall into line with my group and follow Parker to the side door of the hangar. He pats Lizbeth on the shoulder and wishes her good luck.

I find a red circle and sit down. There are soldiers everywhere.

But most of these soldiers are kids, some not much older than Sam. They all look very serious, especially the younger ones. The really young ones are the most serious of all.

You can manipulate a kid into believing almost anything, into doing almost anything, Evan explained in our mission briefing. *With the right training, there are few things more savage than a ten-year-old.*

I have a number: T-sixty-two. *T* for *Terminator*. Ha.

The numbers are called out over a loudspeaker.

"SIXTY-TWO! TEE-SIXTY-TWO! PROCEED TO THE RED DOOR, PLEASE! NUMBER TEE-SIXTY-TWO!"

The first station is the shower room.

On the other side of the red door is a thin woman wearing green scrubs. Everything comes off and into the hamper. Underwear, too. They love children here but not lice and ticks. There's the shower. Here's the soap. Put on the white robe when you're finished and wait to be called.

I sit the bear against the wall and step naked onto the cold tiles. The water is tepid. The soap has a pungent mediciny smell. I'm still damp when I slip on the paper robe. It clings to my skin. You can almost see through it. I pick up Bear and wait.

Prescreening is next. A lot of questions. Some are nearly identical. That's to test your story. Stay calm. Stay focused.

Through the next door. Up onto the exam table. A new nurse, heavier, meaner. She barely looks at me. I must be, like, the thousandth person she's seen since the Silencers took the base.

What's my full name? Elizabeth Samantha Morgan.

How old am I? Twelve.

Where am I from? Do I have any brothers or sisters? Is anyone in my family still alive? What happened to them? Where did I go

378

after I left home? What happened to my leg? How was I shot? Who shot me? Do I know where any other survivors are? What are my siblings' names? My parents'? What did my father do for a living? What was the name of my best friend? Tell her again what happened to my family.

When it's over, she pats me on the knee and tells me not to be scared. I'm perfectly safe.

I hug Bear to my chest and nod.

Perfectly safe.

The physical's next. Then the implant. The incision is very small. She'll probably seal it with glue.

The woman named Dr. Pam is so nice, I like her in spite of myself. The dream doctor: kind, gentle, patient. She doesn't rush right in and start poking me; she talks first. Lets me know everything she's going to do. Shows me the implant. Like a pet chip, only better! Now if something happens, they'll know where to find me.

"What's your teddy bear's name?"

"Sammy."

"Okay if I sit Sammy in this chair while we put in the tracker?"

I roll onto my stomach. I'm irrationally concerned she can see my butt through the paper robe. I tense, anticipating the bite of the needle.

The device can't download you until it's linked to Wonderland. But once it's in you, it's fully operational. They can use it to track you, and they can use it to kill you.

Dr. Pam asks what happened to my leg. Some bad people shot it. That won't happen here, she assures me. There are no bad people at Camp Haven. I'm perfectly safe.

I'm tagged. I feel like she's hung a twenty-pound rock around my neck. Time for the last test, she tells me. A program seized from the enemy.

They call it Wonderland.

I grab Bear from his seat and follow her into the next room. White walls. White floor. White ceiling. White dentist chair, straps hanging from the arms and the leg rests. A keyboard and monitor. She tells me to have a seat and steps over to the computer.

"What does Wonderland do?" I ask.

"Well, that's kind of complicated, Lizbeth, but essentially Wonderland records a virtual map of your cognitive functions."

"A brain map?"

"Something like that, yes. Have a seat in the chair, honey. It won't take long, and I promise it doesn't hurt."

I sit down, hugging Bear to my chest.

"Oh no, honey, Sammy can't be in the chair with you."

"Why not?"

"Here, give him to me. I'll put him right over here by my computer."

I give her a suspicious look. But she's smiling and she has been so kind. I should trust her. After all, she completely trusts me.

But I'm so nervous, Bear slips out of my hand when I hold him out for her. He falls beside the chair onto his fat, fluffy head. I twist around to scoop him up, but Dr. Pam says to sit still, she'll get him, and then she bends over.

I grab her head with both hands and bring it straight down into the arm of the chair. The impact makes my forearms sing with pain. She falls, stunned by the blow, but doesn't collapse completely. By the time her knees hit the white floor, I'm out of the chair and swinging around behind her. The plan was a karate punch to her throat, but her back is to me, so I improvise. I grab the strap hanging from the chair arm and wrap it twice around her neck. Her hands come up, too late. I yank the strap tight, putting my foot against the chair for leverage, and pull.

Those seconds waiting for her to pass out are the longest of my life.

She goes limp. I immediately let go of the strap, and she falls face-first onto the floor. I check her pulse.

I know it'll be tempting, but you can't kill her. She and everyone else running the base is linked to a monitoring system located in the command center. If she goes down, all hell breaks loose.

I roll Dr. Pam onto her back. Blood runs from both nostrils. Probably broken. I reach up behind my head. This is the squishy part. But I'm jacked up on adrenaline and euphoria. So far everything has gone perfectly. I can do this.

I rip off the bandage and pull hard on either side of the incision, and it feels like a hot match pressing down as the wound comes open. A pair of tweezers and a mirror would come in handy right about now, but I don't have either one of those, so I use my fingernail to dig out the tracker. The technique works better than I expected: After three tries, the device jams beneath my nail and I bring it cleanly out.

It only takes ninety seconds to run the download. That gives you three, maybe four minutes. No more than five.

How many minutes in? Two? Three? I kneel beside Dr. Pam and shove the tracker as far as I can up her nose. Ugh.

No, you can't shove it down her throat. It has to be near her brain. Sorry about that.

You're sorry, Evan?

Blood on my finger, my blood, her blood, mixed together.

I step over to the keyboard. Now the truly scary part.

You don't have Sammy's number, but it should be cross-referenced to his name. If one variation doesn't work, try a different one. There should be a search function.

Blood is trickling down the back of my neck, trailing down between my shoulder blades. I'm shivering uncontrollably, which makes it hard to type. In the blinking blue box I tap out the word *search*. It take two tries to spell it correctly.

ENTER NUMBER.

I don't have a number, damn it. I have a name. How do I get back to the blue box? I hit the enter button.

ENTER NUMBER.

Oh, I get it now. It wants a number!

I key in *Sullivan*.

DATA ENTRY ERROR.

I'm wavering between throwing the monitor across the room and kicking Dr. Pam until she's dead. Neither will help me find Sam, but both would make me feel better. I hit the escape button and get the blue box and type *search by name*.

The words vanish. Vaporized by Wonderland. The blue box blinks, blank again.

I fight back a scream. I'm out of time.

If you can't find him in the system, we'll have to go to Plan B.

I'm not crazy about Plan B. I like Plan A, where his location pops up on a map and I run right to him. Plan A is simple and clean. Plan B is complicated and messy.

One more try. Five more seconds can't make that big a difference.

I type *Sullivan* into the blue box.

The display goes haywire. Numbers begin to race across the gray background, filling the screen, like I just gave it a command to calculate the value of pi. I panic and start hitting random buttons, but the scroll doesn't stop. I'm well past five minutes. Plan B sucks, but B it is.

I duck into the adjoining room, where I find the white jumpsuits. I grab one off the shelf and wisely attempt to dress without taking off the robe first. With a grunt of frustration, I shrug out of it, and for a second I'm totally naked, the second in which that door beside me will fly open and a battalion of Silencers will flood into the room. That's the way things happen in all Plan Bs. The suit is way too big, but better too big than too small, I think, and I'm quickly zipped up and back in the Wonderland room.

If you can't find him through the main interface, there's a good possibility she has a handheld unit somewhere on her. It works on the same principle, but you have to be very careful. One function is a locator, the other is a detonator. Key in the wrong command and you won't find him, you'll fry him.

When I burst back in, she's sitting up, holding Bear in one hand and a small silver thing that looks like a cell phone in the other.

Like I said, Plan B sucks.

75

HER NECK IS FLAMING RED where I choked her. Her face is covered in blood. But her hands are steady, and her eyes have lost all their warmth. Her thumb hovers over a green button below a numeric display.

"Don't press it," I say. "I'm not going to hurt you." I squat down, hands open, palms toward her. "Seriously, you really do not want to press that button."

She presses the button.

Her head snaps back, and she flops down. Her legs kick twice, and she's gone.

I leap forward, snatch Bear out of her dead fingers, and race back through the jumpsuit room and into the hallway beyond. Evan never bothered to tell me how long after the alarm sounds before the Stormtroopers are mobilized, the base is locked down, and the interloper captured, tortured, and put to a slow and agonizing death. Probably not that long.

So much for Plan B. Hated it anyway. The only downside is Evan and I never drew up a Plan C.

He'll be in a squad with older kids, so your best bet is the barracks that ring the parade grounds.

Barracks that ring the parade grounds. Wherever that is. Maybe I should stop someone and ask for directions, because I only know one way out of this building, and that's the way I came in, past the dead body and the old fat mean nurse and the young thin nice nurse and right into the loving arms of Major Bob.

There's an elevator at the end of the hall with a single call button: It's a one-way express ride to the underground complex, where Evan says Sammy and the other "recruits" are shown the phony creatures "attached" to real human brains. Festooned with security cameras. Crawling with Silencers. Only two other ways out of this hallway: the door just to the right of the elevator and the door I came out of.

Finally, a no-brainer.

384

I slam through the door and find myself in a stairwell. Like the elevator, the stairs go in one direction: down.

I hesitate for a half second. The stairwell is quiet and small, but it's a good, cozy kind of small. Maybe I should stay here awhile and hug my bear, perhaps suck my thumb.

I force myself to take it slow down the five flights to the bottom. The steps are metal, cold against my bare feet. I'm waiting for the shriek of alarms and the pounding of heavy boots and the rain of bullets from above and below. I think of Evan at Camp Ashpit, taking out four heavily armed, highly trained killers in near total darkness, and wonder why I ever thought it was wise to stroll into the lion's den alone when I could have had a Silencer by my side.

Well, not totally alone. I do have the bear.

I press my ear against the door at the bottom and rest my hand on the lever. I hear my own heartbeat and that's all.

The door flies inward, forcing me back against the wall, and then I do hear the pounding of boots as men toting semiautomatics race up the stairs. The door starts to swing closed and I grab the lever to keep the door in front of me until they make the first turn and thunder out of sight.

I whip around into the corridor before the door closes. Red lights mounted from the ceiling spin, throwing my shadow against the white walls, wiping it away, throwing it again. Right or left? I'm a little turned around, but I think the front of the hangar is to the right. I jog in that direction, then stop. Where am I most likely to find the majority of Silencers in an emergency? Probably clustered around the main entrance to the scene of the crime.

I turn around and run smack into the chest of a very tall man with piercing blue eyes.

I wasn't close enough to see his eyes at Camp Ashpit.

But I remember the voice.

Deep, hard-edged, razor-sharp.

"Well, hello there, little lamb," Vosch says. "You must be lost."

76

HIS GRIP ON MY SHOULDER is as hard as his voice.

"Why are you down here?" he asks. "Who is your group leader?"

I shake my head. The tears welling up in my eyes aren't fake. I have to think fast, and my first thought is Evan was right: This solo act was doomed, no matter how many backup plans we concocted. If only Evan were here . . .

If Evan were here!

"He killed her!" I blurt out. "That man killed Dr. Pam!"

"What man? Who killed Dr. Pam?"

I shake my head, bawling my little eyes out, crushing my battered teddy against my chest. Behind Vosch, another squad of soldiers races down the corridor toward us. He shoves me at them.

"Secure this one and meet me upstairs. We have a breach."

I'm dragged to the nearest door, shoved inside a dark room, and the lock clicks. The lights flicker on. The first thing I see is a frightened, young-looking girl in a white jumpsuit holding a teddy bear. I actually give a startled yelp.

Beneath the mirror is a long counter on which a monitor and keyboard sit.

I'm in the execution chamber Evan described, where they show the new recruits the fake brain-spiders.

Forget the computer. I'm not about to start hitting buttons again. Options, Cassie. What are your options?

I know there's another room on the other side of the mirror. And there has to be at least one door, which may or may not be locked. I know the door to this room is locked, so I can wait for Vosch to come back for me or I can bust through this looking glass to the other side.

I pick up one of the chairs, rear back, and hurl it against the mirror. The impact rips the chair from my hands and it falls to the floor with a deafening—at least to me—clatter. I've put a large scratch in the thick glass, but that's the only damage I see. I pick up the chair again. Take a deep breath. Lower my shoulders, rotate my hips as I bring the chair around. That's what they teach you in karate class: Power is in rotation. I aim for the scratch. Focus every ounce of my energy on that single spot.

The chair bounces off the glass, throwing me off balance, and I land on my butt with a teeth-jarring thump. So jarring, in fact, that I bite down hard on my tongue. My mouth fills with blood, and I spit it out, hitting the girl in the mirror right in the nose.

I yank up the chair again, breathing deep. I forgot one thing I learned in karate: your *eich!* The war cry. Laugh at it all you want; it does concentrate your power.

The third and final blow shatters the glass. My momentum slams me into the waist-high counter, and my feet come off the floor as the chair tumbles into the adjoining room. I can see another dentist chair, a bank of processors, wires running across the floor, and another door. *Please, God, don't let it be locked.*

I pick up Bear and climb through the hole. I imagine Vosch

returning and the look on his face when he sees the busted mirror. The door on the other side isn't locked. It opens into another white cinder-block corridor lined with unmarked doors. Ah, the possibilities. But I don't step into that corridor. I hover in the doorway. Before me, the unmarked path. Behind me, the one I've marked: They'll see the hole. They'll know which direction I've taken. How long can I stay ahead of them? My mouth has filled with blood again, and I force myself to swallow it. Can't make it too easy for them to track me.

Too easy: I forgot to jam the chair under the door handle in the first room. It won't stop them from getting in, but it would drop some precious seconds into my piggy bank.

If something goes wrong, don't overthink, Cassie. You have good instincts; trust them. Thinking through every step is fine if you're playing chess, but this isn't chess.

I run back through the killing room and dive through the hole. I misjudge the width of the counter and flip off the edge, somersaulting onto my back, smacking my head hard against the floor. I lie there for a fuzzy second, bright red stars burning in my vision. I'm looking at the ceiling and the metal ductwork running beneath it. I saw the same setup in the corridors: the bomb shelter's ventilation system.

And I think, *Cassie, that's the bomb shelter's freaking ventilation system.*

77

SCUTTLING FORWARD on my stomach, worrying that I'm too heavy for the supports and that at any second the entire section of pipe will collapse, I scoot along the shaft, pausing at each juncture to listen. Listen for what, I'm not really sure. The crying of frightened children? The laughter of happy children? The air in the shaft is cold, brought in from the outside and funneled underground, sort of like me.

The air belongs here; I don't. What did Evan say?

Your best bet is the barracks that ring the parade grounds.

That's it, Evan. That's the new plan. I'll find the nearest air shaft and climb up to the surface. I won't know where I am or how far I am from the parade grounds, and of course the entire base is going to be in full lockdown, crawling with Silencers and their brainwashed child-soldiers looking for the girl in the white jumpsuit. And don't forget the teddy bear. Talk about a dead giveaway! Why did I insist on bringing this damn bear? Sam would understand if I left Bear behind. My promise wasn't to bring Bear to him. My promise was to bring me to him.

What is the deal with this bear?

Every few feet a choice: turn right, turn left, or keep going straight? And every few feet a pause to listen and to clear the blood from my mouth. Not worried about my blood dripping in here: It's the bread crumbs that mark my way back. My tongue is swelling, though, and throbs horribly with each beat of my heart, the human clock ticking down, measuring out the minutes I have left before they find me, take me to Vosch, and he finishes me the way he finished my father.

Something brown and small is scurrying toward me, very fast, like he's on an important errand. A roach. I've encountered cobwebs and loads of dust and some mysterious slimy substance that might be toxic mold, but this is the first truly gross thing I've seen. Give me a spider or a snake over a cockroach any day. And now he's heading right toward my face. With very vivid mental images of the thing crawling inside my jumpsuit, I use the only thing available to squash it. My bare hand. Yuck.

I keep moving. There's a glow up ahead, sort of greenish gray; in my head I call it mothership green. I inch toward the grate from which the glow emanates. Peek through the slats into the room below—only calling it a room doesn't do it justice. It's huge, easily the size of a football stadium, shaped like a bowl, with rows and rows of computer stations at the bottom, manned by over a hundred people—only to call them people is doing real people an injustice. They're them, Vosch's inhuman humans, and I have no clue what they're up to, but I'm thinking this must be it, the heart of the operation, ground zero of the "cleansing." A massive screen takes up an entire wall, projecting a map of the Earth that's dotted with bright green spots—the source of the sickly green light. Cities, I'm thinking, and then I realize the green dots must represent pockets of survivors.

Vosch doesn't need to hunt us down. Vosch knows exactly where we are.

I wiggle on, forcing myself to go slowly until the green glow is as small as the dots on the map in the control room. Four junctures down I hear voices. Men's voices. And the clang of metal on metal, the squeak of rubber soles on hard concrete.

Keep moving, Cassie. No more stopping. Sammy's not down there and Sammy is the objective.

Then one of the guys says, "How many did he say?"

And the other one goes, "At least two. The girl and whoever took out Walters and Pierce and Jackson."

Whoever took out Walters, Pierce, and Jackson?

Evan. It has to be.

What the . . . ? For a whole minute or two, I'm really furious at him. Our only hope was in my going alone, sliding past their defenses unnoticed and snatching Sam before they realized what was going on. Of course, it hadn't quite worked out that way, but Evan had no way of knowing that.

Still. The fact that Evan had ignored our carefully thought-out plan and infiltrated the base also means that Evan is here.

And Evan does what he has the heart to do.

I edge closer to their voices, passing right over their heads until I reach the grating. I peer through the metal slats and see two Silencer soldiers loading eye-shaped globes into a large handcart. I recognize what they are right away. I've seen one before.

The Eye will take care of her.

I watch them until the cart is loaded and they wheel it slowly out of sight.

A point will come when the cover isn't sustainable. When that happens, they'll shut down the base—or the part of the base that's expendable.

Oh boy. Vosch is going all Ashpit on Camp Haven.

And the minute that realization hits me, the siren goes off.

A THOUSAND WAYS

78

TWO HOURS.

The minute Vosch leaves, a clock inside my head begins to tick. No, not a clock. More like a timer ticking down to Armageddon. I'm going to need every second, so where is the orderly? Right when I'm about to pull out the drip myself, he shows up. A tall, skinny kid named Kistner; we met the last time I was laid up. He has a nervous habit of picking at the front of his scrubs, like the material irritates his skin.

"Did he tell you?" Kistner asks, keeping his voice down as he leans over the bed. "We've gone Code Yellow."

"Why?"

He shrugs. "You think they tell me anything? I just hope it doesn't mean we're taking another bunker-dive." No one in the hospital likes the air raid drills. Getting several hundred patients underground in less than three minutes is a tactical nightmare.

"Better than staying topside and getting incinerated by an alien death ray."

Maybe it's psychological, but the minute Kistner pulls the drip, the pain sets in, a dull throbbing ache where Ringer shot me that keeps time with my heart. As I wait for my head to clear, I wonder if I should reconsider the plan. An evacuation into the underground bunker might simplify things. After the fiasco of Nugget's first air raid drill, command decided to pool all noncombatant children into a safe room located in the middle of the complex.

It'll be a hell of a lot easier snatching him from there than checking every barracks on base.

But I have no idea when—or even if—that's going to happen. Better stick to the original plan. Tick-tock.

I close my eyes, visualizing each step of the escape with as much detail as possible. I did this before, back when there were high schools and Friday night games and crowds to cheer at them. Back when winning a district title seemed like the most important thing in the world. Picturing my routes, the arc of the ball sailing toward the lights, the defender keeping pace beside me, the precise moment to turn my head and bring up my hands without breaking stride. Imagining not just the perfect play but the busted one, how I would adjust my route, give the quarterback a target to save the down.

There's a thousand ways this could go wrong and only one way for it to go right. Don't think a play ahead, or two plays or three. Think about this play, this step. Get it right one step at a time, and you'll score.

Step one: the orderly.

My best buddy Kistner, giving somebody a sponge bath two beds down.

"Hey," I call over to him. "Hey, Kistner!"

"What is it?" Kistner calls back, clearly annoyed with me. He doesn't like to be interrupted.

"I have to go to the john."

"You're not supposed to get up. You'll tear the sutures."

"Aw, come on, Kistner. The bathroom's right over there."

"Doctor's orders. I'll bring you a bedpan."

I watch him weave his way through the bunks toward the

supply station. I'm a little worried I haven't waited long enough for the meds to fade. What if I can't stand up? *Tick-tock, Zombie. Tick-tock.*

I throw back the covers and swing my legs off the bed. Gritting my teeth; this is the hard part. I'm wrapped tight from chest to waist, and pushing myself upright stretches the muscles ripped apart by Ringer's bullet.

I cut you. You shoot me. It's only fair.

But it's escalating. What happens on your next turn? You stick a hand grenade down my pants?

That's a disturbing image, sticking a live grenade down Ringer's pants. On so many levels.

I'm still full of dope, but when I sit up, the pain almost makes me black out. So I sit still for a minute, waiting for my head to clear.

Step two: the bathroom.

Force yourself to go slow. Take small steps. Shuffle. I can feel the back of the gown flapping open; I'm mooning the entire ward.

The bathroom is maybe twenty feet away. It feels like twenty miles. If it's locked or if someone's in there, I'm screwed.

It's neither. I lock the door behind me. Sink and toilet and a small shower stall. The curtain rod is screwed into the wall. I lift the lid of the commode. A short metal arm that lifts the flapper, dull on both ends. Toilet paper holder is plastic. So much for finding a weapon in here. But I'm still on track. *Come on, Kistner, I'm wide open.*

Two sharp raps on the door, and then his voice on the other side.

"Hey, you in there?"

"I told you I had to go!" I yell.

"And I told you I was bringing a bedpan!"

"Couldn't hold it anymore!"

The door handle jiggles.

"Unlock this door!"

"Privacy, please!" I holler.

"I'm going to call security!"

"All right, all right! Like I'm freaking going anywhere!"

Count to ten, flip the lock, shuffle to the toilet, sit. The door opens a crack, and I can see a sliver of Kistner's thin face.

"Satisfied?" I grunt. "Now can you please close the door?"

Kistner stares at me for a long moment, plucking at his shirt. "I'll be right out here," he promises.

"Good," I say.

The door eases shut. Now six slow ten-counts. A good minute.

"Hey, Kistner!"

"What?"

"I'm gonna need your help."

"Define 'help.'"

"Getting up! I can't get off the damned can! I think I might have torn a suture . . ."

The door flies open. Kistner's face is flushed with anger.

"I told you."

He steps in front of me. Holds out both hands.

"Here, grab my wrists."

"First can you close that door? This is embarrassing."

Kistner closes the door. I wrap my fingers around Kistner's wrists.

"Ready?" he asks.

"Ready as I'll ever be."

Step three: wet willy.

As Kistner pulls back, I drive forward with my legs, slamming my shoulder into his narrow chest, knocking him backward into the concrete wall. Then I yank him forward, pivot behind him, and pull his arm up high behind his back. That forces him to his knees in front of the toilet. I grab a handful of his hair, shove his face into the water. Kistner is stronger than he looks, or I'm a lot weaker than I thought. It seems to take forever for him to pass out.

I let go and stand back. Kistner does a slow roll and flops onto the floor. Shoes, pants. Pulling him upright to yank off the shirt. The shirt's going to be too small, the pants too long, the shoes too tight. I rip off my gown, toss it into the shower stall, pull on Kistner's scrubs. The shoes take the longest. Way too small. A sharp pain shoots through my side as I struggle to put them on. Looking down, I see blood seeping through the bandaging. What if I bleed through the shirt?

A thousand ways. Focus on the one way.

Drag Kistner into the stall. Fling the curtain closed. How long will he be out? Doesn't matter. Keep moving. Don't think ahead.

Step four: the tracker.

I hesitate at the door. What if someone saw Kistner come in and now sees me, dressed as Kistner, coming out?

Then you're done. He's going to kill you anyway. Okay, don't just die, then. Die trying.

The operating room doors are the length of a football field away, past rows of beds and through what seems like a mob of orderlies and nurses and lab-coated doctors. I walk as quickly as I can toward the doors, favoring my injured side, which throws off my stride but it can't be helped; for all I know, Vosch has been tracking me and he's wondering why I'm not going back to my bunk.

Through the swinging doors, now in the scrub room, where a

weary-looking doctor is soaped up to his elbows, preparing for surgery. He jumps when I come in.

"What are you doing in here?" he demands.

"I was looking for some gloves. We've run out up front."

The surgeon jerks his head toward a row of cabinets on the opposite wall.

"You're limping," he says. "Are you hurt?"

"I pulled a muscle getting a fat guy to the john."

The doctor rinses the green soap from his forearms. "You should have used a bedpan."

Boxes of latex gloves, surgical masks, antiseptic pads, rolls of tape. Where the hell is it?

I can feel his breath against the back of my neck.

"There's the box right in front of you," he says. The guy's giving me a funny look.

"Sorry," I say. "Haven't had much sleep."

"Tell me about it!" The surgeon laughs and elbows me square in the gunshot wound. The room spins. Hard. I grit my teeth to keep from screaming.

He hurries through the inner doors to the operating theater. I move down the row of cabinets, throwing open doors, rummaging through the supplies, but I can't find what I'm looking for. Light-headed, out of breath, my side throbbing like hell. How long will Kistner stay out? How long before someone ducks in for a piss and finds him?

There's a bin on the floor beside the cabinets labeled HAZARDOUS WASTE—USE GLOVES IN HANDLING. Yank off the top and, bingo, there it is with wads of bloody surgical sponges and used syringes and discarded catheters.

Okay, so the scalpel's coated in dried blood. I guess I could sterilize it with an antiseptic wipe or wash it in the sink, but there's no time, and a dirty scalpel is the least of my worries.

Lean against the sink to steady yourself. Push your fingers against your neck to locate the tracker under the skin, and then press, don't slice, the dull, dirty blade into your neck until it splits open.

79

STEP FIVE: NUGGET.

A very young-looking doctor hurries down the corridor toward the elevators, wearing a white lab coat and a surgical mask. Limping, favoring his left side. If you pulled open his white coat, you might see the dark red stain on his green scrubs. If you pulled down his collar, you might also see the hastily applied bandage on his neck. But if you tried to do either of these things, the young-looking doctor would kill you.

Elevator. Closing my eyes as the car descends. Unless somebody's conveniently left a golf cart unattended by the front doors, walking distance to the yard is ten minutes. Then the hardest part, finding Nugget among the fifty-plus squads bivouacked there and getting him out without waking anybody. So maybe half an hour to seek and snatch. Another ten or so to slip over to the Wonderland hangar where the buses unload. This is where the plan begins to break down into a series of wild improbabilities: stowing away on an empty bus, overcoming the driver and any soldiers on board once we're clear of the gate, and then when, where, and how to dump the bus and take off on foot to rendezvous with Ringer?

What if you have to wait for the bus? Where are you going to hide?

I don't know.

And once you're on the bus, how long will you have to wait? Thirty minutes? An hour?

I don't know.

You don't know? Well, here's what I know: It's too much time, Zombie. Somebody's going to sound the alarm.

She's right. It is too much time. I should have killed Kistner. It had been one of the original steps:

Step four: kill Kistner.

But Kistner isn't one of them. Kistner's just a kid. Like Tank. Like Oompa. Like Flint. Kistner didn't ask for this war and he didn't know the truth about it. Maybe he wouldn't have believed me if I told him the truth, but I never gave him that chance.

You're soft. You should have killed him. You can't rely on luck and wishful thinking. The future of humanity belongs to the hardcore.

So when the elevator doors slide open to the main lobby, I make a silent promise to Nugget, the promise I didn't make to my sister, whose locket he wears around his neck.

If anyone comes between you and me, they're dead.

And the minute I make that promise, it's like something in the universe decides to answer, because the air raid sirens go off with an eardrum-busting scream.

Perfect! For once things are going my way. No crossing the length of the camp now. No sneaking into the barracks searching for the Nugget in a haystack. No race to the buses. Instead, a straight shot down the stairwell to the underground complex.

Grab Nugget in the organized chaos of the safe room, hide out until the all-clear sounds, and then on to the buses.

Simple.

I'm halfway to the stairs when the deserted lobby lights up in a sickly green glow, the same smoky green that danced around Ringer's head when I slipped on the eyepiece. The overhead fluorescents have cut off, standard procedure in a drill, so the light isn't coming from inside, but from somewhere in the parking lot.

I turn around to look. I shouldn't have.

Through the glass doors, I see a golf cart racing across the parking lot, heading toward the airfield. Then I see the source of the green light sitting in the covered entranceway of the hospital. Shaped like a football, only twice as big. It reminds me of an eye. I stare at it; it stares back at me.

Pulse . . . Pulse . . . Pulse . . .

Flash, flash, flash.

Blinkblinkblink.

XI

THE INFINITE SEA

80

THE SIREN'S BLARE is so loud, I can feel the hairs on the back of my neck vibrating.

I am scooting backward toward the main duct, away from the armory, when I stop.

Cassie, it's the armory.

Back to the grate, through which I stare for a full three minutes, scanning the room below for any sign of movement while the siren pounds against my ears, making it very difficult to concentrate, thank you, Colonel Vosch.

"Okay, you damn bear," I mumble with my swollen tongue. "We're going in."

I slam the heel of my bare foot into the grate. *Eich!* It pops open with one kick. When I quit karate, Mom asked why, and I said it just didn't challenge me anymore. That was my way of saying I was bored, which you were not allowed to say in front of my mother. If she heard you complain that you were bored, you found yourself with a dust rag in your hand.

I drop into the room. Well, more a medium-size warehouse than a room. Everything an alien invader might need to run a human extermination camp. Against that wall you have your Eyes, several hundred of them, stacked neatly in their own specially designed cubby. On the opposite wall, rows and rows of rifles and grenade launchers and other weaponry that I would have no clue what to do with. Smaller weapons over there, semiautomatics and grenades and ten-inch-long combat knives. There's a wardrobe section, too, representing every branch of the service and every possible rank, with all the gear to go with it, belts and boots and the military version of the fanny pack.

And me like a kid in a candy shop.

First, off comes the white jumpsuit. I pull the smallest set of fatigues I can find and put them on. Slip on the boots.

Time to gear up. A Luger with a full clip. A couple of grenades. M16? Why not? If you're going to play the part, look the part. I drop a couple extra clips into my fanny pack. Oh, look, my belt even has a holster for one of those ten-inch, wicked-looking knives! Hi there, ten-inch, wicked-looking knife.

There's a wooden box beside the gun cabinet. I peek inside and see a stack of gray metal tubes. What are these, some kind of stick-grenade? I pick one up. It's hollow and threaded at one end. Now I know what it is.

A silencer.

And it fits perfectly on the barrel of my new M16. Screws right in.

I stuff my hair under a cap that is too large for me and wish I had a mirror. I'm hoping to pass for one of Vosch's tween recruits, but I probably look more like GI Joe's little sister playing dress-up.

Now what to do with Bear. I find a leather satchel-looking thing and stuff him inside, throw the strap crossways over my shoulder. I've stopped noticing the blaring siren by this point. I'm all jacked up. Not only have I evened the odds a little, I know Evan is here, and Evan will not give up until I am safe or he is dead.

Back to the ductwork, and I'm debating whether to attempt it, weighed down as I am with twenty or so extra pounds, or take my chances in the corridors. What good is a disguise if you're going all stealthy with it? I turn around and head toward the door, and that's when the siren cuts off and silence slams down.

I don't take that as a good sign.

It also occurs to me that being in an armory full of green bombs—one of which can level a square mile—while a dozen or so of their closest friends are being set off upstairs might not be such a good idea.

I haul ass for the door, but I don't make it before the first Eye goes. The entire room jiggles. Only a few feet left, and the next Eye blinks its last blink, and this one must be closer, because dust rains down from the ceiling, and the duct at the other end snaps free of its supports and comes crashing down.

Um, Voschy, that was kind of close, don't you think?

I push through the door. No time to scout the territory. The more distance I can put between me and the remaining Eyes, the better. I sprint under the swirling red lights, turning down hallways at random, trying not to think anything through, just going on instinct and luck.

Another explosion. The walls tremble. The dust falls. From above the sound of the buildings being ripped and shredded down to their last nails. And here below, the screaming of terrified children.

I follow the screams.

Sometimes I make a wrong turn and the cries grow fainter. I backtrack, then try the next corridor. This place is like a maze, and me the lab rat.

The booming from above has stopped, at least for the moment, and I slow to a trot, gripping the rifle hard with both hands, trying one passage, backtracking when the crying fades, moving on again.

I hear Major Bob's voice on a bullhorn bouncing along the walls, coming from everywhere and nowhere.

"Okay, I want you all to stay seated with your group leader! Everybody quiet down and listen to me! Stay with your group leaders!"

I turn a corner and see a squad of soldiers running right at me. Teenagers, mostly. I throw myself against the wall, and they rush past me without even glancing in my direction. Why would they notice me? I'm just another recruit on her way to battle the alien horde.

They turn a corner, and I'm moving again. I can hear the kids jabbering and whimpering, despite Major Bob's scolding, around the next bend.

Almost there, Sam. Now you be there.

"Halt!"

Shouted from behind me. Not a kid's voice. I stop. Square my shoulders. Stay still.

"Where's your duty station, soldier? Soldier, I'm talking to you!"

"Ordered to guard the children, sir!" I say in the deepest voice I can muster.

"Turn around! Look at me when you address me, soldier."

I sigh. Turn. He's in his midtwenties, not bad looking, an all-American-boy type. I don't know military insignia, but I think he might be an officer.

To be absolutely safe, anyone over eighteen is suspect. There may be some human adults in positions of authority, but knowing Vosch, I doubt it. So if it's an adult, and especially if it's an officer, I think you can assume they are not human.

"What's your number?" he barks.

My number? I blurt out the first thing that pops into my head. "Tee-sixty-two, sir!"

He gives me a puzzled look. "Tee-sixty-two? Are you sure?"

"Yes sir, sir!" *Sir, sir? Oh God, Cassie.*

"Why aren't you with your unit?"

He doesn't wait for an answer, and good thing, because nothing is really coming to mind. He steps forward and looks me up and down, and clearly I'm not in regulation. Officer Alien does not like what he sees.

"Where's your name tag, soldier? And what are you doing with a suppressor on your weapon? And what is this?"

He pulls on the bulging leather satchel holding Bear.

I pull back. The satchel pops open and I'm busted. "It's a teddy bear, sir."

"A what?"

He stares down at my upturned face and something crosses over his as the lightbulb comes on and he realizes who he's looking at. His right hand flies toward his sidearm, but that's a really dumb move when all he had to do was lay his fist upside my teddy-bear-toting head. I swing the silencer in a slicing arc, stopping it an inch from his boyish good looks, and pull the trigger.

Now you've done it, Cassie. Blown the one chance you had, and you were so close.

I can't just leave Officer Alien where he fell. They might miss all the blood in the hurly-burly of battle, and it's nearly invisible anyway in the spinning red light, but not the body. What am I going to do with the body?

I'm close, so close, and I'm not going to let some dead guy keep me from Sammy. I grab him by the ankles and drag him back down the corridor, into another passageway, around another corner, and then drop him. He's heavier than he looks. I take a moment to stretch out the kink in my lower back before hurrying away. Now if someone stops me before I can reach the safe room,

411

my plan is to say whatever is necessary to avoid killing again. Unless I'm given no choice. And then I will kill again.

Evan was right: It does get a little easier each time.

The room is packed with kids. Hundreds of kids. Dressed in identical white jumpsuits. Sitting in big groups spread over an area about the size of a high school gymnasium. They've quieted down some. Maybe I should just shout out Sam's name or borrow Major Bob's bullhorn. I pick my way through the room, lifting my boots high to avoid stepping on any little fingers or toes.

So many faces. They begin to blur together. The room expands, explodes past the walls, extending to infinity, filled with billions of little upturned faces, and oh those bastards, those bastards, what have they done? In my tent I cried for myself and the silly, stupid life that had been taken from me. Now I beg forgiveness from the infinite sea of upturned faces.

I'm still stumbling around like a zombie when I hear a little voice calling my name. Coming from a group I had just passed, and it's funny he recognized me and not the other way around. I go still. I do not turn. I close my eyes, but can't bring myself to turn around.

"Cassie?"

I lower my head. There is a lump the size of Texas caught in my throat. And then I turn and he's staring at me with something like fear, like this might be the last straw, seeing a dead ringer for his sister tiptoeing around dressed up like a soldier. Like he's reached the outer limits of the Others' cruelty.

I kneel in front of my brother. He doesn't rush into my arms. He stares at my tear-streaked face and brings his fingers to my wet cheek. Across my nose, forehead, chin, over my fluttering eyelids.

"Cassie?"

Is it okay now? Can he believe? If the world breaks a million and one promises, can you trust the million and second?

"Hey, Sams."

He cocks his head slightly. I must sound funny to him with the bloated tongue. I fumble with the clasp of the leather satchel.

"I, um, I thought you might want this back."

I pull out the battered old teddy bear and hold it toward him. He frowns and shakes his head and doesn't reach for it, and I feel like he's punched me in the gut.

Then my baby brother slaps that damned bear out of my hand and crushes his face against my chest, and beneath the odors of sweat and strong soap I can smell it, his smell, Sammy's, my brother's.

XII

BECAUSE OF KISTNER

81

THE GREEN EYE looked at me and I looked back at it, and I don't remember what snatched me back from the edge between the blinking eye and what came next.

My first clear memory? Running.

Lobby. Stairwell. Basement level. First landing. Second landing.

When I hit the third landing, the concussion of the blast slams into my back like a wrecking ball, hurling me down the stairs and into the door that opens to the bomb shelter.

Above me, the hospital screams as it's torn apart. That's what it sounds like: a living thing screaming as it's being ripped to pieces. The thunderous crack of mortar and stone shattering. The screech of nails snapping and the shriek of two hundred windows exploding. The floor buckles, splits open. I dive headfirst into the hallway of reinforced concrete as the building above me disintegrates.

The lights flicker once, and then the corridor plunges into darkness. I've never been to this part of the complex, but I don't need the luminescent arrows on the walls to show me the way to the safe room. All I have to do is follow the terrified screams of the children.

But first it would be helpful to stand.

The fall has completely torn open the sutures; I'm bleeding heavily now, from both wounds: where Ringer's bullet went in and where it came out. I try to stand up. I give it my best shot, but my legs won't hold me up. I get halfway up and then down again I go, head spinning, gasping for air.

A second explosion knocks me flat out on the floor. I manage to crawl a few inches before a third blast knocks me down again. Damn it, what are you doing up there, Vosch?

If it is too late, we'll have no choice but to execute the option of last resort.

Well, guess that particular mystery is solved. Vosch is blowing up his own base. Destroying the village in order to save it. But save it from what? Unless it isn't Vosch. Maybe Ringer and I are totally wrong. Maybe I'm risking my life and Nugget's for nothing. Camp Haven is what Vosch says it is and that means Ringer walked into a camp of infesteds with her guard down. Ringer is dead. Ringer and Dumbo and Poundcake and little Teacup. Christ, have I done it again? Run when I should have stayed? Turned my back when I should have fought?

The next explosion is the worst. It hits directly overhead. I cover my head with both arms as chunks of concrete as big as my fist rain down. The concussions from the bombs, the drug lingering in my system, the loss of blood, the darkness . . . all of it conspires to pin me down. From a distance, I can hear someone screaming—and then I realize that it's me.

You have to get up. You have to get up. You have to keep your promise to Sissy . . .

No. Not Sissy. Sissy's dead. You left her behind, you stinking bag of regurgitated puke.

Damn, it hurts. The pain of the wounds that bleed and the pain of the old wound that will not heal.

Sissy, with me in the dark.

I can see her hand reaching for me in the dark.

I'm here, Sissy. Take my hand.

Reaching for her in the dark.

82

SISSY PULLS AWAY, and I'm alone again.

When the moment comes to stop running from your past, to turn around and face the thing you thought you could not face—the moment when your life teeters between giving up and getting up—when that moment comes, and it always comes, if you can't get up and you can't give up, either, here's what you do:

Crawl.

Sliding forward on my stomach, I reach the intersection of the main corridor that runs the length of the complex. Have to rest. Two minutes, no more. The emergency lights flicker on. I know where I am now. Left to the air shaft, right to the central command hub and the safe room.

Tick-tock. My two-minute break is over. I push myself to my feet using the wall for support, and I nearly black out from the pain. Even if I grab Nugget without getting grabbed myself, how will I get him out of here in this condition?

Plus I sincerely doubt there are any buses left. Or any Camp Haven, for that matter. Once I grab him—*if* I grab him—where the hell are we going to go?

I shuffle down the corridor, keeping one hand on the wall to steady myself. Ahead, I can hear someone shouting at the kids in the safe room, telling them to stay calm and stay seated, everything was going to be okay and they were perfectly safe.

Tick-tock. Right before the final turn, I glance to my left and see something crumpled against the wall: a human body.

A dead human body.

Still warm. Wearing a lieutenant's uniform. Half its face blasted away by a high-caliber bullet fired at close range.

Not a recruit. One of them. Has someone else figured out the truth here? Maybe.

Or maybe the dead guy was shot by a trigger-happy, jacked-up recruit, mistaking him for a Ted.

No more wishful thinking, Parish.

I pull the sidearm from the dead man's holster and slip it into the pocket of the lab coat. Then I pull the surgical mask over my face.

Dr. Zombie, you're wanted in the safe room, stat!

And there it is, straight ahead. A few more yards and I'm there.

I made it, Nugget. I'm here. Now you be here.

And it's like he heard me, because there he is walking toward me, carrying—believe it or not—a teddy bear.

Only he isn't alone. There's someone with him, a recruit around Dumbo's age in a baggy uniform and a cap pulled down low, the brim resting just above his eyes, carrying an M16 with some kind of metal pipe attached to its barrel.

No time to think it through. Because faking my way through this one will take too much time and rely too much on luck, and it isn't about luck anymore. It's about being hardcore.

Because this is the last war, and only the hardcore will survive it.

Because of the step in the plan I skipped over. Because of Kistner.

I drop my hand into the coat pocket. I close the gap. Not yet, not yet. My wound throws off my stride. I have to take him down with the first shot.

Yes, he's a kid.

Yes, he's innocent.

And, yes, he's toast.

XIII

THE BLACK HOLE

83

I WANT TO DRINK IN his sweet Sammy smell forever, but I can't. The place is crawling with armed soldiers, some of them Silencers—or anyway, not teens, so I have to assume they're Silencers. I lead Sammy over to a wall, putting a group of kids between us and the nearest guard. I scrunch down as low as possible and whisper, "Are you okay?"

He nods. "I knew you'd come, Cassie."

"I promised, right?"

He's wearing a heart-shaped locket around his neck. What the heck? I touch it, and he pulls back a little.

"Why are you dressed like that?" he asks.

"I'll explain later."

"You're a soldier now, aren't you? What squad are you in?"

Squad? "No squad," I tell him. "I'm my own squad."

He frowns. "You can't be your own squad, Cassie."

This isn't really the time to get into the whole ridiculous squad thing. I glance around the room. "Sam, we're getting out of here."

"I know. Major Bob says we're going on a big plane." He nods toward Major Bob, starts to wave at him. I push his hand down.

"A big plane? When?"

He shrugs. "Soon." He's picked up Bear. Now he examines him, turning him over in his hands. "His ear's ripped," he points out accusingly, like I've shirked my duty.

"Tonight?" I ask. "Sam, this is important. You're flying out tonight?"

"That's what Major Bob said. He said they're vaculating all nonessentials."

"Vaculating? Oh. Okay, so they're evacuating the kids." My mind is racing, trying to work through it. Is that the way out? Just stroll on board with the others and take our chances when we land—wherever we land? God, why did I ditch the white jumpsuit? But even if I kept it and was able to sneak onto the plane, that wasn't the plan.

There's going to be escape pods somewhere on the base— probably near the command center or Vosch's quarters. Basically they're one-man rockets, preprogrammed to land you safely at some spot far from the base. Don't ask me where. But the pods are your best bet—not human technology, but I'll explain how you operate one. If you can find one, and if both of you can fit in one, and if you live long enough to find one to fit in.

That's a lot of *ifs*. Maybe I should beat up a kid my size and take her jumpsuit.

"How long have you been here, Cassie?" Sam asks. I think he suspects I've been avoiding him, maybe because I let Bear's ear get torn.

"Longer than I wanted to be," I mutter, and that decides it: We're not staying here a minute longer than we have to, and we're not taking some one-way flight to Camp Haven II. I'm not trading one death camp for another.

He's playing with Bear's torn ear. Not his first injury by a long shot. I've lost count of how many times Mom had to patch him up. He has more stitches in him than Frankenstein. I lean over to get Sammy's attention, and that's when he looks right at me and asks, "Where's Daddy?"

426

My mouth moves, but no sound comes out. I hadn't even thought about telling him—or how to tell him.

"Dad? Oh, he's . . ." *No, Cassie. Don't get complicated.* I don't want him having a meltdown right as we're preparing to make our getaway. I decide to let Dad live a little longer.

"He's waiting for us back at Camp Ashpit."

His lower lip starts to quiver. "Daddy isn't here?"

"Daddy is busy," I say, hoping to shut him down, and I feel like crap doing it. "That's why he sent me. To get you. And that's what I'm doing, right now, getting you."

I pull him to his feet. He goes, "But what about the plane?"

"You've been bumped." He gives me a puzzled look: *Bumped?* "Let's go."

I grab his hand and head for the tunnel, keeping my shoulders back and my head up, because skulking toward the nearest exit like Shaggy and Scooby tinkle-toeing is sure to draw attention. I even bark at some kids to get out of the way. If someone tries to stop us, I won't shoot them. I'll explain that the kid is sick and I'm getting him to a doctor before he pukes all over himself and everybody else. If they don't buy my story, then I shoot them.

And then we're in the tunnel and, incredibly, there is a doctor walking straight at us, half his face hidden behind a surgical mask. His eyes widen when he sees us, and there goes my clever cover story, which means if he stops us I'll have to shoot him. As we draw closer, I see him casually drop his hand into the pocket of his white coat, and the alarm sounds inside my head, the same alarm that went off in the convenience store behind the beer coolers right before I pumped an entire clip into a crucifix-holding soldier.

I have one half of one half second to decide.

This is the first rule of the last war: Trust no one.

I level the silencer at his chest as his hand emerges from the pocket.

The hand that holds a gun.

But my hand holds an M16 assault rifle.

How long is one half of one half second?

Long enough for a little boy who doesn't know the first rule to leap between the gun and the rifle.

"Sammy!" I yell, pulling up the shot. My little brother hops onto his toes; his fingers tear at the doctor's mask and yank it down.

I'd hate to see the look on my face when that mask came down and I saw the face behind it. Thinner than I remember. Paler. The eyes sunk deep into their sockets, kind of glazed over, like he's sick or hurt, but I recognize it, I know whose face was hidden behind that mask. I just can't process it.

Here, in this place. A thousand years later and a million miles from the halls of George Barnard High School. Here, in the belly of the beast at the bottom of the world, standing right in front of me.

Benjamin Thomas Parish.

And Cassiopeia Marie Sullivan, having a full-bore out-of-body experience, seeing herself seeing him. The last time she saw him was in their high school gymnasium after the lights went out, and then only the back of his head, and the only times that she's seen him since happened in her mind, the rational part of which always knew Ben Parish was dead like everyone else.

"Zombie!" Sammy calls. "I knew it was you."

Zombie?

"Where are you taking him?" Ben says to me in a deep voice. I don't remember it being that deep. Is my memory bad or is he lowering it on purpose, to sound older?

"Zombie, that's Cassie," Sam chides him. "You know—Cassie."

428

"Cassie?" Like he's never heard the name before.

"Zombie?" I say, because I really haven't heard that name before.

I pull off the cap, thinking it might help him recognize me, then immediately regret it. I know what my hair must look like.

"We go to the same high school," I say, drawing my fingers hastily through my chopped-off locks. "I sit in front of you in Honors Chemistry."

Ben shakes his head like he's clearing out the cobwebs.

Sammy goes, "I told you she was coming."

"Quiet, Sam," I scold him.

"Sam?" Ben asks.

"My name is Nugget now, Cassie," Sam informs me.

"Well, sure it is." I turn to Ben. "You know my brother."

Ben nods carefully. I still don't get his attitude. Not that I expect him to throw his arms around me or even remember me from chemistry class, but his voice is tight, and he's still holding the gun by his side.

"Why are you dressed like a doctor?" Sammy asks.

Ben like a doctor. Me like a soldier. Like two kids playing dress-up. A fake doctor and a fake soldier debating with themselves whether to blow the other one's brains out.

Those first few moments between me and Ben Parish were very strange.

"I came to get you out of here," Ben says to Sam, still looking at me.

Sam glances over at me. Isn't that why I came? Now he's really confused.

"You're not taking my brother anywhere," I say.

"It's a lie," Ben blurts out at me. "Vosch is one of them. They're using us to kill off the survivors, to kill each other . . ."

"I know that," I snap. "How do *you* know that, and what does that have to do with taking Sam?"

Ben seems stunned by my response to his bombshell. Then I get it. He thinks I've been indoctrinated like everybody else in the camp. It's so ridiculous, I actually laugh. While I'm laughing like an idiot, I get something else: He hasn't been brainwashed, either.

Which means I can trust him.

Unless he's playing me, getting me to lower my guard—and my weapon—so he can waste me and take Sam.

Which means I can't trust him.

I also can't read his mind, but he must be thinking along the same lines when I burst out laughing. Why is this crazy girl with the helmet-hair laughing? Because he's stated the obvious or because I think his story's crap?

"I know," Sammy says to broker the peace. "We can all go together!"

"Do you know a way out of here?" I ask Ben. Sammy's more trusting than I am, but the idea's worth exploring. Finding the escape pods—if they even exist—has always been the weakest part of my getaway plan.

He nods. "Do you?"

"I know a way—I just don't know the way to the way."

"The way to the way? Okay." He grins. He looks like hell, but the smile hasn't changed a bit. It lights up the tunnel like a thousand-watt bulb. "I know the way and the way to the way."

He drops the gun into his pocket and holds out his empty hand.

"Let's go together."

The thing that gets me is whether I'd take that hand if it belonged to anyone other than Ben Parish.

430

84

SAMMY NOTICES THE BLOOD before I do.

"It's nothing," Ben grunts.

I don't get that from the look on his face. From the look on his face, it's a lot more than nothing.

"It's a long story, Nugget," Ben says. "I'll tell you later."

"Where are we going?" I ask. Not that we're getting there— wherever there is—very fast. Ben is shuffling along the maze of corridors like an actual zombie. The face of the Ben I remember is still there, but it's faded . . . or maybe not faded, but congealed into a leaner, sharper, harder version of his old face. Like someone cut away the parts that weren't absolutely necessary for Ben to maintain his Ben essence.

"In general? The hell out of here. After this next tunnel coming up on the right. It leads to an air shaft that we can—"

"Wait!" I grab his arm. In my shock at seeing him again, I'd completely forgotten. "Sammy's tracker."

He stares at me for a second, and then laughs ruefully. "I completely forgot."

"Forgot what?" Sammy asks.

I go to one knee, take his hands in mine. We're several corridors away from the safe room, but Major Bob's megaphoned voice still bounces and skips along the tunnels. "Sams, there's something we have to do. Something very important. The people here, they're not who they say they are."

"Who are they?" he whispers.

"Bad people, Sam. Very bad people."

"Teds," Ben puts in. "Dr. Pam, the soldiers, the commander . . . even the commander. They're all infesteds. They tricked us, Nugget."

Sammy's eyes are big as pie plates. "The commander, too?"

"The commander, too," Ben answers. "So we're getting out of here and we're going to meet up with Ringer." He catches me staring at him. "That's not her real name."

"Really?" I shake my head. Zombie, Nugget, Ringer. Must be an army thing. I turn back to Sam. "They lied about a lot of things, Sam. About almost everything." I let go of his hand and run my fingers up the back of his neck, finding the small lump beneath the skin. "This is one of their lies, this thing they put in you. They use it to track you—but they can also use it to hurt you."

Ben squats down beside me. "So we have to get it out, Nugget."

Sam nods, fat bottom lip quivering, big eyes filling up with tears. "Oh-kay-ay . . ."

"But you have to be very quiet and very still," I caution him. "You can't yell or cry or twist around. Think you can do that?"

He nods again, and a tear pops out and drops on my forearm. I stand up, and Ben and I step away for a brief preoperative conference.

"We'll have to use this," I say, showing him the ten-inch combat knife, which I'm careful not to let Sammy see.

Ben's eyes widen. "If you say so, but I was going to use this." And he pulls a scalpel from his lab coat pocket.

"That's probably better."

"You want to do it?"

"I should do it. He's my brother." But the thought of cutting into Sammy's neck gives me the squishies.

"I can do it," Ben offers. "You hold him, and I'll cut."

"So it's not a disguise? You earned your MD here at E.T. University?"

432

He smiles grimly. "Just try to keep him as still as possible so I don't slice into something important."

We return to Sam, who's sitting now with his back against the wall, pressing Bear into his chest and watching us, eyes flicking fearfully back and forth. I whisper to Ben, "If you hurt him, Parish, I'm sticking this knife into your heart."

He looks at me, startled. "I would never hurt him."

I ease Sam into my lap. Roll him over so he's lying facedown across my legs, his chin hanging over the edge of my thigh. Ben kneels down. I look at the hand holding the scalpel. It's shaking.

"I'm okay," Ben whispers. "Really. I'm okay. Don't let him move."

"Cassie . . . !" Sammy whimpers.

"Shhhh. Shhhh. Stay very still. He'll be quick," I say. "Be quick," I tell Ben.

I hold Sam's head with both hands. As Ben's hand approaches with the scalpel, it becomes rock steady.

"Hey, Nugget," he says. "Okay if I take the locket back first?" Sammy nods, and Ben undoes the clasp. The metal clinks in his hand as he pulls it free.

"It's yours?" I ask Ben, startled.

"My sister's." Ben drops the chain into his pocket. The way he says it, I know she's dead.

I turn my head. Thirty minutes ago I'd blown a guy's face off, and now I can't watch someone make the tiniest of cuts. Sammy jerks when the blade breaks his skin. He bites down on my leg to keep from screaming. Bites hard. It takes everything in me to remain still. If I move, Ben's hand might slip.

"Hurry," I squeak, mouse-voiced.

"Got it!" The tracker adheres to the end of Ben's bloody middle finger.

"Get rid of it."

Ben shakes it off his hand and slaps a bandage over the wound. He came prepared. I came with a ten-inch combat knife.

"Okay, it's over, Sam," I moan. "You can stop biting me now."

"It hurts, Cassie!"

"I know, I know." I pull him up and give him a big hug. "And you were very brave."

He nods seriously. "I know."

Ben offers me his hand, helps me to my feet. His hand is tacky with my brother's blood. He drops the scalpel into his pocket and then the gun is back in his hand.

"We better get moving," he says calmly, like we might miss a bus.

Back into the main corridor, Sammy leaning hard against my side. We make the last turn, and Ben stops so suddenly, I run right into his back. The tunnel echoes with the sound of a dozen semi-automatics being racked, and I hear a familiar voice say, "You're late, Ben. I expected you much sooner."

A very deep voice, hard as steel.

85

I LOSE SAMMY for a second time. A Silencer-soldier takes him away, back to the safe room to be evacuated with the other kids, I guess. Another Silencer brings Ben and me to the execution room. The room with the mirror and the button. The room where innocent people are wired up and electrocuted. The room of blood and lies. Seems fitting.

"Do you know why we will win this war?" Vosch asks us after we're locked inside. "Why we cannot lose? Because we know how you think. We've been watching you for six thousand years. When the pyramids rose in the Egyptian desert, we were watching you. When Caesar burned the library at Alexandria, we were watching you. When you crucified that first-century Jewish peasant, we were watching. When Columbus set foot in the New World . . . when you fought a war to free millions of your fellow humans from bondage . . . when you learned how to split the atom . . . when you first ventured beyond your atmosphere . . . What were we doing?"

Ben isn't looking at him. Neither of us is. We're both sitting in front of the mirror, looking straight ahead at our distorted reflections in the broken glass. The room on the other side is dark.

"You were watching us," I say. Vosch is sitting in front of the monitor, about a foot away from me. On my other side, Ben, and behind us, a very well-built Silencer.

"We were learning how you think. That's the secret to victory, as Sergeant Parish here already knows: understanding how your enemy thinks. The arrival of the mothership was not the beginning, but the beginning of the end. And now here you are, in a front-row seat for the finale, a special sneak peek into the future. Would you like to see the future? Your future? Would you like to stare all the way down to the bottom of the human cup?"

Vosch presses a button on the keyboard. The lights in the room on the other side of the mirror flicker on.

There is a chair, a Silencer standing beside it, and strapped to the chair is my brother, Sammy, thick wires attached to his head.

"This is the future," Vosch whispers. "The human animal bound, its death at our fingertips. And when you have finished the

435

work that we've given you, we will press the execute button and your deplorable stewardship of this planet will come to an end."

"You don't have to do this!" I shout. The Silencer behind me puts a hand on my shoulder and squeezes hard. But not hard enough to keep me from jumping out of the chair. "All you have to do is implant us and download us into Wonderland. Won't that tell you everything you want to know? You don't have to kill him . . ."

"Cassie," Ben says softly. "He's going to kill him anyway."

"You shouldn't listen to him, young lady," Vosch says. "He's weak. He's always been weak. You've shown more pluck and determination in a few hours than he has in his miserable lifetime."

He nods to the Silencer, who yanks me back into the chair.

"I am going to 'download' you," Vosch tells me. "And I am going to kill Sergeant Parish. But you can save the child. If you tell me who helped you infiltrate this base."

"Won't downloading me tell you that?" I ask. While I'm thinking, *Evan is alive!* And then I think, *No, maybe he isn't.* He could have been killed in the bombing, vaporized like everything else on the surface. It could be that Vosch, like me, doesn't know whether Evan's alive or dead.

"Because someone helped you," Vosch says, ignoring my question. "And I suspect that someone is not someone like Mr. Parish here. He—or they—would be someone more like . . . well, me. Someone who would know how to defeat the Wonderland program by hiding your true memories, the same method we have used for centuries to hide ourselves from you."

I'm shaking my head. I have no idea what he's talking about. True memories?

"Birds are the most common," Vosch says. He's absently running his finger over the button marked EXECUTE. "Owls. During the initial phase, when we were inserting ourselves into you, we often used the screen memory of an owl to hide the fact from the expectant mother."

"I hate birds," I whisper.

Vosch smiles. "The most useful of this planet's indigenous fauna. Diverse. Considered benign, for the most part. So ubiquitous they're practically invisible. Did you know they're descended from the dinosaurs? There's a very satisfying irony in that. The dinosaurs made way for you, and now, with the help of their descendants, you will make way for us."

"No one helped me!" I screech, cutting off the lecture. "I did it all myself!"

"Really? Then how is it, at the precise moment you were killing Dr. Pam in Hangar One, two of our sentries were shot, another eviscerated, and a fourth hurled a hundred feet down from his post on the south watchtower?"

"I don't know anything about that. I just came to find my brother."

His face darkens. "There really is no hope, you know. All your daydreams and childish fantasies about defeating us—useless."

I open my mouth and the words come out. They just come out. "Fuck you."

And his finger comes down hard on the button, like he hates it, like the button has a face and its face is a human face, the face of the sentient cockroach, and his finger the boot, stomping down.

86

I DON'T KNOW what I did first. I think I screamed. I know I also ripped free from the Silencer's grip and lunged at Vosch with the intention of tearing his eyeballs out. But I don't remember which came first, the scream or the lunge. Ben throwing his arms around me to hold me back, I know that came after the scream and the lunge. He threw his arms around me and pulled me back because I was focused on Vosch, on my hate. I didn't even look through the mirror at my brother, but Ben had been looking at the monitor and the word that popped up when Vosch hit the execute button:

OOPS.

I whip around to the mirror. Sammy is still alive—crying buckets, but alive. Beside me, Vosch stands up so fast, the chair flies across the room and smacks against the wall.

"He's hacked into the mainframe and overwritten the program," he snarls at the Silencer. "He'll cut the power next. Hold them here." He yells at the man standing beside Sammy. "Secure that door! No one leaves until I get back."

He slams out of the room. The lock clicks. No way out now. Or there is a way, the way I took the first time I was trapped in this room. I glance up at the grating. *Forget it, Cassie. It's you and Ben against two Silencers, and Ben's hurt. Don't even think about it.*

No. It's me and Ben and *Evan* against the Silencers. Evan is alive. And if Evan's alive, we haven't reached the end—the bottom of the human cup. The boot hasn't crushed the roach. Not yet.

And that's when I see it drop between the slats and tumble

onto the floor, the body of a real cockroach, freshly squashed. I watch it fall in slow motion, so slow I can see the tiny bounce when it hits the floor.

You want to compare yourself to an insect, Cassie?

My eyes fly back to the grate, where a shadow flickers, like the flurry of a mayfly's wings.

And I whisper to Ben Parish, "The one with Sammy—he's mine."

Startled, Ben whispers back to me, "What?"

I drive my shoulder into our Silencer's gut, catching him off guard, and he stumbles backward beneath the grate, his arms flailing for balance, and Evan's bullet tears into his fully human brain, killing him instantly. I have his gun before he hits the floor, and I have one chance, one shot through the hole I had made earlier. If I miss, Sammy is dead—his Silencer is turning on him even as I turn on him.

But I had an excellent instructor. One of the best marksmen in the world—even when there were seven billion people in it.

It isn't exactly like shooting a can from a fence post.

It's actually a lot easier: His head is closer and a heck of a lot bigger.

Sammy is halfway to me before the guy's body hits the floor. I pull him through the hole. Ben is looking at us, at the dead Silencer, at the other dead Silencer, at the gun in my hand. He doesn't know what to look at. I'm looking up at the grate.

"We're clear!" I call up to him.

He knocks once against the side. I don't get it at first, and then I laugh.

Let's establish a code for when you want to go all creeper on me. One knock means you'd like to come in.

"Yes, Evan." I'm laughing so hard, it's starting to hurt. "You can come in." I'm about to pee myself with relief that we're all alive, but mostly because he is.

He drops into the room, landing on the balls of his feet like a cat. I'm in his arms in the time it takes to say "I love you," which he does, stroking my hair, whispering my name and the words, "My mayfly."

"How did you find us?" I ask him. He's so completely with me, so there, it's like I'm seeing his yummy chocolate eyes for the first time, feeling his strong arms and his soft lips for the first time.

"Easy. Somebody was up there ahead of me and left a blood trail."

"Cassie?"

It's Sammy, holding on to Ben, because he's feeling the Ben thing a little more than he is the Cassie one at the moment. *Who's this guy falling from the ductwork, and what's he doing with my sister?*

"This must be Sammy," Evan says.

"This is Sammy," I say. "Oh! And this is—"

"Ben Parish," Ben says.

"Ben Parish?" Evan looks at me. *That Ben Parish?*

"Ben," I say, my face on fire. I want to laugh and crawl under the counter at the same time. "This is Evan Walker."

"Is he your boyfriend?" Sammy asks.

I don't know what to say. Ben looks totally lost, Evan completely amused, and Sammy just damned curious. It's my first truly awkward moment in the alien lair, and I'd been through my share of moments.

"He's a friend from high school," I mutter.

And Evan corrects me, since it's clear I've lost my mind. "Actually, Sam, Ben is Cassie's friend from high school."

"She's not my friend," Ben says. "I mean, I guess I kind of

remember her . . ." Then Evan's words sink in. "How do you know who I am?"

"He doesn't!" I fairly shout.

"Cassie told me about you," Evan says. I elbow him in the ribs, and he gives me a look like *What?*

"Maybe we can chat about how everybody knows one another later," I plead with Evan. "Right now don't you think it would be a good idea for us to leave?"

"Right." Evan nods. "Let's go." He looks at Ben. "You're injured."

Ben shrugs. "A couple of torn stitches. I'm okay."

I slip the Silencer's gun into my empty holster, realize Ben will need a weapon, and pop through the hole in the mirror to fetch it. They're all still just standing around when I get back, Ben and Evan smiling at each other—knowingly, in my opinion.

"What are we standing around for?" I ask, my voice harsher than I'd intended. I scoot the chair beside the Silencer's body and motion toward the grate. "Evan, you should take point."

"We're not going that way," Evan says back. He takes a key card from the Silencer's pouch and swipes it through the door lock. The light flashes green.

"We're walking out?" I ask. "Just like that?"

"Just like that," Evan answers.

He checks out the corridor first, then motions for us to follow, and we step out of the execution room. The door locks behind us. The hallway is eerily quiet, feels deserted.

"He said you were going to cut the power," I whisper, pulling the gun from my holster.

Evan holds up a silver object that looks like a flip phone.

"I am. Right now."

He hits a button, and the corridor plunges into darkness. I can't see anything. My free hand shoots into the dark, searching for Sammy's. I find Ben's instead. He grips my hand hard before letting it go. Little fingers tug at my pant leg and I pull them up, hook one through my belt loop.

"Ben, hold on to me," Evan says softly. "Cassie, hold on to Ben. It isn't far."

I expect a slow shuffle of this rumba line through the pitch dark, but we take off fast, nearly tripping over one another's heels. He must be able to see in the dark, another catlike quality. We don't go very far before we're clustered around a door. At least I think it's a door. It's smooth, not like the textured cinder-block walls. Someone—it has to be Evan—pushes against the smooth surface and there's a puff of fresh, cold air.

"Stairs?" I whisper. I'm completely blind and disoriented, but I think these might be the same stairs I came down when I first got here.

"Halfway up you're going to hit some debris," Evan says. "But you should be able to squeeze through. Be careful; it might be a little unstable. When you get to the top, head due north. Do you know which way is north?"

Ben says, "I do. Or at least I know how to figure it out."

"What do you mean, when we get to the top?" I demand. "Aren't you coming with us?"

I feel his hand on my cheek. I know what this means and I slap his hand away.

"You're coming with us, Evan," I say.

"There's something I have to do."

"That's right." My hand flails for his in the dark. I find it and pull hard. "You have to come with us."

"I'll find you, Cassie. Don't I always find you? I—"

"Don't, Evan. You don't know you'll be able to find me."

"Cassie." I don't like the way he says my name. His voice is too soft, too sad, too much like a good-bye voice. "I was wrong when I said I was both and neither. I can't be; I know that now. I have to choose."

"Wait a minute," Ben says. "Cassie, this guy is one of them?"

"It's complicated," I answer. "We'll go over it later." I grab Evan's hand in both of mine and press it against my chest. "Don't leave me again."

"You left *me*, remember?" He spreads his fingers over my heart, like he's holding it, like it belongs to him, the hard-fought-for territory he's won fair and square.

I give in. What am I going to do, put a gun to his head? *He's gotten this far,* I tell myself. *He'll get the rest of the way.*

"What's due north?" I ask, pushing against his fingers.

"I don't know. But it's the shortest path to the farthest spot."

"The farthest spot from what?"

"From here. Wait for the plane. When the plane takes off, run. Ben, do you think you can run?"

"I think so."

"Run fast?"

"Yes." He doesn't sound too confident about it, though.

"Wait for the plane," Evan whispers. "Don't forget."

He kisses me hard on the mouth, and then the stairwell goes all Evanless. I can feel Ben's breath on my neck, hot in the cool air.

"I don't understand what's happening here," Ben says. "Who is that guy? He's a . . . What is he? Where'd he come from? And where's he going now?"

"I'm not sure, but I think he's found the armory."

Somebody was up there ahead of me and left a blood trail.

Oh God, Evan. No wonder you didn't tell me.

"He's going to blow this whole place to hell."

87

IT'S NOT A RACE up the stairs to freedom. We practically crawl up, hanging on to one another as we climb, me in the lead, Ben at the rear, and Sammy between us. The closed space is choked with fine particles of dust, and soon we're all coughing and wheezing loud enough, it seems to me, to be heard by every Silencer in a two-mile radius. I move with one hand extended in front of me in the blackness and call out our progress softly.

"First landing!"

A hundred years later we reach the second landing. Almost halfway to the top, but we haven't hit the debris Evan warned us about.

I have to choose.

Now that he's gone and it's too late, I've come up with about a dozen good arguments for why he shouldn't leave us. My best argument is this:

You won't have time.

The Eye takes—what?—about a minute or two from activation to detonation. Barely enough time to get to the armory doors. *Okay, so you're going to go all noble and sacrifice yourself to save us, but then don't say things like* I'll find you, *which implies there'll be an I to find me after you unleash the green fireball from hell.*

Unless . . . Maybe the Eyes can be detonated remotely. Maybe that little silver thing he's carrying around . . .

No. If that was a possibility, he would have come with us and set them off once we were a safe distance away.

Damn it. Every time I think I'm starting to understand Evan Walker, he slips away. It's like I'm blind from birth, trying to visualize a rainbow. If what I think is about to happen actually happens, will I feel his passing like he felt Lauren's, like a punch in the heart?

We're halfway to the third landing when my hand smacks into stone. I turn to Ben and whisper, "I'm going to see if I can climb it—there might be room to squeeze through at the top."

I hand my rifle to him and get a good grip with both hands. I've never done much rock climbing—okay, my experience is zero—but how hard could it be, really?

I'm maybe three feet up when a rock slips beneath my foot and I come back down, smacking my chin hard on the way.

"I'll try," Ben says.

"Don't be stupid. You're hurt."

"I'd have to try if you made it, Cassie," he points out.

He's right, of course. I hold on to Sammy while Ben scales the mass of broken concrete and shattered reinforcement rods. I can hear him grunting every time he reaches up for the next handhold. Something wet drops onto my nose. Blood.

"Are you okay?" I call up to him.

"Um. Define *okay*."

"Okay means you're not bleeding to death."

"I'm okay."

He's weak, Vosch said. I remember the way Ben used to stroll down the hallways at school, his broad shoulders rolling, zapping people with his death-ray smile, the master of his universe. I never would have called him weak then. But the Ben Parish I knew then is very different from the Ben Parish who now pulls himself up a jagged wall of broken stone and twisted metal. The new Ben Parish has the eyes of a wounded animal. I don't know everything that's happened to him between that day in the gym and now, but I do know the Others have succeeded in winnowing the weak from the strong.

The weak have been swept away.

That's the flaw in Vosch's master plan: If you don't kill all of us all at once, those who remain will not be the weak.

It's the strong who remain, the bent but unbroken, like the iron rods that used to give this concrete its strength.

Floods, fires, earthquakes, disease, starvation, betrayal, isolation, murder.

What doesn't kill us sharpens us. Hardens us. Schools us.

You're beating plowshares into swords, Vosch. You are remaking us.

We are the clay, and you are Michelangelo.

And we will be your masterpiece.

88

"WELL?" I SAY after several minutes pass and Ben doesn't come down—the slow way or the fast way.

"Just . . . enough . . . room. I think." His voice sounds tiny. "It goes back pretty far. But I can see light up ahead."

"Light?"

"Bright light. Like floodlights. And . . ."

"And? And what?"

"And it's not very stable. I can feel it slipping underneath me."

I squat down in front of Sammy, tell him to climb aboard, and wrap his arms around my neck.

"Hold on tight, Sam." He puts me in a choke hold. "Ahhh," I gasp. "Not that tight."

"Don't let me fall, Cassie," he whispers into my ear as I start up.

"I won't let you fall, Sam."

He presses his face against my back, completely trusting I won't let him fall. He's been through four alien attacks, suffered God knows what in Vosch's death factory, and my brother still trusts that somehow everything will be okay.

There really is no hope, you know, Vosch said. I've heard those words before, in another voice, my voice, in the tent in the woods, under the car on the highway. *Hopeless. Useless. Pointless.*

What Vosch spoke, I believed.

In the safe room I saw an infinite sea of upturned faces. If they had asked, would I have told them there was no hope, that it was pointless? Or would I have told them, *Climb onto my shoulders, I will not let you fall?*

Reach. Grab. Pull. Step. Rest.

Reach. Grab. Pull. Step. Rest.

Climb onto my shoulders. I will not let you fall.

89

BEN GRABS MY WRISTS when I near the top of the debris, but
I gasp for him to pull Sammy up first. I've got nothing left for that
final foot. I just hang there, waiting for Ben to grab me again. He
heaves me into the narrow gap, a sliver of space between the ceiling and the top of the slide. The darkness up here is not as dense,
and I can see his gaunt face dusted in concrete, bleeding from
fresh scratches.

"Straight ahead," he whispers. "Maybe a hundred feet." No
room to stand or sit up: We're lying on our stomachs nearly nose
to nose. "Cassie, there's . . . nothing. The entire camp's gone.
Just . . . gone."

I nod. I've seen what the Eyes can do up close and personal.
"Have to rest," I pant, and for some reason I'm worried about the
quality of my breath. When was the last time I brushed my teeth?
"Sams, you okay?"

"Yes."

"Are you?" Ben asks.

"Define *okay*."

"That's a definition that keeps changing," he says. "They've lit
the place up out there."

"The plane?"

"It's there. Big, one of those huge cargo planes."

"There's a lot of kids."

We crawl toward the bar of light seeping through the crack
between the ruins and the surface. It's hard going. Sammy starts
to whimper. His hands are scraped raw, his body bruised from

the rough stone. We squeeze through spots so narrow, our backs scrape against the ceiling. Once I get stuck and it takes Ben several minutes to work me free. The light pushes back the dark, grows bright, so bright I can see individual particles of dust spinning against the inky backdrop.

"I'm thirsty," Sammy whines.

"Almost there," I assure him. "See the light?"

At the opening I can see across Death Valley East, the same barren landscape of Camp Ashpit times ten, thanks to the floodlights swinging from hastily erected poles anchored in the shafts that funneled air into the complex below.

And above us, the night sky peppered with drones. Hundreds of them, hovering a thousand feet up, motionless, their gray underbellies glimmering in the light. On the ground below them, and far to my right, an enormous plane sits perpendicular to our position: When it takes off, it'll pass right by us.

"Have they loaded the—" I start. Ben cuts me off with a hiss.

"They've started the engines."

"Which way is north?"

"About two o'clock." He points. His face has no color. None. His mouth hangs open a little, like a dog panting. When he leans forward to look at the plane, I can see his entire shirtfront is wet.

"Can you run?" I ask.

"I have to. So, yes."

I turn to Sam. "Once we get out in the open, climb back on, okay?"

"I can run, Cassie," Sammy protests. "I'm fast."

"I'll carry him," Ben offers.

"Don't be ridiculous," I say.

"I'm not as weak as I look." He must be thinking about Vosch.

"Of course not," I say back. "But if you go down with him, we're all dead."

"Same with you."

"He's my brother. I'm carrying him. Besides, you're hurt and—"

That's all I get out. The rest is buried under the roar of the huge plane coming toward us, picking up speed.

"This is it!" Ben shouts, but I can't hear him. I have to read his lips.

90

WE CROUCH AT THE OPENING, tips of our fingers, balls of our feet. The cold air vibrates in sympathy for the deafening thunder of the big plane screaming over the hard-packed ground. It's even with us when the front wheel rises, and that's when the first blast hits.

And I think, *Um, a little early there, Evan.*

The ground heaves and we take off, Sammy bouncing up and down on my back, and behind us the stairwell seems to collapse soundlessly, because all sound is buried beneath the roar of the plane. The blowback of the engines slams against my left side, and I stumble sideways and nearly slip. Ben catches me and hurls me forward.

Then I go airborne. The earth bulges like a balloon inflating and then snaps back, the ground splitting apart with such force, I'm afraid my eardrums have shattered. Luckily for Sam, I land on my chest, but that's unlucky for me, because the impact knocks every cubic inch of breath out of my lungs. I feel Sammy's weight disappear and see Ben sling him over his shoulder, and then I'm up but falling behind and thinking, *Like hell weak, like hell.*

Before us the ground seems to stretch to infinity. Behind us, it's being sucked into a black hole, and the hole chases us as it expands, devouring everything in its path. One slip and we'll be sucked in, our bodies ground into microscopic pieces.

I hear a high-pitched screaming from above, and a drone slams into the earth a dozen yards away. The impact blows it apart, turns it into a grenade the size of a Prius, and a thousand pieces of razor-sharp shrapnel from the blast shred my khaki T-shirt and tear into my exposed skin.

There's a rhythm to this rain of drones. First the banshee scream. Then the explosion when they meet the rock-hard ground. Then the blast of debris. And we dodge between these raindrops of death, zigzagging across the lifeless landscape as that landscape is consumed by the hungry black hole chasing us.

I have another problem, too. My knee. The old injury where a Silencer in the woods cut me down. Every time my foot strikes the hard ground, a stabbing pain shoots down my leg, throwing off my stride, slowing me down. I'm falling farther and farther behind, and that's what it feels like, not running so much as falling forward while someone smashes a sledgehammer against my knee, over and over.

A scar appears in the perfect nothingness ahead. Grows larger. It's coming on fast, barreling straight toward us.

"Ben!" I yell, but he can't hear me over the screaming and booms and the ear-shattering implosion of two hundred tons of rock collapsing into the vacuum created by the Eyes.

The fuzzy shadow coming toward us hardens into a shape, and then the shape becomes a Humvee, bristling with gun turrets, bearing down.

Determined little bastards.

Ben sees it now but we have no choice, we can't stop, we can't turn back. *At least it will suck them down, too,* I think.

And then I fall.

I'm not sure why. I don't remember the fall itself. One minute I'm up, the next my face is against hard stone and I'm like, *Where did this wall come from?* Maybe my knee locked up. Maybe I slipped. But I'm down and I feel the earth beneath me crying and screaming as the hole tears it apart, like a living creature being eaten alive by a hungry predator.

I try to push myself up, but the ground is not cooperating. It buckles beneath me, and I fall again. There's Ben and Sam several yards ahead, still on their feet, and there's the Humvee, cutting in front of them at the last second, burning rubber. It barely slows down. The door flies open and a skinny kid leans out, his hand reaching for Ben.

Ben hurls Sammy toward the kid, who hauls my brother inside and then bangs his hand hard against the side of the vehicle like he's saying, *Let's go, Parish, let's go!*

And then, instead of jumping onto the Humvee like a normal person, Ben Parish turns and races back for me.

I wave him back. *No time, no time, no time no time no time no time.*

I can feel the breath of the beast on my bare legs—hot, dusty, pulverized stone and dirt—and then the ground splits open between Ben and me as the chunk I'm lying on breaks free and starts to slide into its lightless mouth.

Which makes me start to slide backward, away from Ben, who's wisely thrown himself on his stomach at the edge of the fissure to avoid riding the chunk with me straight into the black hole. Our fingertips touch, flirt with one another, his pinky hooks around mine—*Save me, Parish, pinky swear, okay?*—but he can't pull me up by my pinky, so in the half second he has to decide, he decides, flicks my finger free, and takes his one and only shot to grab my wrist.

I see his mouth open but hear nothing come out as he throws himself backward, hauling me up and over, and he doesn't let go, he hangs on to my wrist with both hands and spins around like a shot-putter, launching me toward the Humvee. I think my feet actually leave the ground.

Another hand catches my arm and pulls me inside. I end up straddling the skinny guy's legs, only now up close I see it isn't a guy but a dark-eyed girl with shiny, straight black hair. Over her shoulder I see Ben leap for the back of the Humvee, but I can't see if he makes it. Then I'm slammed against the door as the driver whips the wheel hard to the left to avoid a falling drone. He floors the gas.

The hole has gobbled up all the lights by this point, but it's a clear night and I have no trouble watching the edge of the pit rocketing toward the Humvee, the mouth of the beast opening wide. The driver, who is way too young to have even a permit, whips the wheel back and forth to avoid the torrent of drones exploding all around us. One hits a car length in front of us, no time to swerve around it, so we barrel through the blast. The windshield disintegrates, showering us with glass.

The back wheels slip, we jounce, then leap forward, inches ahead of the hole now. I can't look at it anymore, so I look up.

Where the mothership sails serenely across the sky.

And beneath it, dropping fast toward the horizon, another drone.

No, not a drone, I think. *It's glowing.*

A falling star, it must be, its fiery tail like a silver cord connecting it to the heavens.

91

BY THE TIME dawn approaches, we're miles away, hunkering beneath a highway overpass, where the kid with the very big ears they call Dumbo kneels beside Ben, applying a fresh dressing to the wound in his side. He's already worked on me and Sammy, pulling out pieces of shrapnel, swabbing, stitching, bandaging.

He asked what happened to my leg. I told him I was shot by a shark. He doesn't react. Doesn't seem confused or amused or anything. Like getting shot by a shark is a perfectly natural thing in the aftermath of the Arrival. Like changing your name to Dumbo. When I asked him what his real name was, he said it was . . . Dumbo.

Ben is Zombie, Sammy is Nugget, Dumbo is Dumbo. Then there's Poundcake, a sweet-faced kid who doesn't talk, whether he can't or won't, I don't know. Teacup, a little girl not much older than Sams, who might be seriously messed up, and that worries me, because she holds and strokes and cuddles with an M16 that appears to be carrying a full clip.

Finally the pretty dark-haired girl called Ringer, who's about my age, who not only has very shiny and very straight black hair, but also has the flawless complexion of an airbrushed model, the kind you see on the covers of fashion magazines smiling arrogantly at you in the checkout line. Except Ringer never smiles, like Poundcake never talks. So I've decided to cling to the possibility that she's missing some teeth.

There's also something between her and Ben. Something as in they appear to be tight. They spent a long time talking when we first got here. Not that I was spying on them or anything, but I was close enough to overhear the words *chess*, *circle*, and *smile*.

Then I heard Ben ask, "Where'd you get the Humvee?"

"Got lucky," she said. "They moved a bunch of equipment and supplies to a staging area about two klicks due west of the camp, I guess in anticipation of the bombing. Guarded, but Poundcake and I had the advantage."

"You shouldn't have come back, Ringer."

"If I hadn't, we wouldn't be talking right now."

"That's not what I mean. Once you saw the camp blow, you should have fallen back to Dayton. We might be the only ones who know the truth about the 5th Wave. This is bigger than me."

"You went back for Nugget."

"That's different."

"Zombie, you're not that stupid." Like Ben is only a little bit stupid. "Don't you get it yet? The minute we decide that one person doesn't matter anymore, they've won."

I have to agree with Li'l Miss Microscopic Pores on that point. While I hold my little brother in my lap to keep him warm. On the rise of ground that overlooks the abandoned highway. Beneath a sky crowded with a billion stars. I don't care what the stars say about how small we are. One, even the smallest, weakest, most insignificant one, matters.

It's almost dawn. You can feel it coming. The world holds its breath, because there's really no guarantee that the sun will rise. That there was a yesterday doesn't mean there will be a tomorrow.

What did Evan say?

We're here, and then we're gone, and it's not about the time we're here, but what we do with the time.

And I whisper, "Mayfly." His name for me.

He had been in me. He had been in me and I had been in him, together in an infinite space, and there had been no spot where he ended and I began.

Sammy stirs in my lap. He dozed off; now he's awake again. "Cassie, why are you crying?"

"I'm not. Shush and go back to sleep."

He brushes his knuckles across my cheek. "You are crying."

Someone is coming toward us. It's Ben. I hurriedly wipe the tears away. He sits beside me, very carefully, with a soft grunt of pain. We don't look at each other. We watch the fiery hiccups of the fallen drones in the distance. We listen to the lonely wind whistling through dry tree branches. We feel the coldness of the frozen ground seeping up through the soles of our shoes.

"I wanted to thank you," he says.

"For what?" I ask.

"You saved my life."

I shrug. "You picked me up when I fell," I say. "So we're even."

My face is covered in bandages, my hair looks like a bird nested in it, I'm dressed up like one of Sammy's toy soldiers, and Ben Parish leans over and kisses me anyway. A light little peck, half cheek, half mouth.

"What's that for?" I ask, my voice coming out in a tiny squeak, the little girl's from long ago, the freckle-faced Cassie-I-was with

456

the fuzzy hair and knobby knees, an ordinary girl who shared an ordinary yellow school bus with him for an ordinary day.

In all my fantasies about our first kiss—and there'd been about six hundred thousand of them—I never once imagined it would be like that one. Our dream kiss usually involved moonlight, or fog, or moonlight *and* fog, a very mysterious and romantic combination, at least in the right locale. Moonlit fog beside a lake or a lazy river: romantic. Moonlit fog in almost any other place, like a narrow alleyway: Jack the Ripper.

Do you remember the babies? I asked in my fantasies. And Ben always goes, *Oh yes. Sure I do. The babies!*

"Hey, Ben, I was wondering if you remember . . . We rode the bus together in middle school, and you were talking about your little sister, and I told you Sammy was just born, too, and I was wondering if you remembered that. About them being born together. Not together, that would make them twins, *ha-ha*—I mean at the same time. Not the exact same time, but about a week apart. Sammy and your sister. The babies."

"I'm sorry . . . Babies?"

"Never mind. It's not important."

"Nothing is not important anymore."

I'm shaking. He must notice, because he puts his arm around me and we sit like that for a while, my arms around Sammy, Ben's arm around me, and together the three of us watch the sun break over the horizon, obliterating the dark in a burst of golden light.

ACKNOWLEDGMENTS

Writing a novel may be a solitary experience, but seeing it to a finished book is not, and I would be a total schmuck to claim all credit for myself. I owe an enormous debt to the team at Putnam for their immeasurable enthusiasm that only seemed to intensify as the project grew past all our expectations. Huge thanks to Don Weisberg, Jennifer Besser, Shanta Newlin, David Briggs, Jennifer Loja, Paula Sadler, and Sarah Hughes.

There were times when I was convinced that my editor, the unconquerable Arianne Lewin, was channeling some demonic spirit bent on my creative destruction, testing my endurance, pushing me, as all great editors do, to the shadowy boundaries of my ability. Through multiple drafts, endless revisions, and countless changes, Ari never wavered in her belief in the manuscript—and in me.

My agent, Brian DeFiore, should be awarded a medal (or at least a fancy certificate tastefully framed) as manager extraordinaire of my writer's angst. Brian is that rarest breed of agent who never hesitates to wander into the deepest thickets with his client, always willing—I won't say always eager—to lend an ear, hold a hand, and read the four hundred and seventy-ninth version of an ever-changing manuscript. He would never say he's the best, but I will: Brian, you're the best.

Thanks to Adam Schear for his expert handling of the foreign rights to the novel, and a special thank-you to Matthew Snyder at CAA for navigating that strange and wonderful and baffling world of film, working his mystical powers with awe-inspiring efficiency—before the book was even finished. I wish that I were half the writer that he is an agent.

A writer's family bears a particular burden during the composition of a book. I honestly don't know how they took it sometimes, the long nights, the moody silences, the blank stares, the distracted answers to questions they never really asked. To my son, Jake, I owe hearty thanks for providing his old man with a teen's perspective and particularly for the word "boss" when I needed it most.

There is no one to whom I am more indebted than my wife, Sandy. It was a late-night conversation filled with the same exhilarating mixture of hilarity and fear so characteristic of many of our late-night conversations that was the genesis of this book. That and a very odd debate a few months later comparing an alien invasion to a mummy attack. She is my fearless guide, my finest critic, my most rabid fan, and my fiercest defender. She is also my best friend.

I lost a dear friend and companion during the writing of this book, my faithful writing dog, Casey, who braved every assault, stormed every beach, and fought for every inch of ground by my side. I will miss you, Case.

look for

THE INFINITE SEA

THE SECOND BOOK OF THE 5TH WAVE

coming this fall